XANTERA

XANTERA

GUARDIANS & MONSTERS VOLUME 1

MARIAH MONTOYA
GRACE PEARCE

Cover design and illustration by Wavyhues

Internal design and illustration by Aethrastic Designs

Map by Cartographybird Maps

ISBN: 979-8-9998419-0-2

Authors' Note

This book contains subject matter that might be difficult for some readers, including graphic violence, violence against children (off page), forced partnership and birth control, and threats of sexual assault and rape. This book also contains explicit sexual content.

For everyone trying to break free.

THE UTOPIAN CITY OF

XANTERA

— MAPPED —

IN THE PRESENT AGE

HOUSING COMP

TO SOUTHERN FORESTS

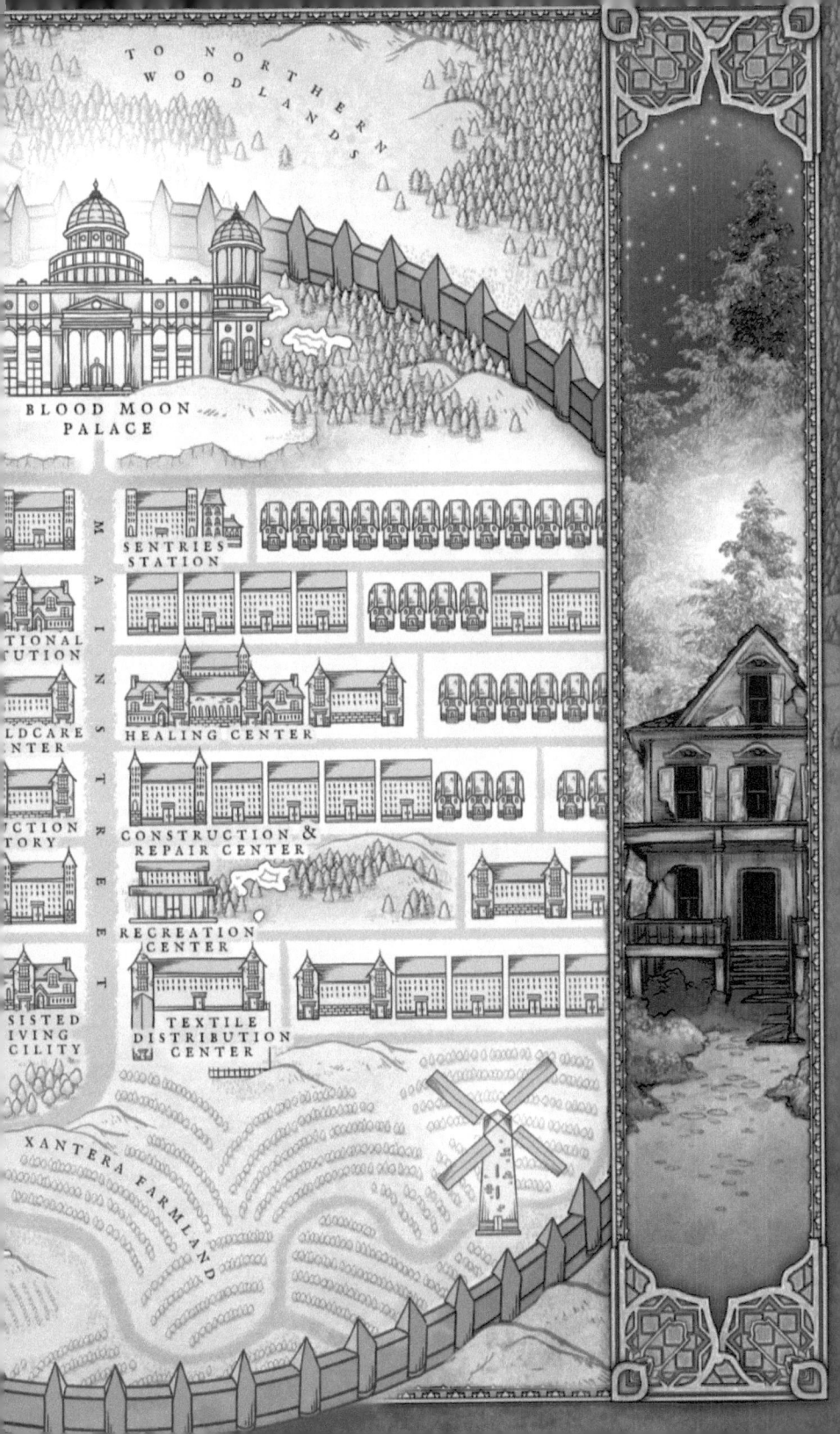

The Twelve
Cardinal Rules

1. Don't question your Guardians.
2. Don't seek out attention.
3. Don't think about yourself.
4. Don't ask unsolicited questions.
5. Don't listen to idle gossip.
6. Don't express personal opinions.
7. Don't engage in arguments.
8. Don't wish for more than necessary.
9. Don't create strife among neighbors.
10. Don't keep secrets from authorities.
11. Don't change without permission.
12. Don't venture near the Wall.

SASKIA

The Choosing is tomorrow night, and I'm more desperate than ever for them to pick me.

Not because I'd get to live the rest of my life in the Blood Moon Palace and be revered from one of those ivory-wrought balconies, a symbol of our city's continued hope and protection of the future. Not even because I'd finally get to see what our twelve Holy Guardians look like up close—their marble skin, their crimson eyes, their pointed fangs.

No, there's another reason I want the Guardians to choose me this time, but it's buried so deep in my bones that I don't allow myself to inspect it. Instead, I focus on blocking out the thing that has been tormenting me every Sunday night since the month I turned twenty-three:

The guttural sound of a man snoring.

Malcolm is my newly assigned civil partner, but neither of us have given each other more than what we're required to in the last six months of our official union. We share the same living space, eat dinner across the table from one another, make polite conversation, and go to sleep in our separate rooms—unless it's Sunday, that is. On Sunday, every couple in Xantera is required to "keep their spark alive."

That's what the Twelve Guardians call what I just pretended to moan through.

Now, I'm slowly shifting aside the rumpled sheets with Malcolm's snores rattling in my eardrums and his cum drying on my thighs. There's no way I'm getting a wink of sleep if I stay here, and as far as I know, there aren't any rules saying I have to let my ears bleed after keeping our spark alive. I'm pretty sure the Twelve Guardians would want me to be bright-eyed and alert for my shift tomorrow morning.

Just as the pads of my feet touch the floor, however, the howling starts.

The noise erupts from the distance, a kind of lonely, echoing peel that scrapes through the air with jagged claws, surpassing the Wall that surrounds Xantera and settling over the city in eerie waves. It lands on my skin, painting me in goosebumps that I can never seem to shake off no matter how many times I've heard them throughout my life.

> *Round and round the Monster prowls,*
> *Starved for meat and bone.*
> *Beware its eyes, resist its howl,*
> *Stay within the stone.*

If it weren't for the nightly howling, I'd almost wonder if that childhood lullaby of ours was nothing but a silly rhyme. If nothing prowled outside the Wall that our Twelve Guardians built for us five hundred years ago. We certainly can't see over the immensity of it, and nobody has gone in or out in centuries.

Well, except for the few citizens who disobey.

But that howling—it's enough evidence for me. It definitely isn't human, and there's always something hungry and yearning in it that makes me want to bolt.

Instead, I continue to my room in the slowest of tiptoes, my weight creaking against the floor until I'm safe in my own cube of a room across the kitchen. Maybe I'll give myself the pleasure that Malcolm is never able to now that I'm alone.

But I'm not alone. The howling continues, and as I fold my arms over my breasts, I can't help but wish, once again, that I'll be Chosen tomorrow night when the blood moon waxes.

Because beyond that secret reason buried deep in my bones, nowhere is safer than with the Guardians who vanquished the Monster in the first place.

"Good morning," Malcolm says just before dawn, when we slide our plates onto the kitchen table and sit down opposite each other.

"Good morning," I echo.

Breakfast today is porridge, peaches, and milk, delivered to us via a pair of graceful hands through the metal slat in our front door. I never get to see the person who makes their rounds before sunrise, distributing even portions of food to everyone in our complex, but their hands are as familiar to me as my own.

I swallow a spoonful of porridge before dabbing at my mouth with a cloth napkin. "How did you sleep?"

"Good." Malcolm nods, running a hand through his mousy brown hair. "You?"

"Good, thank you."

For a few minutes, the only sounds between us are the scraping of our spoons and Malcolm's open-mouthed chewing. I keep wondering if he'll ask why I wasn't in bed with him when he woke up, but he's staring off to the side with an absentminded expression, as if the silent, blackened screen mounted between cabinets is more interesting than me.

I make another stab at conversation.

"Did you dream about anything?"

"No. I don't usually dream."

"Oh, okay."

Malcolm frowns, his gaze flitting back to me. "Do you?"

Yes. Last night I fell asleep to the sounds of those howls dragging down my eyelids and dreamt of the Wall closing in around me, tightening like a cocoon until I couldn't breathe.

"No," I say. "I don't dream either."

"Oh."

At that moment, the screen between the cabinets lights up with a ping. Static skates across the surface, breaking into a half-baked image of a sun rising over a grassy knoll. The familiar female voice that has instructed every moment of my whole life rings out from the loudspeaker above the screen with the usual, *"Eligible citizens of Xantera, day shift starts now. Please proceed to your duty stations, and remember to..."*

"Have a good day," I finish with her.

Malcolm has already shoveled in the last of his breakfast and jumped up, readjusting the scarlet badge pinned to his shirt before throwing his school bag over his shoulder. He works at the Educational Institution, where he teaches twelve- to fifteen-year-olds about the history of Xantera, from when the Monster first overcame it to when the Guardians saved us five hundred years ago.

I don't particularly envy him. To have to talk about that every day... well, that particular wedge of history is always the bloodiest.

And I know a lot about blood.

"Have a nice day," Malcolm tells me.

"Have a..."

But the front door has already swung open and shut.

Alone now, I scoop my hair into a messy bun and tie it in a knot before checking the outline of my reflection in the fading screen to readjust my own scarlet badge—a marker of my place in life right now. Every new couple wears one in public, an indication of the honeymoon stage. In three years, we'll get new green badges to specify that we're in the family-making stage. That we sleep together more than just on Sunday.

Not yet, though. Now, I open the middle cabinet drawer next to our screen and grab the tiny blue pill that keeps my womb empty. I've heard so many women in my age group complain about the medication, but me?

My mother must have dropped me on the head as an infant and failed to report it to the Guardians, because I only ever feel a surge of relief when I pop this pill into my mouth. Maybe it's selfish of me to like the way my body feels as is, to dread those upcoming family-making years, but...

I shake my head. I shouldn't be having these thoughts. And I *definitely* shouldn't be analyzing the shape of my body in the glossy darkness of the screen, wondering why Malcolm doesn't seem as interested in me or my appearance as I secretly crave he would be.

In our schooling phase, we're taught a Cardinal List of Rules that becomes engraved in our psyches, and *Don't think about yourself* is high up there. Number three, to be exact.

Turning away from the screen, I follow Malcolm's footsteps out the door and into the narrow strip of space running between complexes that stare at each other like perfect mirror images. It's always dark in these walkways, every ounce of sunlight blocked by the metal eaves looming overhead. I quicken my pace, eyes straight ahead.

"Good morning."

I nod at one of my neighbors as she passes, and she echoes me with a soft "good morning" of her own. Soon, I've made it to the light spilling from the main walkway, where streams of people do the same to everyone they pass.

Out here in the open, the sun is making a watery appearance between thin films of clouds, and the air has a fresh, clean bite to it that makes me take a large inhale through my nose. A few birds twitter from their perches on the powerlines that run along the street, toward the Blood Moon Palace squatting on the high hill in the distance.

I let my gaze stray to that palace for a moment, its domed crown fluttering with twelve different flags. It can be seen from any vantage point within the city, like a beacon, a symbol, and an expression of all that is good here.

Still, all those ivory pillars remind me of the legs of a spider, as if the entire structure is hunched and waiting for whatever will crawl into its open mouth. But of course, all those balconies need support, and there are a *lot* of balconies—space for the Chosen Ones to wave to their past friends and family during the Viewing on Sundays. Then, they'll lean over their designated railings, gazes sweeping over the city they were once part of, but right now the balconies are empty. Lifeless.

"Good morning," someone says, and I jerk my head back down to nod at them.

"Good morning."

It's the same every day: good morning, good morning, good morning.

Briefly, I wonder if anyone has ever had a *bad* morning.

I continue past the other buildings that make up the spokes of our society's ever-turning wheel: the Sentries Station, the Recreation Center, the Production Factory, the Childcare Center, the Educational Institution, and countless others that I don't bother to glance at.

As I near my own destination, however, that feeling of suffocation, of the Wall closing in around me... it eases ever so slightly. *This* is why I know the Guardians chose the right partner for me, why I had no business questioning my union with Malcolm this morning. The Guardians know exactly what everyone needs at every phase of life. I know so because they chose the perfect *job* for me.

Healing.

I smile up at the building I call home.

Settled between tidy strips of lawn, the Healing Center glitters with windows, its entrance a welcoming spread of sliding glass doors that sweep open of their own accord when I step up to them. The interior is already bustling, some healers in scrubs scurrying to their assigned floors with masks strapped over their faces, others pushing residents in wheelchairs or checking in newly-approved patients in the lobby. The sound of it all—clacking footsteps, beeping monitors, and incessant chatter—is enough to ease the rest of the tightness in my chest.

Even in a perfect world where monsters can't reach us, people get sick or injured. I'm honored that it's my job to fix and heal them. Honored that I get to see so many walk back out those sliding glass doors with repaired bones, cleared lungs, and beating hearts.

I make it to the locker room just as the night shift healers are undressing.

"Morning, Saskia."

"Good morning, Gaia." I smile at the portly woman in the corner. She's a bit slower than the others, mopping her dark forehead with her sleeve before slowly peeling off her scrubs. Meanwhile, I open my locker beside her and pull out mine—freshly washed and dried, courtesy of the Healing Center laundresses. "Any newcomers in the night?"

"Oh, just an older farming gentleman. Fell down in the shower, apparently." Gaia lowers her voice to a gravelly whisper. "Says it was an accident, but between you and me, I wonder if he didn't get a *little* too excited with his partner, considering it was Sunday and all."

I snort. Anecdotes like this are exactly why I have faith Malcolm and I will fall into a groove with each other if neither of us are Chosen in our lifetimes. By the time we're sixty, we'll be doing dangerous things in the shower, too, won't we?

"Well," I say as I shimmy out of my regular pants and hike up my scrubs, "let's hope he didn't bang *just* his head before he had to come here."

Gaia claps a hand over her cackle, her face darkening with a flush.

"Oh, Saskia. What am I going to do with you? You're like a Monster on my shoulder."

"And you're my biggest inspiration," I shoot back with a grin.

It's not entirely a joke. Gaia's badge is bright purple, indicating that she's in the empty nest stage. That her two children are both older than fifteen, living in a complex specifically designated for apprenticeships and other pre-work training.

Maybe that's why she feels so much like a mother to me... I haven't seen my own since I was fifteen, too. Gaia's presence is the steady, nurturing one I look forward to every morning—even if she always seems to toe the line when it comes to the gossiping part of the Cardinal List of Rules.

"Well, let's hope I've inspired you enough to save some lives today," she says now, hefting herself up and hobbling past me.

"No one dies on my watch," I reply automatically. It's been my motto since I first began my training, and I'm happy to say it's held true so far.

"Have a good shift, Saskia."

"Sleep well, Gaia."

I watch her retreating figure until she's gone before changing my shirt and re-pinning my scarlet badge. Fully clothed and ready for the day now, I exit the locker room and fall into my usual rhythm.

I take vitals, administer medications, and change bandages—all under the watchful gazes of the Guardians' portraits, framed and hung up on every wall, as well as the cameras blinking in every corner. When I swish through the curtains to meet the gentleman who fell in the shower, I don't let my eyes so much as blink, even as I feel the surprise ripple beneath my chipper expression.

His face is one giant patch of purple around his eye, with a fresh cut still oozing through the bandage above his left eyebrow. The badge on his patient apron—gold—tells me he's in his sixties: a stage of life where injuries are harder to recover from.

"Hello, Diggory," I say, glancing at the information on my clipboard. "How are you feeling?"

The man looks up at me, lips pinching together. "Like the stains in a toilet bowl, actually."

I stop myself from choking on my next words and breeze forward to wheel the patient monitor closer to him.

"I'm very sorry to hear that. Do you mind if I check your vitals?"

Diggory grumbles something about minding very much but sticks out his arm anyhow. I clip his finger with a pulse oximeter and fasten the blood pressure cuff around the spot above his elbow. The monitor beeps at me, flashing numbers across the screen that make me frown despite the good news they convey.

Perfect blood pressure, strong, slow heartbeat, 100% oxygen saturation... this man is the healthiest gold-badged man I've ever cared for.

"Is your shower slippery, Diggory? Do I need to get a Repair Crew out to your complex to retile it?"

I eye his lean, toned body beneath the apron, more muscular than I would have anticipated. With health and attentiveness like this, my gut tells me he should have had the strength to break at least *some* of his fall, whether a partner was in there with him or not. And how could he have tipped *forward*? What did he even *hit*? The faucet knobs are way too small for a bruise like this.

Diggory blows out an unsmiling laugh.

"I'm fine, thanks. Just a clumsy old fart."

My frown cuts deeper into my cheeks.

"Did someone push you?"

It would be unspeakable, an act of violence like that. If his partner did it, I have no doubt the Twelve Guardians would vanquish her just as they did the Monster five hundred years ago. Just as they do to all the rare civilians who choose to break the guidelines that weave our entire society together.

But Diggory shakes his head with a lazy wave of his hand.

"Nobody pushed me." He closes his eyes and mutters something else under his breath, but I don't quite catch it, and it would be rude of me to insinuate he's lying by prying further.

As I remove his pulse oximeter and blood pressure cuff, though, jotting down his vitals information, I can't dislodge the feeling that I'm missing something.

That the patient I am supposed to keep alive didn't fall in the shower at all.

I don't have much time to ruminate on it, unfortunately. The day whizzes by in a blur, and soon I'm back at the apartment with Malcolm, eating dinner with my knee jiggling in anticipation.

Six hours. Six more hours until the Choosing.

"How was your day?" Malcolm asks in the same tone he does every night, his gaze drifting off to the side.

I swallow a mouthful of broccoli and nod.

"It was pleasant. How was yours?"

"Pleasant as well, thank you."

The sound of his chewing is like fingernails scraping in my ears. I have a fleeting thought that I would tear out my own eardrums if I could, just so I'd never have to hear that sound again. I have another fleeting thought that maybe I won't have to. Maybe one of the Guardians will choose me tonight, and I'll be waving to Malcolm from one of those ivory-wrought balconies by this weekend, and he'll get assigned a new civil partner who can tolerate all this chewing and snoring.

After dinner, we clean our dishes side by side and retire to our separate rooms, but neither of us go to sleep. Not tonight. Tonight, the entirety of Xantera will be wide awake, waiting for that smooth female voice to announce the same thing it does every few months when the sky begins to bleed and the doors to the Blood Moon Palace crack open.

After what seems like an eternity of waiting and staring at the ceiling and waiting some more, static rolls over me. The loud-speakers crackle.

I'm up and out of bed before the announcement can even finish.

"Eligible citizens of Xantera, please report to the Blood Moon Palace for the Choosing."

It's time.

THE MONSTER

My hackles raise as my back arches, and I howl again at the red moon: the largest one I've seen in years.

My life is measured in them.

This year's third quarter brings one in August. At the top of its arc, a sliver of orange fades to white—almost like the moon is being drained of its blood. Like it could die, if it was even alive in the first place.

There's a change in the air, something sweet. I can smell it on the wind that carries between the spikes of the Wall before it twists through the woods.

I want to get in. *Need* to get in. Like it's encoded in every atom humming through me. The white-hot rage that crosses my vision never ceases, but the blood moon only intensifies it.

I will stop at nothing. Otherwise...

No.
Time is running out, but that Wall *will* come down.

SASKIA

E *ligible citizens of Xantera, please report to the Blood Moon*
Palace for the Choosing."

The female voice repeats her message every few seconds, and I'm
a whirl of movement in response.

Hair up. Shoes on. Cloak fastened. Badge pinned. Breath un-
leashed.

Malcolm, on the other hand, takes his time. I know it would
be rude of me to make the long walk to the northern lip of the
city without him, but impatience makes my fingernails dig into my
palms as he takes his time pulling on his shoes in the living room.
How is he so quick to leave for work every day, but so slow to report
for the most important part of our lives? A sliver of me wonders if
he's one of those citizens who dreads the Choosing, who doesn't
want to be picked.

I can't fathom it. Sure, the Healing Center is my home, my safe space, but the Blood Moon Palace has...

"Alright," Malcolm says finally, straightening as he fixes his collar. "You ready?"

I stare at him. Of *course* I'm ready.

He nods, as if he realizes the exact words that would be too impolite for me to say.

"Let's—"

"*—report to the Blood Moon Palace for the Choosing,*" the female voice says, drowning out his.

Out in the street, we melt into the flow of thousands of bodies surging toward the ivory building in the distance. I can practically hear the mixture of a thousand heartbeats and breaths as all the healthy, able-bodied citizens over the age of eighteen make their way to their potential future. But the other sound is louder.

The howling.

It's always extra vicious on nights like these, when crimson slathers the full moon above our heads. As if the Monster can sense all its untouched prey moving like blood in an artery within the walls it cannot overcome.

I bask in the chills it sends down my body. The Monster cannot reach us in here, so let it howl. Let it rage. The Guardians will protect us as they always have, and tonight, twelve of us humans will sustain their strength so that they can keep on protecting. They call it a sacrifice, but it's not a sacrifice in the literal sense. The Chosen Ones must let the Guardians drink from their necks, yes, but they don't die. In fact, they're rewarded—with a lifetime of comfort and ease and a place in the Blood Moon Palace until the day they pass of old age.

As always when I near the giant courtyard before the palace, I find my gaze flitting up to all those balconies for proof.

The Choosing is the only other day the previous Chosen Ones come out besides Sanctuary Sunday. Now, a few dozen of them are leaning over the ivory railings, their cloaks and hair flowing in a slight breeze as they observe the crowd pooling below them. They look poised, regal, strong. A few wave.

I swallow a sudden lump of disappointment.

Turning around, I find that I've lost Malcolm in the flurry, but there's no time to go looking for him. Sentries are stationed in a semi-circle around the courtyard, herding everyone into position until I'm standing exactly twelve inches from my neighbor in every direction.

The movement dies down. The jostling comes to a halt. Even the heartbeats and breaths seem to come to a standstill, silence settling over the night like a shroud.

Only the Monster howls on, and I can't help my eyes from wandering to the Wall stationed behind the palace.

One hundred feet tall, its spiked top scrapes the silhouettes of midnight clouds in every direction. I can almost picture the Monster pacing back and forth on the other side, occasionally sitting on hideous haunches to fling its fury to the bloodstained moon.

The screech of ancient doors rips my attention downward again.

They're coming out.

They're here.

I sense rather than see them. I almost *always* sense rather than see them. There was only one time, after I had just turned eighteen, when I got to observe one of them with my own two eyes: the Tenth Guardian, a beautiful black-haired female with red, red, red lips. She'd passed me by without even glancing my way, but I'd felt the swish of her presence like a whisper grazing my skin. Felt her otherworldly grace and strength that sang of her superiority.

These people are truly a gift from heaven. Our saviors. Our idols.

Now, I feel that kind of presence again, crisscrossing through the crowd. I see my neighbors go even more rigid. All around me, spines straighten and knees begin to shake. I keep my eyes forward, trained on the back of the person in front of me.

Pick me. Pick me. Please pick me.

Nobody ever admits they want to be the Chosen One, but here I am, admitting it.

I hold my breath tight in my lungs, waiting.

At first, I'm almost positive this will be just like almost every other time, where I don't even get a glimpse of those pointed fangs, crimson eyes, or marble skin. The disappointment from earlier is sinking deeper and deeper into my gut until—*there.*

A flash of brightest white.

The people around me stir. Everyone seems to inhale as the beacon of light flows closer, and then I see one of them—*him.*

The Third Guardian.

I'd recognize him anywhere because his picture is everywhere. Hung up on every wall, threaded into every flag, carved into every statue alongside his eleven brothers and sisters. Wrapped in a rich, velvet cloak, he has wavy, golden hair, skin the color of bone, and eyes that flash the color of the moon above us.

And as he moves like silk closer and closer to me, I see them when his lips pinch up.

His fangs.

My breath burns in my chest, aching for me to release it, but I can't. The Third Guardian is moving so close that I can see his nostrils flaring as he smells each citizen that he passes, eyeing the badges pinned to their cloaks. Silver, red, green, purple, gold. His gleaming fangs seem to reflect each of the colors, but it's only when he approaches me that I hear the small, purring sound he makes as he passes each potential sacrifice.

"Hmmmm."

The voice shocks me straight to my core.

Two crimson eyes flick to my badge, and I swear my heart sinks straight to my toes. I can almost *see* the future five seconds from now. His gaze will slide up to my face. He'll tilt his head ever so slightly, golden locks falling to the side, and I'll never move again, never *breathe* again as he'll pin me to the spot with that single glance and realize I'm exactly who he's looking for. Even now I'm entranced. Enthralled. *Elevated.*

But the Third Guardian doesn't lift his eyes to my face.

He simply shifts his gaze from my badge to the person behind me and moves on.

My breath whooshes out of me as if the moon pummeled me in the stomach.

What happened? Was I not good enough? Not worthy enough? Why didn't he pick me?

Heat rushes back up my legs, urging me to turn around and track his progress. I don't, of course, but I can hear him do that purring "hmmm" again from behind me, and my ears don't even process the howling rage of the Monster in the distance as I hear another woman gasp.

"Yes, I think you'll do nicely."

The Third Guardian's voice spins through the crowd, and then there's a shift of movement as everyone stands aside. My head whips around to see him place a hand on the small of another woman's back. Lifting her chin, she lets him lead her through the parting crowd, toward the front doors of the Blood Moon Palace.

I don't see another Guardian all through the rest of the Choosing, but I can sense the stirring of the crowd as eleven other citizens are picked and led into the palace—and all my hope fleeing with them.

The Monster howls on.

"Diggory's gone" is the first thing I hear from Gaia when I walk into the Healing Center locker room the next morning.

"What?"

The bags I can feel under my eyes are still weighing me down, but every healthy, able-bodied citizen over the age of eighteen is probably feeling the effects of the Choosing right about now. The twenty-four-hour period afterward always feels off-kilter, as if someone cut into our routines and scooped out a hearty chunk of it. I'm used to this feeling.

So why am I blinking so long and hard at Gaia, unable to comprehend what she just said?

"What do you mean Diggory's *gone*?" I ask finally. "He... those injuries shouldn't have... he was fine!" I'm reeling, staggering toward the bench and slumping into a position where my hands can cradle my face. No one dies on my watch.

But some die when I'm not on shift. I just didn't think the gold-badged gentleman with the perfect vitals would be one of them.

Gaia surprises me by scooting herself closer to me, passing a quick look at all the other healers either getting dressed or undressed on the other side of the room. We're not supposed to gossip, but I don't stop her when she whispers out of the corner of her mouth, "He's not dead. He disappeared during the Choosing—just up and snuck away when everyone else was looking the other way."

"*What?*"

Again, that question falls out of my mouth. Again, I'm blinking rapidly at Gaia.

The only citizens exempt from the Choosing are sentries, children, and the sick or injured in the Healing Center... plus a very few select caregivers and healers who stay with those left behind. If there was ever a time to run off, it would be during that singular hour when most of Xantera is standing in formation before the Blood Moon Palace.

But I've never, *ever* heard of anyone doing such a thing. It's ludicrous. Horrifying. Unspeakable.

Yet I find myself speaking anyway.

"Did staff report it?" I ask under my breath. This isn't knowledge that should spread throughout the Healing Center. The fact that Gaia even knows about it is just a testament to her spectacular eavesdropping abilities.

Gaia nods. "The night clerk told the nearest sentries as soon as she noticed he was gone. The Twelve Guardians should have been alerted by now."

"They got his exit on camera?"

Another nod. "Footage shows him sneaking out the front doors and into the passageway between Complexes 360 and 361. But he never returned to his housing unit, and as far as I know, he's not showing up on any other cameras after that."

Missing. My patient is missing, and I've never wanted to stitch up a situation as badly as I do now. I must have missed something when I was caring for him yesterday—some sign that the injury to his head damaged his brain, too, because no one in their right mind would risk being thrown over the Wall, fodder for the Monster, for a transgression as perplexing as running away from the Healing Center.

"It's not your fault, Saskia."

It would be impolite of me to argue with Gaia, but I can't help my fingernails from digging into the metal of the bench at her words. Of *course* it's my fault. If I had just asked him some more questions...

I pull a deep inhale through my nose and nod. "Thanks for the information, Gaia. Have a good sleep."

"Saskia." Motherly concern follows every line of my friend's face as she registers my formal response. She's the only person I've ever joked with after turning fifteen and leaving my original family unit.

"Really, Gaia. It's okay. I'm sure the sentries will find him and bring him back to the Healing Center so that we can continue our care."

Yes, that has to be the bright side I can cling to. The Twelve Guardians wouldn't throw out someone who is clearly delusional with a bruised and battered face.

I spend the rest of my shift trying to mull it over, but unfortunately, my remaining patients are too curious about the Choosing they had to miss.

"What was it like?"

"Who was picked?"

"Did you see any of them?"

To that one, I pause with my eyes on the young patient's face. Odette's been in our neurology wing ever since her parents reported her unconscious on the floor about a week ago. We're still running tests to figure out what's wrong.

"Yes," I answer, watching her little eyes widen at that single word. "I saw one of them."

"Which one?" she breathes.

I hesitate before blowing out, "The Third one."

"Oooh. My friend Cheryl has a crush on him." The girl is practically vibrating with excitement, her heart monitor increasing to 105 bpm. "She thinks he's the most handsome of the Twelve. Do you think he was just as handsome in person?"

I glance at the monitor. I should probably remind her of the Cardinal List of Rules right about now. Number four: *don't ask unsolicited questions.* This type of prying curiosity is stamped out of kids by the time they receive their blue badges.

But I also know a conversation like this is one of the only bits of normalcy she'd be able to have in the Healing Center now that she doesn't have children her age to trade improper questions with, so I relent with a soothing, "Yes, he was very, very handsome."

Too handsome, maybe. I don't think I'll ever get that perfect face out of my head.

The girl squeals and claps her hands. "Oh, I knew it, I knew it. Cheryl is going to *die.* Did he notice you? Did he?"

I think of the way the Third Guardian's eyes flicked to my badge before moving on— how he didn't even raise his eyes to my face, but how he inhaled after passing every citizen, as if taking note of each of our scents.

"Of course he noticed me," I whisper. "The Guardians notice everyone."

They're always watching, I keep to myself, not daring to glance to the corner of the room where I know a camera is blinking and recording every moment of this interaction. *They're always watching.*

So how did Diggory manage to disappear?

After hours of taking vitals, administering medications, and changing bandages, I'm finally tearing off my scrubs and sighing off the day of work.

Sweat has dried all over me like a second skin, and I can't wait to get back to my housing unit to lather myself in soap under a scalding shower. Usually, I wish the automatic operation was longer than five minutes, but today I'm pretty sure I'll be grateful for every second until the spray shuts off on me.

I loiter, though, on the steps of the Healing Center, my eyes darting treacherously past the flow of civilians to the complexes across the street: 360 and 361. The space Diggory melted into.

I'm sure the sentries already tried retracing his steps. I'm also sure it's not my place to wonder if they found anything or not.

Still, my healing motto clangs through me: nobody dies on my watch. What if Diggory is somewhere in the labyrinth of complexes, hurt and unable to ask for help? What if this still, technically, falls under the job designation the Guardians gave me? He never checked out of the Healing Center the proper way, after all. He's still my patient.

By the time I exhale, I'm already stealing in between that dark lane sandwiched between Complex 360 and 361.

It's just like any other walkway in here. Symmetrical doors line either side of me, with knobs and metal slats for meal-laden trays to fit through. I've never really studied the corners and edges of these walkways, though. My eyes have always been focused on the light spilling from the end of the darkness, not the darkness itself.

Now, I allow myself to slow my steps and look up. Down. All around.

The first thing I notice is what *isn't* here. Flags. Loudspeakers. Screens.

Cameras.

The lack of color, the monotony, the symmetry—I've always considered it a no-man's land between point A and point B. Now, it seems like a perfect crack for someone to fall through, especially when the end of this walkway splits into spiderwebbing intersections where I waver, uncertain whether to turn left, right, or continue straight ahead. I have a vague idea of the Xantera map etched into my mind from my schooling days, so I know that clusters of complexes bleed into other clusters on either side of the main road. Diggory could be anywhere within the walls of this city.

Up ahead, a door opens. Somebody exits their housing unit, their red badge gleaming in the shadows. I nod politely as she makes her way past me, as if I live in one of these complexes, too, and I'm just heading home after a long shift.

Which, on a technicality, I am. I'm just taking a detour.

To where? I don't know. I don't *know*.

Watching out for signs of bloodstain or a struggle, I continue on a meandering path until something snags my attention, and I stop dead to pivot back around. For a second, I don't understand why the door I'm staring at seems *off*, but unease trickles down my spine.

Then I realize there's no metal slat for food to fit through above the doorknob.

I gawk at the smooth absence of a slat for several seconds, feeling my pulse skitter up my neck. This... this can't be right. Unless whoever lives here doesn't need food, they should have the same door as the rest of us, the same means for receiving daily meals.

Before I can pull myself back, my knuckles are knocking against the door.

Oh, I shouldn't have done that. I *really* shouldn't have done that. Invading the privacy of someone's personal housing unit is reserved for sentries and sentries alone, unless it's Sunday. Sanctuary Sunday marks the day of balance, a reprieve in our routine. The Recreation Center unlocks its doors, the Blood Moon Palace welcomes visitors in the courtyard, and citizens can accept visitors, too.

Today isn't Sunday, though. If someone opens that door and sees a random uninvited civilian in front of their space, the sentries might be knocking on *my* door soon enough with a whole host of questions.

But nobody answers. The door doesn't open.

And when I abandon all sense of courtesy and self-preservation and try to turn the knob, I find that it won't budge.

It's locked.

Now that same unease spikes in my lungs, making it difficult to breathe. Nothing is ever locked except for the front doors of the Blood Moon Palace, but I've never heard of anyone even *trying* to open them anyway. To lock a door is a sign of distrust. And there is no reason to distrust this society the Twelve Guardians have built us from the ground up.

Almost as if something about the door repels me, I find myself hurrying on, taking turn after turn until I'm back in the last remnants of faint sunlight leaking from a pink-tinged sky. Soon, it'll be dark and the Monster will begin its nightly howling. Malcolm will be wondering where I am. Everyone is either back at their housing unit or starting a night shift, so the main road is practically empty as I sneak back onto it.

Which is why, when a scream splits the air, I have a clear view of who's making it.

The patient I thought I'd find bleeding out somewhere in between complexes is currently on the main road, kicking and thrashing, as several sentries haul him away.

THE MONSTER

The deep screams fill my head, and I already know this is over. A taste.

A tease.

Like biting at fucking smoke and trying to rip it between my canines. Useless.

One second, I'm howling, and the next, a man's voice echoes through my skull.

Are you there?

Like he knew. He knew he could talk to me, be present in my mind, communicate beyond the Wall—which means not every citizen of Xantera is an empty, vacuous body to be controlled.

For the first time in my life, I have a link to the inside. How this man found the necklace laced with the blood of my ancestors doesn't matter right now. If the Guardians take him while it still hangs around his neck, he'll die for nothing.

This opportunity cannot be wasted.

Throw it, I yell in my head.

Anyone, anything, would be better than one of those Twelve parasites getting their hands back on the one, tiny part of me I have on the inside.

Rip it off your fucking neck, I urge him further, more vicious, forgetting his name he told me mere hours ago. *Do not let them take it again.*

The man's mental grunts are like punches to my gut, and I take off running through the mist of the forest. It's so thick it feels like rain against my face. A chill follows it. But I need to be closer, to feel the stone against my body.

My veins ignite as I approach it, a chaotic energy wrenching through every nerve. My spine straightens, I stretch my legs, and my arms reach out.

I press my claws against the ten-foot-thick Wall, ignoring the pain that zaps me. There's a path that winds to the left and right from the amount of times I've paced the perimeter. Scratch marks rise above my head from the number of times I've tried to climb it.

I was so close this time. So close to instructing this man how to open the Wall, only to have the hope ripped from my heart.

Anger surges again at the sound of another scream. I slam myself into the stone and growl, *Throw the necklace if it's the last thing you do.*

I'm met with only silence.

5

SASKIA

Immediately, my healer instincts kick in.

I zone in on every detail of Diggory as the sentries drag him toward the Blood Moon Palace, from his ragged screams to the trail of blood splatters he's leaving in his wake to the crooked dip near his collarbone as the sentries tug even harder on his arms.

Guardians, they actually *dislocated* his shoulder.

I don't hesitate this time. Several straggling passerby gawk at me as I sprint toward Diggory, but for once in my life, I don't have time to assess whether my manners are appropriate or not. My focus is *him* and the way his cries of pain are shredding my insides apart.

"Hey. Hey! Let him go!"

The sentries crank their heads in my direction. Like every other citizen of Xantera, they wear badges pinned to the front of their cloaks, but *unlike* every other citizen of Xantera, they get helmets and weapons, too—not to be used against us, but against the Monster in case of a breach.

Now, though, I find my eyes shooting to the rapier swords sheathed against both of their hips as their eyes widen then narrow at me through the slits in their helmets.

"Back away. This man is a danger to society and must be—"

"No, no, no."

I'm close enough that I can see Diggory's face now. The bruises have yellowed slightly, but fresh cuts and scrapes glisten on his cheeks and forehead and...

"He's one of our residents at the Healing Center," I explain as quickly as I can, trying to fabricate a good enough story using what I think is the truth. "He just has a concussion that I missed during my initial assessment. It's made him loopy and disoriented, but I promise if you can just escort him back to the Healing Center, I'll get some meds and fluids in him, and he'll be good as new by next week."

At the sound of my voice, Diggory's gaze travels to my face, blood vessels spiderwebbing in the whites of his eyes. They widen in recognition before glazing over, as if he's straining to listen to something or someone beyond me.

The sentries only pause for a moment.

"Guardians' orders," one of them says firmly, and then they're dragging him away again.

I watch them go, rooted in place and scrambling to come up with something, anything, to say to get them to stop. But a direct order from the Guardians isn't exactly something you can argue with. I'd be better off stealing one of their rapiers and slicing off my own head.

Yet I can't quit staring, evaluating every move Diggory makes and every move made against him, as if I can still fix this by writing a report on his health condition when I get back to work.

And that's why I notice him scrabbling at his throat, tearing something from the folds of his cloak, and chucking it to the side in the midst of his struggle to resist.

The sentries don't stop, don't notice, but I follow the arc of the glittering object as it lands on the ground between the Production Factory and the Childcare Center.

Time seems to waver in the space between my breaths as I try to tell myself to leave it alone. To turn around and hightail it back to my housing unit so that I can eat dinner with Malcolm and tell him that my day was pleasant and ask "How was yours?"

But of course, I can't. I stay glued in place as I watch the last of Diggory and the sentries fade into the distance, until they're no more than three dots before the Blood Moon Palace. Only after the doors open up to inhale those dots do I jump toward the place where the object glitters.

It's... I don't know *what* it is.

I swear I've seen or heard of something like this before, but I can't remember the name. It's a long chain weighed down by what looks like a solid miniature vial bracketed in elaborate swirls of gold. The vial itself is red, as red as the blood moon, as red as the Guardians' eyes, and I can't help but think that it looks like it was cut from a heart that ended up turning to stone.

My fingers stretch out to touch it...

A noise to my left sends me into a flurry of quick movement. I jerk upward. The Production Factory doors squeak open and a stream of manufacturers flows out. One of them glances over his shoulder, eyebrows scrunching at the way I'm standing in the middle of the two buildings. His eyes flick down to the space between my shoes.

"Good evening," I force out with a fixed smile, breezing out of the rich black of the shadows and into the shallow gray of a dying dusk.

"Good evening," he echoes with a smile just as wide.

I walk past him, eyes trained on the road ahead. It's *way* past time for me to head back to my unit, but I force myself to move at a steady pace, to not attract attention, to not reveal how viciously my hands are shaking at my sides.

As far as I know, there aren't any rules against picking up strange chained vials and stuffing them in the inside pocket of your cloak moments before someone spots you.

But I don't want anyone to find out and tell me otherwise.

When I get home, Malcolm is already seated at the dinner table, waiting for me. To my surprise, he hasn't dug into the chicken, rice, and peas that must have been delivered to our unit a good half hour ago. Both of our trays sit there, untouched and no longer steaming.

"Good evening," he says.

"Good evening. I'm sorry I'm late. There was a commotion."

I already decided on the walk over that half the truth would be better than none of the truth at all. Lying would be extremely rude, but my civil partner deserves at least *some* kind of explanation.

Once I'm settled in my chair and we're both eating, therefore, I tell him all about Diggory and the sentries in between bites, and how I hope the Guardians don't toss him to the Monster, and I wish I would have done something at the Healing Center to prevent this from happening, and...

"Are you even listening, Malcolm?"

I don't know where my temper is coming from—maybe last night's Choosing coupled with what just happened—but something is simmering beneath my skin. Agitated. *Angry.* I've only been angry a handful of times in my life, and all of them involved other kids on the playground at the Childcare Center. I've never been angry at another functional member of society before.

Today, right now, I'm angry at all of them.

"What?" Malcolm is saying, stray peas falling out of the corner of his mouth as he gapes.

I can still feel the weight of Diggory's object in the inside pocket of my cloak, but the weight in my heart is even worse. All I want is a civil partner who can *pretend* to care for even a fraction of a minute. Malcolm waited for me to eat dinner, but the absent-minded wander of his attention is clear: our union is a routine for him. Nothing more.

"Would you have chosen me if the Guardians hadn't picked me for you?" I dare to ask.

Tears burn against the back of my throat. Malcolm gawks at me as if he's never really seen me before, his jaw slack, his pupils racing back and forth across my face.

"Well?"

"Saskia." He clears his throat. "I can't... this isn't something we should be... the Guardians never choose wrong—they're... they..."

"But say they *do*," I blurt out. "Say that they *do* sometimes choose wrong."

I bite down on my lip, even as more wicked thoughts race through my mind: *say the Guardians choose wrong because they sit in their palace and view us through cameras and read their pairings through loudspeakers and never feel the actual spark—or lack of spark—between a couple and never realize that you, Malcolm, have always looked everywhere but at me.*

"Saskia," Malcolm says again, an ache beneath the admonishment in his voice.

And I know. I know right then and there, as if I'm making a clinical analysis, that Malcolm does not and cannot and will never love me. Not in the way I want him to. Not in the way that I could ever love him.

I stare at the grayish brown lumps of my uneaten chicken, my anger crashing back down into the pit of my stomach and shriveling up into something else. Something smaller and sadder.

"I understand," I whisper.

"What? You—I..."

I look back up at him and gather a deep breath. Refusing to glance at the camera above the screen in our living room, I lean toward him and whisper so quietly that nobody else would be able to hear if they decided to listen in to our individual unit in this exact moment of time, "We won't be in the family-making stage for several more years, you know. We don't have to... be together on Sundays—not in that way. There's no camera in our joint room. Nobody will ever know if we just take a break from pretending and forcing ourselves." I try to gather the words in my mouth. "We can just be friends behind closed doors."

Malcolm tips his head like he didn't hear a thing I just said. Like he's in as much denial as I've always been. "Are you feeling okay? Did you pick up a fever from your shift today?"

"No," I insist. "I mean, yes, I feel fine, and no, I don't have a fever. Admit it, Malcolm."

"Admit what?"

"That you don't feel for me. Not like you should."

"We shouldn't think like that," he replies much too quickly. "That would be irresponsible of us."

"Irresponsible?" I laugh despite the sadness sitting in my chest. "It's our private life, isn't it? No one else has to know what we do in our own home. Maybe we can start as friends since we were never given the chance to get to know each other." I can't help but glance at the camera this time, and now I lower my voice even more. "Just one little difference behind the door of our bedroom. How would they know?"

Of course, what I'm asking of him is a lot more serious than 'just one little difference.' It's the Cardinal Rule I hate the most, the one I've never been able to fully follow: *Don't keep secrets from authorities.*

"As long as no one asks us," I press, "then we're not lying."

I see the moment all pretense drops from Malcolm's face, leaving nothing behind but that ache that echoes mine.

"Friends?" he says, tasting the word as if it's something foreign that he can't comprehend.

"Friends," I whisper back.

Six long months seem to flash between our eyes. Six months of him pumping into me while I stare at the ceiling and push moans out of my throat, wondering when it'll start to feel good for me, too, or if I'll always have to do it myself. Six months of polite breakfast and dinner conversations that amount to nothing more than the same twelve words recycled over and over again until he's more of a stranger than when we were first assigned to each other.

Finally, relief shutters in Malcolm's eyes.

He nods.

I nod back and settle into my chair again.

Malcolm and I might be civil partners in the system, but we aren't together like that within these four walls. We'll still have to spend a few hours in our joint room together on Sanctuary Sunday, but if we just lie there without doing anything... well, what the Guardians don't know can't hurt them. Or us.

And for the first time in six months, Sunday doesn't sound too bad.

After washing our dishes side by side, Malcolm and I bid each other goodnight with slight smiles on our lips and retire to our separate rooms.

I shed my cloak, hearing the small *thunk* as the thing inside it hits the ground. But I don't inspect that thing yet. First, I shower off the day's events, letting the water blister my pores until my skin flares with patches of red. When it automatically shuts off after five minutes, I take my time drying my hair, slipping into my nightgown, and pulling the covers up to my chin.

Then and only then do my thoughts explode.

Diggory. Oh, poor, poor Diggory.

What could he have possibly been thinking?

What could he have possibly been doing?

Did he really get a concussion, was he really loopy and delusional, or did he have another motive? Was he trying to break into someone's unit? Did he succeed?

And what is that thing he threw as they were dragging him away?

I can't resist much longer. I tip sideways, reaching for my cloak that I tossed onto the floor and dig for that chained vial in the inside pocket to inspect it.

As soon as my skin makes contact with the object, I yelp.

An electric current seems to shoot through me, there one moment and gone the next. I toss it onto my bedspread where I can observe it without touching it, a frown tugging on my mouth as I stare at it in the red-tinged light of my bedside lamp.

I don't remember feeling that same electricity when I touched it the first time to throw it into my pocket. But I grabbed it by the chain then, and this time I swear my fingers skimmed the vial itself. Was the shock just a figment of my imagination, or...?

I touch the vial again, and that same electric shock flits through me, as if trying to connect with my pulse and make it skip a beat.

"What *are* you?" I marvel quietly.

The answer scratches at the inside of my brain. I have a very distinct feeling my old instructors taught us about these kinds of things in our history classes, that similar objects were used as decorative markers of power and prestige. Selfish. Greedy. Excessive.

So why do I want to put it on?

I close my eyes and throw my head back into my pillow, thinking, thinking, thinking.

Diggory had it around his neck, I'm sure of that. He was clutching at his throat when he ripped it off, and while the folds of his cloak may have been hiding a majority of it at the time, I would have noticed it on him in the Healing Center. Which means he found them *after* he ran away—both this strange object and a cloak.

Maybe he really was just crazy. A lost cause.

Or maybe if I mimic his last action, something will click in my brain to prove that he wasn't.

Opening my eyes again, I sit up and grab the object by the chain. Careful not to touch the vial, I raise my hands slowly over my head.

Selfish. Greedy. Excessive. The words clang through me as the vial gleams right in front of my face, its golden bracket winking in the lamplight.

Then a familiar howl erupts from the distant night, jolting me from my trance.

And I let the chain drop around my neck.

THE MONSTER

One second, my heartbeat is my own.

The next, another heartbeat latches onto my pulse, a new, foreign presence sprouting in my blood.

Someone has found the necklace.

If it's one of the Twelve—that third one specifically, here to taunt me—I'll make sure my revenge on him is extra sweet.

What is wrong with me? A female voice fills my head: gentle and warm, like a sunray stretching out to caress you. It's too rich, the timbre too colorful, to be a Guardian, but I know she must feel our connection, too. Must be aware of the electric tether now connecting us from either side of the Wall. *Maybe I'm going crazy too,* she thinks.

I wait.

Whoever this woman is, I need a second to figure out my tactic. If she doesn't have a rebellious spirit like the other one, then how can I use her? I need to find the advantage.

It feels alive, she thinks, *but it can't be. It's not real.*

And I just can't help myself.

Actually, it is, I reply angrily. For too long have the people of Xantera thought of me as a distant threat, a near-myth always prowling beyond their horizon of reality. I'm real. And I will *not* fade away.

Her gasp shoots through me, almost like she's stolen the oxygen from my own lungs, and her thoughts go haywire.

I try to sort through them as I seek shelter from the chilly evening air.

No, that was my imagination. Take it off anyway. I don't even know what it is. No, it had to be Malcom through the wall. Yes, it was Malcolm.

Who the hell is Malcolm? I ask.

Her response is a muffled scream followed by *Get it off! Get it off!*

I'll admit, this is actually a little fun. For two hundred years, I've been tormented by the marble-cold voices of the Twelve. No one so naive has ever graced me with their mental presence, and her mind is better than sitting alone with my own thoughts. It reminds me of a prism, rich with color.

Let's forget about Malcolm, I offer. It goes silent mid-scream. *I'm much more interested in your name.*

Who—who are you?

There's a faint echo, like she whispered her disbelief out loud, and my chuckle turns dark.

That's not how this is going to work.

But I'm the one with this thing around my neck... I could just take it off if you don't answer?

She poses it like a question, almost to herself: a fleeting, threatening thought that she tried to suppress but let slip out anyway.

Perhaps I underestimated her.

Whoever it is that picked up the necklace, she doesn't know who I am. She doesn't know *what* I am.

Maybe she's exactly what I need.

SASKIA

Your name, he demands.

I'm paralyzed—more with fear or curiosity, I'm not sure. When I first put the necklace on, the vial settling against my chest, something within it seemed to reach out and *grab* onto my heart-beat.

Now, there's a literal voice in my head. And even though I'm fairly certain I must be hallucinating, that voice is so dark and rough and *masculine* that I can't help but wonder how my own mind could conjure something so... not me. It reminds me of the rich soil on the southern end of Xantera, where our farmers tend to our fall harvest. And I want to keep unearthing it.

But I shouldn't be curious. It goes against the Cardinal List of Rules for me to wish for more. I should be ripping this thing off my chest and chucking it as far away from me as I can.

I don't know who you are, and you won't tell me your name, I say instead, despite my better judgment. Maybe Malcolm was right earlier when he asked if I have a fever. I must have caught a bug from the Healing Center. Or maybe the vial itself radiates some kind of sickness.

You're not sick, the voice growls in my head, cutting through my own thoughts. A trickle of uneasiness filters into me at how *real* he sounds. *What do you look like then?*

Excuse me?

My patience is wearing thin at how rude this fever is.

You refuse to tell me your name, and I'd like a sense of who I'm talking to, the voice says.

I—I— I stutter, trying to piece together his words and the confusion they pump into my veins. I look down at the crimson vial laying over my heart. *I don't know. I don't know what I look like.*

How can you not know what you look like? he questions me.

Why would I need to know?

What? His exasperation pushes against my mind, holds itself there, daring me. *Haven't you ever looked in a mirror?*

We don't have mirrors, I reply automatically, even though my mind flits guiltily to how I stared at myself in our screen's reflection just a few days ago. *They're self-indulgent.*

There's not a single mirror? he asks sarcastically.

Not in my housing unit.

I swivel my head to catalog my room, as if doing so will help me make sense of this absurd conversation I can't possibly be having. What purpose would a mirror serve? Every morning, I open my tiny closet in the far back corner and put on the same outfit: brown pants, a white linen shirt, and a cloak that fastens overtop. I run a comb through my hair to prevent tangles and knot it at the back of my head. Sometimes, I sit in the chair by the window and read my Healing textbooks or mend my clothes with our standard-issue sewing kit. None of that would require an actual mirror.

I close my eyes and roll to my side. If I'm not sick, then I must be dreaming, caught in one of those dark, twisted nightmares I never tell anyone about.

You're not asleep, he says, his own impatience beginning to lace his tone.

My eyes pop open again. *That's what a nightmare would say.*

Or maybe I'm the one sleeping, he croons, *and you're the thing that haunts my dreams.*

I can't even wrap my head around the concept of that, and for some reason, I'm desperate to prove him wrong. To prove that I'm real. *I'm not nearly as scary as you are.*

How can you be so sure? Considering I don't know what you look like, you very well could be. He laughs a deep sound that rolls down my arms. *Find a mirror, and we'll see who's scarier.*

What? No! Guardians, this is crazy. Maybe Diggory was infectious. None of this is possible or even reasonable, and my mind turns to a more haunting possibility that plunges my heart into fear. *Diggory, is this you? A spirit? A ghost?*

Ah, right. Diggory, he says in recognition. *How do you suppose he fared?*

The sentries weren't gentle, I say quickly, so used to giving reports that the response is programmed. *From the dislocated shoulder alone, it would take a skilled healer to make sure it was placed back properly. But citizens dragged to the Blood Moon Palace, they...* I don't want to dwell on what happens to them right now.

His tone turns slightly... empathetic? *He knew what he was doing. If anything successful comes from this, his name won't be forgotten a second time. I'll make sure of it.*

The sudden earnestness surprises me, and I swallow down a lump in my throat. But underneath that, something in his voice still gives off an air of superiority. A troubling possibility gnaws at me before I let it simmer to the top of my thoughts. *You're not a... Guardian, are you? Is this a test?*

If anyone could make it possible to talk to someone mind-to-mind by means of a chained vial, it would be one of the Twelve. Is this why they didn't pick me at the last Choosing? I failed whatever task they bestowed upon me, and they're testing me again? *I'm worthy!* I want to scream. *I'm worthy enough to join those you've Chosen in the past.*

Worthiness. His scoff scratches at my brain. *I'd rather rip out my own vocal cords than be so worried about the worthiness of others. But that brain of yours... I think I can guess a thing or two about you—other than your name and your appearance.*

Thank you. I like to think I'm predictable, I almost say. That's what makes a productive citizen, one who contributes and does what is expected of them. But the tone of his next words makes me doubt myself, like it's somehow despicable.

I bet you do.

And even if it is a Guardian, I can't stop my thoughts from turning admonishing. *Quit it. It's rude to read my thoughts. What's wrong with giving people what they expect of you?* I try to reason with him. *No surprises.*

Your Guardians wouldn't take kindly to being surprised, would they?

My Guardians? His tone sure doesn't make it sound like he's one of them. But even if he's another citizen, shouldn't he be talking about the Guardians with respect?

You always do as you're told, he continues. I bite my tongue, just in case he really is the Third, testing my response to such blasphemy.

I'd assume you don't have children yet, since there are no remnants of them in your thoughts, so you're probably in your early twenties.

Twenty-three, I answer almost involuntarily.

Twenty-three, he repeats smugly, a hint of interest buried beneath the tone. *And you're surprisingly talkative, but you don't ask the important questions—that makes me think you're a teacher or nurse.*

I ask lots of important questions, I defend myself. *It's part of my job, figuring out what is wrong with people.* Frustration picks at the darkest parts of my mind. Even if he is a Guardian, this voice acts like he knows me beneath the surface. And if there's one thing I've determined from my relationship with Malcolm, it's that the Guardians don't—could never—know the deepest parts of me.

The voice laughs with a mixture of victory and an emotion I can't quite pin down, but I know it makes my stomach spark, the embers swirling in my ribcage. I pull my covers over myself to smother it.

Ahhh, and now we're back to Malcolm, he practically purrs, taunting. *Your boyfriend? Husband? Is he everything you dreamed of?*

I keep my mouth shut, but his smirk slides across my thoughts as he reads them anyway.

Monotonous, isn't it? he tsks. *All that lost passion.*

We're chosen for each other, perfect. It will come with time, I say, clinging to what I told Malcolm—that no one could possibly know what we decided outside of our four walls.

Time, he says, his voice turning to gravel, *is not a luxury we have.* Something frightening and vicious alights within me... or him. *Find a mirror, little nightmare. I need to know what you look like.*

My heartbeat speeds up, or perhaps it's his own. Two rhythms blending into one, woven together for a string of time, a quick but steady *thump, thump, thump* shared between us.

That is, until the tempo of mine picks up faster in my chest at the realization that all of my secret thoughts are laid out bare here in my mind, ripe for his taking.

Whoever *he* is.

Whether this is the doing of a fever, a ghost, or a Guardian, I can't keep indulging.

Wait, the voice growls out. *Don't you dare lea—*

Without a second thought, I tear the chain away from my neck, and I'm alone in my room.

The next morning at breakfast, Malcolm and I sit down across the table from each other with a new energy between us. It's slightly warmer, more relaxed, than ever before, and it gives me the strength to clear my throat over a spoonful of porridge.

"What are you teaching at the Institution nowadays?"

He raises one eyebrow, surprise etching into the grooves between both. "Right now, we're going over the Dark Days."

I nod. I remember that section of my schooling well. It was the time before the Guardians, when all anyone ever did was fight and steal and lie and cheat. When the Monster snatched up anyone it fancied at any time, and there was no Wall to protect us from its teeth and claws.

"Do you remember," I start uncertainly, trying not to fidget, "what people used to wear?"

Malcolm frowns at me. "Like clothing-wise? Some of them went around practically nude, if that's what you—"

"No, no." I shake my head, trying not to imagine why anyone would want to walk around in public so exposed. "I mean, the greedy, self-indulgent things they wore. The shiny objects they hung around parts of their bodies—like their fingers or wrists or necks."

All last night, I couldn't sleep. Every time my eyes started to flutter, I'd jolt awake and stare at my dresser across the room, where I dropped the vial into a drawer by its chain.

Nothing whispered in my mind, though. No dark, masculine voice teased or taunted me. It was as if those five minutes of eternity where I had a conversation in my own head didn't even happen, even though I could still feel the goosebumps that voice seemed to breathe over my skin for hours afterward.

How can you not know what you look like?

You don't ask the right questions.

Your Guardians wouldn't take kindly to being surprised, would they?

Find a mirror, little nightmare.

In all my life, nobody has ever spoken to me that way. No one has ever made me doubt and question and wonder as much as that voice did in the span of mere minutes, which tells me there's no way my own brain could have conjured such outlandish thoughts, even if I was sick.

Not a fever, then. Also not a dream, since I kept pinching myself to no avail.

Someone was speaking to me through the vial. Either a Guardian or... I don't even know. Another citizen? A Chosen One or someone banished from beyond the Wall? Whoever it was, I'm positive that voice must have been the last thing Diggory heard before the sentries dragged him off. Maybe it even drove him to madness, and that's why he was screaming and thrashing by the end.

So for the rest of the night, a new resolve twined around my bones, hardening into place.

I was Diggory's healer. I *am* Diggory's healer. I will find out exactly what happened to him so that I can make an appeal on his behalf and save him before it's too late.

And contrary to what the voice tried to claim about me, that means asking the right questions. Like what those shiny objects that people used to wear even *are*.

"Oh." Malcolm nearly laughs now, and part of me marvels over the way it changes the shape of his face, how it makes him look younger and more carefree. "You're talking about jewelry."

"Jewelry?"

Even though we technically aren't doing anything wrong by discussing the Dark Days, our faces both twist in equal expressions of disgust, as if the word itself is greedy to use.

"Yeah," Malcolm says, lowering his voice. "Back when there was an imbalance of power, the rich liked to flaunt their jewels in front of those who were less fortunate. Some children went hungry and cold while other children's parents wore those jewels on parts of their body—rings and bracelets and necklaces."

Necklaces. The chained vial is a *necklace*. I knew I'd heard the word before, but I never could have guessed how relevant it would become to me. How on earth did Diggory find such a thing from five hundred years ago? The Guardians destroyed all remnants of the Dark Days when they came to save us from our own ruin, building Xantera upon the ashes of everything foul and ugly. How did such a delicate piece of jewelry survive all that... and why?

"Why?"

"*Why?*" Malcolm echoes me. "Because they thought it was pretty. To show off their wealth. Why else would anyone drape riches over their body parts?"

I shrug.

"Saskia?" he asks, peering at me.

"Hmm?"

"Is there a reason you're asking me about this?"

Yes. I have a forbidden necklace in a drawer in my room and I heard a wicked male's voice when it touched my chest and despite every instinct telling me to turn it into the authorities, a darker, deeper part of me wants to hang it around my neck and hear that voice again.

"No, not really. I was just wondering."

For the first time since we were assigned as partners, I feel a nip of guilt for holding back on him. Every other time I've kept something to myself, it's been because I don't want to be rude by talking too much about myself, but now...

"I hope you have a good day," I say before I can let myself dwell on it. Jumping up, I throw my cloak over my shoulders and pin my badge to my chest, refusing to let my eyes wander to my reflection in the screen. *I don't know what I look like* seems to ring through me.

Other people know what I look like, though. Malcolm himself looks at me, day in and day out from across the table, side by side when we clean the kitchen, hovering above me in the dark when he used to be inside me. I wonder what he sees.

"You as well," Malcolm says slowly, almost cautiously. "I'll see you tonight."

I smile and find that the smile is easier than it's ever been despite the secrets swirling in my chest. "See you tonight."

Hopefully by then, I'll be one step closer to finding out where that necklace came from.

And who is speaking to me through it.

After repeating "good morning" nearly a dozen times, I'm back in the locker room, saying hello to Gaia like usual, but this time with a weird mixture of hope and nerves writhing in my gut at what I'm about to ask her.

"Morning," Gaia says back, peeling off her blood-spattered shirt. It must have been a long night. "Did you hear?"

I pull my eyes back to her face, off the red dots dried into the fabric. "That Diggory was found? Yes. I actually saw the sentries haul him off yesterday after my shift."

"You did?" Her eyes pop wide open, hungry for the information.

"Yes." I pause for a steadying breath. "And I need you to do something for me."

For once, my friend seems at a loss for words. Her mouth hangs open, her hands frozen mid-movement. Among the Cardinal List of Rules is *Don't wish for more than necessary,* and I'm obviously breaking it now. Along with *Don't ask unsolicited questions,* of course.

For all my little jokes I've shared with Gaia over the years, for all the small tidbits of harmless gossip we've traded, I've never once asked her to do anything for me. Yet here I am, asking. My conversation with Malcolm went so well this morning that part of me believes she won't even scold me for breaking such an ingrained rule.

But then Gaia sucks in a breath, her eyes narrowing, and her tone morphs into something a little more suspicious than ever before.

"What kind of favor?"

I seem to be speaking in a lot of whispers lately. Even still, I try to keep my words as casual as possible as I pull on my clean, blood-free scrubs.

"Oh, nothing huge—just find Diggory's personal information." I look down at the laces of my shoes. "Who his partner is. Where she lives. That kind of thing."

"Guardians help me," Gaia hisses out. "Tell me you're joking."

"Not today, unfortunately."

"Only the information clerks would be privy to that kind of thing."

My tone stays light when I say, "You have a good ear," but Gaia's face is darkening with every new word I speak.

"Yes, but that doesn't mean I can just go around snooping in files I don't have access—" Gaia cuts herself off as one of the male healers across the room turns to head out the door. His eyes cut to us, his lips turned down in disapproval as if he thinks we're arguing. Maybe we are. Gaia waits until he closes the door behind him before resuming in a lower voice. "It would be improper to dig."

"But—"

"It would be improper to dig."

The finality in her voice is striking. I let my shoulders deflate before the fight can claw its way out of my throat. I've crossed a line, and the fact that Gaia is reminding me of that rather than turning me in is a testament to her loyalty. Yet...

You don't ask the right questions, that voice in my head claimed last night. *Well,* I want to scream back, *look what happens when I try to!* Since Diggory isn't around to give me answers, I wanted to pay a visit to his assigned partner, but I can't do that if I don't even know who she is.

Gaia lets out a grumbling sigh and gives my shoulder a half-squeeze. "This is the first patient you've lost, Saskia. It's normal to feel emotional about it."

I freeze in place. *The first patient I've lost.* As if Diggory is already dead.

And what if he is? What if the Guardians already threw him over the Wall and the Monster tore into his flesh as soon as his body hit the ground? I can practically hear the crack of bones, the tearing of skin and sinew, the gurgle of blood and—oh, I'm going to be sick.

"Right, I'm only emotional. I'll be fine tomorrow. Have a good sleep, Gaia," I intone, my words a bit sharper than I intended in an effort to hold back the tears stinging the back of my nose.

"Saskia, wait—"

I'm already out the door.

I pull back the curtain around my young patient's room, and she turns over at the sound of the metal hooks scraping along the rod.

"Odette," I smile. "How are you feeling today?"

"I feel fine," she insists, sighing into her pillow. "There's nothing wrong with me."

I nod empathetically as I approach her bedside. "Of course, but passing out can be scary. We want to make sure everything is okay before we release you." I muster up a lighthearted tone to mask my impatience. "You'll be back to your regular routine in no time."

Staring at her chart only makes me blink harder, faster. There are no answers. Only the same questions. We've already pestered her with all the standard medical questions that might point us toward a resolution. Are you eating all of your designated meal portions? Have you ever felt faint before now? What were you doing before you passed out? But so far, no part of her daily routine seems abnormal, and her scans are normal and her blood cell counts have all come back within normal range since then, even if they're a bit on the lower end.

As hard as I've tried to turn off every bit of greed and curiosity and selfishness that has been festering in me throughout the day, my mind wanders again for the millionth time to jewelry and mirrors and questions that shouldn't be asked.

Like the one I can't help but voice aloud now out of annoyance because no other questions have given me answers.

"Do you ever dream?"

Odette's head jerks up, and a grin splits her face wide open.

"Yes! All the time. Is that strange?"

"No, I don't think so," I answer honestly, and cock my head at her. Before I can second-guess myself, I sit on the lip of her hospital bed. "Tell me about them. Are they happy? Scary?"

My frustration over Diggory and the Choosing and the mysterious voice from last night is bleeding through cracks that have slowly but surely began fissuring inside me. It feels like I'm losing control of all poise and restraint, but the girl isn't so well-trained in manners yet, so she doesn't appear to be offended by my request. In fact, she lights up as if delighted and props herself up on the pillows.

"Oh, both. I have all sorts of dreams."

"Which one is your favorite?" I ask.

"Sometimes I dream that I have wings and all my schoolmates laugh at me because they don't believe that I can fly, but then I start flapping and ha! You should see their faces when I take off."

I laugh. "It would be fun to fly. What's another happy one?"

"Well, I know the whole thing about *beware its eyes, resist its howl, stay within the stone* and all that, but I've dreamt that I climb up the Wall and stand there at the very tippy top."

"On top of the spikes?" I ask curiously.

"Well, in my dream, they don't hurt me, and when I look down, I find a whole field of rainbows on the other side."

I fold my lips into a smile. I wish that were the truth, what would be waiting for us if the Wall ever fell.

"Or sometimes," Odette continues, unable to hide her new-found excitement, "I dream that I'm the first person in the world who can defeat the Monster because my fingernails can actually turn into sharp knives that stab him to death!"

I raise my eyebrows as she continues, finding myself enjoying the visuals she describes despite the impossibility of them, before she drops her eyes and fidgets with her fingers.

"If only my own dreams were so freeing," I encourage her. "I might be more excited to go to sleep at night."

She looks up at me, hopeful. "You dream too?"

"I do. But mine are less courageous, more constricting. Like the Wall flattening me into the ground, burying me into the earth, or that my heart is a blood moon, pumping crimson moonlight through my body."

I suddenly startle myself, snapping back to who I'm talking to, and how I shouldn't be saying any of this out loud. I'm not a child anymore. I can't just cry about my nightmares in my mother's arms. Besides, I shouldn't scare my young patient.

But then Odette says something that makes my breath pause.

"Just the other night, I dreamed of something like that. One of the Guardians, actually." She wrinkles her nose. "Not the Third one who's so handsome, but... which one has the thing on his neck again?"

"The Eleventh," I answer immediately, knowing what she means: an Adam's apple. All the images of the Eleventh Guardian always depict him with a long neck and a bulging Adam's apple. I squint at her. "Why do you think you dreamt of him?"

She shrugs. "I don't know. Dreams are just funny like that, aren't they? Uncontrollable, just like yours. This one was really vivid, though. I thought I was already awake until I *actually* woke up."

My breath seems to unstick itself in my lungs in one giant exhale. "What did the Eleventh Guardian do in your dream?"

"Just stared down at me and told me to go back to sleep."

A frown drags down my lips. "That's it?"

She shrugs. "Yeah."

"Were you scared?"

"No," she replies, shaking her head. "At first, he was just standing there, protecting me. Like they always do, watching over us to make sure we're safe. It was boring, actually. And then I woke up and he was gone. But I'd rather dream of flying or rainbows. Do you like rainbows?"

"What? Oh. Yes," I say, thinking of the flimsy films of colors that sometimes stretch from cloud to cloud after a bout of rain—how they fall across the sky and land somewhere beyond the Wall, somewhere we can't reach. What I don't say is that I much prefer the deep shade of red that glares from the blood moon against a black-as-ink sky—it's both terrifying and exhilarating. "Well, Odette, why don't you get some rest? I'll be back with your lunch in about an hour."

The girl sighs and lies back down, but her words leave me in a state of confusion that slowly buds into more anger by the end of my shift.

I don't know what happened to Diggory. I don't know where his partner lives. And I don't know why a little girl's dream seems to bother me. All I know is that there's a forbidden necklace waiting for me in my drawer at home.

And this time, I'm going to ask the right questions to figure out who is speaking from the other end.

THE MONSTER

A bolt of lightning strikes, connecting my heart to my head. She's back.

And I've been waiting—impatiently, for sure, pissed off and alone.

They all leave me alone when I'm in this mood. Nobody wants to feel the spitting heat of my temper, which is probably for the best in this particular circumstance. Because it's not *just* my temper that's been burning down my spine over the last twenty-four hours—it's her voice, too. That colorful wave that travels through my body, and the soft pitch that she accentuates with. I couldn't get it out of my head, even after she wrenched herself away from me with hardly any warning whatsoever.

Back so soon, my little nightmare? I ask, though it's felt like a fucking lifetime of wondering if she'd be back at all.

She says nothing in return—except the flooding thoughts of someone desperately trying *not* to think.

I chuckle, trying to coax a reaction out of her. *Curiosity is a strong emotion, isn't it?*

Still nothing comes, and for a second, I simmer on the vile possibility that she actually has turned over the necklace to a Guardian before I catch a fleeting thought through the crisscrossing pattern of electricity between us.

Unmistakably *her*.

But her next gift comes as a surprise—one that ignites my veins and makes me want to bottle up her voice to examine the change in tone. It's not timid or bewildered like it was last night, but demanding, almost as angry as I am. Like a sting to my senses that makes every last one of my hairs perk up on command.

Who are you?

Little nightmare has bite.

SASKIA

Is that how you speak to all your friends?

His voice cuts through me like a heated blade. This time, though, I'm prepared.

I curl up in my chair in the corner of my room, feet under me, blanket draped over my body. I've pulled it off my bed to cover me up in case Malcolm can hear me if I accidentally talk out loud to myself.

Friends? I scoff, anger lashing off my tongue in ways it never has before. Not that I'm even using my actual tongue, but still—my emotions seem so much more honed inside my head. *Hardly. Not until I know your name.*

What will that tell you?

I can't help but grind my teeth because I can *hear* his smirk in my head. *Lots*, I insist.

But will it? A name is nothing of consequence. No matter what he tells me, it wouldn't change anything. Unless I already know him, but there's no way that I do. I'd remember that voice, the way it dips so low and rattles deeply in my core.

Instead, I need to study him.

And what if you aren't happy with what you learn? he prods. *Will you still be my friend then?*

We're strangers, and nothing more, I reply. *Feel free to change that.*

He clicks his tongue. *I feel like you shouldn't need reminding that you also refuse to tell me your name. Which reminds me, did you find a mirror today?*

No, I don't trust you, I say, *and I'm taking a big risk even talking to you. Maybe they took Diggory in simply because he possessed this necklace.*

A flicker of pleasure passes from him to me. *So, you* have *been asking questions. The last time we talked, you didn't seem to have "necklace" in your vocabulary.*

I shake off the sudden satisfaction that melts my insides, at first unsure if it's his or my own. I'm afraid he's already picked up on it, but there's no way I'd feel so pleased that he's pleased. Even if he *is* a Guardian, he's a startlingly rude one.

It didn't get me very far. I've only learned the name for a piece of jewelry. But for every answer I receive from you, I'll return the favor. So, who are you?

I half-expect him to say I don't have the authority to speak to him that way. It's what a sentry would do, and a Guardian would probably just smite me for even daring to make any kind of bargain.

Surprise flickers through me, therefore, when the voice pauses and then says, *I'll answer when you earn it, but so far, you're not working for it.*

I ignore the skip of my pulse.

Then I have no other choice but to hand over this annoying piece of jewelry to the Guardians.

He growls an almost inhuman sound, and the snarl twists tightly around the doubt forming in my head—a Guardian wouldn't react like this.

I'm not risking my life to talk to a stranger, I continue, eager to keep stoking his emotions. Maybe doing so will get me somewhere. *A pretty necklace isn't worth being thrown over the Wall.*

That same growl slowly morphs into a low laugh. *Thrown over the Wall?* he parrots me skeptically.

My eyes drift out the window to trace those spikes jutting up against the dark sky, my imagination nowhere near as bright and happy as Odette's as I visualize myself being pushed through them—my clothes tearing, my skin chilled, the blood moon's light casting across my face, and then the free-fall, right into the Monster's waiting arms. If it even has arms.

His humored tone sinks into me like quicksand. *Pretty sure the Monster has arms. Besides, even if you do turn the necklace in, I'm sure they'll be happy to punish you anyway—without asking questions.*

I know without a doubt he's right. I've already hung on to it too long. Anyone would be suspicious, and rightfully so. Where would I have gotten it from? It's entirely possible that the Guardians are already looking for it, knowing now that Diggory no longer has it. I know for a fact he didn't want the sentries finding it, or else he wouldn't have torn it off his neck like that.

The second I walked home with the thing he discarded, I chose this fate. If I try to do the right thing by turning it in now, it could cost me my life.

There's a shift between the current that connects the voice and me, almost like we've arrived at the conclusion together, and his arrogance becomes palpable. *That's right, little nightmare. You're dead either now or later. May as well choose later. Assuage your curiosity. Ask me more questions—but maybe make them a little more specific than "Who are you?"*

Fine, then, I state emphatically to cover up the fear creeping back in. Clinging to my anger is best, easiest. I haven't felt this type of emotion since I was a child, when the Cardinal List of Rules stifled every one of them that wasn't polite or pleasant, but it feels good to let it out.

Even if I sound insane.

Are you stuck inside this necklace?

No, he says. *But maybe it would be better if I was.*

I shake the visual of this man actually nestled against my chest, touching me, somewhere even Malcolm hasn't bothered to. Maybe he has a necklace as well, picking it up like I am to sweep my fingertips over the deep red vial.

Then do you have a matching one that connects our thoughts?

Wrong again.

I sigh and focus out the window. This man could be in any of the housing units, maybe one step ahead and watching me every time I leave my complex.

I slink back against my chair, away from that clear pane of glass, and curse myself for not turning off the lamp across the room.

Play with me, he taunts, *and take another guess. This is the most fun I've had in years.*

You consider this fun? Guardians, you must be a miserable human. This isn't actually fun at all.

Don't lie. That laugh of his, it's certainly not doing boring things to my stomach as it twists into a knot that pulses behind my belly button. *And I'm not really human, now am I?*

Not a human? Wouldn't that be impossible? Aside from the Holy Guardians who need blood to survive, we're all...

No.

I hear the lullaby play in my head, like a carousel of words that spins around and around and around until I'm dizzy with a horrible possibility, an impossible realization.

Round and round the Monster prowls,
Starved for meat and bone.
Beware its eyes, resist its howl,
Stay within the stone.

Every night, the Monster howls. I've become used to that sound, used to the way it raises chills on every inch of my body. It's as constant as the moon, as the stars, as the Wall itself.

But there is no howling now. I even tug my blanket down to make sure, to strain for a sound that, for once, is not bleeding through the night and scraping down my skin.

There's only the sound of my own heartbeat, and...

No, I say again, a new type of fear hammering in my bones. There is no howling because the thing that usually howls is preoccupied—with me. *You're the M...* Even my internal thoughts seem to stumble over the word.

Go on, he encourages, sounding much too amused. *Say the word.*

I want to resist, but my mind lets it slip out. *Monster.*

His amusement only grows. *That's not what I would call myself, but for the sake of your vocabulary, I'll make an exception for now.*

It's a confession, loud and clear, but still... my brain isn't catching up to the reality of it. It can't be. Someone from another housing unit must be breaking every single Cardinal Rule by playing an elaborate prank on me.

His voice drops to a low, teasing octave. *I play by my own set of rules. And they aren't Cardinal.*

Prove it.

I told you this was fun, he laughs. *Tell me when to stop.*

Stop wha—

A howl splits through the air, reverberating against my eardrums, and doesn't stop. Not when I think it should. Not when it feels natural. Like a tuning fork, it keeps going with no end in sight, and just as you think it must need to run its course by now, it still rings out. The sound lengthens desperately, and I can feel it all the way down to my toes.

Stop! I cry.

The wailing cuts itself off so abruptly, it feels like whatever made that sound had its head chopped off.

But I know it didn't. Because I still feel his presence.

Regardless of what he calls himself, he is what prowls beyond the Wall, waiting with snapping teeth and sharpened claws and—

I can retract the claws, and as for my teeth… trust me, little nightmare, I can do much better things with them than inflict pain.

An inhale snags in my lungs, and I clutch my throat. Guardians, I'm going to be sick.

Your precious Guardians can't really help you in this situation, can they? he replies cheerfully. *You've been fraternizing with me for a whole day now, which technically makes you a traitor.*

My hands do something peculiar in response to those words. They curl into themselves, forming fists that I imagine pummeling into his face. Whatever his face even *looks* like.

You're not just a Monster. You're a… you're a…

I search for a word, but nothing comes close to the insult I want to throw at him for tricking me like this, for luring me in with a pretty piece of jewelry and capturing my mind so thoroughly. I'd always thought of the Monster as something savage and beastly and inhuman, not… intelligent. Not cunning and manipulative, and there has to be a word for what I want to call him right now.

Asshole would probably fit, he muses. *But I prefer my actual name, and I'd say you've earned it.*

The Monster has a name. A *name?* Impossible. I refuse to believe that's truly who he is, that it has a mother who *named* him.

But despite my disbelief, my question escapes as a whisper from its cage of frenzied thoughts. *Which is?*

Lucan, he says as if it's an everyday greeting. Like he's passing me on the main street on his way to his assigned job; as if it's just one of those thousand 'good mornings' I've uttered in my lifetime.

Saskia, I think politely before I can stop myself. Because it's ingrained in my psyche, like everything else, to echo a greeting no matter the circumstance.

Saskia, he repeats in a low rumble, rolling my name across his tongue, savoring every syllable. A dark pause hovers over us. *It's nice to meet you, Saskia.*

Fear rushes back in like a burst dam. My heart thumps, and the vial laying across my sternum rises and falls rapidly with it.

Just as I wrap my palm around it, Lucan—*no,* the *Monster*—calmly chuckles out, *Sweet dreams. You'll be ba*— before I rip the chain off my neck.

For good this time.

I'm on top of the Wall.

My feet are planted between two spikes that rise to my shoulders, and I grip their pointed ends as I brave the dizzying glance downward.

My stomach plummets. There are no fields of rainbows waiting for me on the other side. The ground is nothing but a hazy horizon below me, so far down and so slathered in mist that I can't make out the details of what would await me if I jumped.

Wind whips at my hair, a storm churning around me as if to try to push me off the ledge. I smell blood and salt. Earth and pine. The sweet, cloying scent of rot and a whiff of what I can only describe as moonlight—something simultaneously rich and light. It's calling me, those scents, but just as I lean forward to inhale more of it, the howling erupts around me.

It's loud when I'm safely tucked away in my housing unit, but out here, on top of the Wall, that howl swells louder than the wind itself. It wraps around me, tugs on my wrists, plays with my hair like a living thing, like ropes trying to yank me away.

I'm afraid, but the reasons drop in my stomach like a stone.

I'm afraid I like it.

I'm afraid I want more.

I *want* to wake up, I realize. Or do I?

"*You do not deserve this safe haven.*"

I nearly lose my grip on the spikes as I shriek and whip my head around.

The Third Guardian is there, his head right near my ankles, his fingers gripping the edge of the Wall, as if he climbed it like a spider. His golden waves don't seem to move in the wind. His blood-red eyes gleam hungrily up at me, but there's murder in his expression. Not like he sees me as something to feast upon and cherish, but something to feast upon and then squash.

"What do I deserve?" I cry out over the wind and howling.

Despite the fact that he's supposed to be one of my twelve protectors, I've never been so terrified, seeing him clinging to the Wall like that just below me. *Behind* me. I don't want my back exposed to him, and I have half an idea to turn around when he pounces.

"*You deserve a Monster.*"

The Third Guardian pushes me, and I fall.

And fall.

And fall.

My own scream is tearing apart my lungs. My hair whips around my face. I close my eyes to prepare for the impact of that distant ground when I land against a warm, solid body that breaks my fall.

Instantly, I want to curl up against that chest and cry against his shoulder. I want to let his hands press tight against my body and keep me safe. I want to kiss his mouth as a thank you for catching me.

"*Don't worry, you're safe with me,*" his familiar voice croons.

My eyes pop open—and yet I'm still caught in the dream.

Yellow irises gleam wickedly back at me. A cruel mouth opens to reveal teeth as sharp as the spikes on the Wall. Claws scrape against my skin in a threatening caress. And in the thickness of the mist, it looks like two horns rise from either side of his head.

"*Hello, little nightmare.*"

I wake up with a start, panting heavily.

My throat is dry, my eyes wet. Every inch of my skin tingles, as if despite the horrible dream I just endured, my body wanted it to keep going. To feel what would happen, in the confines of my unconscious brain, if the Monster continued to hold me and touch me.

Not good. Not good at all.

For the last four days, I've wrestled with the choices laid out in front of me: throw the necklace as far away from me as I can, just like Diggory did, and be rid of that deadly, masculine voice in my head, or turn it in and risk the wrath of the Guardians for keeping it in the first place.

I've done my best to push away the sly, third option that whispers in a dark recess of my mind: *keep it. Keep it and wear it and get to know him more. Find out why your pulse quickens at the very thought of him. Push and pull and take and give like a heart that has finally started to truly beat.*

No. No more of this. The longer I have the necklace, the longer I'll be subjecting myself to this special kind of torment, where nothing is straightforward and everything doesn't make sense. I shouldn't be afraid of the Guardians. I shouldn't want to see what the Monster looks like without all that mist shrouding the rest of his features. I shouldn't be dreaming of the other side of the Wall. *Lucan* was so confident I'd run back to him a third time, but the Cardinal List of Rules trained me better than that. I can't allow this to go on any further.

As I lean my head back against my pillow, my breath finally settling, my ears pick up the sound again, for real this time. Howling. Tormented, furious howling, as if the one making the sound is flinging it at me and me alone. For the past four nights, it's been like a morbid lullaby.

Well, good.

I hope he's reeling, unable to forget me—that my brief appearance and sudden departure haunt his mind for the rest of his life, however long that may be. Maybe forever. I hope I *do* become his nightmare. Because my sudden streak of rebellion officially ends here.

I know what I have to do.

The congregation in front of the Blood Moon Palace is as thick as it always is on Sanctuary Sunday.

Instead of going to the Recreation Center, I've come to the Asking, when the Blood Moon Palace accepts visitors. Well, at least up to the front steps.

Some people spread out beneath the balconies and wave up at their Chosen loved ones, while others, including me, form a line leading to the double doors. There, stationed right between two sentries, a human representative sits on an oversized wooden chair to hear requests, questions, and grievances from the citizens of Xantera. Our messages are then passed on to the Twelve Guardians, who will take all the information into consideration when they decide all aspects of our lives.

I'm willing to bet nobody's ever stood in line to hand in a forbidden necklace that connects their mind to the very Monster we're taught to fear since birth. But here I am, doing exactly that.

As soon as I get to the front of the line, that is.

Still, my hand fiddles nervously in the inside pocket of my cloak, rubbing the necklace's chain between my thumb and forefinger, even though I'm careful not to touch the vial itself. A dozen scenarios have played out in my mind regarding how this could go once the Twelve Guardians realize what I have.

They could hear my case and let me go. They could keep me for questioning. They could inflict various types of punishments on me. They could throw me over the Wall—probably the worst option, since then I'd have to come face to face with the very Monster who put me in this position in the first place.

And I doubt I'd actually survive that fall, anyway. Not like how I did in my dream.

Sweat dampens the small of my back as my spot in line inches closer and closer to the door, and my eyes betray me by flicking up to those balconies where a few dozen Chosen Ones are leaning against the railings, looking down at everyone beneath them.

I don't know any of them personally, and disappointment thrums through me like it did on the night of the last Choosing, so strong and hard that I nearly sway on my feet.

Instead, I abandon all pretense and let my neck crank upward, spearing my focus at the Chosen One hanging over the balcony directly above me.

He's middle-aged, fair-haired, and looking just as regal as all his companions as he sweeps a cupped hand through the air. To my right, a woman of the same age is smiling up at him, two children on her other side waving frantically at the man who must be their father.

The man who *was* their father, I should say. Hard to be a real one when the Guardians whisk you away from your family and everyone else you've ever loved under the guise of it being an honor.

And just like that, I'm rooted to the spot, even as the line shifts forward.

I've never really let myself think all the thoughts that press against the forefront of my mind, but now they explode and fracture into a hundred different questions that prick me from the inside-out.

How is *this* considered an honor—staring down at a city you can never be a part of any longer? Why don't the Guardians feed from our necks to get the sustenance they need to protect us and then release us back to the city? What makes them Choose one sacrifice over another? What makes them Choose *anything*? They're never here, among us, unless a blood moon blares from the sky. Even now, it's a human representative who's holding the clipboard and scribbling down a message much slower than an eager, blue-badged boy is talking, trying to plead his case about switching to a new job assignment.

Why isn't he allowed to plead his case on a random Tuesday? Why is his ability to use his voice limited to once a week?

But of course, it's the Twelve Holy Guardians who think they know us better than ourselves, and a human representative who will decide what to do with me when I drag out the necklace from my inside pocket.

Either he'll find my injustice trivial, thanking me and slipping it into his own pocket, or he'll find himself speechless, unable to process the gravity of what I've done. In that case, he'll haul me through the front doors to face the wrath of the Twelve, where one of those dozen scenarios I've played out in my head will become a reality.

"Excuse me, miss, are you still in line?"

The question rattles me from my thoughts, and I whip my gaze back to find the person behind me blinking politely at the way I've glued myself to the stone beneath my feet.

"Oh. Oh, I'm not sure. I just—"

Need a minute, I try to get out, but the words clog in my throat, and I'm spared having to cough them out when a commotion from up ahead jerks both of our heads forward.

"No. No, please, I need to see him."

The voice is high-pitched and strained, reminding me of the Monster's continuous howl he inflicted upon me the other night. There's an unspoken rule in Xantera to never sound distressed, to always keep your voice at a civil pitch that doesn't incite worry or fear. The eagerness of the blue-badged boy was one thing, but this...

This is another.

I already have half a foot out of line, so I lean even further sideways to peek around the people in front of me and find the owner of that voice.

The blue-badged boy must have been sent on his way, because the person at the front of the line is a woman with a gold badge pinned to her chest now, her hair pulled back into a long silver braid. She's actually on her knees in front of the representative, whose face screws up in a look of disgust as he uses his clipboard like a shield from her obvious desperation.

"As I've told you, ma'am, the Twelve Guardians will be in contact once they have made a decision about—"

"But is he alive?" the woman cries, and everyone in line seems to reel in a breath at the way she just interrupted him. "Can you tell me if he's alive?"

"I am not authorized to speak on the matter."

"Then let me talk to someone who is!"

The entire courtyard goes completely still for a second as her shout reverberates in the air. My own heart leaps in my throat, and I swear I can hear our collective heartbeats thrumming in the silence that follows her exclamation.

Then everyone breaks out into horrified mutters and whispers. "Guardians," the person in front of me gasps. "The audacity!"

The representative's face, however, slides back into neutral pleasantness, as if he can combat the woman's behavior by pretending she's done nothing out of the ordinary. "Thank you for voicing your concerns, ma'am. I appreciate your time."

"But I—"

"Next, please."

"But—"

The two sentries on either side of the representative twitch forward, their hands sliding to the pommels of the rapiers in their belts.

For a second, I have the strangest feeling that the woman is about to attack them with her bare hands. That, or try to charge through them, straight through the double doors of the palace.

But after a few hushed seconds, her back straightens, and she lifts herself to stand on shaking legs. She manages to toss the representative a curt bow before turning, pulling the edges of her cloak tighter around her, and walking away.

"Wait," I find myself whispering. Then, shaking my head, I step fully out of line before racing after her, through the crowd and out onto the main road again. "Wait!"

She pretends to ignore me at first, or maybe her hearing is actually failing, because it's not until I've shouted after her a second and third time that she turns, her forehead wrinkling to find my hand outstretched toward her. Her red-rimmed eyes flick to my face, confusion and wariness setting her mouth into a hard line when she realizes she doesn't recognize me. Our paths may have crossed before during one of those endless "good morning" treks to work, and we've no doubt been in the same vicinity during the Choosing, but neither of us find the other familiar.

"Can I help you?" she asks with a sniff.

Yes. No. I don't know. I'm probably making it all up—this feeling that I do know you in a roundabout way.

"I only wondered..." I glance over my shoulder at the Blood Moon Palace. The sentries have returned to their stoic stances. The human representative is already listening to the next person in line. The visitors beneath the balconies are waving at their Chosen loved ones once again. As if everyone just fell back into their place like a gear in a machine. "Are you okay?"

The woman's shoulders stiffen.

"I am perfectly fine. Thank you for your concern."

She turns to continue walking away, but I blurt out, "Are you sure? Did... did a loved one of yours get Chosen?"

Slowly, the woman swivels back toward me, her lips pinching, her eyes narrowed. "Yes, in fact. But that was a long time ago."

A long time ago? She wouldn't be in a frenzy over someone who's already been gone for a while. Plus, nobody just goes up to the Blood Moon Palace asking if their Chosen One is still alive—because of *course* the Chosen Ones are alive. They are among the safest citizens in the entire city.

No, there's only one type of person she could have been pleading for information about: someone who was taken in for a transgression against their will.

"Are you her?" I whisper, my eyes going wide. "Are you Diggory's partner?"

Ever since Gaia declined my request to find Diggory's information, I've put the idea of his partner to rest. I thought I had arrived at the right decisions over the last few days: *don't snoop; don't put on the necklace again; don't keep it a secret from the Guardians any longer.*

But the ironic thing about limiting your people's voices is that those with grievances will inevitably come together at the same place, on the same day, at the same time—head-to-head.

Just like this woman and I are staring at each other now.

"Who are you?" she asks in a voice that brushes the border between suspicious and awed.

My hand automatically slides into my cloak pocket and grazes the necklace's vial. Electricity flares within me for a millisecond before I retract my fingers again, but it only takes that millisecond for me to realize that I don't want to give this up yet. Not just the necklace and my strange, terrifying connection to the Monster, but this *anger* taking root inside me. The questions, the doubts, and the realization that I may as well have been sleepwalking ever since I was a kid, going through motion after motion and letting Rules define my very self.

I don't want to sleepwalk anymore.

"I was the last person to see Diggory," I say under my breath, locking eyes with the woman. "And I think we should talk."

10

LUCAN

L ucan.

It's not *her* voice that calls out my name in my head.

Four days I've been waiting. The moon rises each night and still she doesn't come.

This voice though, these thoughts, are as familiar as my own. Birthrights do that to you: connect you to the ones closest to you, the ones who are there for you, *always.* Even when you don't want them to be.

I could pick out the cadence of Vivian's voice anywhere—distinctly female, yes, but it's not as smooth or soft as Saskia's.

Saskia, I repeat in my head, just as I've done a hundred times since she let it slip. That name is like a whisper of moonlight. The way it rolls off my tongue in a—

Lucan, Vivian says again firmer. *You need to rest. Eat. You've been like this for four days.*

I thought I asked you not to shift?

Well, you didn't exactly command *it,* she says innocently.

Get out of my head, Viv, I growl. If only it was as easy as taking off a necklace.

It's not healthy, she insists. *You need real food and a break.*

I'm fine.

You need to shift back, Vivian bites out. *And then you won't have to listen to my scratchy voice in your head.*

Yeah, but then I'll have to listen to it in real life, I grouse.

A sudden burst of electricity powers through my veins. The hope gathers in my chest, but Saskia's voice doesn't follow. It was just a blip, as if someone brushed the vial with their pinky, and now I'm left wondering if I imagined it. An uneasy craziness settles over me. I know Vivian is right, I need to take a break, but I can't. Not yet.

No, I want to be ready if she comes back, I tell her. *She's our only way in. Our last chance.*

I must have been too hard on Saskia, pushed her too far. No one can process that much information all at once, especially someone who's lived her entire life under the Guardians' creepy pale thumbs, believing that their way of life is the only way.

Over and over, I've replayed what I said to her—and what I didn't.

I didn't tell her I've seen humans like her fall from the Wall dozens of times before over the last couple of centuries, and not because the Guardians throw them over to feed me like their stupid fucking myths say.

No, these humans jump, I'm almost sure of it. In a desperate attempt to escape that hellhole they've been locked away in, they fling themselves off the top, but they're all dead as soon as they hit the ground. No human could survive a fall from that dizzying height. Saskia's the only one I've been able to exchange more than a few words with, and I might have scared her away for good.

There's just something about how her mind races that I can't put my finger on. How her thoughts overlap and clash, as if the buried ones are trying to break free. How she suppresses them and only lets those that have been ingrained in her churn to the top—but she has gears. Rusty, sure, but they're there, desperately trying to turn.

You'll know, Lucan. As soon as the human comes back, you'll know. Please shift, Vivian replies, empathy lining her demand. *Come on.*

I throw one last howl into the night before I *tug* at my form from the inside-out.

The shift is harder than usual after being in this monstrous form for four damn days. My veins twist and tighten. My bones scream as they snap inward, reforming themselves within my skin. My skin itself burns as it shrinks, as my claws retract and my body shudders into place.

Exhaling a shaky breath, I grit my teeth once more at the Wall before turning back toward the woods, away from Saskia and the parasites who keep her imprisoned.

This time on two human feet.

SASKIA

Diggory's partner leads me to a housing unit almost identical to my own.

A mounted screen hangs between kitchen cabinets, its surface a glossy black in the present moment, although the loudspeaker above it is due to announce curfew within the next hour. Four doors lead to two separate rooms, a shared room, and a bathroom, just like mine and Malcolm's. Boxes almost like cages that we shuffle in between without any originality. There's even the same square table with the same ramrod chairs, which I sink into now when the woman gestures for me to do so.

I still don't know her name.

"Belinda," she says curtly, watching that question brew in my eyes.

"I'm Saskia." The answer has always been automatic, but for some reason, I feel the weight of my name on my tongue, as if telling it to the Monster the other night somehow gave it more significance.

"Would you like some tea, Saskia?"

"Oh, yes, please."

I don't ask which flavors she has. Tea is the one thing we're allowed to keep in our cupboard beyond the meals we're provided for breakfast, lunch, and dinner, and the flavor is determined by the season. Right now, it'll be red clover.

Belinda nods and begins busying herself with the shiny aluminum kettle that is, once again, exactly like mine at home. If I could choose, I think I'd like a golden one. Not that Malcolm or I use ours much—up until now, we've kept all our rigid mealtime conversations restricted to the required ones. I'm hoping this conversation will prove different.

"How did you know my partner?" Belinda asks with her back still turned to me.

The silver braid down her back sways, and her shoulders rise and fall quicker than they should, even as she pretends to breathe calmly and evenly.

"I was—*am*—his healer. I took care of him until he disappeared, and then I watched as they dragged him away."

She stiffens for the briefest of moments. "I suppose he didn't go quietly?"

The kettle whistles like a scream, the high-pitched sound cutting through us, and both of us visibly shudder. I wait for it to cease, to die in the air, because it's like a haunting memory of Diggory, one that Belinda doesn't have to relive but can imagine.

"No, he didn't."

I can't tell if there's exasperation or pride or fear on Belinda's face as she turns around with two mugs that twirl with streams of smoke. In any case, her next blink wipes every emotion from her face.

"But he *was* quiet about the injury that landed him in the Healing Center to begin with," I press, taking my mug from her outstretched hand and feeling the heat of it waft up into my face.

"I know what you're thinking." Belinda shoots me something that almost looks like a glare as she settles back into her chair across from me, her knuckles white with how tight she grips her mug. "The answer's no, I didn't push him... though sometimes I want to slap some sense into that man," she ends with a mutter.

I lean forward. "What kind of sense?"

"Just the kind that men often lack." She forces out a chuckle.

Curiosity brews in my chest. I could ask hundreds of different follow-up questions, but I press my tongue against the back of my teeth, trying to choose one that is least invasive. My tone comes out as nonchalant as I can make it. "Was he often reckless?"

Belinda seems to have realized she said too much. My eyebrows drop, but I unscrew my lips, trying not to look too disappointed, as her face tightens back into a neutral shape. She gives a sigh. "Look, I already told the sentries everything when they came to investigate our housing unit after his disappearance, so let me spare you having to ask the same questions." She takes a sip of her tea, lips pursed. "Diggory told me he slipped in the shower, as I suspect he told you. He didn't tell me of any plans to run away or steal certain... objects. I don't know what his ultimate goal was."

There's a finality in her voice, but I think about the way she worded each of those claims as I finally take a sip of my own tea. The sweet, earthy taste melts into my tongue and heats up the roof of my mouth. I swallow.

You don't ask the right questions.

Or maybe I don't peer hard enough at the answers.

"You said Diggory *told* you that he slipped in the shower," I start hesitantly. "Not that you believed him. What do *you* think really happened to him?"

Belinda sniffs, her face paling. "It doesn't matter what I think."

"But it does." She's his partner. Even if they never ended up falling in love, *she's* the one who's been by Diggory's side day in and day out for the last few decades. *She's* the one who knows him and his face and his mannerisms better than her own reflection.

"It doesn't matter what I think," Belinda repeats insistently.

"Well, then, how about what *I* think?" I ask. When Belinda's eyes flare for a second, I hurry on before she can stop me, keeping my voice hushed in case anyone is listening in. "*I* think he injured himself on purpose so that he'd be in the Healing Center, marked as ineligible for the last Choosing. I think he wanted to use the Choosing to do something important while every citizen, sentry, and Guardian was looking the other way."

There. I said it. The suspicion has been brewing inside of me for a few days now. Just like the kettle, my thoughts have been filling my head like hot steam, one on top of the other, until there's so much pressure I can't stand it any longer. And when Belinda says nothing in return, I know she's had the same thought.

I cock my head. "Diggory didn't expressly tell you what he was doing, but you suspected, didn't you? You knew?"

Belinda's hand rattles against her mug. For a second, I'm worried I pushed her too hard, that she's going to chuck her tea in my face for accusing her of keeping a secret. I should have learned my lesson from my interaction with Gaia, shouldn't have dared to even come here.

Then Belinda's elbow pulls back, and the mug goes crashing to the floor in a cascade of tea and ceramic shards.

"Oh, I'm so sorry!"

"Not to worry." I stand up, feeling my forehead pinch in confusion. Does she have a tremor? "I can help you clean it up."

I rush over to the cloth dispenser on the kitchen counter to grab something to wipe the spilled tea with while Belinda herself rushes off to snatch the broom and dustpan.

It isn't until we're both hunkered down on our hands and knees below the table that Belinda's whisper comes out as a low hiss.

"Our daughter was born hard of hearing and had to spend her whole life with hearing aids, but Diggory made up his own language with her using just his hands so that she could take them off when all the noises became too overwhelming. The two of them were inseparable because of that—until she was Chosen five years ago when she was twenty years old."

I freeze, blinking at the woman's face mere inches from mine. Had she just purposely dropped her mug so that we'd have an excuse to talk without that blinking camera picking up anything out of the ordinary? If so, I can't allow myself to waste these precious few seconds of privacy by gawking. I nod at her to keep going.

She continues without looking at me, pretending to sweep up some more glittering shards. "While most fathers would think of this as an honor, Diggory was heartbroken. Enraged, even. He was terrified that no one would be able to communicate with our daughter in the way that he did, that she wouldn't be able to take off her hearing aids and talk in the way that she preferred. So he sought ways to sneak into the Blood Moon Palace and visit her."

"And you think he succeeded?" I whisper back, mopping up the liquid more slowly this time. "You think he got into the Blood Moon Palace to see your daughter?"

"I think it was all talk that I had to smother until about a month ago."

"What happened a month ago?"

"Our daughter quit coming to the balcony." Belinda's voice breaks with pain on the last word, and my chest lurches with a sense of familiarity. There are whispers of Chosen Ones who stop coming out to wave at their friends and family after they've been in the palace for a certain length of time. I've always thought they must get so enamored by the palace life that they forget about their previous one, but what if...

"The sentries searched Diggory's room?"

My head is reeling, thoughts spinning faster than I can catch them, but we can't keep whispering beneath this table forever. I don't have time to think right now. I can think later.

"Yes," Belinda whispers. "They searched his room, and mine, and our joint one."

There seems to be a space at the end of her words, an inhalation as if she doesn't even dare say what she wants to beneath the table. I stare into her eyes and think about the first answer she gave me.

Diggory told me he slipped in the shower.

Slipped in the shower.

The shower.

I stand up, holding wads of soaked towel, and hand them to Belinda. "Do you mind if I use your restroom before I leave?" I ask.

Relief and warning seem to flicker in her gaze simultaneously.

"Of course. Mind your step, though. Some of the tiles are loose in there."

I nod and scurry off to the bathroom situated in the same corner as it is in my own housing unit. Clicking the door shut behind me, I let my attention sweep the tiny box of a room, from the crimson curtain hanging from the shower rod to the sparkling clean toilet bowl to the sink with the curled stainless-steel faucet and drain. There is a single cup with two toothbrushes next to a single bottle of issued hand soap. No drawers. The sentries probably didn't even think to search *here* for anything, knowing that every bathroom is the same and there are no hiding places for other potential forbidden items.

One of the downsides of trying to force everyone to be identical: you miss the loose tiles.

Sweeping aside the curtain, I crouch down once again to run my fingers along the shower floor. Most of them are firmly set in place, but one of them is slightly tilted diagonally, the grout around its far end deeper than the others.

Sliding my fingernails into the crack, I heave, tug, and—*pop!*—the entire tile comes loose.

I stifle a gasp in my throat, forgetting, for a second, that there are no cameras in bathrooms. What I'm doing feels so wrong, so forbidden, that it takes me a second of deep breathing before I carefully lean forward and peer into the dark, empty space beneath the missing tile.

Not empty, actually. Squinting, I can make out several objects that wink back at me. More necklaces? More ways to speak to the Monster? If I touch these things to examine them more closely, will his taunting voice infiltrate my head again?

No. When I dip my hand into the hole and my fingertips graze the object on top, no electricity fills my veins. I grasp it and pull it out into the light, a frown forming on my lips.

It's a dense, round object with a small handle poking from the top. An ornate design wraps around the center, where several numbers form a circle and three long, thin slivers tick round and round at different speeds. I watch the fastest one, mesmerized, until it's ticked itself all the way around before I reach back into the hole for another object.

This one is also round, but much smaller and daintier with a clear-cut jewel that sits on top. Without even thinking, I slip it onto one of my fingers before sliding it back off again just as quickly. Another piece of jewelry, if I had to guess. But one that doesn't connect the wearer to the mind of the Monster... simply meant for wearing and looking pretty.

One by one, I pull out the rest of Diggory's forbidden objects and examine them each with a breath that seems to stick to my lungs like a cold sweat.

There's a long, thin cylinder of wax with a blackened wick sticking from the top. A piece of ribbon so much smoother and silkier than anything I'm issued to tie my hair up with. A box that snaps open to reveal a little figurine in the center, though I don't dare touch the miniature handcrank that juts out from the side.

Finally, there are only two objects left, both of which glint back at me when I peer down at them.

The first has my eyes widening so fast, I swear they're going to pop out of my head. I only know what this is because we're taught from a young schooling age that the Blood Moon Palace is always locked outside of the Choosing. It's a key—silver but tarnished.

And the next object... my fingers seem to know what this is before I even bring it out into the stuttering electric light of the bathroom. My hands begin to quiver as they close around the handle, and I only allow myself half a glance at the clear, reflective surface before I shut my eyes and stuff the thing into the inside pocket of my cloak alongside the necklace.

A mirror.

Something creaks outside the bathroom door, and I jump. Probably just Belinda getting herself another cup of tea, but I have a feeling that my time is up anyhow.

Willing my hands to calm down, I pretend I'm doing something as methodical as stitching up a cut as I place each of the objects back into the hole beneath the missing tile. If I could, I would take them all, just so Belinda doesn't have any incriminating evidence to deal with, but I doubt everything could fit in my pockets without creating a noticeable bulge.

Just as I'm about to put that tarnished key back into its hiding place, however, I pause to stare at it.

Could it be a copy of the key to the Blood Moon Palace? Or to a passageway that leads *into* the palace? If Diggory was as obsessed with breaking into there as Belinda claims, then I'm pretty sure it's safe to guess where all of these objects came from: the Guardians themselves.

Suddenly, I have to bite down on a knuckle to keep myself from letting loose an absurd laugh.

Diggory was stealing from the actual *Guardians*. No wonder they didn't want to let him go back to the Healing Center.

A decision clicks into place within me. I pocket the key, too, then slide the tile back where it belongs. If I'm not mistaken, Belinda won't notice they're gone because she refuses to look too closely, too afraid of what she'll see.

Well, she has a lot more self-control than I do, apparently.

Straightening, I swish aside the curtain to step out of the shower, and make a point to busy myself at the toilet. I open and close the lid, flush, and wash my hands at the sink before I finally allow myself to return to the kitchen.

Just as I predicted, Belinda is sitting at her kitchen table once again, a fresh cup of tea cradled in her hands.

"Stomachache?" she asks dryly. I hear the hidden message beneath her words: *cutting it kind of close, don't you think?* And yes, maybe I was in there for a little too long, but all I can do is clutch a hand against my lower abdomen and nod with a soft groan.

"The red clover's a little strong for my taste," I lie. "But thank you for the visit anyway. I'd best get going now."

I dip my head and hurry to her door, trying not to glance at the blinking camera above her screen. It's only when my hand rests on the doorknob that her voice sighs out at me, "The Monster is no idle threat. He is what awaits transgressors like my partner... and he is hungry."

The way she says it makes me shiver. But after my last conversation with the Monster himself, I'm beginning to think no one is thrown over the Wall at all. And the more I think about it, the more ridiculous the idea becomes. Why would the Guardians waste all that blood? What would be the point? Besides to instill fear in us. The way Lucan practically laughed in my face when I said that echoes in my brain.

I know she's trying to tell me to be careful, to tread more lightly than Diggory did or else the consequences will be severe, but for some reason I can't help the thrill from erupting in where my supposed stomachache is.

Because maybe the Monster isn't the only one who's hungry.

Maybe I'm a little bit hungry, too.

The curfew announcement rings through the air as I hurry back down the main road, trying to tell myself to *not* hurry. To swing my arms at my sides like everyone else and not like someone who has a necklace, a mirror, and a key in her pockets.

"Citizens of Xantera, please return to your individual housing units. Recreational time is over. Citizens of Xantera, please return to your individual housing units. Recreational time is over."

Oh, how I'm beginning to hate that smooth, female voice. It reminds me of the Wall—impenetrable and all-encompassing, squeezing us all tighter and tighter until we don't have any of our own choices left.

Still, as I veer off the main road to head down the darkened alleyway between complexes, I can't help but feel the excitement tingling in my fingertips at the prospect that *I* made a choice tonight. Several, in fact.

I didn't turn the necklace in to the Guardians. I discovered Diggory's secrets that even the sentries couldn't find. I chose which of those secrets to carry home with me. As if on instinct, I slip my hand into my pocket and graze the vial again, just to feel that shock, a reminder that I'm *alive.* As soon as I'm safe in the confines of my own bed, I plan to—

My feet lurch to a standstill as I round a corner and face my housing unit's door.

Fear floods through me, surging from my heart and down my body to the very tips of my fingers.

Because a sentry is already standing in front of it.

12

LUCAN

A douse of fear sparks within me, and I know something's wrong.

I don't just feel it in the marrow of my very bones. I know it in the sparse memories that have woven through the synapses of my brain. Saskia's words replay over and over in my head, like a symphony of clues I can't help but fuse together.

I have no other choice but to hand over this annoying piece of jewelry to the Guardians.

When she said that to me, there was a hint of bitterness in her tone that I didn't catch right away. At the time, I was having too much fun toying with her to notice, but now that I'm obsessively inspecting each and every thing she's said to me over our two very brief conversations... this isn't a woman who likes being told what to do. Maybe she's stifled that part of her in order to survive the fucking zoo she's been bred and raised in, maybe she doesn't even know it about herself, but deep down, she wants nothing more than to be given a choice. A real one.

Which means she wouldn't turn the necklace in to the Guardians, even after I told her I was the Monster. Even if she was paralyzed with horror, her curiosity and thirst for knowledge would overpower her need to obey.

So something's wrong, because the sun is about to set on the fifth day of silence, and I swear I just felt *her* fear spurt through *my* veins.

I sprint back toward the Wall before the others can stop me, but this time, I shift as I go. My pounding footsteps morph into thundering paws. My panting shatters into snarling as the branches of the forest whip past me. My speed increases as the shape of me lengthens, honing my momentum so that when the Wall comes into view between branches, I don't stop.

I launch myself at the one thing that has kept me from my future, my birthright, for my entire life.

Maybe this time, my rage will give me enough fuel to triumph over it.

Just like all the other times, my claws scrape at the surface. I let them take root in some of the spiderwebbing cracks, digging into it deeper so that I can pull myself upward.

Not even two seconds later, pain explodes from the point of contact.

It feels like nails are driving through my paws, up my arms, and straight into my fucking heart. My skull splits. White-hot stars bloom across my vision.

And still I scrabble for purchase, pulling myself upward.

If it weren't for the pain, I would have been able to scale this thing a long time ago, or ram myself through it no matter how thick it is. The spikes at the top wouldn't matter—I'd simply rip them off with my teeth and spit them off the ledge.

But the pain. The pain. The *pain*.

It's like I'm rotting from within.

My vision turns black as it drives deeper into every trembling part of me. Fire licks across my veins, stabbing every organ like pieces of glass. Still, I climb, dragging myself higher than I've ever been before, pushing the pain into a dark cavern of my mind.

Until my muscles spasm and freeze—because it's not just my own fear that paralyzes me. It's what's laced through the Wall.

I slide back down and land in a heap at the bottom.

A fury like I've never known bubbles back to life as the pain slowly leaks out of my body.

I can't get to her.

My father was never able to conquer the Wall, and that has been a stone-cold fact that haunts my every waking moment. But now I *know* one of the people I was born to protect. I know her name and her voice and the secret desires she's trying to bury.

And I. Can't. Get. To. Her.

I wasn't joking when I said she's a traitor simply for fraternizing with me now. If the parasites catch her with that necklace and all her other secrets...

Scrambling upward, I run to the edge of the woods and launch myself at the Wall again.

Again.

And again.

And again.

SASKIA

The sentry knocks twice, her long, slender arm making it look so graceful.

Immediately, I release the necklace, my pulse hammering, to watch what's about to happen unfold.

Her sword rests at her hip, hanging from the leather belt around her waist. Her cloak and rich brown hair blow in the breeze that whistles through the alleyway.

The thick sound of her knuckles against the wood bounces back to me. Then she reaches for the knob without giving anyone inside more than a second to react before the door swings open, like Malcolm was already standing on the other side waiting.

When his face comes into view, his eyebrows knot into confusion.

"Good evening," Malcolm says stiffly.

I don't hear the female sentry's reply, but Malcolm's eyes flit over her shoulder and land on me when I reach up to brush the hair from my eyes.

Guardians.

The sentry notices instantaneously and pivots her neck to find me in the middle of my first step. Hopefully, it doesn't look suspicious, like I'm not hurrying or had just been rooted in place half a second ago.

But I'm flustered, and I have the heart rate to prove it.

My legs want to match the tempo as she watches me approach, but I force myself to maintain a steady stroll. Her doe eyes, deceivingly innocent, never stray from my face, but she stands in a neutral manner with her shoulders relaxed.

When I reach her, I smile. "Good evening."

She looks down at me from the second step, but I think I'd be taller than her if she stepped down. "Enjoying the sunset?"

Panic surges into my throat. Is she testing me? Hardly any light ever filters past the overhanging eaves of the complexes, so the strip of sunset that does make it through is as thin and sharp as the rapier at her side.

"Yes, it's quite beautiful," I reply, turning my face upward at the visible slice of sky. "On the way back from the Blood Moon Palace, I decided to take the long way to get some fresh air and exercise, and I ended up visiting a friend."

"The perfect Sunday," Malcolm adds.

I forgot he was there.

I blink through my nerves and plaster on another smile. "It was." Turning to the sentry, I offer her what is my illusion of choice. "Please, come in."

She steps across the threshold without bothering to wait for Malcolm to step back, so it becomes a weird shuffle of feet and Malcolm muttering "Sorry" multiple times.

I follow like she's invited me into my own home, avoiding Malcolm's concerned gaze as he closes the door behind me.

She walks confidently over to the chair on the opposite side of the room before sitting. Her hand sweeps over the remaining seats, and she encourages us to sit with a pleasant, "Please."

I wonder if the Guardians sent a woman to make me feel less on edge, less threatened. Because she seems almost jovial.

Her wide, brown eyes sparkle in the low light, and her cheekbones are dusted with a naturally rosy hue. It's a face you want to spill your secrets to—a face you want to like you.

But I don't let my guard down as I sit, and Malcolm sits beside me like a dutiful partner before the sentry's eyes bounce between us, waiting.

Waiting.

We're all waiting.

The objects in my pocket feel like lead pressing down on my thigh. I resist the urge to look down to check if they're bulging underneath my cloak. The Guardians can't possibly know that I've taken them. Can they?

"Rosalyn," she says finally. The sentry has a name.

Why does this keep shocking me? She must have a partner, children, a life of her own within the Wall.

Does Lucan have the same outside the Wall?

"Rosalyn," Malcolm and I repeat in harmony, then my voice continues alone. "Would you like some tea?"

"No, thank you." She leans back against the chair and rests her forearms on both armrests. "I'm here because we had a healer report an argument between you and your fellow co-worker."

My brain spins to catch on then tries to right itself. "Gaia?"

"Yes. Gaia. Can you tell me what your argument was about?"

Malcolm shifts, running his palms down his pants, as my own palms start to sweat.

It's a trap question, one I don't know if Gaia's already given an answer to. All I know is that glaring man in the locker room definitely reported us for slightly raised voices.

A pain pulses in my temple, but if I take too long to answer, it will be even more suspicious. "It was over a patient," I start. *No, it wasn't. It was over me begging her to access information about a traitor, one whose housing unit I just stole several illegal objects from.* I clear my throat. "We disagreed on whether the patient should be released or not."

Rosalyn squints at me. "Did you raise your voice?"

"No," I assure her. "It was a professional discussion, at most."

"I see." Leaning back, she nods. "The patient?"

"Odette, a young girl."

"And are you feeling okay? Emotionally?"

"Of course," I say.

"Taking care of unwell people can place a burden on you mentally, especially when it's children and those you feel you cannot help or can't determine what's wrong. Did the stress cause you to lash out?"

"I wouldn't say either of us lashed out."

She stares, a piercing brown look that could pin me to the wall. "Do you remember the Cardinal Rules, Saskia?"

I never told her my name, but she wields it as a threat.

"Yes," I reply cooly, despite my tight throat. I haven't counted how many I've broken lately, but it's more than one. I try to keep the tally off my face as I list them in my head. One glance at Malcolm, and my worry multiplies. Based on his narrowed eyes, I wonder if he would turn me in for asking questions. "I count them to myself every night before bed." Like a prayer to the Guardians, but now I don't know who I've been praying to.

I feel like I'm right back in a rigid metal desk, a yellow-badged eleven-year-old.

"Rule number three, Saskia!" my old teacher would shout—a pop quiz in the middle of history class. I flick my eyes back to Malcolm, wondering if his style resembles Miss Dolores. His eyes look gentle, though, a warmth that lives there like you're stepping into the sunlight on a chilly day. The suspicion lingers in them still, but I could never imagine him drilling twelve rules into someone until they cracked, and I don't think he would turn me in.

"Rule number seven?" the sentry prods.

"Don't engage in arguments," I answer automatically

She raises her eyebrows. "Yet you argued with Gaia."

"It won't happen again. I was mistaken thinking I was doing best for my patient."

Rosalyn stays silent but tips her chin to acknowledge that it most certainly will not happen again.

Malcolm turns his head to study me with an urging look. *Are you telling the truth?* he seems to say.

I've got this, I try to communicate with my eyes.

Rosalyn interrupts our moment. "How is your partnership going?"

Tearing my eyes off Malcolm, I slip my hand through his. My forearm lays across the pocket in my cloak, and from underneath the fabric, the mirror's handle digs into my skin. A reminder of how much risk I'm taking. Lying. And it's not just myself I'm gambling with, but Malcolm as well.

I turn back to her. "It's going well."

"It *is* Sunday," she comments, leaning forward and clasping her hands in front of her. Her lips curl.

A look of sick satisfaction crosses her face like a hologram, and her eyes dart to the blinking camera involuntarily. A hollow, sinking feeling spreads outward from my stomach.

Someone is watching us. Recording this entire interaction. Did they hear Malcolm and me whispering the other night? Our voices were *so* low. But nevertheless, a new fear simmers in my chest—that they know about our forbidden agreement.

"I hope your spark is alive and well," Rosalyn simpers. "We wouldn't want it going out so soon." Her neck cranes toward our joint bedroom door before her tone drops and slows, dripping with amusement. "Would we?"

Unmistakable fear hammers in my chest. She's getting off on her power. I can see it in the creases around her eyes and lips, in the twitch of her fingertips. Like she's happily pulling our strings.

I squeeze Malcolm's hand. He squeezes back.

We both know what she wants. What she expects.

It's not about the sex. It's about the control.

Which we bend to like marionettes.

Malcolm smiles softly. "Rosalyn, thank you for your visit." The slat in our door scrapes open, and I can hear those anonymous hands place a tray down with our dinner, but no one dares turn their head.

Instead, Malcolm rises to his feet, keeping his fingers laced with mine. "We may just skip dinner tonight," he comments to no one in particular, but his tone is one I've never heard before—almost sultry. He tugs gently on my arm to pull me up. Without looking at her, he smiles seductively at me but directs his words at Rosalyn. "I trust you can see yourself out."

"Good night," she replies, still seated.

She's still seated, from what I can tell from my peripheral vision, when I close our joint bedroom door behind us.

Is she still there? Malcolm mouths, all traces of his earlier act dissolving.

I press my ear to our bedroom door, listening for the sound of footsteps, the creak of the floor, or the squeak of hinges to indicate that the sentry is leaving.

Nothing. I can almost sense her held breath, though, the pause of expectation, and I swing my head back toward Malcolm to nod.

Yes, she's still there.

A new emotion steals over his features. It's not fear, exactly, but more like resignation. His shoulders droop, and his mouth becomes a weak line of pressed lips as he realizes, no doubt, what this means: it's our first Sunday as a secret non-couple, and we're going to be forced into having sex by the very authority figures we thought we could dupe.

It's impossible to escape their control. That sentry in our living room is no less of an invasion of privacy than the camera mounted above our screen. She is a whip that the Guardians wield to make sure we stay in line, and for the first time in my life, I'm wondering what that line actually looks like. Is it really just the Wall that contains us, or have they molded us into cages so tight, there's no room to breathe?

Malcolm is actually trembling as he tosses his shirt over his head, revealing the soft planes of his pale chest. It's a chest I've seen so many times before, but it feels different, seeing him undress now. Before our conversation a few days ago, we were still under the illusion that we might grow into wanting each other. Now, this is just an assault on our bodily autonomy. A mockery of the small choice we gave ourselves permission to make.

I watch Malcolm begin to unbuckle his pants when a sudden idea hits me square in the chest.

What if we could still dupe them?

These bodies are *ours*. I won't let anyone else decide what to do with them.

"Stop," I whisper, throwing out a palm and hitting Malcolm in the chest. He freezes in place, and his eyes follow me as I make my way to our shared bed, crawling up to the metal headboard with my cloak still fluttering around me. I curl my fingertips around two metal arches, as if I'm gripping a pair of horns.

Then I begin to rock in place.

The headboard hits the wall. *Bump. Bump. Bump.* The floor beneath us creaks. They're sounds I've heard over and over for the past six months, like the heartbeat of my dissatisfaction. I look over my shoulder to find that Malcolm's jaw has actually dropped open.

It's just a soft thump, but the vibrations travel through the thin walls.

"C'mon," I whisper. "Help me."

He stays rooted to the spot for another few seconds before he shakes his head and crawls onto the bed next to me. Then he takes hold of the headboard and rocks, too.

The *bump, bump, bump* against the wall increases in its fervor. I swear to all Guardians, we've never made our bed rock like this while having real sex before, but I find a laugh crawling up my throat as we increase our vigorous movements in unison.

"Groan a little bit," I whisper out of the corner of my mouth.

"What?"

"You know, the sound you make when you're getting into it."

He pulls a horrified expression, so I take the opportunity to let go of the headboard with one hand, grab a pillow beneath me, and smash it across his face.

"Ugh." His muffled grunt is perfect, and I hit him again. "Ugh."

"That's it!" I hiss. "You're doing great."

"You've got to be kidding—*ugh*," he cuts himself off as my pillow catches him again.

I grin. "Have fun with it."

Now I'm actively clamping down on the laugh in my mouth at the look he gives me in return. It's exasperation and playfulness all in one, something I've never seen on his face before. It almost feels like a privilege to witness it. This is probably the most fun I've ever had with him, no orgasms required.

Malcolm takes advantage of my pause to snag his own pillow and whip it across my face before I can hit him again.

I shriek, more out of surprise than anything else. The soft, fluffy thing does little more than fuel a sense of competition within me, and soon we're both pummeling each other with our pillows, turning our laughs into forced grunts and moans. I think I might hear footsteps outside our room, followed by the opening and shutting of the front door, but we don't stop our pretending, even after the sentry leaves. The camera is still on, after all, recording every sound.

Finally, I whack Malcolm across the face so hard, he falls sideways onto the rest of the bed.

I slump down next to him, breathing heavily as sweat beads against my skin.

"Good work, partner." I lift up a hand. He shakes his head, his lips pinched in a suppressed smile, but slaps my palm anyway.

"Yeah. Good work."

I can still feel the three forbidden objects pressing into me from my cloak pocket, but I don't dare shed it now, even to cool down. As soon as I'm sure the sentry is long gone, I'll sneak them all into my own personal room and figure out what to do with them there.

"Saskia?"

I open my eyes. "Yeah?"

Malcolm turns his head toward me, his smile fading. "I... I hope you know what you're doing."

"Hm?" My heart just calmed down, but now it begins to drum up against my ribs again.

"All the questions about the Dark Days. The deal we made. Now this argument with your coworker and this sentry interrogating you. I know you're up to something. I just can't think of what it could possibly be."

The way he says that has me swallowing thickly. At this point, I doubt he would turn me in, but I'm also not sure he'd want to know the details of what I'm hiding—both in my pockets and in my heart.

What better way to know than to ask him, then?

"Do you want me to tell you?" I whisper. "What I'm up to, I mean?"

He blinks at me, surprise flicking through the rapid movements.

"It's your choice," I say when he continues to gawk at me.

"My choice?"

"Yes."

It's sad that so many choices have been taken from him that Malcolm looks positively awestruck at the possibility.

"It feels good, huh?" I sigh. "To have a choice."

His eyes stick to mine with a raw and vulnerable look, like he wishes he could make a thousand more, before he turns his gaze back to the ceiling, concentration furrowing his forehead as he thinks about it.

"No," he says finally. "Don't tell me unless your life is in real danger. If your life is in danger, then I want to know. But not otherwise."

Now it's my turn to blink at him. I don't think I could ever view Malcolm in a romantic way, but his words are tugging on my heartstrings in an entirely different manner.

"You'd put your own life at risk to help me if mine were in danger?"

The concept is a new, strange one. There are no Cardinal Rules saying you have to lay your life down for someone you love. Nothing that could force anyone into that kind of willing sacrifice for someone other than a Guardian.

Malcolm's smile turns rather somber, but he nods.

"What else are friends for?"

Alone in my own room now, I slip the key from my pocket first.

It's heavier than I think most keys would weigh, but I've never actually had to lock anything, so I'm not entirely sure.

This one looks ancient, with two twirling pieces that merge at the top of the bow, reminding me of a heart. There's so many questions sprouting like weeds in my head again: did it really belong to the Guardians, or someone else? Do they realize it's missing? How did Diggory even know where to steal it from?

I push those away and slide open the drawer of my dresser. The key makes a heavy *clunk* sound when I place it toward the back. I'm going to have to find a better hiding spot because Rosalyn would have found it within a few minutes tops if she'd decided to search our housing unit.

Next, I pull out the mirror.

The handle is warm from being buried in my cloak and pressed against my body for more than an hour.

I can't bring myself to turn it over yet and lay eyes on that silvery surface again. But the gold back and handle are beautiful. Its intricate etchings swirl in a pattern of flowers and vines inside the oval shape.

I place it face down on the top of the dresser before rummaging in my pocket again.

My fingertips could find the necklace on their own, because the electricity is like a beacon that I can feel even before I wrap my hand around the chain and hold it up in front of my face.

It doesn't scare me anymore. Instead, I feel an anticipation more akin to excitement. The satisfaction you get when you learn something, master it. Because your curiosity drove you to grow.

Hurriedly, I remove my cloak, and as soon as the pendent slithers down my sternum and rests above my heart, I feel the connection alight.

Lucan. I finally allow myself to taste his name for the first time.

When he doesn't answer at first, my first thought flickers nervously, but I take a steadying breath and repeat myself with conviction.

I found a mirror, Lucan.

He might be the Monster—and also an asshole—but he also has a name. A personality. A heartbeat of his own.

And that heartbeat crashes into me like a waterfall as his presence suddenly latches onto mine.

Lucan, I say again, finding myself enjoying the sound of his name... if only because it seems to shock the asshole right out of him. I can feel his surprise as if it's my own.

I thought... That gravelly voice of his trails off as if he's out of breath. And then I hear the panting.

What's wrong? I ask, panic momentarily creeping back in. *Do Monsters get asthma, or something?* Merely a week ago, I would have been overjoyed to hear that the thing that howls beyond the Wall has some sort of medical issue, but now that thought fills me with a sudden urge to protect. To heal.

No, I don't have fucking asthma, Lucan gets out between heavy breaths. *Just give me a second.*

My thrill doesn't want to subside, doesn't want to be contained, because as soon as I'm sure his breathing has steadied, I burst out with, *Did you hear me, though?*

His chuckle vibrates against my chest at last. *And here I was thinking you were dead.*

Dead?

You know, the thing that happens when you're no longer alive.

I wish I could glare at him. *I know what dead means.*

What was wrong? he questions, ignoring me.

You could tell something was wrong?

Saskia. He says my name as if he's practiced it a hundred times since the moment we last talked. *What was wrong?*

I sit back on the edge of my bed and lift my eyes to the Wall looming in the distance outside my window. Giddiness bounces through me in a way I haven't felt since I was a child. *I mean, there was something wrong. A sentry came to question me about a tiny little thing, but I lied.* The laugh in my head feels weird. No sound escapes my mouth, but humor bubbles in my mind. Apparently, lying makes me laugh now. *And then the sentry got greedy, like the Rules don't apply to her. She couldn't just leave. She had to make sure we knew we weren't in control. But Malcolm and I chose to have fun.*

What kind of fun? Lucan asks hesitantly.

We went into our joint bedroom—not like that, I say quickly. For some reason, this new euphoric sense of freedom is making me feel like I can spill at least some of my secrets. It's not like the Monster can tell the Guardians that I'm deliberately disobeying them. I almost snort at the thought. *Malcolm and I decided that we're not the right partners for each other, so we just pretended to... you know.* I hurry on before the blush on my cheeks can leach into our connection. *But I felt like a kid again—because I couldn't tell you the last time I chose to pretend.*

Lucan sighs, and for some reason, I feel like he slumped down in relief. *Chose,* he repeats, finally catching his breath. *I like that word.*

Me too. I smile to myself as my eyes cut to the mirror laying face down. The golden metal catches a bit of moonlight and casts reflections across the room. *And I went to Diggory's housing unit. I found all his secrets.*

What?

This time, I'm sure Lucan remembers who Diggory is, because it sounds like he's gone rigid, all of his attention honed in on me and my words—like he knows just how dangerous it is for me to go snooping. The intensity of his tone makes me feel like I actually did something brave.

Under my breath, I tell him what I discovered in Diggory's shower. He listens with rapt quietness until I get to the part where I nicked the key and the mirror.

A mirror. You actually found a mirror. Do I finally get to know what you look like, then? The teasing tone comes back, and it settles low in my stomach like simmering coals. I realize I like the way it ignites my core, simply because it's not supposed to.

No, I say. *I finally get to know what I look like.*

Lucan doesn't respond, and I can't quite make out a complete thought in his mind. He must be better at hiding his thoughts in the folds, somewhere I'm unable to decipher them.

I rise to my feet and take a deep breath as I tip the handheld mirror up.

Adjusting it against the wall, I catch a brief glimpse of myself. *Not yet*, I think, averting my eyes, before I prop it up so that it's at the right angle and take a step back.

My face fills the oval glass surface, and immediately, my lips part in surprise.

They're full and pink. I bring my index finger up to touch them, sweeping the tip across my top lip, and then I watch the flesh bounce back after I press into my bottom lip.

Turning my chin to the side, my eyes follow my jaw line sideways, then up and across my cheekbones, to my nose. I've seen so many different shapes of noses on other people, but this is the first time I'm seeing mine—how it slopes ever so slightly in the middle. Like only a handful of people I've noticed before, I also have a light dusting of little dots that sweep over the bridge of it.

Freckles, Lucan says intently, like he's trying to memorize the shape and color of my thoughts. *You have freckles.*

I have freckles, I agree.

I look myself in the eyes. They're green? Or brown? Greenish-brown, I decide.

That's called hazel, he tells me.

It's... pretty, I say, trying to take my eyes off my own. My pupils are blown, taking in every curve, line, and angle that creates my face. *What color are yours?*

I don't expect him to respond, but he does after a few moments of hesitation. *Amber.*

For a moment I think back to my dream, how I fell off the Wall and opened my eyes to find wicked yellow irises gleaming back. I wasn't far off, then, and suddenly my imagination is conjuring more images of him and what *he* might look like—until I get distracted by my hair.

You have red hair? Lucan asks.

I've always known it was a deep auburn. Obviously, I can see the ends of my long strands when I braid it, but the way it frames my face and the way the reddish color contrasts with my fair skin—I'm enamored.

I take a few steps back eventually, unsure of how much time I've spent staring at my face, to take in the rest of my body. I have on the same plain shirt and pants I put on this morning, but it looks different on my body than it does on the hanger. I have to shift to get the complete picture, but I have curves; my breasts, my hips, my waist. They form an hourglass shape, and when I bend over, the swell of my breasts makes me feel... I don't know. But I like it.

I straighten and let my fingers linger across my collarbones that create a trail down to where the necklace drops into my cleavage. Into the space that I think looks *good*.

My heart jumps in tandem with Lucan's as I abruptly remember he's even here with me.

I'm sorry, I start. *I shouldn't be seeking out attention or thinking about myself like this. I just never realized I'm...*

The word stifles itself in my throat. It's something I shouldn't admit, too selfish to even think, but Lucan finishes my sentence in a growl.

Beautiful. You're beautiful. He pauses. *And little nightmare?*

What? I whisper, but I can feel it. That pesky little emotion we're not supposed to indulge in intertwining around my heart.

I'm jealous of the people who get to lay eyes on you.

LUCAN

E nvy.
An emotion I haven't felt in a long time.

It spreads outward from that dark pit in my stomach, replacing my earlier exhaustion from throwing my body into the Wall over and over. For a brief moment, I'd burn the world down just to have this woman in the flesh before me.

Take in with my own two eyes what I saw through hers. Place my hands where hers just lied.

But it's only lust—wanting what I can't have.

The Guardians have already taken everything from me and my family, and now they have her too. She belongs to me. And it's *their* fault I can't see or touch what's mine.

But rest assured, if she gave me the choice, I'd touch. I'd show her how depraved the world really is—and how pleasurable it can be.

Lucan, she says breathily, likely following the pathways of my corrupted thoughts. I want to fucking *consume* the way she says my name, her own mind a twist of intrigue and desire that I wish I could wrap up in my fist.

A man has never made her come, I pick out from the tangle of emotions. She's always had to give herself her own pleasure—always the one to give, never the one to take.

Yet, she wants everything. Knowledge included.

I might not be able to touch her, but I can give her that. I can tell her what really happened five hundred years ago, when the Wall was built and the parasites took their twelve false thrones.

I tip my head up toward the sky from where I slumped down at the sound of her colorful voice, watching as a cloud drifts over the bright crescent moon. Something about her determination and excitement seems to have healed the echoes of pain that were ringing through me afterward. Now, despite the weariness settling into my bones from what that pain did to me, I stay in my monstrous form.

And pray she doesn't leave me as soon as I utter the words that will turn her into a rebel once and for all.

Do you want to learn the truth about your Guardians?

15

SASKIA

In the Dark Days, we were all prey for the Monster."
I was eight years old when my instructor told me that. She painted scenes of spoil and horror, where a terrible beast prowled among men and attacked the easiest prey—children and homeless beggars—while a corrupt figurehead sat idly by, letting his people suffer with pieces of greed glittering around his neck. He had the means to end his people's agony, and yet he chose to do nothing.

"It was a society heading for disaster," Miss Dolores said. "Until thirteen holy saviors from another land found us in chaos."

I remember her describing the Guardians as stronger and faster than regular humans: their skin harder, their teeth sharper, their bones less breakable. They were the only ones who had the physical ability to fight the Monster, and fight him they did.

When our ancestors witnessed the Guardians vanquish what their leader wouldn't and build the Wall to protect the city for good, they called for a new government. One with thirteen thrones instead of one.

"It was a tragedy when the Thirteenth Guardian perished in the war that followed," Miss Dolores said, and I remember several of my peers and I hanging our heads to mimic her apparent sorrow. "But it was a war that was necessary. You see, the current leader at the time didn't want to give up his place in the Blood Moon Palace, so he sent all his remaining loyalists to fight the Guardians."

"Fight the *Guardians*?" one of my classmates exclaimed in shock.

"Yes. But nobody can fight the Holy Guardians and win," Miss Dolores warned. "As is evidenced by the fact that our current Twelve only lost one of their own while the leader at the time lost *everything*. So the Twelve tossed away his crown and established the superior society we have today, with the Monster forever locked outside of our safety bubble."

First there was corruption, death, and the Monster. Then there were the Guardians who saved us—with Rules and a uniform society. That's all I've ever known.

Now, I utter the single word that will give me more.

Yes.

Yes, I want to know.

Even if I still can't fully trust the Monster, I want to learn what he thinks is the truth. I want to hear his perspective from the other side of the Wall.

Lucan sighs, but not as if he's tired. It sounds like he's reeling in one long breath to prepare himself. Or me.

The Guardians didn't come upon a city of chaos, Saskia. They came upon a kingdom of peace—and realized how much they could benefit from controlling and consuming it.

In the mirror still propped up against my wall, I catch sight of my forehead furrowing in confusion.

What do you mean by consuming? They don't eat us if that's what you—

No, but they do drink your blood, right? Lucan's voice pinches as if such a thing disgusts him.

Only the Chosen Ones, I say quickly, pedaling backward to sit on the edge of my bed. *But it doesn't kill them. It's supposed to be an honor, to give sustenance to the beings who protect us from... well...*

Me, Lucan says.

Yes. You.

Even as I say it, a sheepish blush warms up my cheeks. The more I think about it, the more it all seems rather disproportionate. If the Wall is as strong as they say it is, it should keep the Monster out regardless of whether the Guardians get blood from their Chosen Ones. And while the Monster hasn't actually bitten into anyone in living memory, the Guardians bite into someone new every blood moon.

That's because unlike the parasites who stole my throne, I would only bite you if it would bring you pleasure, Lucan growls. *Not to take your very source of life.*

I jolt in bed, and not just because of what he said about biting.

Your *throne?*

Yes, my throne, Saskia. Possessiveness slides into Lucan's voice, gripping my mind like a vice. *It was not a human who ruled the kingdom from that palace before the Guardians—it was what you'd call a Monster. Only back then, his people didn't fear him like you do me. Back then, they called him king.*

Chills filter down my spine as if the Monster is howling. But it's quiet outside my window, because the Monster is in my head, listening to my thoughts spin as loudly as my own heartbeat.

King, I repeat and lower my head onto my pillow.

Like jewelry, the word is only vaguely familiar, as if I learned it once long ago and never heard of it again. But yes, *king* was the word that Miss Dolores used to describe the figurehead of the Dark Days. I just never imagined that king was anything like Lucan—not lazy or greedy, but full of intelligence and rage.

Back then, Lucan continued, *we had a wall made of wood surrounding the kingdom, not to keep out actual Monsters, but to keep out the wild animals of the forest—cougars and bears and... wolves.* He pauses on that last word, but keeps going before I can question why. *There were no Choosings or Chosen Ones because my grandfather didn't need to take anything away from anyone else to rule. It was a flourishing kingdom, and people were happy. There wasn't any suffering.*

His grandfather? It's a good thing I'm already lying down in bed, because I feel faint. If his grandfather was the king from five hundred years ago, then that would make him...

A wicked laugh. *For simplicity's sake, let's say I'm twenty-five. That would be about the human equivalent. But I've been circling this wretched Wall for a lot longer than that.*

My head spins harder. If Lucan is telling the truth, then that means everything we've ever learned about the Monster is a lie. He doesn't prowl around Xantera because he's starved for meat and bone; he does so because it's his lost kingdom. Or, at least, his *ancestor's* lost kingdom.

Exactly, he growls now. *When the Guardians came, my grandfather was ripped away from his people and forced to watch as they turned our wall of wood into stone. Then he was killed, and my father and his family were forced to flee outside the Wall while the Guardians kept everyone else on the inside like cattle to be bred and slaughtered. And when my father died, he passed it down to me: the mission to tear down the Wall so we can take back our throne and vanquish the* real *Monsters.*

The real Monsters as in *them.* The Twelve Guardians.

I massage the bridge of my nose where my freckles are, not knowing what to believe.

On the one hand, part of Lucan's story clicks into place in my brain, filling in the gaps I've been taught never to peer too closely at. On the other, I can't forget that I'm talking to the *Monster*—at least the kind I've always known. Whatever he is, he's not human, and he could be lying to me, spinning a story to get me on his side so that I'll do his bidding. Perhaps to lure me closer to him.

Clever woman, Lucan says, his tone a mixture of appreciation and impatience. *Not believing what you're told immediately. I'm surprised they ever managed to beat all that curiosity and suspicion out of you.*

They didn't beat anything out of me, I snap back, for some reason irked that his praise sends tingles down my belly. *There is no violence here. We aren't being slaughtered like you think we are.*

There is no violence that you see, Lucan corrects. *There is no slaughtering* that you know of.

I think I'd know if my own neighbors were being killed.

What about the Chosen Ones, then? he retorts immediately. *They cease to be your neighbors as soon as they're dragged into that palace. I caught* that *much from my limited connection with Diggory.*

The Chosen Ones are given a lifetime of comfort and ease until the day they pass of old age, I force out, although the words sound regurgitated even to my own ears. *They only sacrifice their blood so that the Guardians can continue to protect us, and it isn't painful.*

Oh yeah? I can practically *feel* Lucan's angry smirk. *Then why do the Chosen Ones stop coming to the balcony after a few years? Why does Diggory think his daughter is dead?*

The words slam into my chest and stop my heart in its racing track. After all this time of suppressing that secret curled against my heart, it's threatening to rise to the surface once again. Tears spring in my eyes, and I grit my teeth in an attempt to smother the secret before Lucan can sense it and use it against me.

What do you want from me, Monster?

I feel him wince at the name, but I don't care. I need him to get to the point, because as much as I'd love to think otherwise, I know his attention must have a deeper purpose. He can call me beautiful all he wants, but it doesn't change the fact that I'm a means to an end for him. Diggory couldn't give him what he needs, so he's turned his sights to the next person who picked up the necklace. Me.

A quick spark of emotions flares through our connection, but it's gone too quickly for me to catch hold of it. Whatever Lucan feels in response to those thoughts of mine, he's able to suppress it with ease.

Only someone from the inside can open the Wall, he croons, and then his howl erupts from outside my window.

I suck in a breath as the same noise echoes in my own mind, wishing I could hate the overlapping of sounds the same way I hate Malcolm's chewing and snoring. Instead, I find myself only wanting to sink into it, to bathe in goosebumps forever.

He stops all too soon, though, and I find my thighs clenching together as his voice whispers through my mind, like his mouth is pressed right up against my ear.

What do I want from you, little nightmare? A dark, heavy pause hovers between his words. *I want you to let me in.*

Today is one of the rare days that I don't feel like healing.

No, that's not true. I'd still want to be a healer. I just wish I was the healer who was running these tests and studying Odette's blood under a microscope.

Then I'd be more in control over this situation.

I've managed to put all thoughts of last night toward the back of my mind, hidden from the light of today. Besides, I've been so busy I honestly haven't been able to think hard about it anyway.

My frown pulls my lips further down as I stare at my clipboard. The little girl lying on the bed in front of me has a clean bill of health, just like Diggory had. Only I'm pretty sure there's no way she made herself pass out.

I flip the top page up and look through every lab we ran. Her red blood cell count is still on the lower end of normal. Her hemoglobin and hematocrit are both within the lower range of normal, too, although none of these numbers are alarming enough to warrant keeping her here.

But I still feel uneasy.

Nothing about this seems all that *normal*.

Odette, of course, is all smiles. "Is my mother here to pick me up?"

"Soon," I say, forcing a smile of my own. "I promise you're getting discharged today. I just wanted to stop by to make sure you're still feeling good."

No matter what I think or say, I can't defy the order that she be released, but that doesn't mean I can't be concerned.

"School tomorrow is going to be so fun," she exclaims. "Everyone's going to want to talk to me."

Morphing my face, I shoot her an overly toothy grin and try to sound optimistic. "You should take it easy too. First day out and all. Maybe take a nap and dream of rainbows."

"But I want to tell them about all the needles you stuck me with."

"It was a lot," I sigh before a forced chuckle comes out. "Wasn't it?"

Odette shrugs. "It wasn't so bad."

A real smile curves up my cheeks this time. I admire her and her resilience. But that's children, I guess. They're adaptable—pliable. No wonder we put them in schooling while they're still young enough to be molded into the box our society has shaped for them. By the time they become adults, they'll be waving the white flag, too tired to remember why they ever wanted more. Too tired to care anymore.

"Let's get you out of this bed," I say.

She scurries to her feet, excitement rapidly controlling her limbs. Her face pales suddenly, and I reach out to grab her waist just as she sways.

The clipboard in my hands goes crashing to the tile floor. The sound echoes around the room like a drum.

"I'm okay," she insists, laughing. "Just haven't stood up in a while."

Her cheeks return to a rosy color, her eyes more alert, but I shake my head and grind my teeth. Every inch of my body wants to hold onto her for dear life. "Promise me you'll take it easy."

There's nothing else for me to say. Nothing else I can do.

No, there *is* something I can do. Just not at the present moment. I have to let her walk out that door, otherwise, I'll be taken in by a sentry for more questioning. And I doubt they'd send doe-eyed Rosalyn. It'd be a man, one with physical strength, this time.

"I will," Odette promises as she skips toward the door. "Thanks, Saskia."

Lucan flutters to the forefront of my mind. I think harder. Stress harder.

If he's telling the truth, I can't help but think about the stakes. If he's right, then it means we've been trapped inside the Wall with twelve real Monsters this entire time.

Only the older citizens of Xantera are eligible for the Choosing, but children like Odette will eventually have to stand in the courtyard of the Blood Moon Palace once they receive their blue badges. And by that time, they'll be whittled into shape like the rest of us as the Guardians prowl out to Choose their living sacrifices.

What if something *does* actually happen to them after they step through those ancient doors? All of my healing will have been for nothing if my patients are being bred just for some of them to be slaughtered, as Lucan claims.

I can't blindly trust a voice in my head, though. Even when that voice rattles through the most neglected parts of my body and mind, almost like its deep pitch is designed to *ignite*.

Following Odette out to the lobby, I watch as the sliding glass doors open and she runs into her mother's arms.

A breeze gets sucked in through the doorway, causing a chill to seep into my bones. The kind where you can't get warm until you're standing under a hot shower.

But suddenly, I feel on fire.

Because I might know how to find out the truth for myself.

I don't come to the Rec Center every Sunday, but when I do, I usually head straight for the cycling equipment on the second floor. There's something so hypnotizing about the constant motion, the exertion of energy that seems to wash away the stress of the day. It's my go-to whenever I've had a long week at the Healing Center.

Now, though, I step through the Rec Center's rotating doors with Malcolm by my side, my eyes searching for a different target. Nobody talks when they're cycling, so there's no way I'll be able to get the information I need among the exercise equipment.

"Malcolm!"

We're hardly three steps inside when both of our heads jerk up at the voice of a man who approaches from the direction of the indoor game lawn. He's rather reedy and long-limbed, with thick-rimmed glasses, and a silver badge on his chest that means he's only a year or two younger than us. His inquisitive smile washes over Malcolm for a few moments before sweeping to me.

"And this must be your partner."

"This is Saskia," Malcolm says, and I notice that his cheeks have gained an unusual hue to them. "Saskia, this is my coworker, Walter. He teaches mathematics across the hall from me."

I dip my head. "Pleased to meet you."

"The pleasure's all mine." Walter's gaze flutters back to Malcolm as if involuntarily. "Would you two like to join me for a game of croquet?" He gestures at the indoor lawn behind him.

Malcolm looks to me for approval. We've never actually gone to the Rec Center together before, but that incident with the sentry seems to have forged some type of real friendship between us, so he decided to accompany me today.

I give him what I hope is an encouraging smile.

"You go ahead. I think I'm going to try my hand at backgammon." I nod over at the alcove on the far left of the building, where several clusters of people huddle around tables set up with various card and board games. I've never been remotely interested in such things, but what better way to get people to talk than to let it be known I'm clueless about how to play? Men, especially, seem to love to teach women about the way of things.

"If you're sure?" Malcolm arches an eyebrow, and when I nod, his gaze flicks back to Walter with that same hue rising on his cheeks again. "Okay, I'll see you a bit later then."

"Have fun!"

I watch the two of them head off side by side, Walter already saying something that makes Malcolm tip back his head in a laugh. For a moment, I'm stuck in a trance, watching them retreat as the barest tinge of understanding settles in the back of my mind. If Lucan were in my head right now, he'd probably bring it to the forefront so that I'd have to analyze it, but he's not—I told him on Monday night that I needed to sort out my thoughts, and to my surprise, his howling has died down since then. As if he's trying to give me space to do exactly that.

Or maybe his throat is just sore. Centuries of howling in a murderous rage would probably do that to you.

A peal of youthful laughter echoes from the indoor play area nestled in the right-hand corner of the building, knocking me out of my haze. Immediately, I start for the alcove on the left, nodding politely at anyone who makes eye contact with me like I'm supposed to do.

The Rec Center is one of the largest buildings in Xantera, so even though it's several stories high, the ceiling looms high overhead, and the air feels as cool and spacious as outside. A few sentries stand guard against the walls, observing each activity with rather bored expressions. Nobody has ever made a ruckus here as far as I know, and I don't plan to change that today.

Still, I swear I feel the nearest sentry's eyes on me, sticky like glue, as I weave around billiard tables to get to the other side of the floor.

Finally, I'm beneath the dimmer lights of the alcove, among all the people who love to play their games of strategy. I wander among the tables, my attention roving from face to face until I land on one I vaguely recognize. A past patient who was the chatty type, if I remember correctly. Perfect.

I'm willing to bet he'll be the chatty type now, too.

Wafting over to him, I gesture at the empty chair across from him. "Excuse me, is this spot taken?"

"No, no, I was just looking for someone to play w—" His eyes flash up to focus on me. "Hey, I know you! You helped me with my eye infection a few years ago, didn't you?"

I pretend to really study his features, then pop my mouth into a look of surprise. "Oh! Yes! Looks like it's all healed now, huh? No more problems with it?"

Now that he's mentioned it, I do remember all the hours I spent helping him flush out the pus that had been leaking from a particularly swollen stye. Not my favorite moments as a healer, that's for sure.

The man waves a hand, his purple badge jostling with the movement. "No more problems. You did a great job, I must say, a great job. Some of those other healers were squeamish about it, but you?" He belly-laughs, fiddling with a pair of dice on the table. "You didn't so much as wrinkle your nose, did you? Well, I appreciate it, I appreciate it. Say, you know how to play backgammon?"

"No." I slide into the seat across from him smoothly, feeling the first signs of nerves ticking in my neck. "But I've been looking to learn. Do you think you could teach me?"

Just as I suspected, the man's face breaks into a truly joyous beam, and I feel a flash of guilt for using him like this. "Of course! Okay, so there are thirty checkers in a game, and twelve spaces on each side. See?" He points a meaty finger at the thin triangular markings that look like the spikes atop the Wall painted onto the board. "We'll each get fifteen checkers to start with, five here, five here, three here, three here..."

Bemused, I watch him click little round game pieces onto the spikes of the board in a particular fashion, each of them mirroring the other. Then, I try my very best to follow the rules he so enthusiastically describes to me, but my brain doesn't seem to want to process a single one. Not when I have another motive in mind.

"Now," the man warns, "it's easy to follow along so far, right?" I shake my head, but he doesn't notice. "Backgammon takes *years* to truly master, though. So while you might understand the basics now, don't feel too badly about losing on your first try, okay?"

"Okay," I repeat, lining my tone with fake fervor.

"Here, now, we both roll a die."

I take a cube and roll it just as he does. Mine lands on a six, while his lands on a four.

"Great luck, I'll say. You go first." He watches me roll both dice again. "There. You got a three and a two, so you'll move one of your checkers three spaces, and another one space. No—not that way! You can only go clockwise... yes, that's it."

We fall into a rhythm, where he moves his pieces fluidly and I mess up a dozen times before I finally seem to get it right. This game is incredibly boring, but I'm the only one in the near vicinity that seems to think this. Even so, I wait patiently for an opening. It's only when all our checkers are on the home board that I dare stray into personal conversation now that his focus is laser-sharp on something else.

"Your brother—when I was your healer, I remember you telling me he was Chosen, right?"

"Ah, yes." The man's eyes darken as he focuses on his pieces. His response is less enthusiastic than it was in the Healing Center. Back then, I remember he wouldn't quit bragging about what an honor it was to have a Chosen One in the family. "He was the only one who could beat me at this game here, actually."

I force a smile onto my face and let a few minutes of silence go by so that I don't appear too eager. In that silence, I keep thinking the man will look up from his checkers and ask me a question back. *What about your sibling?* he might ask. *Do you have a brother or a sister?* I'd reply, *Actually, I'm an only child,* and he'd raise an eyebrow. *That's rare, you know, to only have one,* and I'd snort because I know. The Guardians require every couple in the family-making stage to try for two children. My mother just had a harder time conceiving, and—

"No, you can't land there, because I already have two checkers in that spot," the man interrupts my thoughts.

Right. Rule number three. *Don't think about yourself.* It's selfish to be absorbed. I shouldn't have been wasting headspace on imagining conversations that'll never happen. I need to refocus.

"Do you still visit your brother every Sunday?" I ask, amending my mistake on the board. "If I remember correctly, you would always go to the balconies first thing in the morning to say hi."

The man's fist shakes as he rolls his dice. "I would, sure. But I suspect he's been busy with palace things lately."

"Busy?" I try to keep my face neutral. "What do you mean by that?"

"You know." The man shrugs, his own face just as carefully casual, but he almost can't help the bitter tone from bleeding through. "I'm sure there are plenty of things for him to do as a Chosen One. The balconies probably get boring after a while. All that waving and staring at the people below you. Well, it's no wonder he hasn't come out recently."

I try not to freeze, forcing my fingers to grab checkers and move them the appropriate spaces.

But he just lets out a sigh, eyes focused on the long black and white triangles between us that jut out like teeth. "He always was a bit selfish, though," he mutters to himself.

I dare not move; breathe. He's so into the game, it's almost as if he's forgotten I'm sitting across from him. Then those same eyes rise to mine and sparkle after he moves his pieces. Like he's bested me.

I couldn't care less.

"When's the last time you saw him?"

Maybe that question is crossing a line—it's an unsolicited one, for sure, an invasion of privacy. Rude. But I've chosen my target well, because the man only frowns for a second before he says, "Around the same time I was discharged from the Healing Center, actually. Your turn."

Around the same time he was discharged from the Healing Center? That was *years* ago. *Years* have gone by since anyone saw or heard from this man's Chosen brother.

My hands feel clammy when I take the dice and roll them, trying to do the math that breathes down my neck.

"When was he Chosen again?" I get two ones, so I'm barely able to move my pieces at all.

"I had just received my purple badge," the man answers, rolling the dice. "So that would have been maybe thirteen years ago now." His hand hits the table, making me flinch. "Look! I win."

His brother disappeared a few years ago, and he was Chosen about ten years before that. *She was Chosen five years ago*, Belinda had said about her and Diggory's daughter, too. And my own secret screams a number at me, too.

"Would you like to play again?" the man asks.

"Oh, no thank you. But I appreciate you taking the time to teach me." I stand up, scooting my chair back with a lump swelling in my throat. "I think I'm going to try a different game to see if I have better luck somewhere else."

The man watches me go with thoughtful disappointment, as if he regrets winning so quickly. Thankfully, though, the alcove is large enough for me to disappear among other tables and games, and soon I find myself playing cribbage with another man with a green badge.

I go through the same motions, expressing my interest in learning, trying to follow the rules, asking seemingly casual questions that he doesn't pick up on as suspicious because he's so focused on winning during the one day of the week he has the freedom to do so.

Again and again and again, I work my way around the room, finding that most people know a Chosen One through some means or another. Children, partners, parents, siblings, coworkers... so many humans have been brought into that Blood Moon Palace.

So many have stopped coming to the balconies anywhere between five and ten years later.

Lucan's voice rings through my memories. *There is no violence* that you see. *There is no slaughtering* that you know of.

Could the Twelve Guardians really be playing such a long-winded game? Could they be murdering their own citizens so many years after reeling them into their palace, just to keep the thousands of other citizens appeased?

If the Chosen Ones disappeared instantaneously, after all, if there weren't any balconies for them to wave from, then all of Xantera would rise up against the Guardians, demanding their loved ones back. But this way... this way, the loss is gradual, barely noticeable. After so many years of only being able to wave from afar, the disappearance doesn't mean quite as much. It's easier for everyone to turn a blind eye. And the Guardians...

Well, if they live forever, then what is five years to them? Nothing. Nothing at all.

With nausea churning in my gut, I finally leave the alcove to go track down Malcolm, ignoring the eyes of the nearest sentry who follows my movement. He's still playing croquet with Walter, the two of them leaning on their mallets, more interested in each other than the balls littered around their feet.

"...the questions! Always so many questions with those kids—oh, hi, Saskia." Malcolm catches sight of me picking my way over the indoor lawn toward him. "Are you alright?" Concern creases his forehead, and Walter mimics the expression as if he's perfectly in-tune with Malcolm's emotions.

"I think I'm going to head back to our unit, if you don't mind?"

He straightens before taking a quick glance at Walter. "Do you want me to come with you?"

"No," I insist, looking between them encouragingly. All I want for Malcolm is happiness. "You stay here, and enjoy your Sunday. I just think I need to lie down. I'm not feeling well."

It's not a lie. The realization dawning on me is so horrible, so vast, that I don't think I'll be too interested in dinner tonight. My stomach is a mess of knots that threaten to surge up my throat.

What *is* a lie, though, is the implication that I need to go to bed. I'm not going to bed. No, I'm going to get out that necklace and the one other object that keeps flashing in my mind's eye.

Because now that I've started down this path, I can't turn around and go back.

If nobody else can unlock the secrets that the Guardians keep from us, then I will.

And that starts with a key.

LUCAN

Looking a little less tired today," Vivian remarks before she can even see my face.

Her footsteps approach from behind me before she pats me on the top of the head like a dog and sits down at the table next to Merrick on my left.

He slings his arm around her shoulder and buries a kiss into her short, dark hair. I bounce my glare between the both of them.

I've been in my human form for almost a week.

Even though it's been much needed, I won't give any of them the satisfaction of being right. Otherwise, I'll have to hear about it for another week.

"He's not in the mood, babe," Merrick whispers, but of course, I hear.

I press my fork into the piece of steak I just cut without bothering to wait for the others. "I'm fine," I say, despite the energy snapping through every nerve ending.

It's not agitation, exactly. It's more like I'm... nervous. Nervous that she'll reject what I told her. Nervous that she'll reject *me*.

But I still have to respect her decision. If she needs time to think, then that's what I'll give her—because as much as I want to use this woman in every way possible, I refuse to treat her like a mindless puppet. If I did, I'd be no better than my enemies.

She needs to want this Wall to come down as much as I do.

For the first few days after I told Saskia about the Guardians, my body was much calmer. I caught up on sleep and rested my vocal cords to give her the space she needs. But one day turned to three, which turned to six. Slowly. So damn slowly.

I swear, this woman drags every emotion out of me like threads that she has looped around her pinky. I haven't had to deal with anything besides rage since my father died.

But I'm sure she's more than overwhelmed with her own.

All I can do is distract myself until she comes to a decision. "How was the hunt?"

"Felt good to run, even in human form," Viv sighs. "I caught a rabbit, still feel bad about it, and Soren and Ashe stayed behind to go after an elk that crossed our path. We lost the others, but I'm sure they'll be back soon."

Merrick smiles down at her. Despite her spitfire personality, Viv barely reaches his chest in her human form, so she looks like a doll sitting next to him at the long dining room table.

The second she starts scrunching her nose at him, playfully stealing a fried potato off his plate, I let my eyes wander out the window to my right—where the last remnants of Veradel have been crumbling away for centuries.

The abandoned houses across the street are cast in the shadow of mine, the same as they are every afternoon. Some windows are boarded, others broken and never repaired. We've cleaned up the glass, but the houses that go unused are all rotting from the inside-out. Roofs sag inward, coated in heavy layers of moss. The ones made of wood seem to lean sideways, as if they're one blood moon away from toppling completely.

They used to give me the creeps when I was young, but my father always told me they motivated him, and now I understand. They aren't creepy—they're sad. That used to be someone's home, someone's bedroom.

Someone's life that was—

I jolt in my chair. The wooden legs creak underneath me, threatening to break, as I must have pushed it back at least an inch or two.

Vivian and Merrick look at me with wide eyes that quickly fill with understanding.

"Here we go." Viv smirks.

I'm already out of my chair and running for the door, halfway transformed—human legs, shirt ripped off, claws out. It happened so fast, I didn't even register it, because I may be able to feel when Saskia puts on that necklace, but unless I'm fully shifted, I won't be able to hear her voice.

Behind me I hear Merrick growl out, "Who stole all my food?" and Viv's fading shriek of laughter as Merrick gathers her in his arms.

And then I'm out the back door, where I don't stop running until I'm fully formed and blanketed by the woods in all directions.

My uneasiness swells, sticking to my skin like wax, because all I anticipate her saying is that I'm fucking crazy.

That her life is fine the way it is. That she'd rather me stay out of it. Because what else do you say to a voice in your head that's telling you everything you know is a lie?

And then she surprises the shit out of me.

SASKIA

I believe you.

It's the first thing I tell Lucan when I make it back to my housing unit, dig through my drawers, and throw the necklace over my throat.

But, I press, because I can feel his shock flare through our connection, and I know he's bound to have some self-satisfied remark up his sleeve, *I only believe that the Guardians are bad. I don't necessarily believe that you're good.*

Never said I was, Lucan replies smoothly. *But I'd never pretend to be good, either.*

Great. Then I don't feel bad about taking you with me. Not that they could actually hurt you if they catch me with the necklace, right? Or could they? For a moment, I pause to wonder what would happen if the vial against my chest was shattered—destroyed. Our connection would obviously cease to exist, but would something happen to Lucan, too? Would it hurt him? I never got around to asking him how the necklace actually works. But now is not the time.

Now, there might never be time.

Lucan seems to be tracking each of my thoughts with increasing uneasiness as I continue digging through my drawers. *What do you mean if they catch you?* he begins slowly. *What are you doing, Saskia?*

I fish out one of the other forbidden objects, bringing it up to my face until I'm staring through the hole in the center of the silver, tarnished bow. *I'm going to the Blood Moon Palace to see if this key of Diggory's lets me in.*

More shock ripples into my veins, nearly halting me in my tracks. *What? Are you insane?* A low rumble emanates from his throat. *I might not live within those Walls, but even I know you can't just walk right up to the palace in the middle of the night.*

Oh, I'm not waiting for nighttime. I'm going right now.

I tie up my hair in a knot, using the mirror to make sure all of my dark red pieces are in place. Then I readjust my cloak and debate whether or not I should keep my scarlet badge on. For the first time, the sight of the badge fills me with disgust. It's just another marker of control—of how the Guardians have dictated every part of my life. Even who I'm supposed to love.

Saskia, stop, Lucan tries to command, and I swear I hear the start of him panting. As if he's begun to run. As if he can actually get to me. *Let's talk about this.*

There's nothing to talk about. I turn away from the mirror and drop the key into my inside pocket, my fingers trembling.

There's probably five hundred things to talk about, actually. You seem to have missed several crucial steps between warranted disbelief and... whatever the hell this is.

I start toward the door. *This is me doing the right thing.*

This is objectively you doing the wrong thing, little nightmare. All you will accomplish is getting yourself killed if you go right now without preparing.

I want to scream at him for daring to tell me the truth but trying to stop me from chasing it.

You keep it up and I won't take you with me after all, Monster.

He ignores my threat. *You can't throw yourself right into our enemy's hand without a strategy.*

I can do what I want.

No, you can't. His voice wrenches at something buried deep within my bones. *You can't do what you want because the Guardians have taken away all of your choices. That's the point.*

There is no point unless I do something. My eyes squeeze shut.

Do something, then, he growls. *But let's make a plan first.*

There's no time for a plan! I scream in my head, my hand grasping my bedroom doorknob. *My mother might be dead right NOW!*

There it is. The secret that has finally burst from the deepest cracks in my heart. The reason I'm so desperate to be Chosen—not because I care about worthiness or honor, but because I'm sick to my stomach about what might have happened to my mother since the very last time I saw her leaning over a balcony, waving to me from high, high above.

Lucan's surprise bolts through me for only a moment before his tone cascades into something low and soothing. Like he's urging me to step away from the edge of a towering rooftop.

Talk to me, baby. His mind skips, almost like that slipped out of his mouth, but he continues softly before I can fully process it. *Sit down and tell me about her. I want to hear.*

I pause with my hand still clasping the doorknob.

Nobody—not once—has ever asked me about my mother after she followed the Third Guardian into the Blood Moon Palace almost ten years ago, her chin high, her steps slow. It's as if the Chosen Ones are as much of a taboo subject as they are an honor. People want to congratulate you for your loved one being ripped from your arms, but they don't want to ask how it made you feel. How you're coping.

How it feels like grief.

Now the *Monster*, of all people, is asking me to sit down and tell him about her.

I release the doorknob, slumping down onto my knees until my forehead is resting against my door.

My mother was sick.

A decade's worth of a carefully-built facade crumbles away as I pick through the past I have tried so hard to keep at bay, even from myself. Lucan is silent, but it's a heavy kind of silence. The kind that tells me he's listening.

My mother was sick, but nobody else noticed besides me. I saw the bags under her eyes and the way she was slowly losing weight and begged her to go to the Healing Center, but she refused. I began to wish that I was a professional healer so that I'd know how to analyze and mend her. But then right before I turned fifteen, right before we could start requesting apprenticeships... I scrape in a deep breath. *My father died, and she was Chosen not long afterward, and I was alone.*

Of course, nobody considered me parentless—not when every other fifteen-year-old left their family unit within the same month that my family left *me*. As soon as my age group received our blue badges, we were whisked away to new complexes, where we roomed with each other and cycled through different apprenticeships so that the Guardians could begin to monitor our skills. In the flurry of excitement, nobody cared that my life had changed so drastically. *Everyone's* life had changed drastically. And just as it is today, just as it's always been since the Guardians took over, it was improper to ask unsolicited questions. Especially about a girl's dead father and Chosen mother.

Your father died?

Lucan's question is prodding, but gentle. There's also a shiver of empathy there, and I remember how he said that his own father had died, too.

Yes, I whisper, my forehead sinking into my hands. *I saw it happen. It... nobody knew why he had died, just as nobody knew my mother was sick.*

I still remember the sounds my father made when he took his last breaths, though. His face has blurred in my memory, and I can't recall anything about his other features, either: whether he had soft or calloused hands, how tall he was, or even what shade of eyes he had. I just remember those last few breaths. Labored. Wheezing. Then a horrible gurgling as he crashed to his knees in the middle of our housing unit, scrabbling at his throat while my mother screamed.

He was the first person to die on my watch, and the last. Ever since the Guardians approved my request to become a healer, I've ensured nothing like that has ever happened in front of me again.

None of my training or hard work has helped save my mother, though.

I thought maybe the Guardians had taken pity on her, I continue in a whisper. *I thought they knew she was sick and needed a reprieve from her assigned job after watching my father die. I thought they'd Chosen her to help her heal. But whenever I saw her waving from those balconies, she looked like she was slowly getting worse—her movements slower, her face paler. And then she stopped appearing at all about three months ago.*

Before three months ago, I never missed a Sanctuary Sunday. I always made sure to make the trek to the Blood Moon Palace so that I could catch a glimpse of her face. In return, she never missed a Sunday, either. She always made sure to shuffle out to the balconies and raise a trembling hand.

Then, right before the last Choosing, I looked up and she was gone. I spent that entire Sunday pacing back and forth beneath the balconies, searching the Chosen Ones for a sign of her face, but she never came out. And she didn't come out the next Sunday, either.

I was so worried she was on her deathbed somewhere in one of those palace rooms, I murmur. *I thought if I was Chosen, too, I could heal her and slowly nurse her back to health.*

Now, I keep seeing Belinda's expression flit across my mind, that split-second of determination in which I could have sworn she was going to try to barge through the palace doors by force. That same determination has grown in me. I don't have to be Chosen to get in, especially if I have the right key. But I can't shake the feeling that I'm too late, anyway.

That my mother is already dead.

She might still be alive, Lucan says, and a scoff catches in my throat. *I'm serious, Saskia. My ancestors didn't get to study the vampires much during the chaos of their short battle*—his tone leaks bitterness—*but they did observe that a vampire's bite didn't kill their victims right away. They didn't know if death came slowly or if... something else happened to them, but she might just be incapable of coming to the balconies for some reason. But still breathing. Still alive.*

The clinical side of me tucks that information away, where I can observe it later. Every other part of me snags on the new word he just let loose, one I've never heard before.

Vampires?

What my kind call the parasites. Our legends claim they're our greatest enemies—and the greatest threat to humankind. Lucan seems to bristle at the very mention of them, each of his words tight, on edge. *It's why my kind was designated as kings in the past. Not to dictate humans, but to protect them. Only, my grandfather hadn't seen any real vampires in living memory, so he forgot what a threat they were.* I can practically feel Lucan's teeth grinding. *He wasn't prepared when the original thirteen vampires invaded his kingdom.*

Wasn't prepared. Just like I'm not prepared now.

Turning around, I gather my knees up into my arms and rest my head back against the doorway. Any minute now, the loudspeakers will announce curfew and Malcolm will return. Lucan has successfully delayed me, but how could I possibly prepare for this? I'm just one woman in a city of twelve thousand people and twelve vampires who have us trapped.

How close can you get to the Blood Moon Palace without being detected? Lucan asks.

I think about the dark alleyways between complexes, how the maze of them winds throughout all of Xantera with no cameras to monitor what happens in between. The giant courtyard in front of the palace is the only thing that stands between the edge of the complexes and the palace front doors.

Close, I say.

Okay. Lucan's tone takes on a note of authority that makes me sit up straighter. *Wait until tonight when it's dark. Get as close as you can and observe the sentries who stand guard. How many are there? When does their shift change? Once we know, we can make a plan for you to try out the key when they're at their most vulnerable. Maybe I can distract them long enough for you to slip inside.*

Distract them? How can you distract them when you're on the other side of the—

A howl fractures the air outside my window, so loud and keening that I'm willing to bet the whole of Xantera just froze mid-step. So rarely does the Monster howl before the moon comes up. So rarely does my body flutter with goosebumps before sunset—like it is now.

Lucan stops howling abruptly, the aftermath making the silence vibrate in my ears.

I have others that can do that with me, if I ask them to, Lucan growls. *I'm sure the sentries will be plenty distracted when they realize there's more than one Monster outside the Wall.*

More than one? I breathe, still tingling all over.

You'll get to meet them one day, but only if you live, Saskia. The male in my head seems to burrow into my heart when he adds, *You don't die on my watch. You understand?*

Tears thicken in my throat and well in my eyes as I think about all the people I've ever healed. All the people whose hearts have continued beating a little longer because once upon a time, I was a fifteen-year-old girl who couldn't save the people she loved most.

Now, someone I've never even laid eyes on is trying to save *me*.

And I want to let him.

I want to be saved.

Got it, I say. *I'll wait until tonight to observe the sentries.*

Then the Monster and I will form a plan.

Three hours after curfew, I'm wearing the necklace again, but now it's tucked within the collar of my cloak so that the vial fits snugly between my breasts.

I crack open my bedroom door to find that Malcolm is still in bed. We had dinner together after he came home from the Rec Center, and then we both went into our joint bedroom, where we laid side by side and stared at the ceiling as if there were stars plastered above our heads. Thankfully, there was no reason for either of us to put on quite as big of a show as last week because there was no sentry sitting in our living room. As long as the camera recorded us going into that bedroom together, whoever was watching would think we were obedient.

Still, it was nice to just lie there without forcing anything. The silence between us almost felt... comfortable. I ended up staying for almost an hour before Malcolm's even breathing broke into those horrible, guttural snores of his, and I tiptoed back to my own room.

Now, our housing unit is quiet and dark, save for a sliver of moonlight spilling through the window—and the blinking camera above the loudspeaker, of course.

Remember, Lucan warns me. *Nice and slow.*

I nod like he can see me and slip out of my room, crouching down and keeping myself pressed against the wall without daring to exhale. The camera is angled in such a way that if I move beneath the screen, I don't think it'll be possible for anyone to see me leave the house after curfew: a sliver of a blind spot as thin as the moonlight at my feet.

One foot in front of the other, I move at an achingly slow pace, half squatting so that my head stays low enough. My thigh muscles burn by the time I'm halfway across the kitchen, not used to the angle at which I'm forcing them to move, but I don't relent. I don't straighten. I—

My foot steps down, and the floor *creaks* beneath me. I freeze.

Malcolm gives an extra loud snore that rumbles through our bedroom door, and then everything goes quiet again.

The camera keeps on blinking.

I'm almost there, I tell Lucan.

He stays silent to let me focus, but I feel his presence like a dark awareness honing in on the movement of my thoughts. I reach out a hand, grab the door handle, and ease it partway open.

A cool gust of night air hits me in the face. I blink, then sidle my body through, not daring to open the door any further. As soon as I'm on the other side, I snick it shut behind me, wincing at the click of the latch that seems to echo through the alleyway.

I'm out, I say.

It's the first time I've ever been outside at night. If I thought the spaces between complexes were unnerving before, now they're downright terrifying—like narrow throats swallowing me whole from every direction. Only the faintest illumination of moonlight filters through the eaves above my head, so it takes a second for my eyes to adjust to this new level of darkness.

When they do, I simply stand here, my heartbeat thrumming, looking left and right at all the doors. So many doors, closed and lifeless for now, but for some reason my imagination tells me they're going to fly open as I pass them, monstrous arms snaking out to curl around me and drag me back.

Saskia? Lucan asks. *If you want to go back in and try this a different night, I—*

No. I straighten. *It's just—I've never smelled the night air before. What?*

It's... crisper. Kind of like mint? But there's also a hint of something mossy. I use the conversation as an excuse to gather a big breath before forcing myself to move—not toward the main road on the right but deeper into the labyrinth of complexes on my left.

You've never smelled the night air before, Lucan repeats, temper simmering beneath his tone as if the idea of that personally offends him. *I'll add that to my list.*

Your list? I soften each of my footsteps as much as I can. There might not be anyone else in these alleyways right now, but I don't want a sentry patrolling the main road to hear even the slightest scuffle from my direction. *Your list of rules?*

No. My list of everything those parasites have done to harm you and the rest of my citizens.

The way he says that, a hint of possessiveness surging through the words, has me almost halt in my tracks. He's right, though. If the Guardians had never taken over Xantera, then Lucan... Lucan would be king right now. He'd be *my* king. And I would be *his*.

The idea of belonging to him sends a shuddering thrill down my spine—one that he picks up on, unfortunately. I feel the sudden satisfaction oozing from his end of our connection, bleeding into my own senses.

You like the thought of being mine, little nightmare?

I scoff in my head, resuming my pace and keeping an eye on all the closed doors to make sure they stay closed. *I like the thought of you keeping quiet, actually. It's rude to read my emotions.*

His gravelly words come out with a chuckle of amusement. *I can assure you, I didn't pry. I would've felt that shiver of yours from three hundred miles away.*

The breeze is strong right now, I say defensively, even though the air is definitely stagnant at the moment—nothing stirring in the shadows ahead of me. *I was just a little cold.*

Or maybe you were wondering what it would feel like for me to rule over you.

I was wondering no such thing, I quip, curiosity like a budding bloom in my core despite my best attempts to strangle it.

Then there's no reason for me to tell you I could make you shiver a lot harder than that.

Now my entire body is tingling, but I realize something as I come to my first split in the alleyway: the banter has made me feel so much less alone in the dark. I can't believe I've already come to the next complex, where I'll need to decide which way to turn.

Right. I need to go right. I don't have a clear mental map of the city memorized, but the Blood Moon Palace is like a compass in my heart. As long as I keep making turns to move toward it, I should be on the lip of that courtyard within an hour.

Glancing over my shoulder, I turn and creep along this new alley, listening for any signs of life besides my own heartbeat. There's nothing. The silence buzzes in my ears much too loudly.

You still want me to keep quiet? Lucan asks mockingly.

I'm about to reply with a biting remark of my own when a particular door catches my eye.

I'm nowhere near the complexes across from the Healing Center where I first started searching for Diggory... but this *door.* It's exactly like that other one was, seemingly normal but without a metal slat for meals to slide through.

Saskia, Lucan warns, his tone dropping from playful back to serious at once. *Keep moving. It would be unwise to linger.*

I know, it's just that... I squint and duck my head, my hair falling to one side as I crane my neck. *There's a keyhole here.* With trembling hands, I try the door handle, but it's locked just like the other one was. *Nothing is ever locked except for the front doors of the Blood Moon Palace.*

An alarm bell blares in my head, a sense of wrongness leaking from this door as if there really might be monstrous creatures lurking behind it. I need to move on before something comes out, but the silver object in my pocket keeps me rooted to the spot. Like a tether has pulled tight between key and lock.

Forget it, Saskia. For some reason, Lucan doesn't sound eager at the discovery like I'd expect. He sounds like he'd give anything to drag me away, actually. *We'll do this another night.*

What? I try to force some humor through the fear spiking in my chest. *You've spent centuries trying to tear this Wall down, and now you want to wait even longer?*

No, I want you to stay on track. If you let a random door distract you, then it means you're not focused, which means you're not aware of your surroundings.

Actually, I think it means I'm extremely aware of my surroundings, given I noticed that this door is different from the others.

A growl rips through my head, pure dominance bristling through it. *Stay on track, or go back, Saskia. We can think about this door another night.*

You're a bossy little Monster, aren't you? I joke. He snarls in my head, but I ignore him, digging into my pocket to pull out the key. I bring the tarnished tip to the lock hidden in the shadows beneath the door handle, my breath frozen in my lungs.

It slides right in.

A gasp rushes down my throat, and I clap my hand over my mouth at the amplified noise. Diggory didn't steal a key to the Blood Moon Palace, so it would be pointless to go monitor the sentries now. He stole a key to... whatever this is.

More snarling erupts in my head, but I ignore Lucan as if I'm in a trance. I turn the key, and when something *clicks*, I try the handle again.

The door creaks inward this time, exposing me to a darkness even richer than the nighttime shadows of the alleyways. This darkness is so thick, I swear it would paint my skin with ink if I stepped into it. Definitely not a housing unit, then, because all housing units have at least one window and a blinking camera to shed light on their interiors. When my eyes adjust after a few blinks, I can make out the outline of what looks like stone steps angling downward.

Where does it lead? Could this be how Diggory disappeared for an entire day—by descending a set of stairs like this one? What could possibly lurk beneath Xantera that the Guardians want to keep locked away?

Lucan's snarling goes quiet as he processes what I'm seeing through the questions flashing across my mind. When I sense a heaviness to his thoughts, I ask, *What is it? You know, don't you?*

It... He clears his throat. *When my grandfather was king, there were underground tunnels and caverns called catacombs, where they buried all the royal families. But I don't know what could be down there now that the Guardians have taken over. They didn't lead out into the city back then.*

Well, there's only one way to find out, isn't there?

Don't even think ab—

A pair of voices drift to me from around the corner of the alleyway, and I shush Lucan.

"—probably just a rat," a man says.

"Yeah, but we've got to check anyway. You know how this year's new group of blue badges is. Always trying to push the boundaries."

"I say we throw 'em over the Wall if they want to be that way. Treat 'em like every other citizen."

"I'm sure the Monster would be happy. It seems to be quiet tonight, huh?"

Sentries. My earlier gasp must have echoed through the alleyways and alerted the ones patrolling the main road to my presence.

I wish there was a word to describe how utterly furious I am with myself for the slip-up. Maybe Lucan was right, and I shouldn't have let myself become so distracted.

But self-loathing won't help me now as their footsteps clack closer. If I run the other way, they'll hear me, but I won't make it back to my housing unit in time if I try to sneak away quietly. And if I stay here, they'll round the corner to find me standing next to an open doorway, outside long after curfew.

Go. Lucan's command sounds like it pains him. *Hide.*

I don't waste time trying to deliberate any longer. The voices are too close now. Any second now, they'll round the corner.

Gathering my cloak around myself, I step into the inky darkness and close the door behind me.

18

LUCAN

I never thought I'd *regret* that someone besides a Guardian picked up the necklace.

But still, why did it have to be her?

She's far too precious, dammit. Too good.

Her heart and mind are too pure for this.

Despite the fierceness that brews behind her careful facade, I've deconstructed her thoughts that she tries so hard to hide, picking away at the deep recesses of her mind.

And while she's angry, yes, her passion for life is blinding and completely surprising. How she's become what she is in spite of being raised in a human farm like cattle, I can't wrap my head around.

But I also can't let myself be distracted. One woman cannot get in my way, no matter how much I like the sound of her voice filling my head.

This has been my goal, my destiny, from the moment I was born, so I can't allow fear to hinder me now.

Yet, I'm still afraid—that she'll be overwhelmed, that she'll be caught, that she'll die, that she'll continue to hate me. The list seems endless.

It certainly doesn't help that her own panic is tearing through me like knives.

If I could, I'd dig under the Wall to get to her right now. But I've tried countless times before. The Wall only seems to sink deeper and deeper into the soil, like it has no bottom, like it sprouts more roots every decade and keeps burrowing further into the ground. If I hadn't known what it was like *before*, I'd have convinced myself by now that it grows from the very core of the earth itself.

Sitting down and looking up at the moon, I push my feelings down and focus on my one task in front of me—the Wall stretching out to my left and right. *Not* a woman.

Because I'm so close, the closest I've ever been. And while there's still so much more to tell her, who knows if she'll choose to continue on this path after I do.

I'm here with you, I tell her, feeling her breath snag in her throat. She acknowledges my presence without words. Instead, it's like a fire crackling, the warmth cascading through my body down to the end of my tail. *I promise, I'm not going anywhere.*

19

SASKIA

Lucan's words steady me in the dark.

And it really is a darkness unlike anything I've ever experienced. I can't even see my own hands moving when I slip the key back into my pocket, as if the lack of light is a cloak clinging to my own skin. My eyes don't adjust. There's nothing to adjust *to*.

I'm not going anywhere, Lucan repeats, and in this darkness, he might as well be standing right beside me—so I let myself pretend he is.

Okay. I nod as if he can see me. *I'm going down.*

The sentries' voices rumble from the other side of the door, but I can't make out what they're saying, exactly. I just know that if they happen to have their own key to this secret space, I'd be a fool to stay right here where they could open it and catch me. If I can just make it down the flight of steps...

I brush my foot out in front of me until I feel the edge of the topmost stair. Then, pressing my hands against the walls on either side of me, I take a step down. And another one. And another.

These are some narrow stairs, I try to say nonchalantly, bringing myself down step by step. *Whoever had it built should have really hired a better architect.*

Of course you'd joke at a time like this, Lucan murmurs, and I can't tell if he's angry or impressed. *So help me, Saskia, if you fall and break your leg...*

Then what? I taunt, eager for more distractions—this place is really creeping me out regardless of what I try to convey to Lucan. My fingers brush against cracks in the wall, the smooth stone turning ragged and rough the further I descend. *You're going to punish me for breaking a leg?*

That depends. Lucan's tone turns thoughtful. *Do you enjoy being punished?*

Enjoy it? I think back to the smacks on the hand that my instructors used to give me whenever I talked out of turn in the schooling phase. *Who would enjoy that?*

You might, if it was someone else doing it. Someone who knew how to wring out the right amount of pain to enhance your pleasure.

My insides flutter, and I nearly lose my footing. I grasp the walls on either side of me, feeling a slice of pain as one of the rocks cuts through my finger. A startled breath tears out of my mouth, and the sound rebounds back to me in waves.

Shit. Lucan's side of the connection explodes with alarm. *Are you okay?*

I'm fine. I can feel the slight pulse of the cut on my finger, and the wetness of blood trickling down my hand. I'll have to sanitize that as soon as I get out of here—there's no knowing what kind of bacteria could be on the stone that cut me. *It's just a scratch,* I tell Lucan.

He doesn't sound convinced. *Okay, but no more distractions for you until you reach the bottom safely.*

I do as he says, focusing on my balance with each step, further and further down until I finally sweep out a foot to find that the ground has flattened out. The darkness in front of me seems more spacious, too, as if the tunnel has widened slightly. I still can't see a thing, but I hear the unmistakable *plink, plink, plink* of dripping water from somewhere up ahead. It seems to pulse in time with the cut on my finger, and in the darkness, my imagination tells me it's my own *blood* drip, drip, dripping onto the ground.

I'm sure the sentries are gone, Lucan starts. *If you want to turn back ar—*

Goodness, Lucan. I shuffle forward, keeping my hands out in front of myself in case I run into anything. *I'm almost starting to think you don't actually want me to do any of this. How am I supposed to sneak into the Blood Moon Palace or bring down the Wall if you keep telling me I can turn back around or try again later? This is obviously where Diggory went when he disappeared, so if we want to find out how he got into the Blood Moon Palace, I have to keep going.*

Lucan stays silent on the other end, and I know I've hit a nerve. As my footsteps begin to swish through thin puddles of standing water, I cast around for a different subject. I need to keep the conversation going or else I'm definitely going to be imagining all sorts of hands reaching out of that water to grab at my ankles, and *that* wouldn't be good for anyone's blood pressure.

What was that word you said earlier? I ask. *Right after I almost fell?*

What? Shit?

Yeah, that one. My fingers brush against a wall in front of me, and when I drag my hand along its surface, I feel the slight curvature of the tunnel—now I'm angling slightly to the left. *What does it mean? Is it like that other word you taught me—asshole?*

Lucan snorts. *Not quite. Technically, shit refers to a bowel movement. Less technically, it meant I... cared. That I was worried something had happened to you.*

My breath squeezes in my lungs. *You were?*

Yes.

Because you need me to get inside, I say.

He's silent again—as if his thoughts have clammed up. As if he himself doesn't even know the answer to that.

I know I'm right, though. It might be a crystallizing fantasy in my head, that the male on the other end of the connection actually gives a... a shit about me. But the truth is, we've never even met each other face to face. If I had fallen and broken my leg—or worse, cracked my skull open—it would be a grievance to him only because his connection to the inside would have been lost with me.

Saskia, that's not—

How does the necklace work? I interrupt, not wanting to hear him flounder around for an excuse to soften that blow. I'm using him too, after all. Because I have a feeling I'm going to need him to get to my mom. *If you don't have a matching necklace,* I continue, *then how does this one connect us?*

A pebble of something cold lands on my head. I flinch and freeze. Another one lands on the tip of my nose, and I exhale when I feel a bead of liquid roll off. It's just the dripping water I heard from earlier.

Still, I resume more slowly, trying to blink away the wavering shapes and shadows that have begun to cultivate in front of my eyes—just my imagination making up images in the absence of anything real to see, I'm sure.

Lucan seems to sense I need his voice to ground myself. He answers my question with the edge of a growl lacing his words.

The blood of my kind is unique, to say the least. When we're in our monstrous forms, it becomes a transmitter of sorts, a conductor of the electrical impulses of our thoughts. We can all communicate like this when we shift.

There's that *we* again, a reference to the mysterious others who are with Lucan physically. For the briefest moment, a pang of jealousy pricks my insides before I snatch at a different thing to focus on.

Shift? You have another form?

He told me once that he could retract the claws, but I never imagined he could actually change his entire self. That he has a form *other* than his Monster one.

Yes, I do, Lucan murmurs. *And you'd probably find it more appealing.*

I swallow the sudden urge to ask him what he looks like when he's not the Monster. All I can really picture are amber eyes. *So when you're in your... more appealing form, your blood doesn't connect you to the others? Or to me?*

Look at you, asking all these good questions. The words might have sounded patronizing if I couldn't feel his emotions swelling through our connection—actual pride. And a bit of admiration that makes my cheeks heat even in this frigid nothingness. *I can sense if someone is trying to connect, like a knock on the door,* Lucan explains. *But I can't actually hear anyone's thoughts until I shift into my monstrous form.*

So whenever you're talking to me, you really are the Monster. And we're connected because...

That vial between your breasts, Lucan says, and I try to tell my nipples to stop pebbling as his voice drops low. *It contains the blood of my grandfather, from when the Guardians slayed him in his shifted form.*

Okay, well that was enough to get my nipples to calm down. My shoulders deflate, and the vial suddenly feels much too cold against my skin. The idea that there's actual ancient *blood* trapped within it...

Whenever that vial of blood is pressed against your pulse, it connects us, Lucan continues. *A clever contraption the vampires made to spy on those of us who escaped.* His tone is so bitter, so biting, that I want to ask him more questions. But something about the space around me pulls my attention away.

I rub my eyes, trying to blink away the shapes in front of me again. I can't imagine how Diggory knew where to go when he escaped down here. Maybe he brought a light with him.

A light...

My body straightens. Is it really just my imagination procuring shapes in the darkness, or is the darkness itself thinning out? I swear I can see the silhouette of the ceiling above my head, and now the texture of the walls ebbs into focus—rough and rocky, like someone carved out this tunnel with a crude knife.

Lucan, I think there's light up ahead.

I move faster now. The further I follow the tunnel along its curving path, the more I can see: the stalactites hanging from the ceiling, the pools of water at my feet, my own hands raised in front of me. The light is flickering now, a jittery orange glow that makes shadows sway along the walls. And when I round a particularly sharp corner—

I stop dead, staring at the open cavern before me.

It's a round space held up by stone pillars, with five or six other tunnel openings forming gaping mouths all around me. A thin film of water forms a glassy sheen across the floor, but I swear it almost looks red, as if someone else's blood dripped into the water. The whole thing is lit by what I can only describe as really, really large candlesticks fit snugly in metal brackets on the wall.

Torches, Lucan says urgently. *Someone's been down there recently to light them. You need to get out of the open, Saskia. Now.*

It doesn't take his bristly tone of command to spur me into action. I surge forward and splash my way to one of the other tunnel openings, letting myself melt into the shadows again so that I can observe the open space from a new angle.

What would this place be used for? As far as I can see, there are no ancient skeletons leaning against any of the walls, so I'm pretty sure this can't be the old royal catacombs. No, this reminds me more of a hollow heart, with veins and arteries running off it from every direction. Leading to where, though? Who could have lit those torches now that Diggory is gone?

An idea is prickling at the back of my head, but I don't have time to analyze it before something clangs from one of the other tunnels across from me.

Get back as far as you can without making a sound, Lucan says immediately, and hearing his fear sends my mind in a whirl. *Press against the wall, cover your bleeding finger, and hold still.*

I do as he says, a dim part of me recognizing that I like it when he takes control, just so I don't have to worry about what to do when my body is already so spiked with adrenaline. Shrinking back and crouching down against the wall, I wrap my stinging finger in the folds of my cloak and wait. Watch. Listen.

It's a smooth sound that greets my ears. Almost like a snake sliding through water, the footsteps glide toward me, closer and closer, until my heartbeat is thudding through my eardrums, louder and louder...

A pale face emerges from the shadows of the tunnel, like a moon rising from a bed of dark clouds.

A *recognizable* face. One I've seen hung up on walls, threaded into flags, carved into statues alongside his brothers and sisters. Marble-white skin. Oily black hair. A long, prominent neck.

The Eleventh Guardian.

The one who was in Odette's dream.

For the next few seconds, nothing exists except for that precious space between the vampire and me.

My heart pounds in my ears, and I wonder briefly if he can hear it, feel it.

If he finds me hiding in the shadows of one of his tunnels right now, I'm dead. I don't know how I know that, but I do. There's a certain glaze in his crimson eyes that I can see from all the way across the flickering cavern, one that reminds me of someone who is never quite satisfied with their meal.

His Adam's apple bulges as his neck tightens before he stops dead in between pillars and cocks his head, like he just caught a whiff of something.

Lucan's snarl floods my brain, but of course, the Eleventh Guardian can't hear it. Just like I'm hoping he can't hear the inhales and exhales I ever so slowly pull in and out of my lungs, either. He *is* smelling something, though, his gaze roving around the cavern, his chin tilting up as he takes a deep breath in.

He's going to find me. He's going to race toward me and grab me by the arms, and then he'll tear out my throat or smash my skull in or rip my body in half or...

The Eleventh Guardian focuses on the tunnel I just came from—the one that leads to the complex a block away from mine—and streaks off into its gaping darkness.

Shit, I curse in my head, finally allowing myself to breathe properly. *He's gone.*

He probably smelled your blood smeared on the walls of that tunnel, Lucan says, a possessive snarl vibrating through each word. *If the coast is clear, you need to try to find another exit point before he comes back.*

Easier said than done, I murmur. Because who knows where any of these other tunnels lead? All I can really do is choose one and follow it into the complete unknown.

For a second, I deliberate stealing one of those so-called torches so that I won't have to plunge back into darkness, but that would be like a flickering beacon leading the Guardians straight to me. And I'm pretty sure they'd notice one of them missing from its sconce if they traverse this place so often.

Which begs the question—why? Why do the Guardians have so many veins running beneath their city? What are they using this underground system for?

We can ask the philosophical questions later, Lucan growls. *Right now, I need you to move for me, Saskia.*

So bossy, I mutter, but I relent.

Passing a mournful last look at all the firelight, I turn around and hurry deeper into this new tunnel, moving as fast as I can without actually running. Still, my footsteps crunch much too loudly over wet pebbles as the pathway twists and turns, and I wince at every footfall. What's even worse? The panic of the moment is beginning to leak into my bloodstream, kicking my heartbeat into a higher gear.

I don't know how much time has passed since I snuck out of my housing unit. Without the moon to travel a path across my window, I'm at a complete loss. What if it's been several hours? What if I don't make it home in time for my healing shift in the morning? Who's going to cover me?

That's what you're worried about right now? Lucan bursts out. *You're trapped underground, in the dark, with walls closing in on either side of you, a Monster in your head, and a vampire after your blood, and you're worried about who's going to cover you at work tomorrow?*

Well, I gasp, *we're short-staffed!*

Lucan groans as if I've personally offended him. *I'll add it to my list.*

What?

My list of grievances, remember? I'll add that the Guardians don't assign enough people to work at the Healing Center so that the ones who do feel even more shackled to their duties—just another way for them to control your sense of freedom.

I don't really have an argument to that, and besides, my breathing has become more labored, my muscles more strained, as the tunnel floor begins to tilt upward. I can still see the vaguest outline of shapes ahead of me, so when I round a corner, elation jolts through me at the sight of a door at the end of the tunnel.

A way out.

A way back—

I tug on what feels like a marble door handle, but it doesn't budge.

Rummaging in my cloak's pocket, I bring out Diggory's key and fumble with the lock, but this keyhole is much too large for the little silver one in my grip. It slides into the gaping hole with several inches to spare, and I yank it back out with a huff.

Fear begins to tighten around me, constricting my airway. This *has* to be a nightmare, me facing a dead end with nowhere else to go. It actually feels like the walls are shrinking around me now, and I have half a mind to start clawing at the door with my bare hands.

Breathe with me, Saskia. It's okay. You are okay.

Lucan's voice doesn't *sound* like it'll be okay—it's jagged and sharp, as if he's just as panicked as I am. But the words themselves jog a memory that unspools in my brain like fine thread.

Breathe, Saskia. It's okay. Take deep breaths with me, sweetheart.

My mother.

She wasn't required to love me. She was assigned to be with my father just like I was assigned to Malcolm. She was forced into motherhood as soon as the Guardians took away those little blue pills and handed her a green badge, even if it took her a little longer to get pregnant than the women around her. She didn't have to give me more than the basic parental requirements.

But she did. Whenever I jerked upright in bed in the middle of the night, shaking and sweating, she was by my side in an instant, rubbing circles between my shoulder blades. Telling me to breathe. *Take deep breaths with me, sweetheart. That's it. Nice and slow.*

And then her voice would tumble into a lullaby, soft and whispery against my hair.

Round and round the Monster prowls,
Starved for meat and bone.
Beware its eyes, resist its howl,
Stay within the stone.

It was the only lullaby anyone ever sang, the only one the Guardians ever approved of. But my mom would make up her own words on nights when the nightmares became too dark, too constricting, too much. When staying within the stone felt like a noose around my neck.

It's that secret second part of her lullaby I repeat to myself now.

> *On and on the girl must march,*
> *Starved for an end to the night.*
> *Beware the Monster in her heart,*
> *For even she can bite.*

The memory calms me just enough that my shoulders stop shaking, just like I would back then in her arms. I blink at the door in front of me again, willing myself to pause long enough to take in the details so that I might figure out where it leads.

It's not made of wood, I realize as I lean closer, trying to dissect the strange texture in this excruciatingly dim lighting. When I brush my fingers against the surface again, the grittiness of *stone* meets my skin. Lines sprout like cracks throughout it, but when I try to trace those lines, I don't feel any kind of indentation. Rather, the cracks are somehow smoothed over, as if someone filled them with... glass?

No, that can't be right. Glass doesn't mend—it breaks.

Lucan sucks in a breath, stealing my own from my chest. *I know where you are.*

What? How could you possibly...

I trail off as his answer blooms in my head, my eyes widening at the realization that I've just broken the twelfth Cardinal Rule. That I'm closer to the edge of Xantera than I've ever been before.

The Wall.

I'm at the Wall.

Stay where you are, Lucan says gruffly. *I'm coming.*

He's coming? The thought sends nervous flutters pouring into my stomach. But beyond that, how could he possibly know which part of the Wall I'm at?

There are dozens of doors embedded in the stone in various places around Xantera, Lucan answers, and now I hear the breathlessness of his thoughts, as if he's broken into a loping run. *I know where each of them are, so you're bound to be on the other side of one of them. But none will open from my side,* he adds as a reluctant afterthought. *It's as if they were fused shut when the vampires took over.*

I can't help but gape and stare at those strange glassy cracks again.

How... how do I open it for you?

I don't know if I'm more terrified to let him in or *not* let him in. Part of me is shaking down to my toes at the idea of facing him in the flesh for the first time—of finding out exactly how monstrous he is in this form. The other part of me knows I need him. Not just so that he can help me get to my mom, but because I have the strangest feeling he'd be able to steady the panic rising up my throat again, threatening to spew out. And if I run into another Guardian down here, Lucan might be my only chance at survival.

Unlike my mother's made-up lullaby, I don't have teeth like either of them.

I can't bite.

I beg to differ, Lucan pants. *You have more bite than I ever would have thought possible. You—wait. I... I think I smell you.*

His voice slows, and I swear I feel a presence approaching on the other side of the Wall. It's less a sound than a change in the air, a prickle along my spine and the slight stirring of the dust motes around me.

The Monster. The Monster is standing just on the other side of this unmovable slab of undulating stone. And he's *smelling* me. Taking in my scent.

I don't know why that's the thing that calms me. It shouldn't make the nerves in my throat drop to the bottom of my belly, morphing back into flutters, but it does.

I quit shaking and press my hand against the Wall, wishing I could feel the pressure of Lucan's hand on the other side. For a moment, we both just stand there, absorbing each other's thoughts and staring at the stone as if it's a window through which we can get a first glimpse of each other.

You smell... Lucan starts hesitantly.

Probably like mud and other creepy tunnel stuff, I say, my cheeks burning.

No, Saskia. Like roses and strawberries.

Oh. I wrap my arms around myself to stave off the shiver of appreciation those words bring me. *I'm sorry, I can't really smell you, or I'd try to return the compliment. Guess I've got a weak human nose.*

He chuckles in my head, and the strangest thing happens when he does. An actual growl rumbles from the ground, rushing up my feet and straight into my core.

I hear you, I breathe. I stare at that massive keyhole again. If I could just figure out how to open it...

You can't, Lucan says, his tone dwindling into something a lot more somber. *Not right now.*

But you said—

That only someone on the inside can let me in, yes. But what I didn't tell you is how.

He pauses, as if the weight of what he says next will drag us both down.

When the Guardians made that necklace to spy on me and my family, they spoke to me, too. He takes a deep, rumbling breath that I feel in my toes as the ground vibrates. *The Third vampire, especially, liked to gloat about all of his accomplishments.*

He taunted you? The thought leaves a bitter taste in my mouth, and I curl my fingers around the vial against my chest, feeling a strange sort of possession take root in my bloodstream.

This necklace is *mine.* To imagine the Third Guardian using it in such a way...

Lucan's sudden smugness washes over me.

Territorial, are we, little nightmare?

I glare at him through the Wall as if he can see me, as if I can wipe the smirk of satisfaction from his tone. But my stomach sinks at the realization that I *am*. Is the lure of jewelry already making me feel greedy?

Trust me, Saskia, he replies to my thoughts, *you can be as greedy as you want with me. I'll return it ten-fold.*

Pure want shoots down my core, but I fight it off. We have a bigger problem to deal with right now. *How do I let you in, Lucan?*

He huffs, a sound I can feel in the vibrations against my fingers still splayed against the stone. *The Third Guardian created a key—made out of the same material as the Wall,* he says. *It is the only thing that can unlock any of the doors embedded within it.*

I glance down at the silver key still in my free hand. *I'm guessing it won't be quite as easy to find it as it was for Diggory to find this one?*

Not that I even know *how* Diggory found this one, but still...

I sense Lucan shaking his head, though.

It's not a question of finding the key. My father told me exactly where it is multiple times—smack in the middle of the old white drawing room in the north wing, on a table, under a glass cloche.

How would he know that? I wonder.

I don't know, he replies, *but he was insistent. Sure. And the Third Guardian loved confirming that it was indeed there, out of my reach forever.*

I don't exactly know what the old white drawing room is, but the bite to Lucan's tone tells me that such a display is a mockery of the highest order: a pathway back to his throne, right where all the Guardians can view it every day like a platter of dead history. Still, I go cold at the thought of what that entails.

Even if we know exactly where the key is...

Give me another word, I say suddenly.

What?

Give me another word, I repeat. *Like shit, but stronger. Something that can reflect what I'm feeling right about now.*

Oh. Lucan's surprised chuckle lands straight in my belly button. *You want another curse word, baby?* Again, that name slips out, but he sounds less hesitant about it this time, and I find myself... liking it. *'Fuck' would be the word you want.*

Fuck. I taste the word on my tongue.

Fuck, Lucan agrees with a sigh.

Because I don't just have to find my way back home tonight. If I'm going to get that key to let him in, I need to find out which of these tunnels leads to the Blood Moon Palace, too. I need to do what Diggory wanted to do ever since his daughter was stolen away.

I need to sneak into the home of the vampires.

LUCAN

Night after night, Saskia explores the catacombs.

And each night after she takes off the necklace, I morph back into my human form and stay up until sunset to map out her discoveries. My pencil strokes have become a cathartic release for me, creating a maze of lines that travel back and forth, split off into forks, and burst into multiple pathways that I now know like the veins on the back of my hand.

Saskia has discovered that the tunnels wind underneath the city in a labyrinth, with multiple entry and exit points located strategically throughout. Several lead straight to the Wall, ending in doors just like the one she ran into the first time. Others rise up to various alleyways between complexes. A few are locked that she can't get past, which only deepens my curiosity at what else they're hiding.

And one—a singular one—leads to the original catacombs directly beneath the Blood Moon Palace, where an ancient staircase ascends to a dungeon door.

Her way in.

I stare at that tunnel on my map now, clenching my jaw at the thought of her inside it.

My nerves are completely frayed. My mind hasn't fully relaxed in months. I'm on edge whenever she's down there, just waiting for another vampire to cross her path and snatch her away.

And yet to both my amazement and my immense relief, nothing has happened to her. Saskia has observed a few more of the parasites creeping along the tunnels long after their citizens have gone to bed, but they've never detected her hiding in the shadows. Somehow, they've never detected the fresh blood humming through her veins.

Still, I've spent hundreds of hours listening to her gasps, feeling her racing heartbeat, and absorbing her emotions, hating that I can't bear the brunt of the legwork. Hating that she's alone.

Maybe it's why I'm being such an ass to my pack members now.

"No touching." I shove Ashe's fingers off the edge of my paper with a growl.

Vivian whistles under her breath at my annoyance, but I just glare at everyone's hands too close to my map, protective over the tangible result of all of Saskia's hard work.

Soren is the first to lift his head from where five of us are hunched over in a circle around the desk in my office.

"Is this really happening?" he asks eagerly. "We're finally going to fight and kill these bastards?"

"Not yet," I say darkly, "but this is the first step."

Soren whoops as Merrick slings an arm over Vivian and grins. "We're going to bring the Wall down with their own fucking key."

But Vivian continues to watch me intently. "She's agreed to open it?"

I cut my eyes to her, narrowing them at her tone. "What does that mean?"

"Do you actually *want* her to?" she presses.

My knuckles turn white from how hard I'm pressing my hands against the cold wood of my desk. "Of course I fucking *want* her to."

Everyone collectively lifts their head, wide-eyed, but Vivian continues. She always continues—because she's forever designated as the one to push my buttons. "It's okay to care about someone, Lucan. We can sense the effect she has on you."

"I've never even seen her or met her in person," I insist, even though my mind keeps straying to that moment when we were merely twelve feet apart, only a slab of God-forsaken stone between us. Fuck, I can *still* smell that sweet strawberry scent of hers. It's like a ghost on my tongue, never enough to satisfy my sudden craving that has grown and grown.

"But you've been inside her mind," Merrick adds tentatively. "For months."

"And?"

"It's possible to fall in love with someone's mind—their soul," Viv says. "I'd say that's more important than her body."

I don't miss Soren's smirk at the mention of Saskia's body, and it takes everything in me not to reach out across my desk and claw his lips off his face for even daring to imagine what she looks like based on the details they've all picked up from my mind.

"It doesn't matter what I think about her soul," I remind them all bluntly, trying not to perseverate on that one word—*love*. I've resisted the urge to stray into any more personal territory with her and lusting will get me nowhere. At least not now. "She's a human who's decided to help us, and she deserves our respect." I level a glare at Soren. That fantasy is *mine*. "No thinking or talking about her body allowed."

"Speaking of humans..." Kyra announces, walking into the office. All of us straighten as her chin lifts to the back wall toward the pane of glass that refracts sunlight across the room.

Out the window, we all watch as the top of the sun kisses the dome of the Blood Moon Palace and disappears behind it. An orange haze spreads outward like a halo. Dusk will be upon us shortly.

My skin prickles, already on high alert, like it's second nature, instinct for my DNA to respond to the bloodshed that is coming.

Because tonight, a blood moon will rise.

Twelve more humans will be sacrificed to sustain life for twelve leeches.

The only good thing to come from it? Saskia will use those crucial few hours when the Guardians are too distracted sucking the blood of their Chosen Ones to steal the key right out from under them.

I can only pray like hell that she makes it out alive.

SASKIA

As I make my way to the locker room to peel off my scrubs from another day of work, I glance at the sliding glass doors of the Healing Center.

The rays of the setting sun rebound off the glass, creating a prism of red and yellow hues that splatters across the desk where the information clerk sits. Slowly, the sun will settle over the Wall like it's being pierced by the sharp spikes before disappearing from view at dusk.

Dusk.

Which will then turn to nightfall. And eventually, midnight.

When another blood moon will rise.

I've never been so nervous for a Choosing before. For the first time since my mom disappeared from the balconies, I'm not anxious to be Chosen, but anxious to get this over with. A tense sort of restlessness buzzes in my bones at the thought of what I'm planning to do afterward—sneak into the catacombs and finally ascend that ancient staircase that leads up to the dungeon of the Blood Moon Palace.

I hurry on, but just as I swing open the door of the locker room, a man crashes into me.

"Excuse me," I rush out softly, but when I turn my head in his direction to apologize, he only glares at me with a dark expression—the same way he glared at Gaia and me for simply talking.

I resist the urge to snarl at him. All these nights with Lucan being in my head must be rubbing off on me. Instead, I move out of his way and let him slink past me with a huff.

Sitting down on the cold bench, I slip off my shoes first.

When I straighten, a warm hand curves around my shoulder. "What's wrong?"

I crane my neck up to see Gaia with that look of motherly concern etched into the lines of her forehead.

We've been polite the last few months. No, *formal* would be more appropriate. The *good evenings* more forced, the *have a good shifts* more airy. We've changed into our scrubs without a word. We've passed off patients' charts without making eye contact. But now it seems Gaia wants to break the pattern we've found ourselves stuck in the last few months.

"What do you mean?" I ask, playing with the fabric of my pants.

Her eyes track the movements of my fidgeting fingertips. "You're shaking like a leaf."

"I'm fine," I insist, giving her my best smile.

"I've been worried about you," she says as I stand to pull my scrubs over my head.

"Worried?"

"Losing Diggory," she explains in a whisper. "Our... disagreement."

My body loosens, a tension I didn't realize was wound so tightly around my muscles softening—because I've missed her. That doesn't stop my nerves from shooting through my limbs, though.

"We weren't fighting," I say, keeping my voice soft. "I asked you for something, you said no. That's okay, Gaia. I wouldn't want you to do something you didn't want to do."

Her lips part as she sucks in a shaky breath. "I don't know. It seemed bigger than that?" It comes out like a question. Like she's unsure what really happened between us. "I'm sorry, though. I didn't mean to be harsh. I know you were struggling."

"I'm sorry, too," I reply, suddenly blinking back tears. Everything in me wishes I could hug her. Instead, I wave her off with a flick of my wrist, trying to downplay the moment. "And the sentry didn't seem to have a big issue with it."

Gaia's eyes go wide, her tone dropping to a low hiss. "They visited you too?"

My heart stops pumping. My throat narrows. I can't swallow down the sand flooding my mouth. Nothing came from Rosalyn's visit, but... what are the odds our stories were the same? *It was over a patient*, I had told the sentry—a lie. *We disagreed on whether she should be released or not.*

"What did you tell them?" I ask, panic rising in my chest, bursting painfully from between my ribs.

Gaia's eyebrows pinch together. "The truth, of course. That you wanted to find out where Diggory's partner lives. So you could console her, I told them."

My eyes search her face. Her eyes search my face.

Gaia's body tenses. "Well—" she stutters. "Right?"

"Right," I echo, too high-pitched to my own ears.

Her shoulders drop with relief, her entire body relaxing as she stands to pull on her scrubs over her undergarments. "They understood how dedicated of a healer you are, and it's only a normal emotion to want to console a patient's partner after what happened, make sure they're okay." She turns to me and places a hand on my shoulder. "It's admirable, I think."

My tongue is swollen and heavy, suddenly too big for my mouth. Our stories definitely didn't line up, so why haven't the Guardians done anything? Why did the sentry act like everything was fine?

It's been *months*. Months of me breaking curfew and sneaking through tunnels without getting caught. Surely, somebody should have noticed my transgressions by now?

I look up at Gaia again. The tears behind my eyes make my nose sting, but I inhale deeply to keep them at bay. The concern that she's said the wrong thing deepens in her eyes, but I plaster on a shaky smile to assure her. "Thanks, Gaia. I mean it."

After pinning her purple badge onto her clean scrubs, she bends to squeeze my hand and her good-natured tone reappears. "Well, have a good night. I can't wait to hear all about the Choosing in the morning—I've been designated to stay behind this time."

She shoots me a wink, like we're past this rut we've found ourselves in. And we are. She's one of the only friends I've ever known.

I just wish we hadn't had this conversation *now*, right before I'm about to break into the Blood Moon Palace.

Rising to my feet, my nerves betray me.

The anxiety in my stomach unravels like a ball of yarn, and I rush over to the corner of the locker room to heave into the trash can.

After walking home on autopilot and eating dinner with Malcolm in a haze, I'm now staring at the off-white ceiling of our joint bedroom.

Fully clothed, we're both under the blanket pulled up to our armpits and our hands crossed over our chests.

My eyes trace a line of something that ripples underneath the paint.

"Malcolm," I start unsteadily. But instantly, relief settles into my bones at the thought that I'm about to let it out. My earlier nerves are replaced with old and newly found anger. "You said I should tell you when my life could be in danger. Is that still true?"

Time slows. His legs shift under the covers.

Until finally, he nods. "I think so."

"You think so?" I argue. "Or you know so? Because I don't want—"

"I know so," he says confidently, cutting me off. His face is open, but there's a mix of fear lurking behind his gaze. "What's wrong? Is your life in danger now?"

"I've... discovered some things about our lives—the Guardians," I start slowly. "And I can't ignore it any longer. I don't know if I'll be coming back to our housing unit after the Choosing tonight."

Malcolm blinks once before blowing out a breath. "How can I convince you to not... do whatever it is you're about to do?"

"You can't."

My resolve is fierce. No one else is going to swoop in and save us. We have to save ourselves. And if I die in the process, maybe I'll change things for the ones who live.

"Okay, then," he says, forcing another heavy breath from his lungs. A tense pause lingers between us until Malcolm closes his eyes. "I knew you were up to something."

"You did?" I ask.

A hesitant smirk pulls one side of his face up. "Since when do you go to the Recreation Center to play backgammon?"

I snort, and that thought tickling the back of my mind rises to the top. "Since when have you been in love with Walter?"

"What? I—" he stutters, his eyes flying open. "I'm not."

"It's okay," I insist softly, laying a hand on his arm where the hair is standing on end. My next words are more of a murmur to myself. "I'm certainly not one to judge who you're attracted to. And maybe..."

Malcolm rolls onto his side, facing me. "Maybe what?"

"Maybe one day, things can be different. We wouldn't have to hide it."

His face falters, his voice dropping to a hushed whisper, even though the camera in the living room can't pick up our already low voices. "What are you going to do, Saskia?"

Taking a deep breath, I slip my hand around his, squeeze tightly, and raise my eyes to his.

"If I'm not here in the morning, just know that I'm glad you were assigned as my partner."

I close the door to my own bedroom and press my back against it.

Lucan's howl cuts through the night.

All we can do is wait.

I'm a ball of buzzing energy, my nerves snapping with even the tiniest of my movements.

Another howl, longer this time, settles behind my belly button. The pooling heat calms and frightens me at the same time—because what I feel is longing. A need to be closer to him, a desire to feel that growl against my skin, have it vibrate down to my core.

I climb into my bed with the idea that it will relax me, distract my mind long enough to feel some relief from every emotion compounding on top of each other.

I *need* the relief.

My hand slips beneath the hem of my pants before pushing back the final layer. My breathing deepens. I close my eyes. And I just let the sound of Lucan's howling wash over me.

The anxiety melts away. For several minutes, that pooling heat tightens and tightens... until I cry out in tandem with his howl.

I lie there, then, breathing in and out as the realization sinks in—that I just felt the best pleasure of my life, imagining that my hand actually belonged to the Monster.

Shit. I'm in so much trouble. If I can get through tonight, that is.

Throwing off my cover, I jump up and throw on my cloak, then re-pin my badge and slip on my shoes. Any second now, the loudspeakers will announce that it's time for the Choosing. There's no more time to wallow in nerves or think about this new... predicament.

Still, I find myself bringing out the necklace and staring at the blood-red vial. Lucan told me to check in with him right before the Choosing, so I try to calm my heartbeat before I finally slip it over my neck. Instantly, the howls from outside my window cut short.

What's wrong? Lucan hurries out as soon as it settles along the length of my sternum. *Why are you breathing so heavily?*

I suck in a surprised breath before I fall back onto the bed. *Nothing's wrong,* I tell him as mortification spreads across my skin in heat waves. Thankfully, he can't see me.

But he can—

Ohh, he chuckles out, pure arrogance overshadowing his worry. I can't shut my brain off, each thought like a firecracker, exploding one after the other. A *tsk* sound echoes in my skull before it travels down between my legs, where I'd imagined him touching me only moments earlier. I clamp my thighs together. *You like the sound of my voice in your head?* My eyes flutter closed involuntarily at how close he sounds. His voice drops dangerously low. *Do you want my help next time, little nightmare? I'd drag moans louder than that out of you—without laying a hand on your body.*

Thankfully, a completely opposite and smooth female voice saves me from having to respond.

"Eligible citizens of Xantera, please report to the Blood Moon Palace for the Choosing."

Drowning her out, his rough, gravelly tone suddenly turns serious. *Are you ready?*

I have to be. I raise my chin, because what else can I possibly do? This is the only time the Guardians are guaranteed to be looking the other way, preoccupied with their new sacrifices they choose tonight. If I falter now, I'll have to wait for the rise of the next blood moon, which would be *months*.

No. For my mother, for Diggory and his daughter, for all the Chosen Ones who don't come to the balconies anymore and all their families who don't know what happened to them, it has to be tonight.

I'll let you know as soon as I make it back, I start, already raising my hands to take the necklace off as quickly as I put it on, *and then we'll go to the catacombs togeth—*

What did you just say?

Um. I blink as the loudspeakers repeat that smooth beckoning and the floor creaks outside my bedroom door—Malcolm is probably waiting for me on the other side. *I'll let you know as soon as I make it back,* I start to repeat.

Hell no, Saskia. Lucan's growl could saw through stone. *I'm coming with you to the Choosing, too.*

My hands pause around the chain. *I can't wear this thing around the Guardians. They might see it as they're passing by.* Even if I tuck it into the folds of my cloak, there's still a chance one of them could glance at me and catch a gleam through my hair or something.

Then hide it on some other part of your body, Lucan says firmly. *As long as that vial connects with a pulse, we'll be able to communicate. Doesn't have to be your heartbeat.*

I cross my arms. *And what other pulse are we talking about here?*

I don't know. His voice flickers, as if he very much does know. *You tell me.*

"Saskia?" Malcolm's voice follows a soft knocking on my door. "You ready to go?"

"One moment!" I call. "Just putting on my cloak!"

Why do you insist on coming with me? I hiss at Lucan. He has to realize that he doesn't really have a choice in the matter. I could just rip this necklace off right now like I've done before and take off without him. There's no way he can make sure I obey him.

I don't need to make sure you obey me, Saskia. Once I'm inside that Wall, you'll be crawling after me of your own accord. My eyes fly open, but he plows on before I can process what he just said. *Now find another pulse, because I can't stand the thought of something happening to you around those parasites. I need to make sure you're okay.*

The dichotomy of his words rattle me, and I try to stumble through my own.

I've been to plenty of Choosings before without your mind inside my own, you know. There's nothing you'd be able to do to protect me even if they randomly decided to attack me. Which they won't.

No, the Guardians attack their victims in the confines of their palace, where nobody can see what they really do to them. My fingers tighten with a flash of anger at the very thought, and then a cacophony of voices washes over me all at once.

"Eligible citizens of Xantera," the loudspeakers repeat, *"please report to the Blood Moon Palace for the Choosing."*

"Saskia!" Malcolm calls again.

Another pulse, Lucan says, his voice dropping into something pleading. *Please.*

I huff out a breath of frustration and rip the necklace off my neck. Instantly, our connection is severed, the Monster in my head cutting out like a slammed door.

"Stubborn male," I mutter under my breath, and quickly slide my pants off before putting one of my feet on my bed so that the edges of my cloak fall back. Then, I slide my foot through the necklace and shimmy it up my leg.

When it's just above my knee, I stop, but it slides right back down, and I grit my teeth. It's not quite long enough to loop around my leg twice, but too big to stay put where it's at, so I pull it up even higher. Higher, higher, higher, until it's secured around the widest part of my thigh, the vial resting right between my legs—touching the part of me I just satisfied minutes ago.

Well, I found a pulse for Lucan, that's for sure. He's going to be so satisfied.

Great. Just great.

His presence reappears in my mind merely seconds later, oozing just as much satisfaction as I expected, but I'm already pulling my pants back on, throwing open my bedroom door, and marching out into the living room to Malcolm's side, determined to give Lucan the silent treatment until he stops feeling so *smug*.

I don't know if that's possible, little nightmare. This connection is so much warmer and wetter than—

"Sorry for the wait!" I interject a little too loudly, forcing myself to smile at Malcolm. "I was having some problems pinning my badge."

Malcolm eyes my badge like he doubts that's true, but nods and gestures at the door.

Together, we join the crowd slipping down the main road toward the Blood Moon Palace. The clatter of thousands of footsteps merges with the ticking of my heartbeat in my throat, and I can feel the necklace pressing against me from beneath my clothes, creating a chaotic mess of confusing sensations that I try to shake off by focusing on the moon: a bloody eye looking down on us from the sky, monitoring everyone's march toward what they think would be an honor if they're Chosen.

An honor, Lucan scoffs.

Shhh, I scold him. The last thing I need right now is to be distracted by how his voice seems to be coming straight from my core.

Too soon, Malcolm and I are in that courtyard before the double doors, herded into positions by the sentries forming a blockade around us. I look down at the rows of people, packed as tightly as crops ripe for picking. Twelve inches apart, shoulder to shoulder, line by line, we stand and wait for the Guardians to come out.

And wait.

And wait.

The ridiculousness of this settles into the marrow of my bones. At how accepting we are. How utterly used I feel. Why I never realized this before.

A few of my neighbors glance up at the sky, their foreheads furrowed in confusion, and I realize that it's a little too quiet tonight. The air is stagnant, almost like it's missing the very thing that produces the wind. During every other Choosing I've been to, the Monster has made his fury loud and clear, but tonight, the blood-red ink stain spilling in a halo around the moon is unmarred by any sound that usually fractures the sky right around now.

You're too quiet, I tell Lucan. *Howl so the Guardians don't get suspicious.*

Look who's bossy now. His voice rumbles between my legs, making me tense with a shudder, but he obliges.

The next second, it's his real voice that splits my eardrums, swooping over the courtyard in wave after wave until my neighbors look back down. The echo inside my head is like the inside of a drum, and I shove down the insane urge to cover my ears and experience it inside myself. Beside me, Malcolm straightens his shoulders, facing straight ahead, and I hear the creak of the doors as they open.

Like always, I can sense rather than see them, as if they're wisps on the breeze that suddenly blows through everyone. The slight stirring in the crowd alerts me to their presence, and Lucan falls silent again as he listens to me concentrate on not moving a muscle—though his fury leaks through me anyway, even more potent than his howls indicate.

Relax, I tell him. *I've only ever even seen two of them before. I probably won't even—*

The people around me tense. Okay, never mind. Malcolm inhales through his nose, and one of the Guardians prowls into view like a flash of brightest skeleton-white among all the black cloaks.

My stomach bottoms out as I catch sight of him again: the Third Guardian, the one with golden, wavy hair, bone-white skin, and crimson eyes. He weaves slowly through his options, eyeing the colors of the badges around him with his hands clasped casually behind his back.

What are the odds that I see him twice in a row? Surely, I didn't accidentally fall into the same exact place I stood last time? In all my times sneaking through the catacombs, I've watched a few other vampires slink past without noticing me hiding in the shadows, but I haven't seen the Third one down there at all.

Don't look him in the eye, I remind myself. *This will all be over in a couple more minutes.*

If one of them fucking touches you... Lucan rumbles.

I can almost see the future five seconds from now. The Third will approach me like he is now, that small purring sound growing louder in his throat the closer he gets. He'll pass me by with a quick glance at my scarlet badge. His eyes will shift to the person behind me, and he'll move on to find his Chosen One.

But the Third Guardian doesn't pass me by.

When he approaches me, he slows, his eyes on my badge—

And then he halts in his tracks and looks *up*. Right into my eyes.

"Hmmmm."

His voice nauseates me, and I try to swallow the sudden acid in my throat. Lucan himself stays silent, but I feel his energy—burning hot with loathing as he realizes who I'm staring at. A savage possessiveness slams into me, so hard and fast that I almost double over. The hatred almost spews from my mouth like they're my own thoughts.

Back the fuck off. She's mine.

But of course, the Third Guardian doesn't hear Lucan's snarling words. He merely tilts his head as he analyzes me, his lips pulling up in a smile to display his fangs.

"Yes, I think you'll do nicely," he tells me.

NO!

Whether it's me screaming in my own head or Lucan, I have no clue.

I don't even have enough breath left to gasp as the Guardian's hand—as cold as ice—places itself on the small of my back and gives me a small push.

I stumble forward, and all I can think through the sudden crescendo of frenzied howling that explodes through the air is that *I have to hold my chin high.* I won't be walking into my potential grave like a trembling coward.

I'll kill him, Saskia. Lucan's voice drags down my spine like claws, as if he's desperate to hook himself into me, ground me, keep me. But I can't do anything except put one foot in front of the other. *Eventually,* he adds, tone grating. *Eventually, I'll rip out his fucking throat. I promise you.*

Beside me, Malcolm inhales and raises a hand as if to pull me back. I glance over my shoulder once to give him a look that I hope conveys what I need it to: *don't risk yourself.*

His eyes widen. His hand falls back down. I return my gaze to the path that forms ahead as the crowd parts for me and the Third Guardian, his hand like a cattle prod against my back.

Everyone's eyes follow my trek to the Blood Moon Palace, mixtures of awe and jealousy and admiration pricking me from every direction as they behold one of the newest Chosen Ones.

And as the Monster rages, both beyond the Wall and from within me, I walk through the courtyard with thousands of eyes on me, up the steps to the enormous front doors looming overhead.

Like a gaping mouth ready to swallow me whole.

22

LUCAN

I feel as if the world has been sucked out from underneath me. All that remains is a deafening stillness that roots me to the forest floor—a rage that pulses in my head as if nothing exists but Saskia's remaining heartbeats.

The. Vampire. Chose. Her.

He's going to put his teeth right where *my* mouth should be.

He's going to inject her with venom that will take her away from me sooner rather than later.

He's currently touching what is *mine*.

And I'm going to rip that hand off his marble body for that. I'm going to pull out his teeth one by one, then turn around and impale every inch of him with his own uprooted fangs. I'm going to claw his eyeballs out of his sockets for daring to look at her and think of her as appetizing in such a sickening way, because she is *mine* to feast upon. Only mine.

Saskia's sudden chuckle shoots through me like a lightning bolt. *Well, at least I don't have to sneak into the Blood Moon Palace anymore.*

Of course she'd try to turn this into a positive, but that lethal rage only sinks deeper into me—so deep that I'd snap someone's neck if they stepped too close to me right now.

Because this is it. All the time it took me to convince her to open up for me, all of her bravery spent traversing the catacombs... they were all for fucking nothing. She won't be able to search for the key while the Guardians are distracted with their Chosen Ones because *she'll* be the distraction. She'll give her blood unwillingly and slowly, so slowly, slip away.

I've lost her before I even had her.

The realization seeps into my heart—of what she means to me. No matter what I said in the past, she's not a means to an end, and she hasn't been for a long time. She isn't just a key.

The others would tell me to give it up. To shift back into a human and sever the connection between us so that I don't subject myself to this kind of agony. Because it *will* be agony to listen to her thoughts as the Third Guardian takes her blood. It will destroy me.

But this is my destruction to bear. I told Saskia I wouldn't leave her, so I'm not going to fucking leave her, even if there's no hope for my kingdom anymore.

Closing my eyelids, I channel her mind deeper, like I'm pulling on a rope fistful by fistful until I'm as close to her as I can get. Until I can feel her determination to see the bright side of things battling against a chilling fear that spiderwebs over her thoughts like frost.

I'm here, I say firmly.

A new goal blooms through my monstrous bones when she grasps onto my words like a lifeline, one so hot and painful that

I wince as it smothers the purpose my father planted in my heart ever since I was born.

But I don't care about saving all of my people anymore. If all of them have to die for her to live, then so be it.

There's only one objective worth fighting for now.

Her.

SASKIA

I step into an entirely new world.

Gone are the metal and concrete of the city. Gone are the symmetrical lines and grid-like patterns I was born into. All of that blandness and uniformity peels away as the Third Guardian prods me inside and new colors and textures spring to life right before my eyes.

The air is warm, like the oncoming winter can't touch here. A lush, scarlet rug spreads out before me, so soft and rich compared to the drab gray carpet I'm used to that I blink, realizing that I've never even thought carpet could be any other color *besides* gray. But this... it's soft underfoot as I force myself to take rigid steps forward, and so thick I feel like I could sink into it.

On either side of me, ivory pillars rise up to form an elaborate archway engraved with way too many designs to count. Something glittery and bright hangs from the ceiling, a sort of light fixture that swoops and swirls and makes me dizzy with the sparkles it shoots into my vision. I've only ever seen the glare of bright fluorescent lights or the stuttering of flames, not this fancy lighting that spreads a glittering glow over the room.

Or maybe *hallway* is more accurate, because this room is *long* and there seems to be no end in sight as the Third Guardian pushes me onward.

Where are we going? A private room where he'll take my blood and then leave me to my own devices? For as many times as I've dreamed about being Chosen, I've never given any thought to what would actually happen once I walked through those front doors. Will it be quick, or will the process take a long time? Will I feel myself fade right away?

I steal a glance behind us to check if any other Guardians are following with their own Chosen Ones, but as far as I can see, we're alone.

"Don't worry, Saskia." The Third Guardian's voice slides out like a snake next to my ear. "We'll be to the dining room in no time."

I jolt at the realization that the Guardian knows my *name*.

They know everything about us, I told Odette months ago. But for some reason, I didn't think it was possible for them to actually keep track of every one of their citizens. Are vampire memories exceptionally superior, or—

No, Lucan says, his voice rumbling up my body from where that necklace is wrapped around my thigh. *This was premeditated. The son of a bitch must have planned to choose you long before tonight.*

If tones could kill, the Third Guardian would be a splinter of bones at my feet already.

But unfortunately, that's not how murder works, and I'm not even sure the Third Guardian's bones are breakable. His hand against my back, forcing me forward, feels more like stone than skin. And suddenly, tears prick my eyes for the first time since I was Chosen.

My mother walked this same hallway. She took these same steps. And now, I am heading toward her same doom.

Except she didn't possess this necklace.

Does he know? I wonder helplessly, not daring to steal a glance at the Guardian over my shoulder, although I feel his presence like a magnet—not a force pulling me toward him, but something that repels every atom in my body. *Does he know we're...*

No, Lucan assures me. *He would rip the necklace off you right now if he knew you had it.*

At that, my step is a fraction lighter. Lucan can stay. I can keep him through whatever I'm about to endure.

I'm yours, he affirms, though something in his voice cracks. *Tell me what you need from me, Saskia. Tell me how I can help.*

I wish I could answer him, but there's nothing he can really do from the other side of the Wall anyway. Which means it's up to me to get through this. I'm the damsel in distress, but I can save myself—the male between my thighs is just an added benefit.

Keep on being the same asshole you've always been and I'll do just fine, I reply with my chin tilted a fraction higher. Because the catacombs wouldn't have been possible without his snarky voice in my mind, goading and guiding me forward. He's not the light in the dark, exactly, but the shadows at my feet, the thing that reminds me how brave I really am in the dark.

And if I can deal with a Monster in my head, I can deal with this.

The hallway finally splits wide open into a sort of antechamber, two massive spiral staircases swooping up and around to a second floor, a polished wooden doorway between them. Looking up, I find a domed ceiling high above my head, the same dome I've looked at from afar for twenty-three years. Except it looks even more enormous on the inside.

Split into twelve sections, each depicts a painting of one of the Twelve Guardians, and the intricate gold swirls catch the light from the windows in all directions. The Third Guardian's portrait is the most intense, peering down at me like an all-seeing god.

Next to me in actual form, he pushes me toward that doorway, and my resolve tightens into curling fists.

"I can walk in myself, thank you," I tell him politely—though there's a bit of bite to my voice as I flash a stiff smile over my shoulder.

The Third Guardian's smile tightens, too, but he removes his hand from my back and gestures. "Of course. After you, then. We wouldn't want to be late, would we?"

His red eyes hook into me as I breeze past him and stifle my smile. Let him be mad. It actually brings me a little joy.

Good girl, Lucan says. *Keep defying the bastard.*

My nerves light up with his appreciation—quickly smothered by a flare of shock as I step into this new room and my senses are assaulted yet again.

A table spreads from one end of the room to the other, longer and grander than any table I've ever seen. Just like carpet, I've never given much thought to the possibility that tables could be anything other than thin metal squares on four spindly legs. But this one stands on clawed legs made of dark mahogany with a beautiful lace cloth of some sort draped over it.

Yet hardly any part of its surface is even visible under the weight of all the *food*.

Silver platters of steaming chicken and ham and steak. Ornate bowls of rice and pudding and soup. Little glass plates overflowing with grapes and other colorful fruit I've never seen before. Goblets filled with a burgundy liquid that looks too strong to be tea. And so many other types of food or drink I wouldn't be able to name even if I tried. The smells wafting up make my mouth water against my will.

The sheer enormity of it makes me dizzy in comparison to the perfect little proportions everyone else gets back in the city. Who would ever need this much abundance? What purpose does it serve? And why is it laid out before us right now, when we're supposed to be giving our blood to the Guardians? Do they need to eat regular food before they sip from us?

I blink for several seconds before I realize there are already several others in the room.

Three other Guardians are sliding chairs out from under the table... but rather than sit in them, they gesture for their Chosen Ones to sit instead.

Two of the humans—a man with a green badge and a man with a purple one —glance nervously around before taking a seat. The third one, on the other hand, a woman with a scarlet badge like me, keeps her chin high and her posture stiff, refusing to flinch as she settles into the cushioned chair.

I find myself staring at this Chosen One for what feels like an eternity as I take in her expression, how it reflects the one I feel stamped on mine. She looks at me, too, and we share an emotion that has always been forbidden in the city of Xantera.

Defiance.

"I thought you said you could walk yourself?" the Third Guardian croons from behind me. I almost flinch, but stop myself just in time.

That's it, little nightmare, Lucan says with pride. *Don't give him what he wants.*

Bolstered by his words, I turn my head an inch to pin a glare straight into the Third Guardian's face. Because yes, I can walk myself. But I can also *run*.

If I can just get to that key in the white drawing room before he catches me, I can...

At that moment, the other Chosen woman suddenly pushes back her chair in a flurry.

The legs screech against the floor and she takes off, her cloak flapping behind her, her arms pumping, her breaths sawing the air as she tries to make a break for it.

Faster than I can even blink, her Guardian streaks after her, his body nothing more than a blur.

A vicious *CRACK* vibrates through my very bones the next second, and when the blur of motion stops, the woman lies limp in her Guardian's arms.

The adrenaline in my stomach flares and flatlines. I know what I'd put in the system at the Healing Center immediately: patient deceased.

Her eyes pop out of her skull, glassy and unseeing. Her head hangs from her neck by a thin scrap of skin, collarbone poking out of the side. The only movement in the entire room is her blood, squirting in several separate jets from the wound in her neck and splattering the floor.

"All this wasted food," her Guardian breaks the silence with spitting venom in his words, his crimson eyes following the jets with equal parts disappointment and repulsion. "She could have regenerated the blood after this first time, but *no,* she had to be a runner."

One of the other Guardians down the table gives out a little chuckle that scrapes away the breath in my lungs. "Better get to work then, Rufus."

In evil's case, "get to work" must mean mutilate a corpse even further. Without even dragging his victim out of the room to give her privacy in death, Rufus lowers his head and tears into her right then and there, ripping and squelching and sucking and oh, I'm going to be so fucking sick.

In my head, Lucan has gone carefully still and heavy, like an anchor to my soul.

Don't keep defying him, actually, he says slowly, like we're both caught in the gaze of multiple rabid dogs. But dogs wouldn't be nearly so threatening as the smile that slowly stretches across my Guardian's face as he inclines his head toward the seat right in front of me.

"I see that your legs are shaking, Saskia. Better take a seat."

Okay, so running isn't an option. I'll have to play their game and beat them by breaking the Rules later.

Because here in this palace, the veiled threat isn't actually veiled.

Gripping the edges of my cloak, I force myself forward and sink between the arms of the seat, trying to ignore the feast staring me in the face. There's no way I could be hungry with the sucking and squelching sounds still emanating from my right, especially when the Third Guardian moves to stand right behind me like a solid bar of iron.

Caging me in.

You're doing so well, Lucan says soothingly, though I can tell by the murderous quiver in his voice it's a farce for my benefit. *It'll all be over soon.*

Is that what my mother had to tell herself when she faced this? Did she witness any of her fellow Chosen Ones running and dying just as quickly? What will that woman's family think when their beloved daughter never comes to the balcony? My fists clench in my lap.

Before long, the remaining Guardians drift in with their Chosen Ones, and gasps prick the air as my fellow humans witness the mangled mess of blood and guts that I refuse to look at. When their Guardians urge them all to take a seat, there are no more raised chins. No more defiance.

By the time the eleven of us are staring at each other from across the table, a vampire standing guard behind each of us, the energy in the room pulls tight, the presence of the Twelve Guardians pressing in on us from every direction.

Somewhere behind me, an echoing boom signifies that the double doors have officially closed, locking us in. For the rest of our lives.

Silence stretches and flexes. No one dares breathe. Even Lucan remains silent, as if he's afraid his words in my mind will bleed out into the air for the vampires to hear.

My skin prickles, all too aware that it could be pierced at any moment.

Finally, it's the First Guardian—the eldest-looking one with his hair tied back in a braid—who breaks the nauseating silence swelling throughout the room.

"Eat."

We all glance at each other, more confused than ever. Another Chosen One across from me catches my eye, eyebrows high in silent question. I wish I could say something back, but the Third Guardian is breathing clouds of icy vapor down the back of my neck, watching my every movement.

They're nourishing you before they take your blood, Lucan says in disgust, and he doesn't have to finish the thought for me to fill in the dots myself: *like pigs before a slaughter.*

"Eat," the First Guardian says again, this time more forcefully.

Jolting, we all reach out and grab our silverware.

Try to get something down, Lucan encourages me, his tone morphing back into something soft, as if he forgot his manners. *You'll need your strength. Besides, this is real food. Not the cardboard they regularly feed you.*

I'd prefer to not ever look at food again, not as the dead woman's Guardian finally begins to drag her deflated sack of skin and bones out the door, the sound hissing across the floor. But I don't want to join her, so I shakily grab a bowl of pudding and take a bite.

A wretched sweetness coats my tongue. Maybe in another lifetime it would be enjoyable, but now I'm forcing myself to take tiny spoonfuls even though I can hear each of my swallows. The chewing, the lip smacking from an older Chosen One to my left, the scraping of knives and forks—it grates on my eardrums even worse than my lonely dinners with Malcolm.

Maybe some sounds have always bothered me because of what they represent. With Malcolm, it was endless, meaningless routine. With this, it's the false promise that our Guardians are giving rather than taking.

Did I ever tell you about the first time I turned into a Monster? Lucan asks conversationally.

I cling to the distraction as I swallow the slimy, too-sweet pudding. *No, Lucan. You're not really the mushy-tell-childhood-stories type.*

He chuckles for my benefit. *You know me so well.*

Apparently not well enough, because curiosity is sprouting amid all my fear and anger and grief for the life that was just lost right in front of my eyes. *What happened? How old were you? Did you freak out?*

I was eighteen, and I only freaked out because I didn't know where my balls had gone for a moment. A cough travels up into my stomach from where the necklace touches me. *Sorry. Bad table manners.*

On the contrary, thinking about Lucan's balls rather than the blood to my right or the vampire at my back is helping me get all this food down better. I swallow another bite and say, *Did you find them? Your balls, I mean?*

Yes. They'd just moved slightly in comparison to my... well, we don't have to go into detail. I halfway want to tell him to go into as much detail as he can conjure up so that I can picture his male anatomy after I take the necklace off tonight, but that would be *really* bad table manners, and he's already hurrying on. *As soon as I had settled into my new body, it's like all my senses just exploded. There was this energy in the air that I could taste. And I just started running before anyone could stop me.*

I allow my eyes to close for a second, getting a bite of roasted meat down but imagining that I'm far away, running through the mist of the woods with Lucan.

I didn't stop for three whole days, just ran and ran and ran—around the perimeter of the Wall until I'd memorized every part of it and just about collapsed from exhaustion.

My eyes flash open. *You ran for three days straight without stopping for food or sleep?* The healer in me is both mortified and awed. What kind of body does he even have if he's able to do such a thing?

And what wouldn't I give to possess that same kind of strength? I could have stopped that Guardian from snapping his Chosen One's neck. I would run right through all the vampires holding us hostage and free every Chosen One who's still alive in this palace.

Tell me more, I plead Lucan before more tears can prick the corners of my eyes. *More sweet, sentimental childhood stories.*

I prefer the adjectives gruff and grizzly. There's nothing sweet or sentimental about me.

You're the sweetest Monster I've ever met, I argue.

He growls in response, one that feels so real that I almost yelp and shift in my seat.

The Third Guardian's voice slithers over my shoulder. "Is something the matter?"

"No," I gulp, reality slamming back into me as I shovel in another bite of something much too flavorful. I wish I could glare at Lucan, but the best I can do is clench my thighs together.

I'm sorry, he says immediately. *Sweet, sentimental stories coming right up.*

And he follows through, giving me tidbits of his life that he never has before until I've completely gorged myself, so consumed by his voice that I'm able to block out all the other scraping, sucking, chewing noise.

At last, even the Chosen One to my left pushes his plate back, but he doesn't give a satisfied sigh. Instead, his hands clench over the table, as if preparing to have to fight off the Guardian behind him at any moment. I tense up, too, waiting for something, anything, to happen.

The First Guardian claps his hands, a sound like stone clacking twice against stone.

"Now that you are fed and nurtured, Chosen Ones, it is time for you to perform your duty to Xantera. In exchange for our protection from the horrors beyond the Wall, you will provide us the sustenance we need with honor and dignity. If you will please sit up on the table."

My stomach clenches, sickeningly full from the meal they just forced us to eat. The command couldn't be any clearer, though.

Get up on the table because now *we're* the food.

It's just as humiliating as it is frightening when I stand up and turn around to face the Third Guardian's fanged grin, his lips pulled tight as he assesses me.

Before he can ask, I spit out, "I can lift myself."

Scooting all the dishes away to clear a spot, I plant my palms on the surface of the hard table behind me and hoist myself up. All around me, I can hear the other Chosen Ones struggling to do the same, some clambering up on chairs to do so, others lifted forcedly by their Guardians. One of them on the other end of the table is crying, her sniffles radiating through me in waves of fury.

My mother had to do this.

Diggory's daughter had to do this.

Every Chosen One before me had to do this—face a reminder of the feast we're not allowed to have back in the city and then become that feast for others.

The Third Guardian sits in the chair I just vacated and slides it forward an inch toward my knees. He tilts his head at me, his pupils tracing my neck and then my arms, his nostrils flaring. His golden hair falls just below his wide shoulders. He's built so much differently than the men I typically lay eyes on. That plane of a chest, his shoulders carved from stone—it's like a trap for women everywhere. No one would be able to deny how striking he is, how eerily beautiful he looks, like a snare ready to snap its prey when they're lured in.

His own knees widen.

He can't possibly expect me to sit in his lap and straddle him... can he?

A smirk forms across his vampire lips before he licks them. "Any part of your body will do, Saskia—whichever part you prefer. No need to take off your cloak... unless you want to, of course."

I clench my teeth at the suggestive tone, but Lucan stays utterly silent, as if giving me the choice to react how *I* want to. Because the Third Guardian is actually giving me the option to drop myself into his lap and offer him my neck, I realize. Like it's a game to him—getting his Chosen Ones to fawn at his feet after a few sultry words.

Unfortunately for him, creepy crimson eyes and cold marble skin aren't really my type.

Even though I know defying him could very well send me to my grave, I can't help the words from spilling through my teeth. "You're the last monster in the world I'd remove my cloak for," I say in a low voice that nobody else in the room would be able to hear—besides Lucan himself, who inhales with an emotion I can't quite name.

The Third Guardian's pupils burn blood-red, but before he can decide whether to kill me or not, I roll up my sleeve and stick out my arm.

"I'm sure it tastes just as satisfactory from my wrist—but only if I'm alive, right? Might taste a bit stale if I'm dead."

I've got him. I can see by the way his eyes shutter and drop to my wrist, his tongue darting out a few times to wet his lips again. Oh, gross. I squeeze my eyes shut when he reaches out his hand, not wanting to see it happen but feeling every movement anyway.

Long, clammy fingers lock around my wrist. A pair of rock-hard lips press against my skin, even colder than I expected. He's chosen to keep me alive despite my insolence. For now.

You foolish, brave, stubborn fucking woman, Lucan chastises, finally exhaling. *How the hell am I going to survive you?*

I don't have time to wonder what he means. Sounds erupt around me from my fellow Chosen Ones—gasps, whimpers, shouts, even a scream. But contrary to the underlying assumption that a Guardian drinking from you would be more than just honorable, these all sound like noises of pain to me. Only pain.

And when two sharp needles pierce my delicate skin, I can confirm it: there's no rush of gratification or pleasure. Only a feeling like hot poison leaking into my veins and rooting its way up my arm like snakes of fire.

I stay quiet. I won't give the Third Guardian the satisfaction.

But his light hum travels up my forearm, like he just can't help himself.

I'll make you forget, Lucan promises desperately, his voice mimicking the pain I feel. *Every second of this nightmare, I'll bury it so deep, Saskia, it won't be able to haunt you.*

I nod inside my own head, focusing on Lucan's words, on his presence. That warmth that stamps out the iciness of everything around me. The muscles in my face relax as I block out my surroundings and the siphoning of my blood goes numb.

Just you and me, baby, Lucan whispers, and I believe him.

In this haze of a nightmare, it's only the Monster and me.

When the last vampire, the Seventh to be exact, finally unsuctions herself from a man's neck with a sickening pop next to me, the man tips forward slightly.

Without thinking, I reach out to catch him just as he slams his hands down onto the table so he doesn't fall right off.

My own movements feel like electric zings through my nervous system.

"Are you okay?" I gasp out as a drop of blood beads from his wound before trickling in a zigzag down to his collarbone.

The man groans in response, his skin paling instantly.

"Are you going to faint?" I rush out.

"He's fine," the Seventh Guardian says curtly with a hand on his shoulder.

Her eyes, though, aren't on me.

They're on the Third Guardian—who's wiping my blood from his lips with a fingertip and watching me curiously with a groove between his eyebrows.

A rock weighs my stomach down. Sweeping my head around to assess the room, I find that everyone else seems to be off-kilter, like they've been administered general anesthesia at the Healing Center.

One man hangs his head to bury his face in his hands. One woman slumps against the Eleventh Guardian as she clings to his neck and that sickly-looking Adam's apple.

Lucan, I hurry out, *everyone else looks...*

Hungover, he finishes, though I don't know what that means.

...like they've lost too much blood. But I don't feel like that? I say, focusing on my toes. I flex them inside my shoes and a snap echoes up my legs. Every tiny movement shocks me, as if I'm running on electricity, and I blink. *Whoa. I can feel the tips of my eyelashes.*

So you're basically high then, Lucan says, worry lining his tone. *I suppose it affects everyone differently.*

I raise my hand in front of my face, and I swear the venom and blood pulsing there are speaking to me. When my hand falls to my lap, the Third Guardian's face materializes in front of me, fading slowly into clear view.

Lucan's concern grows deeper. *Saskia, are you okay?*

Actually, I feel great, I reply, practically smiling.

The Third Guardian and I stare at each other, both of our eyes narrowing in unison, until my head suddenly fills with air. I almost tip right into his lap, but lurch back just in time.

The laugh that comes out of him isn't amused or humored—it's triumphant.

"There it is." He reaches out a finger as if to stroke a strand of my hair, but even in my current state, I have enough sense to jerk back. I clamber to my feet, trying to put as much distance between us as I can manage, but bump into the chair beside me. His laugh deepens, chiseling a cold pit into my stomach. "Don't worry. It won't last forever."

And neither will you, Lucan grits out, and I swear his words must have hardened something in my eyes, because the Third Guardian's own eyes widen just an infinitesimal amount—as if somehow, Lucan's threat hangs in the air between us.

Before either of us can respond, the First Guardian commands the room again with a sharp clap. "Chosen Ones will now be shown to their rooms where you can rest and regain your strength. You will be called upon when needed by your Guardian, but until then, do not leave your room. A servant will be assigned to you. Anything you need, request it from them."

Lucan's relief that this is finally over is a tangible thing inside my heart.

Another clap and a handful of side doors in every corner of the room fly open. Blinking away electric stars, I gape as dozens of servants stream out—*human* servants. They rush toward us to clear off the table in a flurry. I've never even given any thought to the possibility of non-Chosen humans living within the palace, serving our Guardians. Where did they come from? Have they always been here? Were they assigned to this job or born into it?

One of them approaches me and dips her head, gesturing for me to follow her, but the Third Guardian steps between us like a towering wall.

"You're relieved of your duty this evening," he tells her.

Curtsying, her eyes fall quickly to the floor, but I catch a glimpse of relief when she pushes her short, blonde bangs out of her face before she turns and scurries back through the same door she came through.

It's not until the Third Guardian's hand is cradling my lower back again to guide me to the door that I realize what he's done.

The other remaining Chosen Ones are each stumbling away after a servant, but not me. My vampire presses me forward, making sure I'm steady and upright as we step over the dead Chosen One's bloodstains still smearing the floor.

When we break off from the single file and take a grand staircase lined with gold and red carpet, he finally speaks.

"Saskia, you can call me Arad."

I snort. "I'd rather not."

That's probably something I would have held in before the whole blood-sucking thing made my head feel like it's floating off my body. I whip around to gauge his reaction and just barely catch the tail-end of his jaw tightening in anger. "It will make it sweeter then, when you change your mind."

"Excuse me? I won't."

The Third Guardian takes a step into me. I take a step back against the railing, my body now frozen by the intimidating snarl that rises from his throat. "Mark my words, Saskia, you're going to end up screaming my name just like the rest of them. Either from pleasure or pain. To beg for release or mercy." He shrugs, as if he's said this a thousand times before and watched his wishes come to fruition. "I don't care which."

For a moment I wonder if it would actually be possible for me to explode from the surge of Lucan's white-hot rage.

I got it, I tell him. And I do, because with the current coursing through me, I feel as though I could burst through the Wall right about now.

"I feel sorry for you then, because your name will never leave my lips," I promise, twisting out of his caged presence and resuming our trek up the stairs.

Arad clicks his tongue after we reach the last step like each one progressively helped to reel himself back in. "That's the thing about all of you humans though. You *are* mine for the next few months, and longer if I so choose. You'll fall in line with the rest of them." A pause thickens the air. Then his red lips lift into a half-smile that exposes one long fang like he's imagining me bending to his will. "Eventually."

I swallow, swallow again. The lump grows like a ball of energy, and I may just vomit on his shoes. But he stays silent, just a moving statue using his fingertips to turn me right and the base of his palm to turn me left when the hallways split.

Finally, he stops in front of a wooden door intricately carved with roses and unlocks it with a large brass key he produces from the folds of his velvet cloak.

My heart leaps, even though I know instinctively that it wouldn't fit in any of the doors I'm most interested in.

That one's in the white drawing room in the north wing. Under the glass cloche. That I'll steal from right under his sharp nose as soon as he's looking the other way.

Like he knows what I'm thinking, Arad's nostrils flare.

"Did you know you smell like strawberries and roses?"

Lucan growls. *I know you've got this, little nightmare, but when it's my turn, this motherfucker is going to get two spikes up his nose before I kill him for even daring to breathe you in.*

A smirk forms on my lips as I imagine that exact scene playing out.

"Something funny?" Arad asks.

I clear my throat. "You're not the first one to tell me that," I say before I can think about the logistics of what I'm confessing. "That I smell like strawberries and roses."

The Third Guardian audibly grinds his teeth, eyeing my neck. "Too bad you'll never see your partner again," he says, and I realize with a relieved jolt he must think I'm talking about Malcolm, "except from a balcony." He licks his lips like he's savoring something, and a new sensation washes over me: murderous rage. Except this time, it's my own. "And by the way, your blood tastes even better. You're lucky I have such self-control—unlike the others."

I swear the necklace vial jumps against my thigh before Arad's long fingers wrap around the doorknob and he swings the door open.

"And the thing about me," he adds above my shoulder, "is I learn my Chosen Ones intimately. Everything you find in here has been handpicked by me." I sway on my feet before he gives me one good shove across the threshold. "Enjoy. I know I will."

Then the monster locks me in my room alone with my guardian.

24

LUCAN

E ven though we both just heard that heavy key slide the dead-bolt into position with a loud thunk, Saskia immediately whips around to try the doorknob just for the hell of it.

She balls up her fists and slams them into the door over and over when it won't budge.

Hey, I try to soothe her, even though nothing about me feels even remotely soothing right now.

Don't 'hey' me, she bites back. *That asshole has my mother—and the key.*

I wish I could rage and claw at the door alongside her. Her anguish and confusion and anger feels like they've fractured every part of me that matters, but I can't let her know how much this has affected me. It isn't about me. And I have to be her voice of reason, her foundation when everything's falling apart.

We're going to find both of them, I say. *Your mother and the key. But first, you need to rest.*

She scoffs. *This was supposed to happen tonight. It needs to happen tonight.*

Squeezing her eyes shut, she curls her fingernails into the wood hard enough to leave a mark. The pain shoots down her arms and cuts into my own heart.

We're inside, I assure her. *First step accomplished. But you can't go anywhere right now, especially when you need to sleep this off.*

I feel fine, she says, and I believe her. Her mind has calmed, settled back into her somewhat normal rhythm, but it's still accompanied by the occasional zap to her brain. She's in her right mind—everything is just heightened. *We don't have time to wait around.*

The me from three months ago would have agreed with her regardless of her condition. But I can't risk it now, not when she's still in such a fragile state. She needs to stay put for now. That newfound fire pumping through her veins has made her feel invincible, but if she finds a way to break out right now, she'll be putting herself in even more danger than she already is.

And that's simply unacceptable.

I need to figure out how to calm her down. Relieve her stress. Take her mind off everything that just happened and *recover*. A dozen wicked things I can say to her, do to her, flick through my mind, but I swallow them down for the time being. I'll let her take the lead on that.

Let her relinquish her beautiful control whenever she wants me to take over.

You can't accomplish anything if you get yourself killed, I say softly, knowing she deserves logic and reason even if the words taste like acid on my monstrous tongue. *Rest is more important right now so that we can find your mother and the key.*

When she pauses, I take the opportunity to tug her attention in a different direction.

Saskia, I tell her, *just turn around and open your eyes. Because I'm sure your room is unlike anything you've ever seen. And you deserve to see what you've always deserved.*

25

SASKIA

Lucan is right. My room is unlike anything I've ever seen. Pressing my back against the door, I gape at the enormous scope of it.

I have no frame of reference for whether this is ancient or futuristic. What I do know is that it's gaudy and I shouldn't be so enamored with it—but I am. And I wish everyone back in the city had the same chance to experience laying eyes upon it... without having to sacrifice their blood, of course.

Three pristine sofas form a semi-circle around a polished coffee table crowned with a vase of fresh roses. Standing lamps cast warm glows throughout the room, highlighting an elegant desk with drawers against the wall behind them. On an ornate bedside table, a handheld mirror exactly like the one Diggory had sits beside a familiar packet of blue birth control pills that I've been taking my whole life. For a moment, I wonder why I would still need to take them now that I'm no longer with Malcolm, but then my eyes stray to the actual bed.

It has to be the most lavish thing I've ever laid eyes on. Four wooden posts thick as my waist jut up to the high, high ceiling that's carved with intricate floral designs, winding outward in a circular pattern. Deep crimson curtains hang around the bed, probably to block out the morning sun from the enormous lancet windows that line the back wall.

At the sight of those windows, I bypass all the other furniture and beeline toward the nearest one to search for a latch or opening. I feel along the windowsill and edges, but the colored glass is just as solid as it is thick with no crack or indication that it even opens at all. Escaping through them isn't an option, then.

And it wouldn't be even if they could *open,* Lucan growls. *Considering you're several stories high.*

I could've made myself a rope, I mutter.

With what clothes? You haven't even checked your closet.

I have the distinct impression he's trying to lure me away from the window, and it works. Curiosity tugs me toward the armoire on the far back wall.

Throwing open the doors, I'm met with dresses upon dresses upon dresses. *Dresses.* I've only worn one outfit my entire life, but these... these are nothing short of decadent.

Rich silks, delicate lace, velvets, something soft and shiny I don't have a name for. My hands sweep across them of their own accord. Sinking into the fabric's smooth texture.

Although he stays silent, Lucan's pity seeps into me—pity that this is the first time I'm experiencing something outside of the carefully curated Wall and my rigorous schedule and my mundane belongings, that this is the situation in which I finally get to experience the things of the world I've been deprived of my entire life.

They gave us the Cardinal Rules, I murmur, *so that we wouldn't realize we were missing out on all this.*

And yet there is so much more they're missing out on by stifling you, Lucan muses, his thoughts drifting up and down my body, tightening my throat.

Before I can respond, a rustle behind me makes me whip around—

—and find myself face to face with a pair of squinting, watchful eyes.

Fucking hell. Lucan's heart pounds in tandem with mine, but I realize it's just the servant from earlier, the one Arad dismissed.

Practically face to face, nose touching nose, she curtsies stiffly.

"Oh, that's not necessary," I tell her in a hurried voice. I glance at the locked door. "How'd you get in here?"

She straightens, blinks. Those narrow brown eyes feel like they're slicing into me, like whatever they've witnessed have sharpened them into permanent slits.

Still, she doesn't say anything, but she gestures to a space between the armoire and the bed, where I blink at a door I didn't notice in my earlier attempt to escape, its pallid color blending into the wallpaper around it.

I furrow my brow. "Is that where you came from?"

She shakes her head, and with a strong hand, tugs at my arm, leading me to that sliver of white I can see through the crack.

I gasp as soon as she pushes the door back to reveal a bathroom. But the word bathroom doesn't justify whatever this is.

White marble, floor length mirrors, and gold upon gold accents. My eye-line latches onto some sort of basin with clawed feet in the center of the room, where my servant turns two knobs and water flows from the faucet in a rumbling start.

Lucan senses my confusion. *It's a bathtub, little nightmare. Like a shower, but better.*

The gears in my head click, but instead of responding directly to Lucan, I use my voice. "I get to sit in the tub? For as long as I want?"

Steam unfurls from the water, calling to my muscles that have been on edge for the last few hours.

My servant looks up and nods curtly before motioning to my clothes.

"Oh." I startle when she reaches for the edge of my cloak. "I can do it myself. Thank you though."

With a disapproving pinch of her lips, she busies herself with the hot water: plugging the hole in the bottom, testing the temperature, adding a floral-scented liquid that hits my nose as it swirls around like oil.

"I haven't gotten your name," I say as I remove my cloak and lay it over a chair in the corner.

She glances at me from behind her bangs, and I catch a flare of longing on her face before she turns away.

Saskia, Lucan starts slowly, hitting every syllable. *I don't think she can speak.*

A haunting feeling settles in my gut. *You mean...*

I can't even bring my inner voice to say it. I let my eyes linger on her mouth, too long, apparently, because a muscle in her jaw tics from how hard she's keeping it shut.

Yes. I think her tongue has been removed, Lucan says carefully.

My breath catches as the truth barrels into me, horrible and vicious. All with the idea to silence these people, forbid them from communicating. And a tongue being removed... it would require instant cauterization or else the patient—servant—would die.

To think that the Guardians do this on *purpose,* that they must have a palace healer on standby to attend to the wound they inflict on their own supposed *people...*

Taking a deep, shaky breath, I ask, "Can you write your name for me?"

She snaps her head up as she lays a towel on the cushioned bench on the other side of the tub, scowling at me like I've asked for something impossible. Yet as I sidle up next to her and she smooths the towel flat, I see that she's tracing something over the plush cotton.

"E," I say, watching her strokes closely, "l—e—n—i." I look up. "Eleni?"

She shakes her head at the way I said it—El-uh-nigh—and points to her knee.

"Eleni," I correct myself with a smile. "It's nice to meet you. I'm Saskia."

I'm met with a deeper scowl. But her eyes betray her—a trace of happiness glimmers through before she shutters her emotions again and crouches at my feet to untie my shoes.

"Please," I insist. "There's no need for that."

Eleni huffs under her breath as she rises and fusses with my shirt.

But I step back—because I don't think she should be waiting on me and I have a necklace between my legs that might seem rather strange.

"Really, Eleni," I laugh awkwardly. "I can do it myself. You don't have to... serve me."

She throws her hands up, worry creasing into her face, before she gestures with her hands in an indecipherable motion.

I'm sure she's just as worried as I am about you, Lucan offers. *You just had some of your blood replaced with venom. She's seen this hundreds of times.*

"I'm fine," I tell them both. "I promise."

While my muscles do feel like they're on fire, it's a good kind of burn—like a light snaking through my veins, a power activating some deep recesses of my mind.

My limbs still zing with every movement, but the world around me has slowed. I feel more alive than ever. Which definitely means I need to sleep this off, because I shouldn't be feeling so exhilarated after the murder I just witnessed and the pain I just felt.

"Eleni." I smile. "I'm going to take a bath and go to sleep, and you need to rest yourself. It's almost two in the morning."

She hesitates, but I see the exhaustion seeping out of her move-ments. It doesn't take another word from me—just a gentle, reas-suring touch to her arm and a once-over from her, and then she's retreating from the bathroom.

Before I close the door, I watch her cross over the plush rug to the other side of my bedroom, slip something out of her pocket, and press it against the wall.

A panel pops inward, silently swinging on hidden hinges.

Just before Eleni steps through into the dark, she looks over her shoulder at me and flashes me a quick smile.

I suppress my laugh and say to Lucan, *I think I just made a friend.*

Warmth envelops me.

From my neck down to my toes sticking out the top of the water.

The steam clears my senses and my pores. The scent of lavender calms me, pulling me far away from images of that dead Chosen One on the floor and sliced tongues and the two pinpricks of blood that have dried on my wrist. Hopefully tomorrow, when the venom has faded a bit, I'll remember to hate anything and everything that comes from the Guardians, but for now...

Lucan, baths are my new favorite thing.

I'm met with cold silence.

Lucan?

Panic flares—a worse feeling than vampire venom flooding your heart—until I realize I left the necklace on the stool next to the tub after I undressed and forgot.

The Monster has become such an ingrained part of me, it's almost natural to just assume he's in my mind.

I sit up and pick up the blood-red vial, the chain uncurling from its little pile, before I slip it over my head. The pendant slides down my slick skin and hits the water, where it floats for a second before sinking down between my breasts.

The curve of them looks so sensual against the surface of the water, and when it ripples, my peaked nipples alternate between the warm liquid and the cool air.

I run a wet fingertip over my right one.

Saskia, Lucan says firmly through my thoughts.

Baths are my new favorite thing, I say again, for some reason unbothered. I feel like I should be embarrassed, but I'm not.

Lucan chuckles. *I figured that's why you forgot about me.*

I think it would be impossible to forget you at this point.

Is that so?

His voice is so thick it feels like it's coating me. All these little places that have always felt neglected and empty, they're bursting with fire out of my control.

Yes, I exhale. *Are you going to forget me? If I end up like that other Chosen One?*

That *will never happen.* He pauses. Almost like he's taking a slow, steady breath that matches the rise and fall of my breasts. *Your voice is etched into my brain.*

My voice, I echo, both with hope and a little disappointment thrumming through my words.

I stare at my body through the water, the outline of my curves fragmenting with each tiny wave. I can't help but wish it could be etched into Lucan's mind just as well. That he could see me in the flesh, that I could feel his hands on my skin, his real voice in my ear.

How... much does this work from your end exactly?

What do you mean? he asks, and I can tell his curiosity has perked up.

Well, I assume you're better at the mind communication than me. For instance, can you see through my eyes?

It doesn't really work like that. He hesitates. *More like a hazy second-hand view of the pictures you form in your mind, and even then, I'm lucky if I get that deep. It takes concentration from me and openness from the other person.*

Ah, I say, tracing the surface of the water with my fingertips, *so you've become good at shutting your own mind off then? Because I never get any of your mental images.*

I've been practicing for centuries, he laughs. *When your obnoxious family and friends are constantly invading your space, you have to learn.*

Do I invade your space?

No, Lucan scoffs. *You're the best part of my days.*

I fold my lips into a smile and continue to swirl my palms along the top of the water directly above my stomach, wishing with every fiber of my being that Lucan could actually see me right now. Because I have a sinking suspicion that, in a way, he *can* see me. That if he wanted, he could scrape away every thought I'm thinking and discover where they're wandering. Maybe he already knows.

And could you... control me? If you wanted?

A beat of silence. A drip of water from the faucet.

Finally, his gruff voice fills my mind. *If you let me.*

My subconscious doesn't even have time to goad him. I gasp when my hand moves to trace my collarbone, because I didn't tell it to.

Earlier didn't satisfy you enough? Lucan says, voice rough.

No! I want to scream as heat rips through my core with a dangerous intensity that I didn't know was possible.

Is it me? Or him? I can't wrap my mind around it. All I know is I want more.

I try to move my hand downward, but I'm only given an inch of leeway before I'm met with resistance and Lucan clicks his tongue.

What's the rush, little nightmare?

I can only manage a whimper when his smirk is practically a living thing inside me.

How badly do you want to touch yourself right now?

You know how badly. A helpless plea, I already know.

I do, but I want to drag it out, he counters. *If I can't touch you. If I can't taste you. If I can't use my own fingers and lips and tongue. If all I have is time with you like this, then I'll make the most of it.*

Now I'm wetting my own finger. Just placing it on the pad of my tongue, closing my lips around it, like it's of my own volition. Which, I realize, it kind of is. Anything he's commanding me to do, I could easily overpower. He can't manipulate me into doing anything I don't want to do.

It all lies in how freely I open myself to him. And I want *this.* Full trust with him in a place where I can't trust anyone else. A slice of pleasure after all that physical and emotional pain I just had to endure.

Let's go back to the beginning, baby, he says, removing my finger from my mouth and trailing it along the chain of the necklace. *When you were teasing me.*

I wasn't meaning to... I trail off when my hand reaches my breast.

Lucan groans, a low rumble in my head that I feel below my belly button.

You've been teasing me for months, though. My thumb and index finger roll my nipple, pinch. My eyes flutter closed, my head falls back. I'm lost in the sensations of pleasure twining down my body, connecting between my legs. This is more than I've hoped for, wondered about, always questioning if I was lacking something. Nothing in my past has ever felt this good—and he hasn't even touched me. *It all started with that goddamn mirror,* he growls.

My mind wrestles for control, so I can snap back, *That mirror you demanded I find.*

And that mouth that always talks back, Lucan chuckles. My eyes are forced open. *But admit it. You needed that mirror as much as I did. Didn't you like what you saw? Look at you.*

I don't just look. I stare down at myself. The way my curves dip and valley, rise and peak. The way the water casts the light across my skin. Both of my hands now caress my breasts at Lucan's insistence. The pulse between my legs has grown so strong that it aches.

There's this gnawing acceptance of myself that society has demanded I never face. I'm not supposed to think of myself as beautiful, because they don't want me to believe I'm worthy of more. But underneath my heavy cloak and simple clothes, *this* has been there the whole time. Unappreciated. I look like I was made for pleasure, like I was made to be worshipped.

You were, he replies. *For me. By me.*

A low moan slips out of my mouth, bliss and frustration mixed together. I try to ease the fire by clamping my thighs together, but my knees widen an inch instead.

Lucan, I start to protest, but I'm only met with his brewing satisfaction.

You can't lie to me, he teases. My right hand drops to my belly button, my middle finger circling around it with the slightest touch. *Not right now. I can feel how much you like this. And fuck, if I don't love this so much more. When you get out of that godforsaken place, I'm going to make you pay for this.*

I'm going to make you *pay for this,* I argue, watching my hand drop mere centimeters from where I'm craving friction only for it to travel back north. I'm simultaneously aching and fascinated by how much I secretly love it. I didn't know sex could be like this.

And all of a sudden, I pause, overcoming Lucan's control with nothing more than a moment of hesitation on my part.

Sex *shouldn't* be like this. I technically have an assigned partner back at home, and even though we broke it off months ago in secret, surely this level of intense pleasure is wrong... even if it feels so right. If anyone found out that I'm—

No one will find out, Lucan says firmly, though he doesn't try to regain control of my movements yet. *Your pleasure—what we're doing here—it's not wrong. But it's between you and me. Nobody else. Just our little secret.*

Our secret, I whisper back in a haze. Because this part of me is for Lucan and Lucan only—the position I'm in, the lust for more that I've always suppressed, the hidden thoughts he coaxes out.

It's terrifying and freeing all at the same time.

I want it all, he says, gently starting to guide both of my hands down the curves of my hips again. A path of goosebumps bursts out across my skin as my fingers go down my outer thighs and up my inner thighs. *Your good, your bad. Every part I'll hoard and protect, and no one else will know, because you're mine, Saskia. You always have been.*

His. I like the sounds of that, because it means that he can be mine, too.

And at that thought, I relinquish all my control to the Monster with a gasp. My hands move further and further down, and finally, my hand dips between my legs.

The burn ignites as two of my fingers press and circle once. My legs widen, and immediately, I'm trying to press harder, circle faster, but Lucan keeps me at a slow pace.

One of my fingers enters me slowly, pressing against the exact spot that I always search for and stealing the breath from my lungs in surprised pleasure.

Do you forget I'm inside your head? Lucan teases, as he sets the perfect pace and rhythm. *I know exactly what you need. I can read every thought, every memory, desire, wish.* A flame licks up my spine as I arch my back, and my moan echoes off the marble. Lucan brings my left hand up to play with my pebbled nipple. *I know what you want before you want it. Now close those eyes.*

Obeying, my head falls back and another moan, louder this time, reverberates around the room. The water splashes slightly when he has me add another finger and the pace increases.

Lucan's right. He does know exactly what I want before I try to manifest it, exactly how I'll respond to something before I do.

So wet, Lucan murmurs. *So tight. So perfect.* No one has ever spoken to me like this, but I'm immersed, so turned on by every word. *The things I would do for you to be in front of me, to actually be inside you, to feel you come around me... unspeakable fucking things, baby.*

I'm so close, and it's almost as if his voice alone could bring me to the edge.

"Lucan," I moan desperately out loud, the loudest I ever have. My breath is ragged, my legs shake, and I'm falling.

As if into him. He's surrounding me, filling me, my presence and his merging as one.

If this is what it's like with a partner you choose yourself, I may just never come up for air.

26

LUCAN

After Saskia dresses in her silk pajamas and slides between her sheets, I wait until her thoughts slip into dreams before I address the others I can feel hovering on the outskirts of our connection.

Mist beads against my face as I turn my monstrous head to find three pairs of amber eyes, one wolfish, two human, tacked onto mine with their heads dipped before Vivian bursts into questions.

Are you okay? Is she okay? What can we do? I thought you'd look like dog shit, but you're oddly smiling—oh. If a wolf could grin, that's precisely what she'd be accomplishing. Partly because she never listens and insists on shifting whenever she thinks she should for my benefit.

Shut up, Viv, I snarl as Merrick raises an eyebrow and Soren barks with laughter, everyone sensing how turned on I am, but those images are for me alone.

I tug on the bones that hold my form together to shutter my pack off from the tortuous images of Saskia's naked body in the water that will probably haunt me for the rest of my goddamned life.

To see through her eyes but not be able to *touch*, to feel with her fingers but not be able to wrap my own hand around that beautiful throat...

I turn away from them, resisting their prying thoughts. As soon as I fully shift into a human, my dick's already straining against my pants.

Great. Just one more problem I need to fix.

Vivian's smile falters as my scowl cuts through the shadows of the night. Within a blink, she shrinks and straightens into her own human form, too.

"She didn't get into the Blood Moon Palace, did she?" Vivian whispers.

"Oh, she did." I scrape a hand through my hair in an effort to realign myself in this body. "But only because the prick practically dragged her inside. It's like he could sense..."

I trail off, blinking against the memories that threaten to sprout in the darkness of the woods: the Third Guardian, standing on his own balcony that looks more like a perch above the Wall, grinning down at me as I try and fail, try and fail, try and fail, to scale the thing that shoots pain into my limbs whenever I so much as graze it, that blood-red necklace always glinting from around his marble neck.

Remarkable, he would whisper into my mind while his crimson eyes peered down at me. *All that muscle and strength and power, and you're nothing more than a beetle scrambling to climb up a ledge. It really does prove we're the superior species.*

He would say it as if it was a physical ability that kept me from scaling a simple wall rather than a magical one. But the truth is, I've climbed every building, jumped from every rooftop, scaled every tree in the vicinity with the ease of lifting a finger.

And when I finally do meet him face-to-face, I can't wait to find out which of us is truly superior after all. One month ago, I might have been uncertain.

Now, with Saskia as my reason, all of my doubts have crumbled away.

An hour of tossing and turning in my own bed later, and I can't take it anymore.

I step out of my house and onto the abandoned street, the wind whistling through the open doorways and windows. Everything seems to creak as I walk what used to be downtown—past an old tavern, a bank, and finally the church.

The rusted iron gate in front of the cemetery hangs off its hinges, slightly slanted with just enough room for me to step past it without needing to force it open more.

Weaving through the century-worn tombstones, I find the one I'm looking for in the center toward the back. I come here so often my footsteps have created a rutted path almost as deep as the one that circles the Wall.

All of the gravestones have succumbed to time no matter how often we all come here to take care of them. Hundreds of years is a long time. And some go even further back than that, to before the Wall.

"Hello, Father," I say, laying a hand against the cold stone. My other reaches out to the opposite side. "Grandfather."

The guilt that kept me up wrings through my gut. How do I admit my priorities are shifting? I can feel them realigning themselves every second more that passes.

"Can't sleep?"

Nearly jumping out of my skin, I whip around and exhale, "Mom." Her white hair glistens in the moonlight as she drifts toward me, all the soft features of her face lifted in a smile. She looks so fragile, unlike the woman I remember in my youth—her hair always running wildly in the breeze, her spirit louder than anything. "You know better than to sneak up behind someone in a fucking graveyard."

She shrugs, chuckles a little at my misfortune. "Language, son... and I couldn't sleep either." My mother backs up until she grazes the small iron bench and sits, making sure to leave enough room for me. She pats the seat next to her and bursts out, "I fucking miss him."

"Language, Mom," I laugh and lower myself beside her, then add, "You and me both. I wish he were here to finish this."

A beat of silence passes as she rubs my forearm. "What's bothering you, Lucan?"

"Besides the usual leeches draining our people's life away while we can't do anything but howl and haunt this dying ghosttown?"

She huffs out a sad little laugh. "Yes, besides that."

The sigh I stretch out is purely to stall. "This family legacy," I start. "What if I can't fulfill it?"

"You mean what if you don't want to?"

"I didn't say that," I insist, but still grapple with the thought. "It's not that simple. I still want to bring down the Wall. It's just for a different reason now."

Sure, in an ideal world, I'd have it all. Saskia would live, the citizens of Xantera would be liberated, and the Twelve wouldn't even have a tombstone to be remembered by.

But the world isn't ideal. I know that, and it never will be.

"Love," my mother says, "is a feeling. Loving someone, though—that's where you make a choice."

"And if my choice is... cruel even? What happens if I abandon the very people I was born to protect?"

Just so she lives.

My mother's gaze strays toward the tombstones again, her features pinching. Unlike me, she actually lived out the details of the war, the blood and screams and dead bodies that stacked up when the vampires invaded. She remembers my grandfather's head rolling off his shoulders. She remembers the Wall slowly turning into stone until our exile was permanent.

And she remembers how my father decided, one day, that enough was enough. That he would reclaim his lost kingdom or die trying.

She remembers how he died trying.

During the rare times she shifts, I can see the memories plague her mind as if they're my own: my father, in his monstrous form, sinking his claws into cracks in the Wall and climbing, climbing even when electricity tore through his bones, climbing even though his howls of pain were turning into tortured shrieks. Climbing until a single paw made it to the top of the ledge, where the Third Guardian smiled down at him—and snapped his neck.

My father was dead before his body hit the ground.

And that would have been me, too, if Diggory hadn't somehow gotten hold of the necklace and threw it for Saskia to pick up. I would have climbed and climbed until I got to the top, most likely too exhausted to fight back against the Guardians when I got there. Now, I know my death would do her more harm than good.

And I can't die for my people if I can live for her.

"Some people choose the world," my mother finally whispers. "And for some people, the world is one person." She lays a soft hand over mine without looking at me. "Choosing your love over yourself—no matter what that may look like—will never be cruel."

Love. I've lived for centuries and don't know if I've ever chosen it over hate and revenge. And I've certainly never truly loved a woman. I've been a Monster for so long that I'm not sure I even can.

But I do know that a world without Saskia isn't a world I want to save.

I'd gladly watch it all burn to fucking ash if it meant I could finally get ahold of her and never let go.

SASKIA

The next morning, I wake up to a peculiar sound.

For a moment, grogginess weighs down my eyelids and I stretch out in bed, the soft touch of silken sheets rippling over my body. I moan at the luxurious feel, wondering if I'm dreaming and hoping I never wake up.

Then I jolt upward, my blurry vision slamming into those narrow brown eyes of the servant from last night.

"Guardians, you keep scaring me," I gasp as Eleni huffs with exasperation near the foot of my bed. The sight of her crossing her arms between those rich velvet drapes, a streak of sunlight slicing across her features, makes everything come rushing back into my skull.

The Choosing. The feast. The dead Chosen One, her blood smeared on the floor. The Third Guardian drinking from my wrist. The *bathtub*.

At that last thought, I jerk my head down and my hands scrabble at my chest, where—

The necklace is gone.

For the second time since I was prodded into this prison of a palace, terror rips through my veins where Lucan's electric presence usually resides. I may have been in blissful oblivion after my... experience with him last night, but I distinctly remember getting out of the bathtub, throwing on the nightgown laid out for me, and falling into this immense, heavenly soft bed with the necklace *on*.

My breaths become ragged as I search the sheets and pillows around me, until Eleni gives another huff, lifts up the corner of my mattress, and points.

I scramble out of bed to find the vial just barely peeking out from where it's been stuffed deep between mattress and frame, the chain coiled tightly around it.

"Oh." I exhale at Eleni. "You took it off of me and hid it. Because..." I glance at her and catch her eye roll. "Because I'm stupid and I should have done that myself. Do the Guardians regularly make unannounced visits?"

She nods curtly, her lips twitching, and I can't help but smile in a flood of relief—not just because Lucan is still here, but because apparently, I lucked out with a servant who's going to help me rather than rat me out, regardless of all her glares.

"I'm sorry," I say as she gives me an even fiercer glower. "I was just tired, but I feel better now. Thank you for—"

Eleni doesn't let me finish. She pulls me toward the armoire, where she rummages inside and pulls out one of those velvet dresses. Before I can even blink at her, she's attacking me with the fabric, slipping my arms and head through, lacing, cinching, and patting me until I feel like one of those women during the Dark Days, in lavish finery that was probably made by the same people who get strips of brown linen and tiny little rations in their cube of a housing unit back at home.

And just like that, all my good cheer is gone again, especially as Eleni gestures aggressively for me to follow her and I realize she probably has a hundred words she'd like to spew out at me but can't.

"Okay," I breathe out. "One second." Lifting up the corner of the mattress again, I clamp my hand around the vial of the necklace, feeling that familiar spurt of electricity connect with my bloodstream and Lucan's rough, masculine presence invade my brain.

Hey, I say quickly. *I'm fine. Eleni wants me to follow her so I'm hiding you under my bed for now. I'll talk to you again as soon as I make it back to my room.*

After a moment of surprised silence, in which I can feel Lucan's emotions war between lecturing me for scaring him and thanking me for keeping him updated, he exhales with, *Does this mean I'm literally the Monster under your bed now?*

I refrain from saying I wish he was the Monster *in* my bed—especially after last night's bath—and remove my hand from the vial, stuffing it even deeper inside.

"Okay." I straighten and nod at Eleni. "I'm ready."

As she leads me out of my new room, I take a last glance at my bed painted in streaks of sunlight and realize what that peculiar sound I woke to was: silence. I'm so used to jerking awake to the robotic trill of that female voice through the loudspeakers that waking up to silence felt like a sound in and of itself.

"We could be sharing all these clothes and riches and everyone could be happy," I mutter. "But instead, too much is hoarded by too few."

Eleni throws me a look over her shoulder that looks a lot like *tell me about it.*

She takes me down a labyrinth of halls and staircases that I do my best to memorize, until we're back in the same dining room as last night and my nerves are kicking into high gear again.

Especially when she abandons me at a chair with a stiff curtsy and hurries off through one of the servant doorways again, leaving me alone with a few other Chosen Ones and the First Guardian standing at the head of the table.

Are they really going to feed from us again so soon after the first time? Judging by the sways and bleary blinks of the last remaining Chosen Ones who stumble to the table after their own servants, I'm the only one who's recovered from the venom so far. I'm not sure the others would be able to handle another feeding so soon.

At least Arad isn't here to breathe icicles down my neck. Only the First Guardian stares at us over the mountain of new breakfast food that I'm much too full to even look at, waiting until everyone is seated before he claps his marble hands together.

"Attention, Chosen Ones." His voice scrapes through the room. "On behalf of the rest of the Guardians, I would like to thank you for providing the necessary sustenance for the safety of our people—your friends and families that you have so graciously protected with your blood. I hope that you all feel refreshed and fulfilled after a night of such wholesome sacrifice."

Such pretty words to describe an ugly lie. I narrow my eyes and soak up the hidden meanings wavering behind every careful syllable.

"Now that you are Chosen, you are free from the burdens of regular toil. You may enjoy the commodities your Guardians have left you in your private room or wander the palace as you please... except the north wing where *we* preside. In that case, you will have to be invited by a Guardian to enter."

My heart sinks straight to the lush carpet beneath my feet. The north wing—that's where the white drawing room is, where the key to the Wall is. If I want to get to it, I need to convince Arad to invite me into his living space.

I almost laugh. Of *course* it couldn't be as easy as tiptoeing around until I find it. I bet that north wing is guarded by sentries who would deny me access if I tried to get in.

"Breakfast, lunch, and dinner will be provided here in the dining room for all Chosen Ones," the First Guardian continues, "unless you prefer to take your meals in your room, in which case your assigned servant will deliver it to you. Access to the balconies will be opened every Sunday for you to wave to your loved ones."

One of the men down the table dares to fix the First Guardian with beady, angry eyes. "Where are all the other Chosen Ones? If we're all allowed to wander the palace and eat meals down here, how come I haven't seen any of them?"

It's already a question that's been tugging at my brain, my eyes constantly flitting sideways as if desperate that every shadow is actually a sign of my mother or maybe even Diggory, but the others around me seem to perk up, nodding and grumbling amongst themselves.

"As I've said," the First Guardian answers in a tone that sounds like he's patiently sweeping a bit of dust off his cloak, "if you wish to reside in your private room all week until the balconies open up, you may. The same applies to the Chosen Ones before you."

The meaning couldn't be any clearer, though it fills me with prickles of dread. In the span of their first few months in the Blood Moon Palace, every single Chosen One before us has decided to stay in their rooms until they're forced to go to the balconies and wave.

Or until they're no longer able to.

The First Guardian doesn't let anyone else ask any questions. He simply gives what appears to be a patient, fatherly smile and says, "One more thing. From now until the next Choosing, *you* are the source of your Guardian's strength. You have chosen to honor Xantera, and as such, you are not to deny your blood whenever or wherever they seek you out."

He eyes his own living sacrifice with a sliver of hunger shining through those crimson eyes before turning on a heel and sweeping out of the dining room, leaving the eleven of us with nothing but a wasteful feast and horrified silence.

Because while we were Chosen, yes, this is anything but our choice.

Good news, I tell Lucan when I get back to my room and slide the necklace up my thigh again, *my door's no longer locked. Bad news, the north wing is. Worse news, I'm going to have to get invited in.*

Your mother comes first, Saskia.

A thud goes through my heart. I'd been steeling myself to try to convince him that finding my mom before trying to break into the north wing would somehow be beneficial to our mission. I hadn't expected for him to already prioritize her over the key.

Of course I do. His scowl forms in my mind like a shadow, but it only makes my smile stronger.

Okay then, I sigh. *Find my mom, find the key, open the Wall.*

How hard can it be?

After stepping back out into the hallway, though, my optimism fades away.

Which way? Lucan asks.

To the left, the hallway ends with a wide window and a hard ninety degree corner. To the right, the hallway doesn't seem to end at all. It just tapers into a hazy black hole with two staircases that jut upward in different directions.

Is it strange that I like the stairs so much? I ask, gravitating toward them. *I didn't realize they could be so pretty.*

My hand skates along the banister, the cool, dense wood smooth beneath my palm. It curves up high above my head without any indication of what lies on the next level. And the one above that.

And the one above that... I'd never wondered before how many stories the palace has or how many rooms. There are countless doors, the first of which I knock on before I try the handle.

Locked.

But there's no shortage of doors to try. One after the other, they remind me of the doors of the complexes but fancier, like rows of polished teeth ready to snap at me.

I guess this is as good a path as any, I say, *and odds are I get lost anyway.*

I got you, baby. Just like the catacombs. You walk, I map. And when you get lost, I'll guide you back to your room.

I scoff. *You make it sound so simple.*

'*How hard can it be?*' Lucan mimics me.

Has anyone ever told you that you're insufferable?

He hums in defiance. *Wasn't so insufferable last night, was I?*

I don't even have time to register excitement at the first unlocked door I find. Heat rushes through my cheeks, down my spine, as I open it only to find a mundane linen closet.

Am I ever going to be good enough at this to read your thoughts and see through your eyes? I blurt out distractedly.

His voice drops low. *Want to watch me?*

No, I stammer. That's not what I meant, but immediately, I know my response is a lie. And, of course, Lucan knows too. Two more locked doors later, I reply, *I meant I'm curious what's on the other side of the Wall. What your house looks like... what you look like.*

My mind keeps trying to stifle, *don't think about him naked, don't think about him naked* unsuccessfully. But I have no concrete image to work with here—just my vivid imagination.

Trees, he chuckles. *Just so many trees. And what was once a lively town on the outskirts of the main city.* He pauses. *Time is a bitch.*

A female dog? I laugh.

No. In this context, more like something that's difficult. He pauses, as if preparing to broach a tentative subject. *Are there a lot of
dogs within the Wall?*

What? I try another door to no avail. *No, not many. The rehab
portion of the Healing Center keeps a regulated breed for occupa-
tional therapy. Why?*

Well, I—

"Oh," I gasp, almost toppling over when a man throws open his
door and runs right smack into me. "I'm sorry."

The man peers down at me, confusion sitting between his
bushy eyebrows. I don't recognize him as one of the twelve—now
eleven—I was Chosen with.

"Who are you?" he drawls, each syllable stretching out lazily.

I raise my chin to meet his leveled gaze. "Who are *you?*"

"Tristan." His bemused expression muddles into some kind of
sick satisfaction when his eyes drop to the neckline of my dress.
"New Chosen One then? Who knew the palace was like *this*, huh?
Not a bad deal. Give up some blood and you no longer have to live
in that wretched city." He cocks his head in the general direction
of the rest of Xantera.

This asshole, Lucan mutters.

A useful asshole, I reply.

"Right," I tell Tristan slyly. "For just a little blood"—*figuratively
and literally, then throw in your pesky little ethics and morals on top,*
I don't add—"you get all this. How long ago did you get Chosen?"

He crosses his arms and leans against the doorframe. "Four
blood moons ago."

"I was beginning to wonder where everyone was. You're the first
person I've seen who wasn't Chosen with me."

"Not surprising," he laughs, although it sounds as languid and
lazy as his drawl, "and actually, I'm impressed. Usually, the newcomers are too scared to come out at first. Takes a couple of months
for them to realize we don't *all* bite."

"So, you all socialize with each other?" I ask curiously.

"Well, yeah. There's not much else to do."

"Do you know Maribel?"

My heart squeezes as the words slip out. I haven't said my mother's name in years. I used to whisper it to myself sometimes before falling asleep, like I was reminding myself that she existed, that she hadn't been a figment of my distant imagination.

But no recognition crosses Tristan's face. He only chews on his thoughts and shrugs. "Can't say that I do."

The hope building in my chest deflates. One whole year seems like too long to be allowed to freely move about the castle every day and not know everyone in passing.

"Is she one of the older Chosen Ones?" he asks with disdain.

"I guess," I answer, hesitating. I don't know if that's what he wants to hear. "She's lived here for eight years now."

He snorts. "Figures. Those Chosen Ones are too good for everyone else. Most of them just sleep all day. If you ask me, they should throw them back out onto the street, into their housing complex. Let them trade places with someone who appreciates this." The pause ticks in the air between us, until Tristan exhales between his grinning lips and slips his arm around my shoulders. "At least, they're up on the highest floors in the smallest rooms, away from everyone else. Now come on, stick with me and you can't go wrong. I never got your name."

I duck out of his grip, my heart pounding wildly. "I just remembered... I need to pee! In my room!"

Smooth, Lucan comments, amused.

Tristan blinks, then laughs awkwardly as he backpedals. "We'll be in the billiard room playing poker. Just ask your servant to bring you. And don't forget to bring something to bet with." His eyes drop to the neckline of my dress again, tracing it, lingering down to my hips. "That's always the best part."

I stand rooted in my spot until he rounds the corner completely. Then I slowly count, *one, two, three,* before I take off running to the nearest staircase in sight.

Did I say I loved stairs before? I huff, gathering the skirt of my dress and dragging my legs up the seventh flight. My butt burns, my thighs ache, and I can barely breathe. The first three were quick. The last four have gotten progressively slower. *Never mind. They're torture devices. No wonder no one comes up here. Who would willingly climb all this?*

I gaze longingly at the last stretch of steps, wishing there was some necklace that could magically transport me to the top.

One more, Lucan encourages me as I let out a breath and climb. *If I were there, I'd carry you. Then work out all those knots in your muscles after.*

Too bad you're not here, I breathe, unattractively.

And uncontrollably, his claws make an appearance in my daydream. I imagine my skin denting from the slight pressure. The sting of pain lighting up my nervous system. His enormous hands leaving scratch marks along my inner thighs—

Focus, Lucan says hoarsely, like he can't take it anymore.

I clear my head when I stop at the top and look to the right down the long hallway, refocusing on the task ahead of me.

After knocking softly on the first door, I try the handle, only to be met with a deadbolted door.

Lucan, I sigh. *What if these are all just more locked doors? We get freedom to move about the palace, but it's not like they're going to let us just see anything they don't want us to see.*

The only thing we can do is keep trying.

I nod to myself and push on. The next is locked, and the next, until the sound of door hinges squeaks across the hallway.

I stop dead in my tracks and press my back against the nearest door, sucking in as much of my body as I can behind the wide door frame. Thankfully, the footsteps recede, and I poke my head out just as a servant enters another room at the far end of the hall.

Before I can think twice, I'm beelining for the room she just exited.

I can sense Lucan's hesitation, how much he wants to tell me to turn around, but instead he says, *Quickly, Saskia.*

Slipping inside, I blink against the darkness. Tristan was right. These rooms are much smaller, with minimal furniture and a small bed in the center of the room.

It eerily reminds me of the patient rooms in the Healing Center. Sterile. Cold.

The human-sized lump under the covers looks unnatural. Holding my own, I wait to see the rise and fall of a breath, proof that they're alive.

Finally, a slow drag shatters the unnatural stillness. They're alive. Just sleeping.

I creep toward them, a face coming into view. And though it's not my mother, relief still washes over me.

They're only sleeping, I reiterate to Lucan. *But it's not my mom. I'm going to keep looking.*

Careful, he says, despite how much I can sense he wants me to return to my room and never leave again.

I peek out into the hallway to find it empty once more. The next two rooms I find unlocked are more of the same—a bed, a sleeping body, and a chill in the air that feels like stone.

After hearing the servant's footsteps retreating now down the stairs, I slip into the last room of the dead-end that she left unlocked.

This one is a little brighter from the sun peeking through the curtains of the only window I've seen so far.

I can already see the peaceful face of a woman lying on the bed, sleeping. Maybe caught in a dream from the faint smile on her lips.

I watch her for a minute, unnerved by how still she seems—and how familiar, too. She's not my mom, either, but there's something about her features that rings a bell in the back of my head.

Taking a step forward to reassure myself I'm not seeing things, the floorboard underneath my foot creaks.

And her eyes fly open.

LUCAN

On the peak of the tallest mountain, where I can overlook the entirety of what used to be Veradel, I come to a halt at the same time that Saskia's breathing does.

Up here, the air nips at my skin, but the frigidity taking root in my bones doesn't come from the elevation. Something hasn't felt right about the Chosen Ones—and what happens to them—this entire time.

Back in the ghost town, I grew up hearing stories from the elders who survived the war. Rumors and superstitions. Pure guesswork that boils down to two impossible options: either the Chosen Ones die, or they turn into vampires themselves.

Well, obviously the first one isn't exactly true. If the Chosen Ones died immediately, the people of Xantera would have risen up sooner than now, revolting in the face of true, random sacrifice.

The balconies give them false hope—and planted evidence—that all is well.

But now we know the Chosen Ones don't turn into vampires, either. They seem to react strongly to the Guardians' bites, yes, but nothing that doesn't end up fading. Almost like a drug that has to circulate their system before their bodies metabolize it.

The thought has my vision flashing with red. If anything's going to get Saskia high and giggly, I'd rather it be my cock driving her out of her damn mind, orgasm after orgasm, but...

Focus, Lucan, for fuck's sake.

I hone my focus downward, spearing the Blood Moon Palace with my eyes as if I can see Saskia through the walls. Through our connection, I can feel that she's trembling as she stares at the Chosen One in bed, and frankly, I am, too. Because I have a feeling that vampire venom isn't just degrading their bodies until they pass away in their sleep. I just wish I could wrap Saskia up and keep her blissfully unaware of her reality until I find a way to get to her.

But that isn't right either.

Although a part of me wants to shield her from the horrors of the world she knows nothing about, she deserves to know what the vampires she thought she could trust are doing. She deserves to know what happened to her mother, what's going to happen to *her* now that those fangs pierced her skin and flooded her veins with venom. And she isn't weak. Despite being molded since birth to cower, to suppress herself, to fall in line—she wants to fight.

Or no. More precisely, she wants to heal—heal others physically, yes, but also hearts and minds and broken spirits.

But this? The way this woman's haunting eyes track her as she approaches? I don't think Saskia can heal whatever the fuck she's about to discover.

29

SASKIA

I swallow my inhale as the woman's eyes lock onto mine.
"Oh, I'm sorry, ma'am. I was just—I'm one of the new Chosen
Ones and... I hope I didn't startle you."

I back up a step to avoid frightening her any further, but in
truth, *I'm* the one who's startled. Because this woman still hasn't
moved a muscle, only her pupils falling to track the movement of
my mouth while her chest rises and falls in a steady rhythm.

With a pause, I glance over my shoulder at the door I left cracked
open. I'm obviously intruding on a moment of rest, but something
about the way she looks so *alert* clashes with the way she's lying
there, unmoving. Like there's a panic scrabbling its way out of her
peaceful expression, begging me not to leave quite so soon.

"Is it okay if I sit with you?" I ask when her attention doesn't
leave my mouth, suddenly feeling like I'm one of the caretakers at

the Assisted Living Facility. This woman can't be much older than a green-badge, but there's a stale mustiness emanating from the sheets, as if the dust motes in this room have settled long ago.

Ever so slowly and painstakingly, her chin rises and dips with a strange grinding sound I might have imagined. A nod. I settle on the edge of her bed and, after a moment of hesitation, lay my hand over hers, shivering at how cold it is. How brittle.

She's dying, I tell Lucan with a healer's certainty, sorrow and frustration ripping through me at the realization. *Whatever the vampire venom does to us, she's had too much of it. She's near the end.*

Out loud, I plaster a smile on my face and say, "I'm Saskia. Can you tell me what your name is?"

A few seconds tick by. Her mouth twitches, like she's chewing on a mouthful of words. Then, as if it costs her the greatest effort, she shakes her head. The same grinding sound pierces my eardrums. I definitely didn't imagine it this time.

My heart squeezes painfully, but her free hand trembles as she lifts her wrist, and my gaze snaps to her fingers as they pinch together. Her hand rotates with creaking slowness, then falls back into her lap with a defeated slump.

I cover the back of her hand with my palm, not wanting her to move even an inch. "I'm sorry, I don't understand what you're trying to tell me..."

My gaze returns to her face, her nose and mouth and the color of her eyes, and suddenly, my heartbeat drums against my ribcage as I realize why she looks so familiar. And why she keeps staring at my mouth as I form words.

"Are... are you... having trouble hearing me?"

She gives me a meaningful blink that I think might mean yes.

Our daughter was born hard of hearing and had to spend her whole life with hearing aids, but Diggory made up his own language with her using just his hands so that she could take them off when all the noises became too overwhelming. That's what Belinda had told me back in her housing unit, and even though this woman doesn't have any hearing aids in, I can *see* the resemblance. She's a perfect mix of her mother and father.

"Are you Diggory's daughter?" I ask.

Her eyes widen at the way my mouth moves, reading the question on my lips. She doesn't even have to nod. I'm already getting up, shutting her door, and returning with an idea brewing in my head. In the space Lucan occupies, to be exact.

You can talk to anyone who's touching this vial? I ask him.

Yes. He sounds surprised yet impressed as he catches wind of my unfurling idea. *But I'm not sure if I can talk to two humans at the same time.*

Only one way to find out, then. If Diggory's daughter can't speak and I can't understand her attempts at sign language, then maybe I can talk to her mind-to-mind just like I'm talking to Lucan. *Just...* I hesitate. *Maybe don't reveal that you're the Monster. That might actually give her a heart attack in her current condition.*

Who am I supposed to be? Your sexy imaginary friend?

I suppress a smile. *Something like that.*

Before our conversation can drag on too long, as it so often does, I dig under the skirts of my dress to slide the necklace down my leg and over my foot. The woman's eyes flare with shock when I hold it up, the blood-red vial catching a beam of sunlight from the window. A million thoughts seem to swirl behind her irises, so I don't waste time to give her an ability to communicate.

Gripping the necklace tight, I grab the woman's hand and press the vial against her skin, sandwiching it between our clasped palms.

Instantly, a new presence zaps my bloodstream, joining Lucan's rich, dark aura. Hers is surprisingly strong but panicked, like the branches of a tree grabbing hold of both of us in a vice-like grip, reeling herself in as if she's on the cusp of drowning.

It's okay, I say as soothingly as possible. *I know it feels funny, but this will help us communicate.*

Diggory's daughter gives a slow couple blinks in my direction, then her questions explode in my mind. *Who are you? How did you get that necklace? What happened to my father? Is he alright? Why are you here?* Fear bursts through her pupils. *How did you get that necklace?* she repeats.

Praying that Lucan stays silent like a good imaginary friend until I can calm her down, I tighten my grip on her hand. *Your father actually gave this to me.*

The woman swallows thickly and furrows her brows, wrinkles spiderwebbing like cracks in marble across her forehead.

If I know one thing about my father, it's that he didn't trust anyone. He didn't give that to you. So let me ask again—how did you get it?

I frown down at her as I mull over her question, her tone, and her general urgency. When I first heard Lucan's voice in my head, I was going in circles trying to figure out if I'd gone crazy, but Diggory's daughter doesn't seem even remotely surprised to be communicating mind-to-mind. Only suspicious of my motives.

Your father... I start hesitantly. *The sentries were taking him, and he threw the necklace. I picked it up and have been hiding it this whole time. Do you know how* he *got it?*

She doesn't answer the question. Not yet. Her eyes gloss over, a single tear welling in one of the corners. *They took him? The sentries really took him?*

I don't try to sugarcoat the expression on my face, not when she deserves to know the truth. *Yes. I don't know if he's still somewhere here in the Blood Moon Palace or...*

My thoughts trail off, and she swallows thickly again, her presence already sinking into a hollow type of grief. Her gaze travels down the length of my arm to where the vial is clasped between our palms, though no part of the rest of her body moves.

That necklace. I gave it to him.

My mouth drops open, and judging by the rustling in my mind, I can tell Lucan is struggling to keep his thoughts reined in. *You gave it to him?*

I guess I should say I hid it for him. He must have found it. It's a long story. As she thinks those words, a foreign memory flashes across my mind: my—her—hands, grasping this very necklace by the chain.

Trying to don my healer's persona, I snap my mouth closed and put on my most comforting smile. *Well, I'm a Chosen One now, too. Seems like there's nothing to do until the balconies open up again, right? Might as well listen to a story.*

Diggory's daughter glances at the closed door over my shoulder. *If you're new, you've still got a chance. You should try to escape while you've got your strength left.*

My smile falters ever so slightly. *Believe me. I'm trying.*

You call this trying? she snaps. *If either of our Guardians walks in here and finds us with this necklace, we're dead sooner rather than later. They don't think anyone notices, but there's been quite a ruckus among them ever since I stole it from the Third one.*

Another foreign memory flashes across my mind: the sound of thumping footsteps, shouts, the hallway blurring past. But it's gone as quickly as it came.

You stole the necklace from the Third Guardian? I ask in disbelief. *Why? How?*

Apparently, Lucan has just as many questions, because his thoughts burst past his mental barrier before I can stop him. *Now that is a story I'd like to hear.*

Diggory's daughter shrieks internally, and I have the distinct impression that if she could move, she'd be swatting at her ear right about now. *Who was that?*

Don't pay him any attention, I grit out. *He won't harm you.*

The tone of my voice is more of a warning to Lucan than any consolation to her. If he starts pulling out snide comments like he did to me when we first met, she won't want anything else to do with us.

Don't worry, Lucan agrees. *I don't bite.* After a slight pause, he adds, *Usually.*

If I could smack him right now, I would.

Even though her face hasn't moved, Diggory's daughter seems to narrow her gaze at me anyway. *It's him, isn't it? The one the Third Guardian was always talking to? I never knew who was on the other end, but I thought it might be someone who could save us all. That's why I...*

Her thoughts fade away, and a few memories flash across our connection, too fast for me to grab hold of them. I rub my thumb over her knuckles in soothing circles.

You don't even have to tell me. Just... close your eyes and reimagine what happened for me. I think I'll be able to see it through your memories. And then I promise you, I won't just try to escape. I'll help you and your father escape, too.

She doesn't need to read the earnestness in my eyes to know I'm telling the truth. There's an implicit relay of honesty using this method of communication, and I can already feel her mind caving as she lets her eyes drift shut again.

And her memories burst to life.

A too-warm breeze picks up over the Blood Moon Palace courtyard, making the sticky sweat prickle on my—no, Diggory's daughter's—skin. It must be a summer night, when the humidity is so dense you can almost taste it on your tongue.

The Monster's howling sounds extra vicious tonight. Usually, it's one of the only sounds Diggory's daughter can pick up on, especially from the vibrations, and right now it only grows louder when the palace doors open with a booming echo.

My own goosebumps crawl up my arms at the sound of Lucan's voice, the cadence and tone, and the fact that I now recognize it. It baffles me that it used to frighten me.

But everyone else is frightened, that's for sure. Just like my own Choosing, a Guardian's presence stills the crowd. Diggory's daughter fidgets, her fingers curling and uncurling repeatedly... until the Fifth Guardian appears with a hum in his throat and a red-eyed stare that hammers her still.

"You are perfect."

Diggory's daughter reads his lips, her heart stops, and she's yanked away before she can even remember to look over her shoulder for a last glimpse of her mother and father.

But she can hear her father's scream behind her.

"SYLVIA! NO! PLEASE! TAKE ME INSTEA—!"

A sentry is already muffling Diggory's voice, and the sound cuts off abruptly. With the Fifth Guardian still yanking her forward by one wrist, Sylvia throws her free hand behind her back and gives her father one last goodbye in the language they made together: "Stop making a fuss. I'll find a way to talk to you."

The memory fades to black, replacing itself with a new one—and this time, I'm staring into a pair of eyes that aren't mine through a reflective surface.

It takes a second for me to orient myself, but finally it clicks. A mirror. The one that I ended up pulling from Diggory's shower, to be exact.

Sylvia blinks at herself, angling the mirror to each side just as I did, as she takes in her features. Her hand drops to pick up the jewelry sitting on her dresser, the same piece I slid on my finger in Belinda's shower, too.

I knew it, she thinks with disgust. *I knew they don't follow their own rules. If only the rest of Xantera could see all this wealth they keep from everyone else, they'd realize...*

Her thoughts morph into an idea, and the room swirls into a new memory. Now, we're on a balcony—reliving a long-ago Sanctuary Sunday.

Faces peer up at us from below, just close enough to make out their doleful smiles and waves. Diggory and Belinda are there, mimicking the motions of everyone else, but Sylvia watches the way her father's hand moves through the air and deciphers the coded message.

"Are you okay?"

Sylvia leans over the railing, plastering on a face of happiness and exhilaration, while she waves her own arm regally and brings her fingers snapping down against her thumb. "No."

Immediately, Diggory's hand movements get sharper.

"What did they do to you?"

"Besides the obvious?" she signs, thinking about the puncture wounds that already litter her body, courtesy of the Fifth Guardian. "I'm not sure yet, but I know they're not being completely honest with us. Here. I can prove it."

"Prove it?" Diggory asks, his forehead wrinkling in confusion even from afar. Beside him, Belinda is blatantly gazing off into the distance, choosing to remain in ignorance rather than acknowledge that her partner is doing more than waving at their daughter. Or maybe she's watching out for any sentries, making sure nobody else notices the strange exchanges. Either way, Sylvia chooses to risk it.

She reaches into her cloak, whisks out the mirror, and *drops* it.

Diggory's hand flashes out to grab the object before swiftly hiding it within his cloak, and Sylvia lets out a satisfied breath.

I catch her thoughts and feelings just as the memory begins to morph: a rush of adrenaline that she's already addicted to. She's going to do it again—find more evidence of their hypocrisy and give it all to her father. Just to defy them.

The memory swirls into another one. Now, my pseudo-heart is pounding nails into my ribcage. Sylvia looks over her shoulder, and I stamp the hallway into my brain, somehow aware that we're entering the Eleventh Guardian's bedroom, before she clicks the door shut behind her and turns around.

If a new Chosen One's bedroom is massive, a Guardian's is simply unbelievable. Spreading into more and more rooms, the place has to be bigger than a handful of housing units put together, brimming with furniture, drapes, decorations, and other gaudy, elaborate things that make the rest of Xantera look like the barest of bones.

But Sylvia doesn't hesitate as she starts toward the bedside table by the colossal, four-poster bed filled with rumpled sheets. She's been sneaking or sleeping her way into every Guardian's bedroom over the last six months, and she knows they all have a key they keep beside them when they sleep. Just last night, she saw the Eleventh Guardian glance at his before he continued sucking on her neck, but she didn't dare nab it. Not then.

Now, the Eleventh Guardian is off tormenting other Chosen Ones, and Sylvia sets her sights on the little open box where a key lays horizontally on a red cushion. So out in the open. So stealable. She doesn't know what it unlocks, but she knows her father will figure it out when she drops it to him.

Her long slender fingers trace the heart-shaped end.

I jump when a door handle twists, a metal sound scraping my nerves. Whipping my head around, I realize it's the memory, not reality. Sylvia snatches the key, drops to the ground, and squirms her way to a plank underneath the Eleventh Guardian's bed.

Chest heaving. Heart hammering.

Two footsteps click inward. If the Eleventh Guardian realizes his key is missing, he'll tear the room apart and find her trying not to breathe beneath his bed frame. Cursing herself for her stupidity, she clenches the key in trembling, sweaty fingers, feeling the Guardian's presence pulsing like the opposite of a beacon. And then—

"Felix, you're needed in the library."

It's Arad's voice from the hallway, loud enough for her to hear.
The vibrations of the Eleventh Guardian's footsteps recede, the
door slams shut again, and Sylvia exhales against the floor with the
key still tight in her grip.

The memory spirals into a new one again. This time, Sylvia
crouches in some kind of internal courtyard, where rose bushes
circle a set of benches and a fountain tinkles merrily in the middle
of a placid pond. When she peeks out from behind a thorny bush,
it becomes apparent who she's here to spy on: Arad himself.

His laugh reaches us, a darkness vibrating through it that makes
acid rise in my throat.

Peering up at Arad through the leaves, we watch as he holds up
my necklace, and a sick smile twists his lips.

The chain graces his throat. The vial now trapped in his
clenched fist.

And he can't help but speak aloud, angled in a way that Sylvia
can read every word on his lips.

"You know, it's such a beautiful day. I really wish you could see
it. The sun is shining, the birds are chirping, everyone in my city
adores me, and they all loathe you. How wonderful is that?"

Lucan. He's talking to Lucan, and hatred crackles in my bones
as I get my first taste of the taunting my Monster has had to endure
for centuries. I'd give anything to rip the necklace from Arad's cold,
undeserving fingertips so that past Lucan wouldn't have to hear
the slimy words dripping from his lips.

But this is Sylvia's memory, so all I can do is listen with curdling
disgust.

"Oh? You loathe *me*? Well, why don't you do something about
it, then?" Arad waits for a response with a smile widening his face
before he brings the vial close to his mouth and says, "That's right.
Because every time you try, you just end up whimpering like a little
puppy. You are not a Monster. You are just pathetic. And there is
nothing left for you to try. I *always* come out on top."

I want to swing my fist into Arad's face, but Sylvia just cocks her head at him through the leaves of her hiding place, eyeing the necklace with gleaming interest. She doesn't know why he's talking into it like it's an intercom, but it might be the most interesting thing she's had an itch to steal yet. And maybe whoever's communicating with him on the other side can *help*.

Slowly, she rises from the bushes, pretending she'd been bending over to smell the roses. Arad jolts and stuffs the necklace away, his mouth opening as if to admonish her—or perhaps worse—but Sylvia throws on her most flirtatious smile and begins her game.

The next memory *feels* different. Sylvia's resolve has hardened, but so has she. Almost physically. Sluggish, disoriented, and exhausted, her limbs seem to weigh a ton. But her desire has never wavered, and she'll do anything to take the necklace.

She's lying on a bed, counting in her head, and when she turns slowly, I'm horrified.

Arad is sleeping shirtless next to her, his chest moving in a slow rhythm, the sheets rising and falling with every breath, as if even they obey him.

I'm not the only one horrified. Sylvia hates herself—for liking what just transpired between them. The feeding. The sex. The multiple orgasms. She's drunk on power and revenge, loving that Arad became putty in her hands over the last several weeks. Loving how easy it was to manipulate him with a few fluttering eyelashes and wiggling fingers.

Sylvia's eyes travel south along the grooves of his stomach muscles, somewhat sad she won't experience this again.

She smiles, thinking *what a waste.*

When she reaches one hundred and one in her head, she reaches over his body and plucks that gold necklace off his bedside table. For a second, she eyes another silver chain hanging around his neck, but taking that one would be too risky. So she simply leans over to place her puckered lips at the corner of Arad's mouth, knowing she'll pay for this steal.

And slips away.

Afterward, I tried to run away from the Blood Moon Palace and found myself in some kind of dungeon, Diggory's daughter says finally, opening her eyes again. *But the sentries caught up to me before I could find my way out, so I dropped the necklace in the tunnels. Just so the Third Guardian wouldn't ever find it again.*

I gape at her, the pieces clicking together.

Diggory... I shake my head, gripping the chain tighter. *Your father went missing two Choosings ago, right after you stopped coming to the balconies. Since you'd already given him a key to the catacombs, I'm willing to bet* that's *where he went. Down in those same tunnels. And he found the necklace right where you dropped it, and put it on...*

Pride shines through Sylvia's eyes. *I knew he'd stop at nothing to try to save me. He was too late, but he tried. And that's all that matters to me.*

She closes her eyes with a slight smile on her face, but the absolute horror of all her memories and everything she went through still has me disoriented, blinking down at her as I try to remember who I am and where we are.

In a small, coffin-like bedroom, relatively safe. For now.

Did the Third Guardian... I can hardly bear to form the question in my head. *Did he find out you were the one who stole the necklace?*

As sadistic as Arad seems, I can't imagine how Sylvia is even still *alive* after defying and betraying him so openly.

Oh, yes. Her eyes shutter. *I was already in trouble for trying to run away, but when he realized one of his necklaces was gone... let's just say I didn't break. I never told him where it was.* She clenches her jaw. *Finally, the Third Guardian told me death was too easy for me, and then he drank. Drank from me within an inch of my life—calculated, strategic—and when he was finished, he brought me here, more than happy to watch me fade away. He still comes just to watch sometimes and smile.*

My shoulders slump as I take it all in. The Guardians know what they're doing, then, using their venom like a weapon in small or big doses to get to their desired result. The only thing I can offer is *I'm sorry,* but it will never be enough. Diggory's daughter is more courageous than I could ever be.

No, Lucan interjects for the first time since Sylvia shared her memories. *Courage can be used in different ways. And you're the most courageous person I know.*

Sylvia's eyes flit between me and the necklace as my cheeks grow warm with Lucan's praise. I can hear the echo of all her questions, but her eyelids are also growing heavier by the second, as if sleep is trying to wrap her up in dreams—or nightmares—once more.

I chew on my lip, glancing down at the shape of her body lying there beneath the sheets. *Do you mind if I take a look at you? I'm a healer.*

She opens her eyes again. *You* were *a healer, you mean. Now you're a prisoner, just like the rest of us.*

My brows furrow at her. Although it's clear she's just as rebellious as her father is, something about her wording is tugging at the back of my mind. Because being Chosen is supposed to be an honor. Yet Sylvia obviously doesn't think it is, and neither did that other Chosen One who tried to run away last night. In fact, none of the Chosen Ones have appeared to be enjoying themselves like they're supposed to, save for maybe Tristan.

Sylvia seems to tilt toward me as much as she physically can. *Why do you think the Guardians choose us, Saskia?*

When I blink at her, she gives a long, languid sigh into my mind. *They're watching us from the start, of course. They know who's starting to have questions and doubts. They know who's suspicious and who's angry. Who's breaking the Cardinal Rules and going to cause them trouble in the future—who might cause a stir among other content civilians. So why do you think they choose us?*

This time, the answer tastes like ash on my tongue as I remember my misgivings about Gaia, wondering why nobody had punished me for lying to the sentry.

This—being Chosen—*is* the punishment. The Twelve Guardians must have known I was up to no good all along, but rather than make a big scene by hauling me in like Diggory, they saved me and the other dissenters for the Choosing.

Because if they dragged us *all* in kicking and screaming, everyone else would realize that Xantera isn't the utopia they make it out to be after all.

See? Sylvia whispers. *The Blood Moon Palace isn't just the home of the Guardians and their living sacrifices. It's a prison for the only ones who would dare to stand up to them, a place for them to keep us under lock and key away from everyone else. And slowly drain us until any threat we carry just... withers away.*

My eyes rack her body again, noting just how withered she truly looks, almost as if any second could be her last breath.

But nobody—*nobody*—dies on my watch, regardless of the circumstances. I need to help this woman, and to do that I need to figure out what, exactly, is wrong with her.

Prisoner or not, I say finally, *I will be a healer for the rest of my life.* The Guardians may have assigned me my job and then ripped me away from it, but they'll never be able to take away the love I feel for taking care of other people.

I hold out my hand. *May I?*

After a brief staring battle, Diggory's daughter relents with a grumbled sigh, reminding me so much of her father lying in the Healing Center bed that my throat clogs with emotion. But now isn't the time to shed any tears. Now is the time to analyze my patient and determine what's wrong.

First, I peel back the bedsheets to take a look at her body—and it's so much more rigid than I expected. Although her chest still moves up and down in a slow, feeble rhythm, her posture is so stiff that no part of her sinks into the mattress.

Frowning, I lower my head to place my ear against her chest. Her heartbeat pulses consistently, but it's slow and weak. And her chest itself... it's rock-hard. Not at all what I'd expect from a middle-aged female.

I lift my head and give her stomach a gentle push. Unyielding. It's abdominal distention to the max, but she doesn't look bloated, and when I run my hands down her arms and legs, the skin feels nothing like skin at all. There's nothing supple or pliable about this woman in the slightest. Almost as if her body has started to...

Swallowing a gasp, I wrench the vial away from her palm so that she can't access my thoughts before I have time to make sense of them.

The grinding sound her movements make. The chill from her skin. The cracks in her features. How is this even possible?

What is it? Lucan asks. There's something about his tone that sounds reserved—distant. But maybe our connection is a little strained with a third person on the line, so I shrug off any misgivings for now. *She's not just dying, is she?*

No. I press my lips together to keep them from shaking. None of the Chosen Ones are dying in the regular sense. The reason the Chosen Ones eventually quit coming to the balconies, the reason *I* will be just as bed-bound as Diggory's daughter one day, too, if I can't claw my way out of this prison...

It's because the vampire venom is slowly fossilizing us.

The Chosen Ones are turning to stone.

LUCAN

The guilt racks my chest with each step Saskia takes back to her room.

She's turning to stone as we... well, as we *don't* speak. I don't dare lower my shields to let any of my emotions taint her more than I already have.

I'm no good for her.

The Chosen Ones are chosen because they're rebels the Guardians want under control, but Saskia wasn't a rebel before me. *I* planted these little seeds of doubt in her mind. *I* stoked those thoughts she tried to suppress. And she never would've strayed from the unknown rigidity of her day-to-day life if she hadn't met me. She never would have been Chosen.

She could have been content for the rest of her natural life. She could've died of old age—happily, without me, because I didn't go fucking up her life.

I am a poison to her just as much as that vampire venom. And yet here I am, leeching onto her as if my fucking life depends on her existence, listening to her descend all those staircases with quick little breaths that steal mine from my lungs.

If Saskia notices my withdrawal, she doesn't say anything—directly—until she's safely tucked away back in her bedroom.

Lucan, are you there? What's wrong? She slams the door behind her and paces around the perimeter of her room, waiting for my response. When I don't reply right away, her internal thoughts branch out to me, too. *Did I do something wrong?* An empty chill scrapes through her. *Maybe I shouldn't have shared the necklace...*

No. I cut through her thoughts. *You didn't do anything wrong.*

There you are. Her foreboding bursts into a laugh, the sound twisting knives into my ribcage. *I was beginning to think you'd fallen asleep or something.*

How could I, when *she's* my dream?

But I don't say that, instead chewing on the words I have to get out—the honesty she deserves. A part of me wants to throw out insults, make her believe I'm truly a monster once again so that she pushes me away, stops defying them, plays it safe.

But if being alive for a few hundred years has taught me anything, it's that lying will only make everything so much worse.

So instead, I dredge up my most harsh, commanding tone, the one that makes the others bend their necks on the rare occasions I use it.

Promise me something, Saskia.

What's wrong? she asks again, stressing her words.

I need to shift into my human form for a while. And I need you to be good. Her thoughts bristle, but I plunge on before she can protest. *No acts of rebellion, no smart mouth. Don't give that bastard a reason to drink more from you or to kill you.*

My father and grandfather both kept journals during the war, ones I haven't touched in decades. I've already flicked through them, but maybe I missed something. Maybe, somewhere between the pages, there's information about the nature of vampire venom and how to reverse the effects or slow the fossilization process.

It's the only thing I can think to do to be of any use, but I can't exactly flip through centuries-old journals while I'm the Monster.

Oh, Saskia says as she processes what I'm saying. *Oh. You're leaving me?*

My chest cracks wide open. *Never, baby. I'm always right on the other side of the Wall. But we won't be able to communicate as much while I'm in my human form, and I... I wanted you to be prepared before I went silent on you.*

So much for using my commanding tone. My voice has dissolved into a soft, whimpering mess.

Promise me you'll be good, I beg when she doesn't say anything, her internal thoughts dropping into a glacial stillness, like the water under the surface of a frozen pond.

Even to my own ears, my words sound a lot like goodbye. The nightmare was never her—it was a world *without* her. And I'll go back to living in that world if it means I can keep her safe. But I need her word that she won't keep playing with fire while I'm away. What if the Third Guardian finds her sneaking around and poking into information she shouldn't and decides to drain her dry? Or what if another Guardian stumbles across her and takes more blood than her body can handle?

Still, she says nothing, and I clear my throat. *I need to hear you say it, Saskia. That you promise me.*

Finally, she clears her throat right back. *Well, I don't.*

Excuse me?

I don't promise you, Lucan. I won't. You can go on and shift into a human all you like, but I'm going to keep looking for my mother and Diggory and that key in the meantime.

Saskia... A warning growl rises in my tone now.

You can make me behave when we meet face-to-face, she taunts. *Until then, I won't promise anything.*

My blood heats. A snarl rips from my chest, shooting through our connection. *You're going to regret saying that one day, little nightmare.*

Am I? I can practically feel her stubbornness pushing back at me, a radiant aura I wish I could catch and cradle forever. *Prove it.*

Fine, then. I'll just have to work fast. And if she won't give me a promise, then I'll give her one.

I will.

Then I'm gone.

SASKIA

The days here blend together. Floor after floor, room after room, I keep exploring. The higher I go, the smaller the bedrooms become—and the more statuesque I find the Chosen Ones lying in their beds.

On the topmost floor, I find most of the rooms empty, and the few people I do find are so rigid under their sheets, with the faintest, slowest heartbeats I've ever witnessed, that it takes me minutes to even be certain they're alive at all.

While there's been no sign of my mother or Diggory, I won't give up until I've searched every room in this godforsaken palace.

I take my meals in my room, thanks to Eleni, to avoid running in to any of the vampires in the dining room. But asking her any further questions has proved fruitless. She doesn't make any more attempts to communicate with me, despite my rambling, and I've hidden the necklace away from her in fear that she'll feel obligated to turn me in to the Guardians.

Most importantly, I haven't run into Arad—well, until today. My first Sanctuary Sunday as a Chosen One.

Even though I can sense him as soon as I open my bedroom door, I still gasp when my eyes find him comfortably splayed out in my armchair in the corner.

A sharp pain of fear cracks inside my stomach, but I won't be the first to speak—because I know as soon as I open my mouth, I'll keep pushing. And even though I didn't promise Lucan anything, my heart still wants to be good for him.

I wish he were here now. It takes everything in me to keep my eyes trained on Arad and not glance at my mattress, where the necklace is hidden underneath.

Arad's crimson eyes lazily take me in, his elbow perched on the armrest, his fingers pressed against his disturbing smirk.

"I require more blood, Saskia." His voice slides into the air between us, more soft and soothing than the angry way his face contorts at the sight of me. "And I don't like having to wait."

"You'd think someone who's supposed to live forever would have a little more patience," I dare to say, striding over to the edge of my bed with my head held high.

My confidence wavers when Arad rises and situates himself next to me on the mattress. It dips deeply from both our weights, and I have to lock up my muscles to avoid falling into him.

I bite back a gag when his fingers skim down my arm until he grips my wrist and pulls it to his freezing cold lips.

I jerk my head away, refusing to watch as those fangs pierce my skin and the suction tugs at my arm. Instead, I let my mind wander to the only one who makes any of this bearable.

Lucan checks in with me every night to make sure I'm okay, but my poor attempts at flirting to get him to stay go absolutely nowhere. Each time he leaves me again, a new weight seems to drop into my stomach.

I miss him. And I shouldn't. I shouldn't want him this much. Because if I ever do find a way to escape, I'm still going to turn to stone, and Lucan will blame himself—even though he shouldn't. I don't want to go back to the way I was before, blissfully ignorant.

So if I have to endure *this* as a means to an end, then so be it.

After Arad retracts his razor sharp fangs from my vein, his tongue swipes along the two reopened wounds along my inner wrist. His pleased hum vibrates up to my shoulder before he releases me.

"I want this more than once a week, Saskia," he says, dropping my arm back to my side. He doesn't let go, though. His thumb rubs a circle over my pulse, and I imagine vomiting all over his lap. "But at the same time, I want to savor you."

Actually, good thing Lucan's not here right now to overhear this.

Scoffing, I wrench my arm away. "And if I refuse? What? You'll throw me over the Wall?"

"Don't tempt me," Arad replies smoothly.

My heart ticks against my sternum as Diggory flashes through my mind. Maybe, if I can get Arad to keep talking... "I thought only prisoners go over the Wall. That's what they teach us in school."

"Prisoners are disposed of," he says, "in any manner we see fit. The Wall is just my favorite option."

I briefly wonder if anything that comes out of his mouth is ever the truth. My anger hardens. "What happened to all of those Chosen Ones who lie in bed all day? Which option is that?"

Arad sears a look into me, his pupils like pinpricks that make me want to shutter my eyes. I resist.

"If they want to laze around in bed all day, then who are we to stop them? It's their choice. They don't have to explore the palace." He pauses briefly to lick his lips. "Unlike you. I've noticed you're taking advantage of your freedom. Tell me, Saskia, what's your favorite part of your new home?"

The way he says *home* makes me shudder, as if what he meant was graveyard instead. But an idea pops into my head, so I force my mouth to move.

"I don't know yet. I haven't seen it all. I'm sure your wing is the most beautiful, though."

Arad laughs with a click of his tongue. A scraping sound that makes my eardrums vibrate with disgust. "You'll have to try harder than that."

Before I can respond, a crackle cuts through the air, making me jump, and the same voice that's dictated my entire life blares through my room.

"Eligible Chosen Ones, please report to the balconies for the Viewing. Newly Chosen Ones, please report to your hallway for further instruction."

I didn't realize there were intercoms within the Blood Moon Palace as well. I swivel my head around, wondering where they must be hidden. Behind the furniture? Within the walls?

Arad stands, holding out his arm as if the bastard actually wants to pretend he has manners.

I don't take it. I simply march to my bedroom door and try not to cringe as the chill of his presence sweeps after me.

As soon as I exit, I see that the other newly Chosen Ones—as well as a few I don't recognize—are standing in front of their own doors up and down the hallway, wringing their hands as the voice blares on. This is the first time I've seen them all since the blood moon, and I blink at them, my vision suddenly swaying.

The vampire venom. It must be snaking through my system again, making everyone and everything appear hazy around the edges. I need to ground myself before my body floats away.

Before I can figure out how to do that, though, the culprit himself snaps the door shut behind me, and dozens of heads crank in our direction.

Curious eyes up and down the hall rove over us. Some people smirk, others shoot daggers. My stomach bubbles like acid.

Their eyes are full of judgment, envy, misconceptions—take your pick—after watching us emerge from my room together.

Arad's breath washes over my neck when he angles his head down toward me. "They're jealous of you. Maybe we should make that into another Cardinal Rule—don't be jealous of a beautiful woman."

I actually might throw up at his attempts at... what? Flirting? Flattery? I'm not even sure what his goal is, but I manage to blink up into his face innocently and make a retort under my breath. "Thirteen rules don't really work when there's only twelve of you."

As soon as I say the words out loud, I realize it's more of a threat than I intended. A reminder that one of the original Guardians died during the war with Lucan's kind.

That a vampire can be killed.

Before Arad can voice the rage brewing in his eyes, the First Guardian sweeps into view, stopping before a pair of large, stained glass windows at the end of the hallway. He claps his hands, and everyone turns back to face him with expressions that melt back into fear.

"This will be the one and only time I address you before each Viewing, so it would be prudent to remember my advice." As if even the robotic female voice obeys him, the speakers fall silent as soon as his words permeate the air. "Just as it is your duty to provide sustenance to the protectors of Xantera, it is also your duty to put on a smile. To wave at the lesser humans who don't have it as good as you do."

The warning in his voice couldn't be more clear. This is a show, one that requires us to participate. And if we dare step out of line, we'll find ourselves like the Chosen One they dragged out of the dining hall on the first night.

"You will file out these doors behind me in a moment," the First Guardian continues, and I realize that the stained glass windows behind him are actually a double door that must lead out to this hallway's balcony. "Do not give us a reason to step foot outside."

Then the First Guardian whirls around and throws open the doors. A breeze catches the hallway, and my hair flutters over my shoulder.

Arad inhales before his fingers graze down the column of my neck. I jerk away, but I can still hear his whisper, "Remember, Saskia, how happy you are here. This is a dream come true. Show everyone that I'm the best thing that has ever happened to you. Show them in how you smile and how you wave."

My fists are wound so tight that my nails are digging little crescents into my palms, drawing blood.

Arad laughs. "I'll come back to taste that later."

"Follow me," the First Guardian announces before I can get in the last word, and we all shuffle forward toward the fresh air.

Out on the balcony, the sun kisses my skin for the first time in almost a week.

I've never been this high up before. To my amazement, I can actually see a slice of the world over the Wall. A blanket of treetops spreads over the valley beyond, and to my right, I can spot part of a river winding at the base of the mountains. Or at least, I think it's a river. I've never seen one before, except in textbooks.

Lucan is out there right now, somewhere in those same forests. Doing what? I have no idea. I haven't even heard his howls over the last few nights. He was so determined to get me to promise him I'd be good that he didn't give me a chance to ask.

Up until this point, my heart has ached at the thought of him, but now my fingers clench over the railings of the balcony as I watch the trees sway and the water churn beyond the Wall—until an elbow nudges me in the side.

"Wave," the Chosen One beside me mutters out the side of her mouth.

I jolt out of my daydream of streaking through the woods to find Lucan and bang him over the head, silently thanking the Chosen One for bringing me back to the bleak present.

Nobody down below would notice that my hand trembles as I lift it to wave.

Examining Xantera from this angle puts the city into a different perspective. The main road stretches out in front of me all the way to farmland, where twin windmills twirl in the distance. The uniform rows of housing complexes look too much like a chicken coop. Too unyielding. Too harsh. Too cramped.

I switch my sights to the courtyard. A sea of faces peer up at us, all with matching expressions of awe and wonder, as if they really do think of us as honorable heroes. From my current balcony several stories up, I can just make out their features: toothy smiles and wide eyes, hands waving frantically whenever they spot their loved ones.

Desperately, my gaze hesitates over each man's face with mousy brown hair, desperate for a slice of familiarity. For a moment, I worry that Malcolm didn't even show up...

And then my eyes land on his smile, right next to Walter and someone else so familiar that my stomach clenches with homesickness.

Gaia jumps up and down when I spot her, smacking Malcolm and pointing me out excitedly.

"Hi!" I yell, my heart jackhammering in exhilaration. It's only been a little less than a week since I've been in here, but I feel as if I knew the three people below me in another lifetime.

But they can't hear me. And I can't hear them.

Between the distance and the murmurs around the courtyard, it's impossible to make anything out. Sylvia and Diggory's way of communicating must have given them a tremendous advantage that others don't have. I just can't figure out how none of the Guardians spotted their hands moving in anything other than these repetitive waves.

Now, I zero in on Malcolm, wishing so badly I could communicate with him in the same way—tell him everything I've learned and what it means for the people of Xantera. Maybe, if the Guardians' secret could leak out to the public, there would be too many rebels to drag into the palace and suck the life out of...

I turn away to reel back my emotions, right as a familiar face sidles up next to me.

"Look who it is," the Chosen One—Tristan—teases, continuing to wave and smile with slow, graceful movements down at his own loved ones. "Your arm already tired?"

I rest my back against the balcony, taking in heavy breaths. "I can't do this."

"Do what? Smile and wave?"

"No," I say. "Lie."

Tristan lets an uncomfortable laugh slip out. "You'll be punished if you don't. I've seen it." He pauses to let out an overenthusiastic whoop before he drops his voice. "I suppose maybe you won't if you're already the Third's little pet."

I turn my face up at him in disgust. "What?"

"Heard he came out of your room earlier. The Cardinal Rules don't matter here, so gossip spreads fast." Once again, his eyes make their lazy way across my chest, down my waist. "Not that I blame him."

It hits me. His slow movements, his leisurely drawl. If I hadn't discovered it already, I'd think he was drunk on venom.

He's not, though. He's in the beginning phases of turning to stone.

"That wasn't what it looked like," I insist.

Tristan shrugs. "No one blames you. I've slept with my Guardian plenty of times. They're undeniably attractive. Though it took me months to be invited into the north wing... not a week." Again he can't keep his eyes off my body. "You're undeniably attractive yourself. Also, you never came to play poker. I was looking forward to your company."

"I was busy," I mutter.

"Busy? There's nothing to do in this place besides—"

"Wait," I interrupt, my mood ticking up, "you've been in the north wing?"

"Yeah." His brow creases in confusion. "I just said—"

"What's it like?"

Tristan peeks over his shoulder to make sure nobody's listening in.

"More palace," he jokes.

"*Specifically*, what's it like?" The irritation seeps into my voice. I want to shake him awake, shout in his face that I'm trying to save him and everyone else here.

"Well," he says before a pause. "There's more rooms."

"Twelve? For each of the Guardians?"

"No. Way more than twelve. Like a maze of them. And there's a huge room filled with books up to the ceiling—not even kidding. I don't know who would want to read like we had to in schooling, but.... oh, and there's this garden with their own personal court-yard and their own personal balconies. I was actually having a *great* time with the Tenth Guardian up against the railing when one of those servants popped out of nowhere and interrupted."

I keep my face neutral, though excitement shoots through all my bones—or maybe that's my own vampire venom working its way through my system, trying to fossilize me, too.

"Anyway," Tristan continues, a smile snaking across his lips as he recalls his dirty memories. "Had to cut that short but we made up for it later. You know, Chosen Ones sleep together, too. Like I said, not much else to do."

Lifting my head, I turn back to face the Xantera cityscape with a renewed energy. Now, I wave like a princess in all her glory. Smile like I have everything I've ever wanted.

"Like I said, Tristan," I tell him. "Busy."

I certainly *will* be busy after this is done. Because I don't need to convince Arad to invite me into the north wing.

I can just sneak in through the servant corridors.

LUCAN

The hours wax and wane around me until I'm itching in my human skin.

I've been in my father's old office, my head buried in his journals for the last five damned days. It doesn't matter if I read rapidly or slowly, soaking it all in, whether I'm in his ripped leather armchair he used to love so much or the moth-eaten sofa jammed up against the far side of the room next to all those filing cabinets no one has touched since he died.

I've gone through them all, sifted through every drawer, rifled through every page, scoured every single *word* I may have missed in the past, but I don't feel any closer to a solution.

The parasite was right on my tail, I read now for the tenth time, my eyes burning with exhaustion, *and though the others shouted at me to keep going, I could feel his breath on my skin. I whirled to claw his eyes out, but he lunged, his fangs sinking into my shoulder right before I got him back. Fire exploded through my veins, but he shrunk back just as much as I did.*

They don't like the taste of our blood.

It's nothing I haven't heard before. Genetically predisposed, my pack and I are all resistant to the venom—it causes us excruciating pain to come into contact with it, so says my father, but it doesn't affect us the same way it affects humans.

Now I know what that really means: if any of the Guardians were to bite me, I'd probably yelp an embarrassing amount like I do when I touch the Wall, but I wouldn't turn to stone. Not like Saskia will.

If only I could turn her into a werewolf, I would in a heartbeat. But werewolves are born, not made. She'd have to have the were-wolf gene.

After turning the last page on the sixth journal, I heave it across the room. It slaps against the office door before falling to the ground with a soft thump.

Seconds later, a creak follows a soft series of knocking, and my mother opens the door slowly like she's testing my mood.

When she steps over the threshold, she studies the book now laying at her feet.

"There's nothing in that one either," I say, my words laced with anger that I shouldn't take out on her. I flex my fingers, raking in deep breaths until I feel my face soften. "Do you know where Grandfather's journals are? His go farther back."

Closer to a time when he actually saw a vampire with his own two eyes and witnessed their destruction.

My mother reveals a leather-bound book from behind her back. "I've been reading, too. Since our last talk." She holds it out, her hand trembling slightly. "It's not an answer or a cure," she insists, "but it might provide you some new insight."

I eye the journal, twin scratch marks marring its surface. "I don't think I've seen that one before."

"You haven't. Your father—he told me not to let anyone read it. To keep it safe and hidden. But given the circumstances with you and your..."

She doesn't even have to finish her sentence before I'm shooting onto my feet, taking the journal she offers me and flicking through the yellowed pages stiff with age.

"I don't understand. Why'd he want *this* one hidden?"

My father had never been a quiet male, exactly. He'd been loud about his rage, his stories, and his goals, roaring out at the world until his very last breath. I was the one to take it all in, to hoard the anger he spewed out and stuff it in a bottle somewhere at the bottom of my soul. I can't fathom that he actually kept a *secret* from me. That there was anything he wanted to stay quiet.

"Page sixty-eight," my mother whispers, tugging on my shoulder and rising to her tippy toes to lay a kiss on my cheek. Then she turns around and creeps back out of the room.

I stare after her for a few seconds, the ticking of the clock above the desk like a drumroll for my pulse. Outside the window, the dying sun permeates the clouds, casting an orangish light over the journal in my hands.

When her footsteps recede down the hallway outside, I jolt into action, thumping the journal down onto the desk.

And turn to page sixty-eight.

SASKIA

As soon as I'm back in my room, I scramble to the bed and slide my hands under the mattress. My fingers find the warm gold chain, and I waste no time gliding it up my thigh.

Lucan! Are you there?

He told me he's here for me, that he's just on the other side of the Wall. And I believed him. I *believe* him. So I wait for the spurt of electricity patiently, confident that he'll sense me knocking on the door of our connection. Any second now...

The clock ticks.

And ticks.

And ticks.

I glance out the painted panes of my window, realizing how low the sun has dropped since I was out on the balcony. Any minute now, he should be morphing back into the Monster so that I can tell him what I learned.

But my pulse doesn't skip. No dark, rich presence reaches out to latch onto my heartbeat.

Lucan, I whisper into the void. *I have news. If you can sense me, come back.*

Silence.

Nothing but a horrible, haunting silence.

The clock ticks some more, and soon I can't stand the sound without doing something to fill the static void Lucan usually fills. I yank the necklace off just as quickly as I slid it on, stuff it back under the mattress, and begin to scour my bedroom with new eyes.

Fine, then. If Lucan doesn't want to be here for me, I'll have to do this without him.

But first, I need to form a plan before Eleni arrives to bring me my dinner.

By the time the servant door pops open and Eleni emerges from the dark corridor, I'm sitting on the edge of my bed with a placid expression. To anyone else, it probably looks like I'm drunk on vampire venom, but truthfully, that feeling of wanting to float away already dissolved hours ago. And I doubt anyone would notice that I ripped a tiny strip of fabric off the hem of my dress.

"Hello, Eleni," I say pleasantly when she looks up. She doesn't answer, of course, but I use the half-second it takes her to give me a quick bow to peer over her shoulder for a quick glimpse of what could lie beyond the paneled door. It looks dark and...

All too soon, Eleni lifts her head again and shuts the door with a swift kick of her foot.

Oh, well. I'll get a better glimpse soon.

Shuffling over to me with my dinner, she places the tray in my outstretched hands and begins to unwrap the utensils from their napkins.

"Thank you." I paste a smile onto my face. "It must be exhausting for you to climb all those stairs just to bring me a meal. I'd be happy to help you next time."

Eleni glares at me and shakes her head, setting my fork and spoon down on the tray with distinct clinks. I wonder why they don't give us anything sharper. It's not like I'd be able to stab through the Third Guardian's marble skin with a dainty little butter knife.

I could fantasize about that, of course, but now's not the time to lose focus. This whole thing will be a lot easier if I can convince Eleni to just let me into the servant corridors.

Pretending to gaze absentmindedly toward my window, I take another stab.

"It really is such a bore here. Nothing to do. I've already explored the entire palace from top to bottom." *Literally.* All those stairs have now joined the horrors in my nightmares. "I'd really be happy to help you out, Eleni. I miss working."

It's the truth, but whether she can pick out the vulnerability in my tone or not, my servant just clamps her lips together. Without looking up, she removes the silver cloche covering my plate to reveal a plate of roasted lamb, sizzling vegetables, and golden potatoes sprinkled with what looks like parsley.

My stomach clenches as my eyes stay glued to the silver cloche.

The glass cloche in the drawing room.

That's where I'm going to go first. If I can't find my mom, I'll find the key, open the Wall, and let Lucan in. And when the Guardians are no longer breathing, I'll be able to tear the palace apart to find her.

I take a deep breath and place my tray on the bed, standing up and pretending to stretch.

"Well, anytime you need my help, you just let me know, okay?"

I walk toward the servant door as if I'm escorting her out. Narrowing her eyes, Eleni follows, and I watch her whip out a tiny skeleton key and insert it into the lock embedded in a panel of the wall. The door swings open, and I catch hold of it....

Eleni whips toward me, eyes full of warning.

A sudden urge to shove past her and sprint into the darkness races through my limbs. But I can't do that to her—force her to choose between her life and mine. Because I'm sure she'd be expected to alert the Guardians if I ran into a place I am obviously not allowed to be.

"One more thing, Eleni." I lean in close and lower my voice. "I just wanted to tell you that what the Guardians did to you, it isn't right. Fuck honor and duty. None of this is honorable."

Eleni's eyes widen before briefly closing, and I use the mere second to case the doorframe. There, just below my right hand, is a hole that looks exactly where a door would catch.

"You're my friend, Eleni," I whisper, at the same time I stuff the ripped piece of cloth from the hem of my dress into the hole.

All or nothing.

Eleni's eyes drift down to the movement for the briefest of seconds. If she saw me, she doesn't acknowledge it.

Then she nods and closes the door.

Just as Sylvia did in her memory, I count to one hundred and one as I pace the perimeter of my room.

Then I stop in front of the hidden doorway.

I trace my fingers up and down the outline, trying to find a groove.

Nothing catches. With flat hands, I push my weight into the door multiple times, hoping it joggles something, but it doesn't swing inward either.

Again, I trace the outer edge until I feel the tiniest lip—two pieces of wood that aren't flush. *Yes.* I dig my nails into it like claws, getting as deep as I possibly can with all eight fingers, before I finally tug it open.

A cloud of stale air hits me, making me cough. I suppose the corridor doesn't have any working air supply since it's sandwiched in between the walls.

Flashbacks of the catacombs shuffle through my memories, but this time I have to travel alone, without Lucan's voice to drive me crazy and keep me company.

Glancing over my shoulder one more time to glare in the direction of the necklace I'm leaving behind, I step into the stale darkness, drag in a deep breath, and pull the door shut behind me.

Flimsy light flickers from a hanging bulb up ahead, casting a faint yellow glow that hardly illuminates anything outside of its immediate vicinity. But I can see the outline of other hatches up ahead, as well as splits in the walkway where I'll have to make a choice between left or right.

The catacombs 2.0, indeed.

I cough and start forward, passing the other hatches without stopping to investigate. North. I need to go north—which, judging from where I know my room is positioned in the palace, means I need to take a right at the next branch.

I do, and now I'm met with a staircase that spirals downward. Right. To get to the north wing, I probably have to be on the main level.

Clutching the edges of the wall, I descend what feels like several stories until I'm back in a corridor, this time with actual doors lining either side. Muffled voices rumble on the other side of them, and my heart begins a steady beating against my ribcage at the realization that any of them could open at any moment and catch me sneaking past.

North. Which way is north?

Shit. The spiral staircase erased all sense of my direction.

I don't have time to figure it out. At that moment, one of the nearest doors flies open, and I flatten myself against the wall with my heart plummeting straight to my toes.

The door swings shut again as my ears ring, nerves alight, but I let out an inaudible breath when I lay eyes on the back of two servants.

They're each pushing a large cart of what looks like dirty, blood-splattered laundry and linens—away from me, thank the Guardians.

Or... no. Maybe I shouldn't thank the Guardians anymore. They've obviously cut out the tongues of these servants, too, because rather than whisper and gossip to each other as they push their carts farther and farther away from me, the hallway only echoes with the squeak of their wheels.

Hoping the sound will cover my not-so-stealthy footsteps, I follow like a shadow, holding my breath and tiptoeing in time with their steps.

Maybe they'll lead me to where I'm hoping to go.

The servants make turn after turn, never looking back, and I try to memorize the directions as best as I can until their wheels cut to an abrupt stop.

Sinking into the shadows around the corner, I close my eyes and focus on the sounds.

A click. Hinges. More squeaking.

As soon as the carts seem to roll out of the narrow passageway, I muster every ounce of courage I can and sprint to the door as it begins to swing shut. Just before it does, I jam my fingers into the sliver of space still remaining. The door squeezes my fingers, but I bite my lip to avoid letting out a yelp.

With my fingers stinging and my throat so tight it's hard to breathe, I peek through the tiny opening.

Across a grand hallway, through a wide glass doorway, large, ornate chairs with spiked backs sit in a line at the far end of the elaborate red and gold room.

Thrones.

I count them: thirteen.

One for each of the living Guardians, and one for the Guardian who met his demise.

The north wing. It has to be.

The sight makes me sick, so I glance to the next doorway over. Stacks and stacks of *books* rise to the ceiling.

Up, up, up, my eyes follow columns of shelves. The books rise so high, they hit windows that are actually a part of the ceiling. The rays of a bloody sunset bounce around, hitting glass and mirrors, refracting off surfaces that give the books an unearthly but beautiful quality.

You're missing out, Lucan, I whisper into the glaring absence in my own mind, although the truth is, *I'm* the one missing *him* right now. He probably realized that I'm a lost cause and decided to stop checking in. Or maybe he was actually starting to care for me and wanted to cut ties before I turn to stone and break his heart with my new sharp edges.

Either way, I haven't come this far just to turn back now.

My resolve tightening, I slip through the doorway, out into the entrance of the north wing... and gasp when I turn my head and take in the unmistakable profile of the Third Guardian—in statue form.

My stomach slowly travels back to where it belongs, but my nerves still tingle as I behold the eleven other statues, six on each side, of all the Guardians. They're terrifyingly lifelike, as if they're watching my every movement even though I'm the only one here at the moment.

I don't know where to go, but before I can flip a coin in my mind and decide, the door at the very end of the hallway opens with a loud creak.

I dive behind the Third Guardian's statue, taking in the irony of this situation, as two servants appear carrying what is unmistakably a body on a stretcher—more than likely a *dead* body.

The outline of a face, a strong nose, jutted chin, and round head protrudes from the white sheet covering it, and four fingers poke out from beneath the sheet. As they pass in front of me, a servant notices the exposed body parts and tucks the sheet over them respectfully before they enter through another doorway that leads outside, judging by the cold gust of wind that sweeps through.

Sweat trickles down my back, and my hands ache as I clench them at my sides. I don't like dead bodies. Beyond the obvious reasons, I'm quickly learning that they fill me with a sense of failure, like I didn't do my job properly even though I was never called to heal whoever died. Did a Guardian snap their neck because they misbehaved? Or...

A female voice cuts through the air.

And not the robotic one that blares from the loudspeakers.

"....thinks that it might still be somewhere in the palace, but I'm not so sure."

My chest pinches. I'm certain it's an actual Guardian by her smooth tone, the cadence of her authoritarian words. And if she discovers me here, hiding behind this statue, I'll be the next person carried on a stretcher.

Ever so slowly, I turn around to retreat back into the servant corridor—

Only to find the door has swung shut behind me. And when I press against it... locked.

Shit. Adrenaline lights up my nerves as the Guardian's footsteps click closer.

"How could it be anywhere *besides* the palace? It's not like the Chosen Ones can leave."

"No, but they might have dropped it to... him. He's been especially quiet these last few nights."

Another female Guardian. I don't dare glance around the statue's bust to check, but if I had to guess, I'd say it's the Eighth talking to the Tenth—about Lucan and... what?

"Maybe he's finally dead."

"Or maybe he's planning—what was that?"

I pray she's talking about something else, not the shadow of me scurrying behind the next statue over and slipping into the first unlocked door I come across. On the other side, I wait with bated breath for the two Guardians to barge in after me...

But after several seconds, it seems they've shrugged it off and moved on.

I blow out a breath of relief. For such a strong, immortal species, they certainly don't seem to have the same sense of smell that Lucan does. The thought makes me smile, but any smugness I feel quickly slips off my face as soon as I turn around to take a look at this new room I've found myself in.

A bluish light emanates from the far back wall, but there's some sort of soundproofed wall blocking my view of whatever's casting it. It doesn't reach either wall to my right or left, or the ceiling, so there's just enough room for someone to slip around it.

Cautiously, I creep to the side and poke my head around the wall.

I blink.

And blink again.

Rows and rows of screens, just like the one that sits in my dining room, are stacked on top of each other. But instead of the familiar image of a half-baked sun rising over a grassy knoll, these show something entirely different:

Alleyways, housing complexes, living rooms, kitchens. There's the Recreation Center, the Blood Moon Palace courtyard, the Educational Institution, and what looks like the Production Factory, though I've never been inside. My heart squeezes when my eyes gloss over a patient's room in the Healing Center, then the locker room.

In front of the screens, one woman stands with her arms crossed behind four men who sit in swivel chairs with their backs to me, all of Xantera laid out before them. They shuffle through these views on the screen like a slideshow, inspecting the 'privacy' of other people's homes and workplaces.

"That one," the woman says suddenly, turning to point at one of the screens on the far left. My stomach curdles at the sound of her voice and the shape of her profile...

It's Rosalyn, the sentry who visited Malcolm and me, the one who loves control.

On the panel in front of his chair, one of the men maneuvers some type of stick, and a video of a couple inside their housing complex enlarges across multiple screens. He presses a button, and their voices fill the dark room.

"...just seems like you're not happy with the Guardians' choice sometimes. Or with me."

"I never once said that! I would never question their decisions!"

"Then why are you always *complaining*? It's like you're not..."

The man presses another button, and the couple freezes mid-fight.

"Send it to the Guardians," Rosalyn instructs, an unnatural joy trilling through her voice. "I'll go speak with them."

The sound of clickclacking fills the room as the man types something out, and a message pops up on the screen in bold red letters. **SURVEILLANCE VIDEO LOGGED FOR GUARDIANS.**

Then it disappears.

In its place, an image of a courtyard emerges, one I haven't seen before—one where two people walk around a fountain, before it switches to another couple drinking tea in the comfort of their home.

Another man rolls his chair to the edge of the desk and turns a dial, a soft click associated with each time he rotates, and then with his palm, he bears down on the button and a female voice blares out through the monitors.

"*Citizens of Xantera, please return to your individual housing units. Recreational time is over. Citizens of Xantera, please return to your individual housing units. Recreational time is over.*"

I jump, my heart in my throat. The same voice I've heard my whole life is really just an imprisoned man selecting a phrase and pressing a button.

My elbow jolts out from my side, hitting the screen and sending a metal clunk reverberating around the room.

All five heads crank so quickly in my direction that I don't know if they saw me as a blur diving for cover or if they saw me at all.

I throw myself back into the grand hallway and push my legs even faster than before.

But before I can make it back behind a statue, a hand grabs me from behind.

And yanks me away.

34

LUCAN

I storm in circles around my father's office, my eyes hooked on all the journal entries that don't make any fucking sense the further I read.

> *April 29, 52 AX*
>
> *They must have kept Father's blood like a goddamn trophy, because one of the parasites spoke to me today. I heard his voice in my skull, just like I hear the rest of the pack when they shift. He asked me what my name was, so I told him to fuck right off.*

I frown, assuming my father was talking about the Third Guardian. But he never mentioned that Arad taunted him the same way he used to taunt me, so my eyebrows furrow in confusion as I flip the page to the next entry.

May 16, 52 AX

He wants to repent, the parasite does. To change the ways of what he and his fellow vampires are doing to my people. I don't know why yet, and I'm not sure I believe him, but he told me how he's communicating with me: a vase. They put Father's blood in a fucking vase. They don't even like the taste of our blood, so it's more like a decoration they can laugh over.

I swear, I can feel my own blood boiling at the thought. But somehow, the parasite in my head discovered that if he dips his abomination of a hand into the vase, he can connect to my thoughts.

I told him to steal a few drops and put it in a vial that he can wear around his neck. It will make communication easier.

If he's trying to trick me, at least now I can spy on him.

I gape at the page, at the realization that my own *father* came up with the idea of the necklace that brought me to Saskia. And whoever actually made the necklace... he doesn't sound like Arad.

June 02, 52 AX

I told the parasite my name, and he told me his.

Graham. The Thirteenth Guardian.

He claims he's fallen in love with one of the humans, and that's why he wants to change things. I'm still not sure if I believe him or not—it might all be one elaborate ruse—but he says the rest of the Guardians won't budge anyway. He can't convince them to stop. And he's afraid they'll kill his lover if they find out.

If we want to free my people, he's going to need to let me in.

I reread that particular entry over and over again, trying to make sense of it. As far as I've always known, the Thirteenth Guardian perished in the war between the vampires and my grandfather. But according to my father, he was still alive fifty-two years later, apparently in love with some human within the Wall and betraying his fellow vampires by trying to help my father reclaim his kingdom.

What I don't understand is where it all went wrong.

Because they obviously failed. Both my father and the Thirteenth Guardian are dead, the Wall is still closed, and the necklace somehow fell into Arad's hand before Saskia found it.

Saskia. I squeeze my eyes shut, resisting a sudden urge to shift right here and now and make sure she's okay. For the last few nights, I've been doing exactly that, and every time I've breathed a sigh of relief to find her as safe as she can possibly be, taking dinner in her private room.

The sun has barely dipped below the windowsill of my father's office, which means she hasn't gone to sleep yet. A few more journal entries can't hurt.

Pacing in circles again, I flip the page...

35

SASKIA

If eyes could kill, I'd be dead on the spot, courtesy of the look spewing from Eleni's glare.

All that nervous tension subsides for a split second when I realize the hand gripping my forearm belongs to her. Then she drags me back through the grand Guardian hallway, in the direction I just ran away from, and it all comes roaring back.

Is she going to turn me in? We've never actually established that she thinks of me as a friend, too. Maybe it was just wishful thinking on my part, and she's about to march me straight to the Third Guardian himself.

I stumble after her without much choice. If I resist, the ruckus will attract the Guardians anyway. Her hand only tightens around my arm with every step she takes until she stops abruptly in front of a particularly wide door, the nearest one in our vicinity, and presses her key into… something. I still haven't figured out how the doors work.

But nonetheless, the lock clicks, and Eleni pushes the door open to expose a massive kitchen.

Long, bright fluorescent lights hang from the ceiling in rows. I have to squint against the reflections bouncing off all the stainless steel around me. More unnerving is the amount of people—hundreds if I had to guess—toiling away without so much as a whisper in the air.

Dragging me behind her, Eleni mazes through the workstations, where we pass others chopping up an assortment of vegetables and stirring pots of boiling stew. Without fail, each of their heads rise curiously as we pass, then their eyes go wide and their mouths gape, before they quickly cast their faces down and return to their task like they don't want to know.

To my surprise, Eleni presses me into a corner. A young woman about my age turns her back to us and continues stirring vigorously, the slop in her pot squelching loud enough to drown out my next whispered words.

"I'm sorry, Eleni."

Without the chatter of human voices, the sounds that follow already grate down my spine. Metal clinks against metal. Knives slice through meat. Food plops into bowls.

Finally, Eleni shakes her head like my apology isn't good enough. Maybe it isn't. Risking not just my life but hers without clueing her in might have been a little too reckless for me. I at least owe her the truth.

"I need to find something," I start quietly, "in the palace."

Her eyes stay trained on me intensely. She's listening, albeit angrily. Even as the servants around us start to move as one, forming a line that winds itself through the kitchen like a multi-headed serpent, Eleni arches an eyebrow, waiting for me to continue.

"Do you know where the white drawing room is? In the north wing, exactly? There's something I need there. Desperately. Something that could help all of us."

Eleni shakes her head, pupils contracting in an emotion I can't decipher. I don't know if it's fear or indifference or more hatred.

"Please," I beg.

But Eleni shakes her head again, more insistent this time before she releases her hold on my elbow and points back to the servant door.

My shoulders fall. Like I'm right back in the Educational Institution getting scolded for not reciting the third Cardinal Rule word for word, I nod, defeated, and start to make my way to the door we came through.

Eleni follows closely on my heels, but I take my time observing the servants as I weave in and out of them.

At the front of the kitchen, each of them picks up a tray and files through what looks like an assembly line, where they scoop and deposit portions of food onto each section of the tray.

When it hits me, I trip over my own feet. Those are *our* trays. The citizens' trays. The same ones that are slid through the slat in our housing complex doors each morning and each evening. The same ones I've eaten off of my entire life, unknowingly delivered by the hundreds of servants of the Blood Moon Palace.

And somewhere in here, one of these servants delivers food to *my* housing complex.

To Malcolm.

Not even thirty seconds after Eleni drags me back through the corridor and deposits me back in my room with a huff, the door barges open.

Arad flows in with rage dripping off him. His eyes scour my room wildly before landing on me, and for a second, surprise widens them.

Like he didn't think I'd be here.

"Saskia." He slams my door behind him, causing the decorations on my shelves and side tables to wobble with the vibrations. "How very pleasant to see you still awake."

I don't say anything, so afraid that the tone of my voice will give something away. His gaze roves over to the tray on my bed—all the food untouched. His nostrils flare.

"Not feeling hungry, are we?"

I swallow the dryness in my throat. "No."

"That's funny." He prowls closer. "Because I fed from you mere hours ago, and usually that makes you humans very hungry."

The words are out before I can stop them. "Unfortunately, you just make *me* nauseous."

Stupid Saskia. This is what Lucan meant by keeping my head down. It was an unnecessary comment that makes Arad halt, his hands quivering at his sides, as if he's imagining wrapping them around my throat and squeezing tight.

But the moment passes. His hands calm, and a smile tilts up either side of his lips as something even more dangerous takes over his expression. I take a step back, and he takes one forward.

"Saskia," he purrs. "That's no way to talk to a male. Especially on Sunday."

Sunday? What does that have to do with...

I know as soon as I catch sight of the gleam in his eyes. Sunday is the day every couple in Xantera is required to "keep their spark alive." A glittering phrase to cover up how crude and disgusting the Guardians' control is.

"Do you know why we chose that particular system, Saskia?" Arad asks with a tilt of his head.

"Because you're a bunch of creeps?" I dare answer.

Again, his fists tighten for a breath of a moment before loosening again.

"On the contrary, it took years of patience and experimentation. Let the humans fuck whenever they want, and they start to develop feelings for each other—whether it be love or hatred. That seems to be the only thing humans fight about anymore—love and attention. Or lack of it. Some would want to go at it every day, while others would fight about the frequency. And then there would be passion and discord, and all the little lines..." He raises his hands, walking his fingers over an open palm. "...that we've so carefully built would crumble." He smashes his fist into his hand.

Sweat trickles down the back of my neck as I try not to breathe or trigger him in any way. Because the truth is, the Third Guardian looks like he's on the brink of madness as he steps even closer and I lean back.

"But... don't let the humans fuck at all," he continues, pupils zigzagging wildly over my face, "and their animalistic nature starts to come out. They hear whispers from the family-making couples about how good it is and wonder why they have to wait for that primal urge. They all decide they want to fight for their *rights*." He shakes his head with a humorless laugh. "So once a week was ideal. Give the couple their own bedrooms and one shared room, order them to rip each other's clothes off for one day, and everyone is content."

"No," I whisper back immediately. "Not everyone is content, or else you wouldn't have to pick out the rebels from the crowd, would you?" I watch the pale marble of his face actually *flush* with a mottled pink in anger, but I don't stop. "Forcing people to be together or not be together—regardless of the frequency—is an assault to our humanity and our choice."

Arad laughs at that—actually throws up his head and laughs at my ceiling, his fangs protruding.

"Saskia, my dear, when will you learn that you don't *deserve* a choice? I let you waltz around this palace and deny me my pleasure because I think it's fun to play games with you, but I could just as easily lock you up and let you wither away into a skeleton after I suck every last drop of blood from your body. Because you've been a little too defiant now, haven't you? Like you know more than you actually should—more than possible."

He pivots and throws open the topmost drawer of my dresser. Flinging my undergarments over his shoulder, I watch in horrified silence. He moves on to the next two drawers, pulling out my clothes and shaking each folded piece of fabric before letting it fall to the ground.

Then he turns back around and sets his sights on me.

Tears spring to my eyes as he leans ever closer and glances down at my chest. I bite the inside of my cheek to keep from screaming.

Or maybe I *should* scream. Maybe, somewhere over the Wall, Lucan will hear me.

But there's nothing he would be able to do, anyway.

"Take off your dress," Arad says quietly.

The tears flow down my cheeks freely now.

"Please," I whisper to him. "Don't make me do this."

"I SAID TAKE OFF YOUR DRESS NOW."

I flinch at the spit that flies from his mouth and sizzles when it makes contact with my skin. Each droplet is burning hot, fiery like poison—vampire venom. Something inside me stirs, raising its head at the sensation, but I don't have time to think about it. Arad has no patience left.

He lunges forward and rips my dress by the hem, sending it to tattered pieces on the ground and leaving me standing before him in my undergarments. His frantic gaze roves over my entire body, every curve and dip, until his expression retreats back into polite contemplation.

With a fist to his mouth, he clears his throat.

And *backs away.*

"My apologies. I thought you might be hiding something underneath there." With horror, I think about the necklace stashed underneath my mattress merely a few inches away. If I had put it on my thigh before I'd snuck into the servant corridors, Arad would have found it just now...

Instead, he swipes a finger along my cheek, collecting a tear.

"You will forgive me for that little outburst, won't you, Saskia? It's just that I have lost something very important to me, and I need to explore every avenue in order to find it."

When I don't reply, he clears his throat.

"You *will* forgive me for that, *won't you*, Saskia?"

Every ounce of me begs my mouth to spit back in his face. But if I want to survive tonight, I have a feeling I need to be more patient than him. Get him to leave for now so that I can plan my revenge.

"Of course," I force out.

He smiles. "Excellent."

And giving my body a last sweep before twirling around, he bursts out the door in the same manner he came, leaving me alone.

LUCAN

My gaze races across the last few pages of my father's secret journal, the ticking of the clock like a gong in my heart at this point, counting down the seconds until I have to shift. At this point, I crave that connection with Saskia more than any addiction, so I'm not sure I could go much longer even if I *did* feel comfortable leaving her alone this long.

October 28, 52 AX

The Thirteenth Guardian has been telling me more about the nature of his kind as we plan for my pack to breach the Wall. Everything makes so much more sense than it used to.

Vampire venom, for instance, is a magical substance
that interacts differently with a variety of...

"I don't actually fucking care," I mutter, rifling to the next page
with my jaw clenching. I just want to find out what the hell happened to the Thirteenth Guardian and get back to Saskia. Make
sure she's alright. And get a refill of her colorful presence. Flicking
to the last page, my eyes land on a final entry.

November 09, 52 AX

We were supposed to meet at one of the doors of the Wall
last night. Graham was supposed to open it for me, but
he never showed, and my connection with him went
silent.

I don't know if he betrayed us or was playing us
all along or if the other parasites found out and
killed him. I'm hoping the latter. At least that way, I
wouldn't feel so fucking stupid.

If anyone asks, I'm going to say the Thirteenth
Guardian died in the war. I'll erase him from my
memory, because none of it mattered anyway. It's over.

SASKIA

I t's not over yet. Just as I reach for my clothes, humiliated and angry, Eleni appears out of nowhere on the other side of my bed.

My anger reflects back at me, her eyes so dark they scare me. She heard what happened from the other side of the door, and she's not going to let it go.

"I'm alright," I insist, turning away and hurrying over to my armoire to find a new dress, one that isn't torn to shreds.

Tears sting behind my eyelids, but I blink them back. Eleni doesn't need anything more to worry about, and the last thing I want to do is burden her.

"You can go," I tell her.

But she doesn't listen. Instead, she waits patiently for me to redress, and even without the ability to speak, I know she wants to throw my own words back at me: *what the Third Guardian did to you, it isn't right. Fuck being a Chosen One.*

When I'm clothed, I expect her to give a satisfied nod and leave me be. Instead, she nods over her shoulder toward the servant door behind her, and I raise my eyebrows, the tears in my throat swallowed with surprise.

"You want me to go back through?"

She nods.

"You'll take me to the white drawing room?"

She nods again, this time with her fists curled at her side, and whips around.

I don't hesitate before following her into the servant corridor. I'll take help where I can get it, because I don't think any of this will be possible without it. Not to mention, Lucan is too busy to even keep me company.

It isn't until we round the second corner that I become brave enough to speak.

"Thank you, Eleni," I say.

For everything, I don't say. For not judging me. For not turning me in. For bringing me food and drawing my baths. For standing in solidarity with me, even the tiniest bit.

She waves a hand through the darkness like she's dismissing what she's doing for me, as if it's trivial. But the weight that falls on both of us is crushing.

"Whatever happens, it won't be for nothing," I tell her. "I know a secret, one the Guardians think they've protected. And as soon as I find it, I'm going to—"

Eleni whips around and smothers my mouth with her palm. Eyes wide, searching my face, she shakes her head rapidly.

She doesn't want to know.

I nod against her hand until she slowly pulls back.

Like all the kitchen staff I encountered, ignorance is bliss. Or maybe safety, actually. What the servants don't know they can't be tortured over.

We continue meandering the narrow passageway. Down those same spiral stairs, past the same light bulbs and doors, I trudge after her for what seems like longer than the first time. Until finally, we come to a door that looks exactly like all the rest, except it has a white outline.

The white drawing room.

Watching carefully, I try to get as close as I can so I don't miss a single twitch of Eleni and this mysterious door. Of course, she glowers at me when I step on her foot, before a long slim key materializes out of her sleeve.

It looks nothing like Diggory's key. This one is needle-like, long, sharp, and silver.

I quickly find out that's by design when Eleni presses it into the wood, not a keyhole, just the wood right where I imagine the latch would be. Her movements are purposeful as she lets me observe exactly what she's doing. The key slides in like butter, and then to my horror, she sinks her thumb into the razor sharp edge still slightly sticking out from the frame. And the door pops open.

Blood. She offered her blood to the door.

Swallowing down my stomach, my eyes cut back to Eleni. My mouth gapes, but I struggle to get any words out.

"Thank you," I say again, stilted.

She retrieves the little silver key, presses it horizontally into my palm, and pushes me through the doorway.

I blink against the brutal change of light.

The white drawing room is everything the corridor isn't.

And yes, it's definitely white. White sofas, a marble white fireplace, a white wooden coffee table, white flowers in white vases.

Bright sunlight streaks across the room, illuminating the room in an angelic way. My eyes bounce to and from every surface.

Books on the side tables. Busts of faces I don't recognize sitting on each side of the mantle. Lamps on the two desks that sit on opposite sides of the room. A tufted circular ottoman with a tray sitting atop it with what looks like a quill and ink.

But no paper, I notice, when I make my way toward it out of curiosity. I weave the sharp servant key through the hem of my sleeve as I take in the room.

Glass cloche. Glass cloche. Where is the glass cloche?

My heart burns. My hands tremble in anticipation, at how near I am to the very thing I need to bring the Wall of my nightmares down once and for all.

I close my eyes and channel Lucan's voice, trying to remember his words. They feel like forever ago, when I was in those catacombs. The same ones below my feet. The same ones I'll need to escape back through to find the nearest door.

Smack in the middle of the old white drawing room in the north wing, on a table, under a glass cloche.

My eyes fly back to the table sitting in the middle of three sofas arranged in a square around the fireplace.

I take a cautious step toward it, as if I could set off some type of trip wire, and *there*.

My hesitant steps become leaps, my heart ticking like a bomb. There's a glass cloche there, sitting on the coffee table, previously hidden behind a tall porcelain vase.

I blink when I reach it, confused. Lightheaded. This can't be right. Right? Is it a trick of the light?

My hands fly down so quickly, I almost knock the glass over, but I'm able to lift it in my sweaty palms.

And still, it's empty. There's nothing under it. No key. No *anything*.

Not even a speck of dust.

I'd diagnose myself with catatonia.

Cognitive: slow.

Mood: melancholy.

Muscular: stiff.

Behavioral: reckless.

But what I thought I knew no longer applies in this situation.

In all of my schooling, I've never learned about the effects of vampire venom or humans turning into stone. I've been living in the dark, but in reality, that is what's happening to me.

And now, it's officially over. No key. No hope. No change.

I'm back to the beginning, except this time I have the knowledge, the truth that's been concealed from me my entire life.

My laugh echoes around my bedroom, high-pitched, somewhat scary.

The necklace is nestled back in between my legs, but unfortunately, Lucan's voice doesn't rumble out of it to satisfy me the way I want.

What does one do when there's nothing left to do?

Swiveling my head around this disgustingly ornate bedroom, my eyes land on the rose-engraved door that leads out to the hallway

I march straight out of it without even bothering to close it behind me.

My legs lead me randomly through the hallways. I stare out windows. I sweep up and down staircases. Without a destination, I wander aimlessly, but this is my life now.

No Lucan, who must be regretting what transpired between us in the bathtub. Who is removing himself from this helpless situation.

No mother, who must be a stone by now. Dead.

No partner. No friends.

No telling how many minutes—or hours—later, I finally come across a random servant dusting the banisters.

She glances up at my footsteps as I approach her, space closing between us, uneasiness swelling.

As soon as I reach her, the words spew from my mouth without forethought. "Hello." I smile, though my teeth feel like chips of ice. "Could you please show me where the billiard room is?"

She nods, her body visibly loosening.

I traipse after her. Poker could be fun, and Tristan seems fun enough—unburdened and likely purposely oblivious to what's going on around him.

I can be like that.

After weaving through the hallways for a few minutes, the servant brings me to a pair of pretty double doors and gestures to them before turning on a heel and scurrying away.

"Thank you," I call after her, throwing the heavy doors open with a clunk.

While it's nothing as grand as the white drawing room, I'd say the musty yellowness of the wallpaper is still several, several steps above a housing complex.

Five heads snap toward me, but only one face changes from confusion to excitement.

"You finally came!" Tristan exclaims, smile wide enough to crinkle his eyes.

I walk around the entryway table, examining the art on the walls that depict faces I don't recognize.

When I reach them sprawled over the leather sofas, I shrug. "Betting seemed like a good time, suddenly."

One man eyes me up and down skeptically. "You look new. You didn't bring anything to bet with."

"Ah," I laugh, fluttering my eyelashes toward Tristan. "I thought it was my clothes you wanted me to bet with... or myself rather."

Tristan's smirk unfolds slowly, along with the other three men's.

"Saskia, this is Andreas, Geo, Victor, and Claudia," Tristan says, introducing me with a gesture toward each of them.

The men's names go in and out of my ears like vapor. Claudia, the woman across from me, studies me with a tilted head as I sit. She has thick, dark brown hair and full eyebrows that she raises at me skeptically.

Rolling my eyes playfully at her, I try to convey, *There's more than enough to go around, don't you think?*

And I'm not interested in them anyway. The one male I *am* interested in isn't anywhere to be found.

Be good, echoes in my skull, but I push it out. There's no reason to be good anymore. Arad can kill me. He can turn me into stone faster than 'normal.'

Whatever.

"How long have all of you been Chosen Ones?" I ask conversationally.

Victor, I think, speaks first. "Three short years."

I assess his body movements as he leans back on the sofa, crossing his ankle over his knee.

"Geo and I were Chosen with Tristan," Andreas says.

I do the math in my head again based on what Tristan told me. "So, a year ago then." Claudia just stares at me when I smile. "What about you?"

A beat passes where I think she won't answer. "Last blood moon."

A laugh almost bubbles out of me. The blood moon where I wished so hard to be Chosen.

"What's so funny?" she asks, catching the dark humor in my expression.

Shaking my head, I press two fingers to my lips. "Nothing. Just thinking about how much things change in such a short amount of time. What did you all do back in the city before you became palace prisoners?"

Everyone's narrow eyes cut to me, but Claudia's are the first to soften.

"Repair Crew," she says. "I was assigned to the screens and cameras for Complexes 500 to 600. What about you?"

"Healer," I say before a pause. "I miss it already."

"Not me," Tristan drawls. "This beats farming any day."

"I bet it does," Geo laughs.

"Now," I cut in, already eager for the next distraction, "who's going to teach me how to play?"

Tristan's face ticks up in delight, as a man's often does when he has the pleasure of teaching a woman something. Just like backgammon all over again. Hopefully this game is a little more exciting.

He explains the object of the game and how to make combinations with the cards that I'll hold and the cards he'll eventually put down on the table.

I'm half-listening as my mind wanders to my future, wondering if this is what it'll look like everyday... that is, until I'm confined to a bed.

"I'll deal everyone two cards," he says, slinging the red cards face down around the table until each of us has two. "The little blind..." Tristan points to Claudia on his left, who taps an index finger down on the table. "And the big blind..." Which must be Geo to my right because he throws down two fingers instead. "...they put up a bet before even seeing their cards. Now, all of us can look to see what we were dealt and decide if we want to call or raise."

"Call or raise?" I repeat, bemused.

"Call, you bet two," Andreas explains. "Raise and you're upping the bet to three or more."

I throw up two fingers, mimicking Geo the best I can.

He laughs. "Do you even have two to bet with?"

Looking down at myself, I can count at least three articles of clothing, so he must mean something else. "What are you betting with?" I ask.

All of them chuckle before Claudia whispers ominously, "Secrets. It's not like out there in the city, where we're not allowed to keep them. In here, secrets are our gold."

"Oh." As I check my cards, it takes a minute to register. I smile wide, arching an eyebrow. "I think I like poker already. And yes, I have two."

Around the circle, everyone watches me closely, and everyone, except Victor, who folds, matches the two-secret bet.

"Then I'll burn one," Tristan says.

I raise my eyebrows in fascination, waiting for him to physically light something on fire, but Tristan only takes one card off the top of the deck and places it off to the side.

Weirdly, disappointment flutters through me. A real fire would have been more interesting.

"Then the flop," Victor adds.

Tristan turns three cards over in the middle of the table. The first is an eight with what looks like a bunch of clovers, and the other two have faces on them.

"Eight of clubs," Tristan says for my benefit, I'm sure, "Jack of hearts, and Queen of hearts."

I check my cards against the three 'community' cards. I have a two with diamonds and a four with what looks like a pointy clover. I'm fairly certain these are shit cards when I recall the best combinations that Tristan told me, but I don't care.

Hard to care about anything when we're just playing silly little games in our graves.

They all look to Claudia, who takes her time calling before we all do the same. They sure must value their secrets here. Maybe because they're the only thing we truly own.

It all repeats again when Tristan places the "turn," a nine of spades—as I'm told the pointy clover is called. But when he places the "river," a three of hearts, down, I catch Claudia's almost imperceptible tilt of her lip, a tell that she has something good.

When she raises her bet with another secret, I fold with a shrug. I already owe the winner two secrets, and if I want to keep playing, I need to ration them wisely.

Everyone else folds as well, but Tristan raises her another secret.

"You're bluffing," he teases Claudia, then winks at me.

To my shock, that wink ignites me where it shouldn't, and I clamp my thighs together, trying to douse the heat creeping up my belly.

"Maybe *you're* bluffing," I say playfully, nudging his arm.

A rough vibration replaces the heat, confusing me more as it rumbles like thunder between my legs. Why is this man turning me on? He's an oaf.

I shift... until a low voice in my head makes me jolt in my seat.

What exactly are you doing, little nightmare?

LUCAN

Oh, she answers after her heartbeat slows and her head clears, realizing it was me—not fucking Tristan—making her ache between her legs. *Look who decided to come back.*

I'll always *come back*, I stress. *Preferably when you're not flirting with other males.*

Jealous? she goads me.

If you thought I wouldn't care, then you haven't been paying attention. Do I need to remind you whose name you moan?

She hesitates. But despite the desire flooding her senses, she doesn't stand up and march straight back to her bedroom like I hoped. Instead, she simply observes the poker game playing around her with a stubborn little purse of her lips that I can feel more than see.

Maybe I need reminding more than once a week, she observes.

I can't wait to do that—as hard and as often as you want—as soon as I figure out how to fucking save you.

You can't save me, she says, ignoring the singe that travels up her spine, *and I can't save myself.*

My heartbeat slows, my attention honing in on the slight change in her tone. Is she mad at me for being so absent lately? Maybe she needs a more detailed explanation...

I've had my head buried in books, reading journal after journal until my eyes burn—

No, Lucan. She cuts me off. *The key. It isn't there. I snuck into the white drawing room, looked under the glass cloche that was sitting right there in the middle of the room, just like you said.*

You did what? I seethe, my lip pulling back at the picture she's painting for me. Saskia talking back to a cold-blooded parasite is something I can barely tolerate by itself. Saskia actively *putting herself in danger* by sneaking into enemy territory is going to piss me off for centuries. *Were you hurt?* I ask, trying not to quiver as an explosion builds within me.

No. She scoffs. *And don't act so surprised. You weren't here to stop me, and I told you I wasn't going to stop looking.*

It's so very hard for her to lie to me. The war within her—being good for me versus her bratty little mouth and will—rages like night and day struggling for control, which only deepens my satisfaction, makes me wish I could have her in my bed this very second.

But there's something new: a terrifying little seed of indifference that's sprouted roots in her heart and taken hold.

What happened? I ask, dropping my voice carefully.

Like I said—no key in the white drawing room.

My entire world collapses as she confirms what she said before. A year ago, I would have seen it as the end of any hope for rescuing my kingdom. Now it's like a knife through my chest at the realization that rescuing *her*...

No. The key has to be somewhere. The vampires wouldn't just discard it.

Arad was probably lying to you about where it was this whole time, Saskia whispers. *Letting you believe what your father said was true.*

At the mention of his name, her memories bloom like weeds.

I hear the rip of her dress like I was standing right next to her, feel the fear crawling over my own skin.

The fucking *monster.*

Inhaling through my nose to try to keep my emotions from bursting through my ribcage, I clench my canines together so hard, I slice through my own bottom lip, and the copper taste of my blood fills my mouth.

I'm trying to find a way to get you out of there. To stop you from turning to stone. To set you free of this damn cage. And I'm doing everything in my power I can possibly think of as quickly as I can do it. If you can't promise me you'll be good, then promise me, Saskia, the first chance you see to escape, you take it. Without hesitation. No questions asked.

I've never felt so helpless in my life.

Her doubt and indifference, though, still leak from her like thick sap, sticky and hard to remove, because she doesn't believe she'll ever find an escape.

And what did you find? she asks with an edge in her voice.

My anger at myself swells again suddenly. What am I supposed to say? I found out some Guardian was fucking a human? Of course, this isn't news. Apparently, they do it all the time. And it means absolutely nothing. It has no bearing on our current situation that the Thirteenth Guardian was likely killed by his own kind as soon as they found out he was conversing with my father. They still won.

I swallow down my dread and tell her, *I'm still looking.*

Her inner laugh comes out forced. She doesn't have to tell me she told me so.

But vampires aren't all bad, I decide to add. Maybe that'll give her some kind of hope again. *The Thirteenth in particular, he wanted to help my father. He wanted more for humans. He even loved one.*

Shock oscillates through her. Yes. Maybe it'll jumpstart something in her again, give her enough oxygen to stoke that fire she's back to suppressing.

But Saskia quickly shutters it.

Look how that turned out, she says, her voice sarcastically saccharine. *There's still the Wall. We're still bred to be slaughtered. And the Thirteenth Guardian is still dead.*

Okay then. I may need to find something with a tiny bit more shock value to bring her back to me.

SASKIA

F lush," Claudia says, grinning.

Eyeing both of their cards now face-up, I see she indeed has all hearts and Tristan has a sad pair of threes.

I chuckle, and Tristan jerks his head back with a smirk.

"You lost just as bad," he teases me.

"It was my first game," I say, blinking innocently.

Claudia sits back against the sofa, relishing in her winning hand. "Time to collect."

One by one, the men rise to their feet and sit beside her. Her eyes stay trained on my face, making me shift uncomfortably in my seat, as they each whisper in her ear.

What did you put up? Lucan asks me hesitantly.

Well, my clothes at first. But they were betting with secrets.

Lucan snaps his teeth. *I'm late by twenty goddamn minutes and you find yourself in the middle of a strip poker game. Great.*

I fold my lips into my smile, just a little too happy to keep it off my face. *You're cute when you're angry.*

If you could actually see me, he growls, *you wouldn't think so.*

My thoughts convey that I very much doubt it. In fact, I think it'd be even sexier—amber eyes and a hulking monstrous form stalking over me, making me obey. What else is there to dream about now that all hope is gone?

After Tristan returns to his chair, Claudia levels me with a stare. "Well?"

Glancing down at my cleavage, I joke, "Do you want my dress or..."

She huffs. "This girl's got nothing. Tristan, next time you need to consult us before inviting someone to play. This isn't social hour for your dates."

"I have secrets," I insist, raising my chin as I rise and walk around the table before I mumble, "Along with a sense of humor."

Saskia... Lucan warns. But if I understand correctly, a bet is a bet. You don't go back on one.

Claudia tracks my movements, watching me settle next to her, and she doesn't back away when I lean in closely.

I don't know the quality of the other's secrets, or if mine are even relative, but they're all I have.

"I snuck into the north wing," I whisper in her ear so that the others can't hear. "And we're all turning to stone."

Claudia tenses. For a moment, she pulls away from me, blinking into my face while the others watch on uncertainly. Then she lets out a harsh laugh. "You're lying."

"I'm not," I say, sitting back.

"You figured that all out in a week?"

I throw my hands up. "It's not my fault if you don't pay attention."

"I pay attention," Tristan interjects, jokingly placing a hand over his heart like I've wounded his ego.

I'm quick to roll my eyes, no longer worried about who might be offended by what. "You're the *worst,*" I quip. "All those people lying in bed all day sleeping. Right."

"What people?" Geo asks.

I shake my head. Fuck it. They can all know my secret. It pertains to their own futures anyway, and whether I trust them or not has no relevance. Death is inevitable. "The people turning to stone."

They blink back at me before all five of them bark out laughs. I just blink back, exasperated, until only Claudia's chortle dies.

"What people?" Claudia asks with a darker tone to her voice.

Standing, I fluff out the skirt of my dress. No one moves as I step toward the door.

"Well, are you coming?" I ask, turning around.

Tristan scrambles to his feet.

"Not you. Claudia."

Claudia takes a moment, her eyebrows creasing deeper. "Where?"

"To prove myself."

Maybe she doesn't want to know the truth, Lucan offers, which makes me pause.

"Only if you want," I add sincerely.

Geo shrugs. Andreas bounces his eyes between everyone. Victor isn't paying attention. And Tristan pouts.

Patiently, I wait—the room seems to freeze in place, everyone held in a moment of uneasiness—until, finally, Claudia rises slowly without a word and follows me out the room.

My steps are quick, purposeful. I know exactly which path to take, down the identical hallways, up the thousandth staircase.

Claudia, half-intrigued, half-skeptical, stays right on my heels with her anticipation palpable against my back.

I don't even bother trying to step lightly when we come to the last set of stairs. I'd tell Arad to his face that I discovered the effects of his venom, and I'd know he'd laugh in *my* face and ask me what it feels like to see into my future.

Knocking lightly on Sylvia's door, I try to prepare Claudia before I open it.

"Her name is Sylvia. She can barely move, and she's hard of hearing, so try to enunciate so she can read your lips."

Claudia's face tightens with a hint of fear, like whoever we're about to encounter could rip her head off.

In a moment of panic, I question whether this is the right thing to do. If you could see the future, would you actually choose to know when and how you were going to die? Or would you just live every day to the fullest?

The problem is, though, I'm not sure this is living. And Claudia could have easily discovered this herself if she'd just cared about her fellow Chosen Ones. Their suffering has always been only ten floors above her head. All she's had to do is look up and see.

Clenching my jaw, I push open the door.

The light from the tiny window cuts a sunbeam across the room, the dust illuminated as it hangs in the air.

And the tiny bed in the middle of the room is...

Empty.

Nothing but a bare mattress—no trace of Sylvia except the outline of her body pressed into it like a stone stamp.

My gasp claws out of my throat, my voice ragged and stilted. "No."

"Where is she?" Claudia whispers over my shoulder, surveying the room like someone still might pop out of the blank walls.

"*No,*" I sob out again, rushing over to the side of the bed. "She's... gone."

I can't bring myself to say it—dead—but I know in my bones that her fossilization must have reached its last phase. In a way, she died on my watch—just like her father.

As I fall to the mattress, Claudia watches me intensely, chewing on the inside of her cheek in shock. Unsure of what to say, what to do.

I'm sorry, Saskia, Lucan murmurs. *I'm so sorry. She knew, though, in the end that you would continue what she started. That it wasn't for nothing.*

Wasn't it, though? I bite back, tears wetting my face now.

All of this has truly been for nothing. My mother is gone. Diggory is gone. Now Sylvia.

Instantly, the image of that body on a stretcher rolls through my mind. That person was stone, I'm sure of it now, and the servants put them somewhere in the north wing.

Claudia crosses the room and sits somberly in the wooden chair angled in the corner. Each of my breaths drag through my lungs like gravel, my face buried in my hands, until she speaks out of nowhere.

"About six months ago, I started waking up every morning exhausted. Like I hadn't gotten a second of sleep despite a full eight hours passing. My partner, who is such a heavy sleeper, thought I was sleepwalking. So, I brought home a tiny camera out of the Repair Inventory and set it up in my bedroom. I rewired it to my screen to record one night, just to see. I thought it couldn't hurt." She takes several deep breaths that mirror the panic in mine. "But instead of finding out that I was in some drowsy trance, I watched a Guardian drink my own blood right from my neck as I slept."

I gape at her, trying to process what she just said. A Guardian was sneaking into her housing unit? To drink from her while she slept? Before she was even Chosen?

Claudia nods at the disbelief on my face. "That was just the beginning of the end. I set up a few more stolen cameras between the complexes and caught more than one Guardian stalking in and out of doors in the alleyways. Always at night, never lingering too long in one part of the city. I don't know how they were getting around..."

"The catacombs," I say, horrified.

"What?"

"There are catacombs beneath our city." I swallow. "Tunnels from the palace leading to the complexes. They must have been using those to..."

I can't even finish the thought, but a young face swirls in my mind, a patient whose blood pressure was too low, who'd woken up dizzy even though we could never find out what was wrong with her. But I know now. *Just the other night, I dreamed of something like that. A Guardian, actually... just stared down at me and told me to go back to sleep.*

That had never been a dream. I grab my throat, as if that'll help me breathe better, the enormity of how vile the Guardians actually are crashing into me. They aren't just taking from us in a legal way. They're taking from us in illegal ways, too.

They created the law, Lucan mutters angrily. *Of course, they feel entitled to breaking it. They think they're above it.*

"What did you do when you found out?" I ask Claudia.

"Told my partner, thinking that he would help me figure out how to stop them." Claudia shrugs noncommittally. "But it was like talking to the Wall. My partner didn't want to hear it. He thought the Guardians must have a reason. That they needed extra strength to continue to protect us from the Monster. And what did it matter anyway if they took a little of my blood while I slept? It was an honor, he said. Told me to forget it."

My gaze lands on Sylvia's empty bed, and grief buries itself into my stomach all over again. Would *everyone* think this is an honor if they found out what happens to the Chosen Ones and what happens to the innocents while they sleep? Or would some stand with Claudia and me, knowing that it's wrong, knowing that we can't keep being complacent?

I lift my chin and wipe the tears clinging to my cheeks with the heels of my palms.

"You couldn't forget it, could you? That's why they Chose you?"

Claudia nods. "I tried to go back to normal, but the secret festered inside me. I couldn't stop questioning everything about this city and life. But there's nothing I can do in here."

"Actually..." I muse, exhaling a shaky breath at the thought of that tech room in the north wing. At the thought of those servants delivering food to the housing complexes.

Claudia cocks an eyebrow. "What?"

Lucan's presence stills, too. *Yeah... what?*

My fists curl in my lap, my nails digging into my palms. "The thing about stripping us of everything means now we have nothing to lose. And there's one last thing we can try."

"Are you sure she'll even listen to us?" Claudia asks when we're safely tucked away back in my bedroom, both of us sitting nervously on the edge of my bed.

Eleni is due to deliver my dinner at any moment, and I wring my hands in my lap.

"I'm sure she'll listen for at least the first few seconds. After that..." I grimace.

Claudia snorts. "Maybe you're making her do too much work. Have you even eaten a meal in the dining room yet?"

"Not except for that first night and the next morning, when they made us."

She raises her eyebrows. "Usually, the newly Chosen Ones take all meals downstairs until they're a few months in. The Third Guardian must be going out of his mind."

I scrunch my nose. "I don't really care. His obsession with me will be his downfall."

My downfall, too, Lucan's voice drifts out to me for the hundredth time, although I don't acknowledge it. *I don't want to lose you. I can't lose you, little nightmare.*

The first time he'd said it with conviction, actually pleading with me, but I realized somewhere after the tenth occurrence that his subconscious was bleeding through, struggling to be contained.

What Lucan doesn't realize is that he's already lost me. He has been losing me from the very moment he met me.

Lucan, I say softly. *I need to do this.*

His pain shoots like a bolt of lightning through my core. Almost like an acknowledgment that he knows, but he can still be pissed off and angry.

Alone, I add, *for right now. I'll be back when they leave, before I fall asleep. I promise.*

And is this a promise you'll keep?

Only if you're good, I try to tease, but a lump swells in my throat anyway.

Lucan doesn't respond, but I feel his acknowledgment, his distressed thoughts latching onto me like claws trying to keep me grounded. As I slip the necklace underneath my mattress, a howl whips through the evening air, loud and distressing. As if the Monster is in mourning.

I blink back my tears as Claudia jumps at the sound. She stares at me for a beat before rubbing her arms like the wail raised gooseflesh along her skin.

Then she nods.

The gravity of what we're going to attempt settles over us like a heavy, uncomfortable blanket. Fidgeting, we wait until the servant door finally pops open, and Eleni emerges with my tray of food.

When she sees both of us, she stops dead in her tracks and lets out an angry sigh. She cuts me a look that says *what did you do now?*

"Hear us out," I blurt, standing quickly and taking the tray from her arms.

My stomach twists, too wound up to eat anyway, and I practically drop the tray onto my dresser from my fraying nerves.

Steadying my trembling hands, I twist around to face the two other women in my room, who are staring at each other with mirrored expressions of uncertainty.

"Eleni, this is Claudia." I don't mention the fact that we've just met, that I'm fully aware of how insane what I'm about to propose sounds... and that I likely won't make it out alive to see this plan come to fruition.

Claudia smiles reassuringly at Eleni, who flicks a glare in my direction

"I know," I start with a breath, "about the Chosen Ones turning to stone. What I don't know is where they take them." My voice turns desperate, a pleading tone that burns my lungs, and I clench my teeth to keep it from breaking. "We want to find it. Expose it. But to do that, we need your help."

Eleni's pupils dilate in shock. She looks between Claudia and me with a firm shake of her head.

"There's cameras within the palace, aren't there?" I continue.

That fountain I saw on the screen in the tech room, two servants walking around it. I'm sure of that now, how it looked identical to the one in Sylvia's memory. Originally, I thought the Guardians wouldn't want cameras in their own private hallways, but they're recording—everything, all the time—even within these walls. Even each other.

Without waiting for Eleni to confirm it, I power on. "Claudia was a camera technician on the Repair Crew. With your help, we can show the people of Xantera what's really happening. We can reveal the truth, Eleni, on each and every screen that the Guardians use to control us." I grimace. "But I need you to lead Claudia through the servant passageway and show her where the tech room is. She'll take over from there. Without more people standing up to the Guardians, without more people rebelling against this system, nothing will ever change. It's the only way to end this."

To her credit, Eleni doesn't bolt right back into the servant corridor as soon as I stop to take a breath.

"I'm willing to do this," Claudia says. "I'm willing to die if they catch me or find out it was me. I'm dead now or later." She shrugs. "Either way."

Eleni tilts her head, waiting for us to continue with a flaring intensity in her eyes, like she knows there's more. Like there's one more problem we all know needs fixed.

"And when they do find out, the people are going to need a leader," I push on. "Someone who knows exactly what's happening and can organize a rebellion. I think that could be my assigned partner, Malcolm."

As a teacher, I couldn't imagine anyone who'd better fit the role. And Malcolm has something to fight for, too: the freedom to love who you want.

"But first," I hurry on, "I need to get a message to him, and I realized that day you dragged me into the kitchen that I can do that. It's possible, Eleni. All these palace servants who deliver food through our door slats. I just need you to put a letter for me on his tray. He lives in Complex 189, and it just needs to be under his plate. I'll write it and tell him everything if you can make sure it gets there."

Her jaw ticks, and one side of her lips twitches up into a hint of a smile. But it vanishes as quickly as it appeared.

"That's all we ask. No one will ever know you helped us. If this goes sideways, Claudia and I will take it to our stoned graves. I promise."

"I promise," Claudia echoes.

Eleni's gaze stays on me, her eyebrows furrowed in a question. She motions toward me with a flick of her wrist.

"What am I going to do?" I ask, and she nods her confirmation. I swallow down the lump that forms in my throat before my voice comes out thick. "Well, I'm going to be the distraction."

LUCAN

I don't dare shift back into my human form and break my connection with Saskia even long after I feel her consciousness slip into dreams.

As the mist thickens around me and the cold settles across my skin like a shroud, I curl up as best as I can and try to stay awake. To bask in these last few hours with the woman I never even got to have for a second, let alone forever.

Soon, though, a tug on our connection has my ears perking, my nostrils flaring as I sense Saskia's emotions rise and her mind whirl. Dreaming. She's just dreaming.

And I can't help but close my eyes and experience it alongside her.

Darkness churns through her brain, eddying like a windstorm. I frown, trying to find Saskia in the middle of it all. Rain begins to pelt me from above, pounding down and crashing against the floor—no, not rain. Objects. Clocks and jewelry and mirrors. Buttons and lightbulbs and keys. They shatter, crack, and clang at my feet, and I throw an arm over my head to squint into the darkness.

"Saskia?" I call.

She whimpers somewhere to my left, and I jerk my head, but—nothing. The ground rumbles beneath my feet, and suddenly, walls are cracking from the ground all around me, rising up with shuddering force until I'm surrounded by four of them.

Not just trapped within the Wall, but trapped in a cube of a housing unit. One spotless living room, one square kitchen, one blank screen, four symmetrical doors. A lightbulb pops on above my head, and the noise of the storm cuts off abruptly.

"Saskia?" I ask again, this time whirling around.

She's not there, but voices murmur from beyond one of the bedroom doors.

Fuck, it's utterly soulless in here. It's a wonder Saskia developed a personality at all, being raised in this uniformed prison her whole life. My heart rips itself in half when I realize I'll never get to show her what a true home looks like, where the light glows warmly, where the fire flickers in the hearth, where the seats are ripped and worn and the beds creak in welcome when you climb in.

"Saskia," I say, this time more firmly, trying to find her subconscious within this dream, but the voices only grow louder on the other side of the door.

And I don't think either of them belong to her.

"You have to," a female voice wafts out, shaking and scared.

"I can't keep doing this to you, Maribel." That's a male's voice. Harsher. More firm. "You're sick."

"I'm fine."

"You're *not* fine. You're going to die if it happens again."

"Well, *you're* going to die if you don't."

"Then so be it. I can't..."

The voices fade, the ground rumbles, and moonlight slices into the housing unit as thick as blood. So thick that I actually feel the wet touch of it graze my skin. But before I can try to wipe it off my arms, my hands, that same bedroom door bursts open.

A woman stumbles out after a man, and even in this lucid state, I can tell it's Saskia's parents. Her father has the same shade of hair, her mother the same splattering of freckles. Both would be beautiful, if she didn't look so ghostly pale and he wasn't clutching his throat. Spluttering. Coughing. Gagging.

Dropping to his knees, Saskia's father begins to convulse.

Screams bounce around the room from every direction, coming from nowhere and everywhere all at once. Saskia's mother shakes her father, trying to get him to wake up, and then she does something so peculiar I have to rub my eyes: she jams her arm into his open mouth, where... no, the foam building around his lips is too thick.

And then his convulsing stops.

But the screaming continues, finally streaming from one source.

When I whip my head to the right, I finally find Saskia—not as a little girl, when this happened, but as herself, cowering in the corner, covering her own ears while she screams.

"Saskia, hey. It's okay." I sprint to her and grip her shoulders. "I'm here. It's just a nightmare. You just have to wake up for me, okay? Wake up, baby."

She doesn't see me, but I see her. I see her more clearly than anything I ever have before, and I grab her jaw with one hand and swallow her scream with my lips.

"Lucan," she sighs into my mouth, eyes still clamped shut. I drop my head to her neck, skimming my teeth over the sensitive skin below her ear.

I groan. She gasps.

"I'm here," I whisper against her racing pulse.

It's not real. It's her imagination, my imagination. Our minds intertwining desperately, trying everything to manifest this into existence while the heat of my body presses her against the wall.

Her hips grind against mine as if she could bring this dream to actual life. Her hands skate up my chest before she grasps the back of my neck tightly. My fingers lace into her hair, tugging her mouth back up to mine.

Saskia pulls me closer, clinging to me, not wanting to let go. Because as soon as we do, our fantasy will end, the illusion we've created will crumble, and once again, we'll be two people who can't reach each other.

Her lips part.

Instantly, the world collapses around us, our tongues meeting in this subreality.

"No," she cries softly as darkness fades.

And then she's gone.

SASKIA

Opening my eyes, I find myself tangled in the sheets, sweaty and disoriented.

I lie on my back, and with a calming breath, melt back into the mattress.

My mother sick, my father dying. That *kiss*.

It was only a dream, Lucan whispers hoarsely, filling my mind. His voice sounds strained, tired, like he hasn't gone to sleep all night. *And you don't have to do this.*

I do, though.

His voice drops to a chilling octave, one worthy of belonging to a Monster. *And what if I commanded you not to?*

My breath hitches. *I thought you said you couldn't control me, not if I didn't want to be.*

Care to find out? he growls. *A battle for your mind.*

After a split second of internal debate, I sigh out, *You would never do that.*

Lucan's anger that he knows I'm right, that his own morals would never allow him to command me without my consent, bursts out as if I lit him on fire.

He pivots with a different, deeper tone that I feel all the way down to my toes. *Then I'll just make you* want *to stay in this bed all day, little nightmare.*

A spark zaps up my spine, and Lucan chuckles darkly.

You can't hide that desire from me. Pain. Pleasure. Mixed. I'll drive you out of your mind with it. If that's what you want, what you need. You want to feel alive? I'll shock you back to life. You want to feel reckless? I'll absolutely wreck you.

Filthy images flicker through my mind, thanks to Lucan, and I fist the sheets in response as my own dark fantasies morph into his, merging together when he picks them out of the recesses of my mind. Even though he's miles away, the sensation of his teeth drags down my thigh.

I gasp. *If only you could actually touch me,* I can't help but think.

A whimper leaves my lips when the feeling dissolves into claws up my inner thighs, and his canines sink into my shoulder. I breathe through my nose, my mind on fire, as if I'm pinned to the bed.

Get up, I tell myself uselessly.

Everything in me wants to lie here.

Overpower him, I tell myself weakly.

But I don't mean it. So I stay.

Because I want this. I want him. And sadly, this is the only way I'll ever have him.

And then a pressure falls between my legs, as if Lucan is actually circling my clit with his thumb. My own arms lay next to me like boulders.

A moan rips from my mouth, my back arching off the bed, my legs widening.

My mind's suspended in a lucid dream, one where Lucan controls every aspect of this alternate reality in which I've submitted all control to him.

Lucan, I breathe when the pressure increases, the pace quickens, and then scream in frustration when it all comes to a crashing halt.

You want to come? he asks roughly. *Then stay put. Don't get out of this bed. Don't walk out of this room. And I'll pleasure you until you can't fucking think straight.*

Frustration winds around my ribcage, squeezing tightly. I'm facing death, and he's withholding orgasms. But I can't promise to be good. I never could. My mind is made up.

I let my body recover. Wait until my heartbeat slows. Cursing him the entire damn time.

No, Saskia, he begs out in agony when I throw back my blankets and march to the armoire. *Please. I'm sorry I ever told you to do this. I take it back. I take it back.*

There's no other way, Lucan. My heart squeezes at his desperation, but I slip out of my pajamas and into a green silk dress I've been saving for the perfect occasion. The neckline rises higher than all the others, with an ideal collar that can tuck away the vial of my necklace. I slide it behind the lace, concealing it perfectly against the curve of my breast. *I won't leave you behind though. Every step of the way you can be with me... if you want.*

I'm not going anywhere, he says, voice hardened. *For the last time, I'm not leaving you.*

So I pull back my hair into a bun and knock once with my knuckle against the servant door to alert Eleni.

Then I tell Lucan, *Promise you won't distract me,* and throw open my bedroom door.

Probably for the last time.

I follow the hallway path Eleni mapped out for me exactly as I memorized. But nothing could have prepared me for actually laying my eyes on the entrance to the north wing.

The massive double doors, black and white marble etched in elaborate swirls of gold, stretch high above my head at least two stories up. In the middle of each door hangs a knocker, a heavy-looking circular bar that appears to be pure gold.

Two sentries flank the entranceway, their expressions almost happy as they mutter back and forth to each other.

Their swords hang casually from their belts, their uniforms much more extravagant than the sentries' who roam the city.

They straighten when they notice me heading straight for them, a hand flying to the hilt of each of their weapons as if I pose a threat to them. As if I'm not just some human woman who can so easily bleed.

But my footsteps never waver. My limbs don't ever go numb. In this moment, I feel as if I could take on a vampire—just as strong, just as powerful. As if my eyes leak their own venom. Each step feels invigorating.

"Is a Guardian expecting you?" one of the sentries demands as soon as I'm within twenty feet.

"I need to speak to the Third."

The other sentry takes a step toward me. "That wasn't an answer to his question."

"I don't answer to you."

His eyes flare briefly before he huffs out a laugh. "You Chosen Ones think you're all special. You don't get in without an invitation."

I eye the door, searching for a knob that doesn't exist.

Of *course*, there's no doorknob. What do I have to do to make it open? Slice my palm and offer it my blood? Drop to my knees and pledge my allegiance to the Twelve? Sacrifice my body for their eternal pleasure?

Instead, I fling myself at the door before the sentries can react and pound my fist against the door with a heavy thud.

Once, twice. And then strong arms pull me back, holding me steady against his armor.

The other sentry's face goes red with rage, then white with panic. "What do you think you're doing?"

Lucan growls out a warning they can't hear. Thrashing against the tight grip around my waist, I raise my voice to a level that hopefully reverberates past the door.

"I want to speak to the Third Guardian!" I reach for the gold knocker. "I need him!"

I didn't realize before, but it has tiny spikes jutting out from all directions—exactly like miniature vampire fangs.

They prick my skin when I grab hold of it, the sting traveling up my arm at the surprising burst of venom that infiltrates my bloodstream. Fuck. But I clench my teeth and manage to knock again.

This time, the echo booms loud enough to vibrate the polished floor.

Yes. Someone had to have heard that. Based on the blanched face of the sentry who rips my arm away from the knocker and slaps a hand over my mouth, he's scared one of them is going to come investigate.

"Get off of me!" I scream into his palm, kicking the sentry's shins. Upping the theatrics.

I hope the Third Guardian is watching this play out right now on a screen. I hope every single tech servant turns their entire focus onto this scene, not the one unfolding elsewhere. Not Eleni and Claudia.

As soon as the sentry loosens his grip over my mouth, I spit, "The Third Guardian will have your head on a pike for handling me like this."

There. Let Arad think I'm desperate for him.

Before the sentries can reply, the door cranks open with an echoing screech.

As the Seventh Guardian steps through the opening, I don't waste time revamping my performance. Twisting, I knee one of the sentries in the balls and rake my fingernails down the other one's arms locked around me. Both of them shout. I scream. And the Seventh Guardian looks on, clearly torn between amusement and disgust.

"What seems to be the issue?" she asks, tight lipped, when I finally fall still. Her gaze roves down my body, then up to my face. Her dark eyebrows tick up in recognition.

"This Chosen One," one of the sentries stumbles, tightening his hold on me with a punishing grip that is surely going to leave bruises. "She insists—"

More footsteps approach from behind the Seventh Guardian, making the sentry snap his mouth shut. This time it's the Ninth, his hair slicked back over his head, who eyes the scene with glittering interest.

"Emrys," the Seventh says over her shoulder. "Please tell Arad his Chosen One has arrived." She cocks an eyebrow at me. "Unless you're looking to expand your taste?"

I cough into my fist. "Oh. No, thank you. I'm here for the Third Guardian."

She sighs. "Very well." Fanning her arms out in each direction, she waves the sentries off. "Back to your post."

They release me and scramble against the doorframe, standing rigidly and staring straight ahead, leaving me in an awkward silence with the Seventh Guardian. Like all the other vampires, her presence cascades over me, thick and cloying and dangerous.

"Quite the feisty thing, aren't you?" she says around a close-lipped smile. "I can see why he's become fixated on you." She tsks, crossing her arms across her chest. "So emotional, males. They never learn."

Then she turns on her heel as Arad approaches from behind, and with my eyes now locked on his, she gets lost in my peripheral vision.

"Saskia," he murmurs, clearly pleased. "This couldn't wait?"

"No," I say confidently. "It's now or never."

The sentries' eyes flick toward me, and I give them a smug grin, but my victorious mood quickly sours as soon as Arad inhales through his nose. Breathing me in.

Once again, he places his cold, deadish hand against the small of my back and directs me down the hallway, unable to hear Lucan's possessive snarl that rips through my head.

I pretend to be enamored with the Guardians' statues, swinging my head left and right like I've never encountered anything so grand before in my life, like everything erected here is completely new to me.

"I commissioned these myself," Arad says into my ear. "I'm a big supporter of the arts."

"The flags, the statues, the paintings everywhere in the city? That's all you?" I ask loudly. So loudly, my voice echoes, and I hope all the cameras are pointed toward me.

He hums. "Of course."

"Perhaps I underestimated you."

"Creativity is important," he says.

"For the select few," I reply, voice strained.

Arad tightens his fingers against my back. "For the worthy."

I swallow my scoff, but Lucan's is loud and clear. And I can't help but throw my next thoughts at him. *For someone who's supposed to be quiet, you sure do make a lot of noise.*

I never promised I'd be quiet, actually, he quips back.

I swallow a sad smile. *Looks like we both need to work on our promise-making abilities.*

When we come to Arad's door, I hesitate. It's surprisingly simple. No elaborate design etched into the wood. My uneasiness heightens when he slips a key out of his pocket and into the keyhole, unsure if this is even his bedroom. Maybe he's leading me straight to a dungeon...

I exhale in relief when the door opens to reveal the same place I saw in Sylvia's memories—more like a sprawling home inside a palace than a bedroom, but definitely not a dungeon.

We step into a foyer which breaks off into multiple rooms where leather sofas surround thick mahogany tables. Oil paintings hang in rows along the wall, and shelves upon shelves display a variety of objects: glass vases filled with dead flowers, animal skulls, sculptures that look carved from bone, and mirrors. Mirrors everywhere, reflecting our trek into the room from a dozen different angles.

"I want you to be comfortable here," Arad says softly over my shoulder. He crosses the room and settles into a brown, oversized leather loveseat situated underneath a stained glass window. He places a flat palm down beside him. "Come sit."

Listening isn't really my strong suit anymore. Instead, I meander along the perimeter of the room.

I stop and cock my head at a portrait hanging from the wall. A young boy with short golden hair sits in a wooden chair with an imposing figure looming over him, a hand placed on his shoulder. The man's fingertips seem to dig into him like hooks, and the boy's eyes almost have a haunting quality. Staring blankly.

I freeze, realizing—

"That's me as a child," Arad offers proudly. "With my father."

Vampires as children? The thought is horrific—them learning to drink the blood of humans, to slowly kill them.

"No wonder you still force those pills on us," I mutter, somewhat relieved.

"It's rare for our species to have children together, but not impossible. Better safe than sorry." He chuckles as if I've missed the punchline of some kind of joke. "Wouldn't want a hundred other Guardians running around, would we?"

I can't clamp down on the bite to my voice as I continue meandering throughout the room. "What, your eleven other brothers and sisters are too much competition as is?"

His teeth freeze in an icy smile. "The other Guardians aren't my true brothers and sisters. We simply decided to come together to protect and serve you... valuable humans."

For a moment, I stare at the blatant lie written all over his face. The Guardians came together because one vampire wouldn't have been able to defeat Lucan's grandfather, more like. Then I run my hands, as if absentmindedly, over an ornate box sitting on a tall, circular table and murmur, "Of course. And you protect us *so* well, don't you?"

I hold my breath and flip open the box by its little silver hinge. Disappointment floods through me when my gaze lands on a pile of small, flat objects inside—not a key like the one Sylvia stole from the Eleventh Guardian. Not *the* key.

"They're coins," Arad says when I pick one of the round objects up and examine the face engraved on its surface. "Money from a long time ago. Not that you need to worry about such things."

I drop it back into the box with a clink.

Arad cranes his neck as I walk, lets me take my time running fingers over books, picking up stone carvings, and rifling through drawers before his voice takes on an impatient edge. "As amusing as it is to watch you touch everything that belongs to me, I said *come sit.*"

I slam the drawer shut, and without much choice, settle beside him. Trying not to let our arms brush, even though I'm so close I smell the chilled, minty scent wafting off of him.

Arad gives me a smile that makes me think he truly considers himself the god worth worshiping. "I'm very happy you finally came to your senses. This is so much better than simply taking it. After yesterday, seeing you..."

He picks up my hand, then examines my fingers where the door-knob pricked me. Little droplets of blood bead against my skin.

His eyes brighten. "...tasting you."

With a crazed look, he licks his lips and then dips his head to do the same to my tiny wounds before moving down my palm and piercing my wrist with his icy fangs.

He drinks and drinks. So long that my worry knocks around in my chest, and I can feel Lucan's presence surrounding me, holding me close because that's the only thing he can do. The venom heats my bloodstream, stronger than the laced doorknob, flooding into my heart with a potency that feels dangerous.

Until finally, Arad pulls back with lust-filled eyes, drunk on my blood.

A hum forms in the back of his throat as his eyes drift down to the gold strappy heels I'm wearing. "May I?"

I nod, gagging in my throat as I lift my leg up.

Arad takes his time undoing the little buckle resting against my ankle bone. He dips his head further when the strap releases, unable to restrain himself.

One of his fingers trails along my shin, followed by his nose. Smelling me.

"Saskia, you are my most delicious prize," he murmurs, his tongue sweeping out along my knee. Then he slowly undoes the other shoe until I'm barefoot. "Something about you... I'm consumed."

He smiles, his lips against my skin. His head exactly where I want it.

Saskia, no! Lucan pleads with me a millisecond before my decision is solidified in my own mind. His entire being seems to shatter into a million pieces within my heart.

"And finally, I'm going to bite into that precious neck. When I'm finished with you, you'll be completely devoted to me—"

Picking up the heavy vase on the table next to me, I smash it over Arad's skull and run straight for the door.

Out in the hallway, through the Guardian statues, I burst through the open doorway at the very end, feeling a gust of fresh air against my face for the first time since Sanctuary Sunday.

Now, though, I'm not leaning over a balcony from up high but panting on the ground floor, in some kind of outdoor courtyard bordered by hedges and overflowing with rosebushes—the same garden from Sylvia's memories.

When I look up, the underside of a balcony blocks my full view of the sky, boxing me in.

Like I just ran straight into a trap.

With my heartbeat shooting up my throat, I streak down a cobbled path that winds between perfectly pruned shrubs, searching for the back of the courtyard... but stop when I come face to face with a barrier too great to surpass.

Not just any wall, but *the* Wall, looming over me with those same spiderwebbing veins that I came face-to-face with down in the catacombs.

Permission granted to speak again, I say, attempting to distract both of us from the fact that I've solidified my death sentence. His voice will be the last thing I hear—the only way I want to go.

I can smell you again, little nightmare. Roses, Lucan says in a voice that has every hair on the back of my neck standing on end for him. *I'm right on the other side. Right here.*

Our connection pulls taut, as if we're trying to reel each other in, but Arad's voice drifts out from behind me on the next gust of wind.

"Saskia. Oh, *Saskia.*" His voice drips with barely-suppressed wrath. "I've been so patient with you, but I'm afraid you've gone too far this time."

Shit. I glance around, desperate for a place to crouch and hide. But I can feel his presence strolling closer, and my eyes land on a marble staircase on the far side of the garden, vines crawling up the railings as it twines up to the balcony above.

I sprint toward it and take the steps two at a time.

My least favorite thing in the world, I remind Lucan, trying to breathe through my panic. *Fucking stairs.*

Focus for me, Saskia. Don't...

His voice catches and crumbles, like he doesn't even know what he can say in these last few moments before I finally meet my doom. At the same time, Arad's footsteps quicken behind me, and I muster a burst of strength to throw myself onto the terrace above.

Please be a way out. Please be a way out.

There's not. Instead, this second level of the garden tinkles with fountains and smooth, lifelike statues situated between hydrangeas every few feet, just as boxed in as the first level was. The Wall still surrounds the back half, while yet another terrace hangs above us, cutting off everything but a few ribbons of sunset that streak through the gaps. The overlapping of light and shadow makes the whole space look like a backgammon board.

With me as a pawn.

And Arad the hand reaching in to grab me.

"You can run, Saskia," his voice drifts out from behind me again, heavy footsteps clunking up the stairs, "but I will catch you. You can hide, but I will find you. You can scream, but no one will hear you."

I WILL, Lucan roars through our bond. *I'LL HEAR HER SCREAM!*

And then the world trembles as he slams himself into the Wall and a roar tears out of his throat, sending a flock of birds bursting from the nearest hydrangea bush.

Arad's footsteps pause on the marble staircase, and I'd be willing to bet I'd see surprise flicker across his face if I looked back. But I don't.

I shoot straight for a second staircase on the opposite side of the terrace, blurring past all those fountains and statues and taking these stairs even faster.

Does the Wall hurt you? I ask through each drumming beat of my heart.

Does the Wall hurt me? Lucan repeats, disbelief cracking in his voice. *Do you really think I wouldn't have clawed through it if my limbs didn't lock up when I touch it? Do you think I wouldn't have spent every second trying to climb it if it didn't make me go blind with pain? Do you think I wouldn't have torn it apart to get to you? Yes, it hurts me. But this is the most painful thing of all.*

This as in my death. I know he means it, deep down, even though his mind refuses to conjure up the possibility. His heartbreak winds its way into my veins, fracturing my own heart more and more with every breath.

Lucan thinks I'm going to die.

And if he does, then I guess I have no hope left.

But if today's my last day, I'm going to leave this world as close to the sun as possible, hoping that Claudia and Eleni are able to complete their tasks while I draw the Third Guardian's attention elsewhere.

I fling myself onto the next terrace, where even more statues sit between bright pink and purple hyacinths, the stone busts coated in thick layers of moss. Some have weeds growing from them. Some are broken in half, crumbled from years, possibly decades, of neglect. Something about them makes me pause, even more dread sinking deep into my gut as I realize...

But no. Arad's too close behind, so I don't stop to investigate, to confirm if my suspicions are true. I just keep sprinting up, up, up, Lucan's presence keeping my arms and legs pumping, my muscles working, my bones from shattering.

It isn't until I'm five flights up, on a terrace with too many statues to count, that I have to double over and scrape in deep breaths right in front of one of them.

This statue isn't formed regally, like the Guardians in the great hall. The face is frightened, eyes squeezed shut, lips parted like it's eternally about to say one last thing. And although the surface is as gritty as gray stone, there's too much texture, too many realistic dips and curves of the face to have been made by a mason.

This is a Chosen One.

Fossilized.

They're all Chosen Ones, fossilized.

This isn't just a garden. It's a graveyard. *The* graveyard, where thousands of victims of vampire venom are stretched out before me, below me, and most likely above me. Some of their faces are etched in fear, others peaceful, as if they're only sleeping.

A sob tumbles out of my mouth, just as Arad emerges from the staircase behind me, not even a hair out of place. He's not panting like I am, not doubling over in an attempt to catch his breath, but his eyes glitter with calm malice. He knows I can't go anywhere, not really. He's just chasing me into exhaustion.

Don't give up, little nightmare, Lucan begs. *Keep going for me. Until the very last moment, keep fighting.*

He doesn't have to tell me twice. If I was alone here, I'd probably curl into a ball right now and accept my fate, but his soul feeds mine, and I spring into another run. Up, up, up, until I finally burst onto the topmost terrace, where the last rays of daylight beat against my face as the open sky welcomes me, and the statues of the Chosen Ones stand so close together, there's no more room for flowers or anything beautiful at all.

The end of this terrace doesn't run into the Wall here—it bleeds into the spikes themselves, like a morbid railing, a final rounded balcony jutting out over the edge of Xantera itself.

For a moment, I gape at what I see beyond: trees upon trees coated with mist, the smell like a zap to my senses, waking me up. Moss and pine and freedom.

And the Monster.

I'm closer to him than ever before. Nothing separates us—no stone Wall or ancient locked doors. Just air.

But just as I'm drifting toward the scenery, my foot snags on a crack in the terrace and I almost stumble into a statue that stabs me with pain all over again.

Familiarity constricts my throat. The curve of her cheeks, the slant of her nose. Even if I haven't seen her in eight years, it's almost as if only a second has passed.

My mother.

Time slows to a drip. I can tell it's her, even though her time in the palace must have drained her of all nutrients, her face clearly gaunt even in its fossilized state, her shoulders bony, her arms raised as if she was trying to defend herself. Her mouth open in an everlasting silent scream, and I crash to my knees as my greatest fear stabs me in the chest.

"*Mom*," I cry. "No, no, no. I'm so sorry." I grip the edges of her statue, my fingers digging into the rubble. "I wanted to be Chosen sooner. I wanted to save you. I'm sorry. I'm sorry. I..."

Clinging to her, I sob into the rock of her shoulder, thick tears falling and soaking into the stone. I don't know what to do to ease the pain forever engraved on her face. The woman who wasn't required to love me, but did anyway. The woman who sang me lullabies to ease me out of the nightmares I'd wake up from in a cold sweat. The woman who must have rebelled against the system long before me, since she was Chosen and dragged away from the daughter she loved...

Now, I can't even reach up and close her eyelids to give her peace.

But I can sing her to sleep, like she used to do for me.

"On and on the girl must march," I sing against her fossilized stomach now, each syllable cracking in my throat, "starved for an end to the night. Beware the M-Monster in her heart, for even she can b-bite."

"Touching," a cool voice reaches me as my tears splatter at her feet.

I scramble to a stand and wipe the wetness from my cheeks with the back of my hand, unaware of how long he's been standing there watching me. Backing up at the sight of Arad emerging onto this final terrace, I glance around wildly, searching for a door, an escape, anything that can help me.

Arad's lips tilt up and he cocks his head at me, eyes bright as blood.

"Looking for this?"

Then, like a scene in a dream, he reaches into his collar and pulls out a chain that makes my heartbeat freeze, sure, suddenly, that he somehow stole Lucan from me.

But—*I'm still here, baby*, Lucan whispers, and when Arad pulls the rest of the necklace out, it isn't a glistening red vial dangling from the end, but a...

"Key," I whisper.

The key to the Wall. A small, simple, silver key, tarnished with age.

No, I zero in on it, realizing with a jolt that it's laced with the same spiderwebbing veins as the Wall—almost like it was cut from the stone itself.

It was around the Third Guardian's neck this whole time.

"We have cameras everywhere, you know," Arad says, stepping toward me with the key clutched in his fist, "including in the north wing. I don't know how you snuck in, but I saw you in the white drawing room. Looking under a very particular glass cloche that used to hide our way in and out of the city."

I exhale, a sense of numbness crawling up my legs at the realization that the way out—and the way for Lucan to get in—is *right in front of me*. So close, the reflection of the sunset glints off the key and bounces right back into my eyes. That same silver chain I remember from Sylvia's memories. That key was settled against Arad's chest along with the blood of Lucan's ancestors.

It's okay, Saskia, Lucan breathes. *You tried. You tried harder than I could have ever dreamed. You* are *a dream, and I'm so sorry I woke you up.*

The words tug at something in my bones, a kind of determination that has my hands closing into fists as Arad steps even closer. Because I'm awake. And I'm above the city that has imprisoned me now. And this is the end.

I'd better make it count.

"I'm sure all your fellow Guardians are *so* happy about the fact that you've taken the one and only key," I say. "Wasn't it there, where everyone could access it, because you're all equal? Or are you trying to become a dictator over them, too?"

If the cameras are everywhere, even in this graveyard, I hope Claudia is recording this very exchange, so that all of Xantera can hear every word.

Arad's eyes narrow at my sudden change in tone, at the hardness in my gaze. His pupils sharpen into slits that slice into me like twin blades.

"I'm just protecting them, like I protect all of you. Ever since the Thirteenth Guardian tried to steal the key to let the Monster in—to destroy everyone—we've all agreed it's safer in my hands."

I blink at him, now certain he's slipped far past all reason and logic... because he just confessed, without even realizing it, that the Thirteenth Guardian didn't die in the war. The rest of the Guardians must have found out what he was planning to do with Lucan's father and murdered him for it.

Arad tilts his head at me, oblivious of my thoughts. "What I can't figure out is why? Why are you looking for the key? How did you know it was once there?" When I don't answer, and I'm sure my eyes are gleaming with satisfaction, his jaw clenches. "I would never set the Monster on you, Saskia."

I snort, the irony of those words resurrecting a manic kind of humor within me.

"I wish you would."

He narrows his eyes. "And why is that?"

"I would *love* to feel his teeth scrape against my neck. Yours are far too tiny for my taste."

Lucan stirs within my heart. Arad freezes, his expression clouding over with an earnest confusion that makes a laugh bubble from my throat as I back away a few more steps.

"Oh, and his name!" I add. "I'd love to find out the Monster's name so that I can moan it while I dream of him. I'm sure he'd make all mine come true."

"Don't taunt me," Arad hisses. "The Monster is a cruel, mindless beast who would rip you limb from limb as soon as it sunk its claws into you."

"No." I smile, and my eyes flick over his head as I finally catch sight of one: a small, blinking camera jutting out from the cornice shelf of the palace dome—angled right in our direction. "The Monster would rip *you* limb from limb," I continue, determination settling in my chest like a stone. "That's why you built the Wall, right? Not to protect the people of Xantera, but to protect *you* from his wrath."

For a moment, the air strains between us, and Lucan holds his breath alongside us, suppressing all his thoughts and emotions to allow me to focus.

Then it snaps, and the facade crumbles away. No more illusions. No more pretending. Arad knows I'm aware of everything, and I won't hide my rage anymore as I stumble backward onto the balcony gated by the spikes of the Wall.

Arad glances at my feet. His face splits into a nauseating grin at the realization that he's backed me into the last possible corner—that there is nowhere else for me to go.

"Do you know why we built the balconies, Saskia?" he asks casually. "Not this one, but the ones in the front of the palace."

"So that you can trick people into thinking everything's okay with their Chosen loved ones," I spit.

"Trick them?" He throws a hand against his heart, as if personally offended by the idea. "We're not tricking anyone. In the back of their minds, every citizen of Xantera knows that the Choosing is wrong." He takes a careful step toward me. "But if you make things appear *just* right enough, everyone can breathe a sigh of relief and pretend they don't have to do anything about it. They can trick themselves into believing that if no one else is speaking up about it, they don't have to either."

My chest squeezes as one of my feet hits a towering spike behind me. The metal digs into my spine as I flatten my back against it. "You get *rid* of anyone who speaks up."

Arad waves a hand, taking another leisurely step toward me as if he has all the time in the world to play with his prey—because he does. "It's like dousing the sparks of a newborn flame." He laughs, his fangs glinting in the sunset. "Now come back in the cage, Saskia."

Lucan, I plead, braving a quick glimpse behind me that makes my stomach swoop at the sight of how far away the ground really is—I can hardly even see him down below, what with the thick layer of mist hugging the tree line. He's nothing more than a shadow pacing desperately beneath me. *Lucan, I'm going to...*

I know, baby, he promises. *I've got you.*

Okay, I whisper back. *I trust you.*

And then our connection severs like someone cut it with a serrated knife.

I turn back to Arad and steel my voice. "I'm not going back into the cage."

"I'm afraid you don't have much of a choice." Arad cocks his head, his tongue darting out to flick over his lips. "Whether you decide to waltz right into my arms or give me another fun little chase, I am going to drain you dry until you are just as much of a stone as your helpless mother. Well, except for your heart. The only thing that can't turn to stone is your useless human heart, but I'll make sure that stops beating."

As if in response, my *useless human* heart clenches painfully, and I glance over Arad's shoulder to lock eyes with my mother again, her lips parted in that silent scream. I wish so badly I could take her with me and breathe life back into her fossilized corpse.

"And then," the Third Guardian continues, taking another step toward me until I'm backing up into the space between spikes, clutching each of them with a trembling hand, "I am going to come look at you every single day and stroke the frozen tears on your cheek and tell you that everything is okay, because you are safe here. With me. Forever."

Forever. I reel in a deep breath and close my eyes for a moment, letting the breeze send strands of my hair whipping over my face. When I open them again, I chew on the words in my mouth before I spit them back out into Arad's face.

"Go fuck yourself."

His eyes boil with crimson hate, every part of his marble body tightening with shock. He lowers himself into a crouch, preparing to pounce.

To buy a few more seconds of precious time, I seize this moment to surprise him with the only thing I have left, the only thing I cling to for any hope, even when hope doesn't exist.

Digging beneath my collar, I whip out the necklace and pinch the blood-red vial between my fingers, relishing the half-second of pure shock that ripples across Arad's face.

"How?" he seethes, wide-eyed.

Which only fuels my happiness. Even in the last seconds of my life, I'm elated that I'll drive him out of his mind for the rest of his life.

"You'll never know. Just like your name never left my lips. And I promise, one day soon, I'm going to be your biggest nightmare. Because even when I'm dead and can't come after you, *Lucan* will."

I take another step back, until my heels are hanging off the edge of the Wall. A piece of stone crumbles beneath the sole of my foot, plunging to the ground below.

Arad eyes my body, his gaze flicking between the necklace and my feet, understanding dawning across his face as he realizes what I'm about to do.

"No human could survive that fall, you know. I've chased a few other Chosen Ones to this exact spot before. You're nothing new."

My heart flares in shock. Other Chosen Ones have stood in this exact spot before? And taken the leap?

Arad nods, as if he can see my heartbreak for them etched all over my face. "If you try to escape, your fragile little body will splatter at the bottom like all the others—even if someone were to try to catch you."

I smile sadly, because: "I know." And I'm confident when I grip the vial tightly in my palm and tell him, "But I'd rather die in my Monster's arms than in this graveyard with you."

Then with a last glance at the camera and a whispered goodbye to my mother, I launch myself backward.

Arad lunges, his fingernails scrabbling at the scrap of air between us.

But I'm already falling.

Beyond the Wall.

At last.

End of Book 1

Saskia and Lucan's story will continue in *Veradel*, book two of the Guardians & Monsters duology, coming soon.

ABOUT THE AUTHORS

Mariah Montoya has always spent her days imagining stories about the fantastical. She is the author of the Esholian Institute series and currently lives in Idaho with her husband, children, and wiggle butt named Posy.

Instagram: mariah_author

TikTok: mariah_author

Grace Pearce is the author of *Leigh Makes Three, The Ex List, Perfect Praise*, and *Xantera*. She lives in southern Louisiana, but her husband may one day get his wish to move to a state with less humidity.

gracepearcebooks.com

Instagram: gracepearcewrites

TikTok: gracepearcewrites

TITLES BY MARIAH MONTOYA

The Esholian Institute Series
By the Orchid and the Owl
By the Moonbeam and the Mist

TITLES BY GRACE PEARCE

Leigh Makes Three
The Ex List
Perfect Praise

www.ingramcontent.com/pod-product-compliance
Lightning Source LLC
Chambersburg PA
CBHW051948240626
47153CB00005B/1671